# COUNTDOWN: CHAOS

To Ellie & Richie,

Hope you enjoy

Ed

# COUNTDOWN: CHAOS

Edward A. Zanchi

iUniverse, Inc.

New York Lincoln Shanghai

# COUNTDOWN: CHAOS

iUniverse, Inc.

For information address:
iUniverse, Inc.
2021 Pine Lake Road, Suite 100
Lincoln, NE 68512
www.iuniverse.com

ISBN: 0-595-30233-5

Printed in the United States of America

To My Family.

# Contents

# CHAPTER 1

▼

# MOSCOW
# THREE P.M.,
# SATURDAY
# DECEMBER 18, 1999
## FOURTEEN DAYS TO 0 0

In the center of Moscow stood a drab, gray building that once housed the powerful, feared and respected Russian intelligence agency, the KGB. Now the building was crumbling, its paint peeling and its steps missing bricks—just another bitter reminder of how far the country and the agency—now called the Federal Security Services—had fallen since the Soviet Union's collapse in 1991.

On the fifth floor of the building, on a cold day a fortnight before the new year, FSS agent Ivan Malenkov hesitated a moment in the doorway of Director Boris Stepovich's office. The large, sparsely furnished and dimly lit room was uninviting. It was said Director Stepovich's goal in office décor was a bear's den, which made him comfortable and intimidated others. Stepovich had been appointed director in 1995 when the Russian federation increased the powers of FCS, the Federal Counterintelligence Service, to combat rampant crime. At that time, it was renamed FSS, the Federal Security Services, and its responsibilities of crime prevention, intelligence, and counterintelligence became more like the old KGB. Unlike the old KGB, though, whose 15 directorates reported to the Council of Ministers, the FCS Director reported directly to the President. This gave the President—like Josef Stalin before him—the power to direct the day-to-day activities of the secret police.

As Malenkov scanned the room, he was disappointed to see the dingy walls in dire need of paint and the mismatched scatter rugs, no doubt hiding holes in the carpet.

"Don't just stand there, Ivan. Come in," Stepovich said as he stood up and came from behind his desk to greet his subordinate. Even though he was in his late sixties, at five feet ten inches tall and 250 pounds he was broad shouldered and bear-like. With a large stomach, filled by too much borscht, and a red, bulbous nose from years of Stolichnaya vodka, he was a formidable looking man.

"It's good to see you, Director Stepovich," Malenkov said as he cautiously approached his superior.

"It's good to see you too, Ivan." Stepovich hugged Malenkov, Russian-style. At 43, the taller, leaner agent contrasted sharply with his director. Malenkov was in good physical condition, but he could still feel the strength of the older man.

"Sit," Stepovich said, pointing Ivan to a chair and returning to his own. "I've brought you here because I have an important task for you."

"As always, Director Stepovich, I'm at your service." Malenkov replied without hesitation, careful not to betray the caution he felt when summoned earlier that day. He was always wary when in the presence of Boris Stepovich. This man, who had worked in Russian intelligence all of his adult life, had earned his reputation for the swiftness and cruelty with which he dealt with incompetence and disloyalty. "It's been too long since I had something important to do. I look forward to it."

Malenkov's enthusiasm was calculated to please Stepovich, but there was some truth to it. Any sense of importance or urgency in the agency's duties had been missing since its official demise Nov. 6, 1991, 44 days shy of its 74th birthday.

"Perhaps you will not look forward to this." Stepovich leaned forward and showed a slight trace of a smile. "There are times when one must do things that are...distasteful."

Malenkov's body involuntarily tightened. He did not imagine there were many things distasteful to Boris Stepovich. He hoped his reaction had gone unnoticed.

"You must eliminate Yuri Petrov." The Director spoke coldly, staring hard at Malenkov. His delivery was calculated to instill fear. He had learned over the years that respect from one's subordinates was useful, but fear was essential. So he cultivated it whenever possible.

The words struck Malenkov like a kick in the stomach. "But Director Stepovich, Petrov is a dedicated and capable agent. And his father has had a long and distinguished career with the agency. What has he done?" Malenkov had heard of agents being eliminated, but he'd never known them and always assumed they'd defected or sold secrets. In any case, he'd never felt comfortable about it, and had never been called upon to do the dirty work himself. He couldn't imagine what Yuri Petrov had done.

"Yes, Ivan. What you say is true. Dimitry Petrov has been a loyal comrade for many years. I told you it would be unpleasant. But it must be done!" His stern tone and cold look told Malenkov there was no room for discussion. Still, he couldn't help himself.

"Didn't I see Dimitry leave your office just before I came in?"

"Yes."

Malenkov felt the knot tighten in the pit of his stomach. He knew he was on dangerous ground questioning the head of the FSS, but the assignment had caught him off guard. He needed a reason to take the life of a fellow agent. If for no other reason than he didn't want to make the same mistake. But more than that, his target was the son of Dimitry Petrov—one of the KGB's, and now the FSS's most powerful and respected agents.

"Has he done something? Has he revealed something to you that causes us to eliminate his son?"

"Enough, Ivan!" Stepovich pounded his fist on the desk as he leaned forward and glared.

Director Stepovich saw no need to tell Ivan that he wanted to ensure Dimitry would be available to him once his son had been eliminated. He would have to watch Dimitry closely to monitor whether or not he suspected Boris' involvement. If he did, Dimitry would have to be eliminated too. And he preferred not to do that. To kill his son was dangerous enough, but to kill a man of Dimitry's stature involved a great deal more risk.

"Do you question my authority?" Stepovich's glare intensified. His body tensed and appeared to rise slightly out of his chair.

"No. Never, Director Stepovich. I will do anything you order. It is just that the assignment to kill a fellow agent took me by surprise. As you said, it will not be pleasant."

"Take Egor Skulsky with you," Stepovich said, easing back, the hint of a smile lighting his weathered face.

Malenkov caught himself before speaking his mind. He had already come close to overstepping his bounds. He would not do it again. He knew Stepovich was aware he didn't care for Skulsky. Egor was a man who killed for pleasure. "I would rather work with anyone else but Egor," Ivan thought.

"It will be hard for you to kill Yuri. But it will be easy for Egor." Stepovich's smile widened. He was pretty sure he knew what Ivan was thinking. He took pride in knowing his agents—and in making them uncomfortable when it suited his purposes. Ivan Malenkov was intelligent, good looking and dedicated—all traits that helped make a good spy. But he lacked the one trait that would keep him from ever occupying the director's office—the killer instinct. He could be soft.

"As you wish, Director," Malenkov said, involuntarily shifting in his chair.

"Petrov's project has been completed, but I am informed he is still at the Kalingstaad command complex. He will be on his way to Moscow later tonight. You will be notified when he leaves. You are to intercept him a few kilometers outside the city and make it look like a gang robbery and murder. It must look messy and unprofessional so that we will not be suspected."

"I understand," Malenkov said as he stood to leave, a somber look on his face.

"Take heart, comrade. This will be of great service to me, the agency and, most of all, to Mother Russia." Stepovich shook Ivan's hand, squeezing it hard. "I know you will not disappoint me."

In the basement five floors below, Dimitry Petrov, still reeling from what he had heard, tried to put the pieces together. His hunch to leave a bug in Stepovich's office at the end of their conversation had been well founded. He had thought it strange that Stepovich wanted to know his whereabouts for the next forty-eight hours. The excuse he gave had been inadequate. It saddened Dimitry that he could plant a bug so easily. In the past, the office of the KGB chief would have been swept for electronic listening devices at the beginning of each day and then every time a visitor exited. But in the new Russia, with budget constraints, the FSS office was now only swept in the morning, if at all.

The main reason Stepovich had summoned him was purportedly to discuss today's nuclear weapon's system test—a test that would determine if the country would have nuclear capability on Jan. 1, 2000. Until the Year 2000 problem became widely recognized, most computers used two-digit numbers to keep track of dates. Consequently, in the year 2000, computers could mistake "0 0" for 1900 and this could cause systems to stop running or to generate erroneous data, resulting in massive malfunctions.

The millions of lines of code that had to be reviewed made correcting the Y2K problem a major undertaking. Russia's resources were stretched so thin, and the fear of an erroneous early warning signal or other critical malfunction so great, they were forced to accept funding and technical advice from the United States. The Y2K problem had created unlikely bedfellows—something neither country wanted to admit. It had also opened up a rare opportunity for Boris Stepovich—with the help of Dimitry Petrov—to gain control of the Russian nuclear weapons arsenal. Combined with the failure of the American nuclear system, which they expected, this would give them the power they needed to bring Russia back to her place of honor in the world—and the FSS with her.

Stepovich needed Dimitry because his son Yuri was the best programmer in the FSS. He was the only agent capable of being planted on the team responsible for correcting the system's highly sensitive internal security programs. Given the lack of talent available, placing him on the team wasn't difficult. This access afforded Yuri the opportunity to sabotage the system's security and put the control of the nuclear arsenal in the hands of Boris Stepovich.

The plan was a simple one once Stepovich had his men in place. The most sensitive levels of the systems security program could only be accessed when there were two approved programmers present, each of whom would have his own access code of the day. This was to prevent any unauthorized changes to such a critical area. On the day the full test was scheduled, it only required that the other programmer working with Yuri was also one of Stepovich's men. Again, this was not a difficult task for the chief of the FSS. Then all that remained was for Yuri to make a slight adjustment to the system and insert the security code provided by Stepovich.

Once accomplished, the security program would allow the system to operate normally only once. After that, the system would only operate with the new secret code. Without it the system would "freeze" and become inoperable. Then Stepovich would wield control of the country's nuclear arsenal and of President Sokolov. Stepovich could then show the people that it was necessary to bring the communists back to power and end the existing financial crisis and the hunger that gripped the country.

When Stepovich first approached Dimitry, he thought it was a desperate measure by a desperate man. Once asked, though, he could not refuse him. He also knew that sometimes the boldest plans were best. He, too, longed for the country to return to the power and prestige it had held for most of his life. Yes, life was hard under the communists, but life had always been hard in Russia. It was hard now. And, yes, it could be better, but not under the control of men like Boris Stepovich.

That is why Dimitry had determined to adjust the plan. The adjustment was a delicate and dangerous matter and would be put into place tonight. Even though it was not unexpected, when he heard Stepovich order his son's death sentence, he felt a stabbing sensation in his heart. He knew, then, he had done the right thing. Stepovich would never let anyone live who knew the secret code. The plan to have Yuri killed on his way from the complex was calculated to prevent him from passing the code to his father. Stepovich knew Yuri would not risk relaying the code by telephone. The agent who passed the code to Yuri would also be killed as soon as he reported back to Stepovich, leaving the code solely in the director's hands.

Dimitry again felt a stab in his heart as he realized what danger he had put his children in. He would have to put his contingency plan quickly into action to save Yuri. Then he would have to disappear, because Stepovich would know he had been betrayed. Dimitry Petrov, like his son, would be a wanted man. That at least meant he needn't worry about how to remove the bug, but he faced yet another problem. Dimitry had precious little time to warn Katya.

# CHAPTER 2

▼

# THE RUSSIAN COUNTRYSIDE ELEVEN-THIRTY P.M., SATURDAY DECEMBER 18, 1999

## FOURTEEN DAYS TO 0 0

The Kalingstaad nuclear power plant, some fifty kilometers south of Moscow, provided most of the city's electricity. It also contained the top-secret Russian nuclear command complex—the nerve center for the country's nuclear weapons arsenal. Tight security was normal for a nuclear power facility, making it an ideal cover. The heart of the command complex was the computer control center, four levels below the Earth's surface. That's where Yuri Petrov worked feverishly, typing the last of the instructions to complete the task given him by his father—a task that, if discovered, would cost him his life.

As Yuri worked, he reviewed last night's clandestine meeting with his father. It was just after midnight when he slipped into the motor pool building at the north side of the Kalingstaad facility. Because his car was garaged there, it would give him an excuse for being there at such a late hour, if seen. Feeling as if he were being watched, Yuri had stopped three times and waited, but saw no one. He broke into a cold sweat. Moving in the shadows was unfamiliar territory for him. Most of his work had been as a computer expert, holed up in the bowels of FSS headquarters. Once inside the motor pool door, Yuri stood flat against the wall. He waited, motionless, as his eyes adjusted to the dim light of the bulb hanging from the middle of the garage.

"It is good to see you, son," Dimitry Petrov said, stepping into Yuri's field of view

Yuri breathed a sigh of relief. "It is good to see you, father." The two men hugged for a long moment without speaking, then remained close and spoke in whispers. Yuri looked nervously around.

"Do not worry, Yuri. We are alone here—except for my men."

"I was careful not to be followed, but I felt I was being watched," Yuri said, continuing to scan the garage.

"You were. But we only saw you because we were expecting you. Now, the test is still scheduled for tomorrow?"

"Yes."

"Do not be offended, Yuri, but are you absolutely certain the test will be successful?" Dimitry put his hand on his son's shoulder. He did not question his son's computer abilities, but he had to be sure. His many years in the KGB had taught him it was never prudent to assume anything. One needed to double— and triple-check facts and always be ready with an alternate plan. That is why he arranged to receive reports from the project's senior technician and also get access to the progress evaluations from the American consulting team. Both sources indicated the test should indeed be successful. One had to be as certain as possible, because failure could mean death.

"Yes, father, the test will be successful." Yuri was not brash, but extremely competent in what he did. Nonetheless, he was sensitive to any criticism from his father. He wondered if all fathers had difficulty accepting their son's expertise.

"Good. If I did not have the utmost confidence in you I would not have trusted you with such an important project. And I would not put you in even greater danger by asking you to do more—" he said, his grip on Yuri's shoulder tightening, "but I'm afraid there is no other way. Stepovich must not be allowed to gain control of the arsenal.

"Don't worry, I'll be careful," Yuri said, placing his hand on his father's shoulder and returning the pressure. "I'm prepared to do whatever is necessary."

For a moment they stood facing each other, and Dimitry smiled as he saw himself 25 years younger. That the two men were related was obvious: Both had piercing, almond-shaped black eyes, finely cut features and jet-black hair. With Dimitry's added years had come traces of gray at his temples and an additional 20 pounds.

"I am afraid I have one more task for you. A dangerous one." Dimitry's smile disappeared.

"Whatever's necessary," Yuri repeated, his voice firm and steady. His father had dedicated his life to serving his country and had sacrificed much for it. And he would, too. Just as he had been taught, and just as he had always done.

"When the test is completed, you will be able to get back into the system undetected?"

"Yes. As you instructed, I have learned everything there is to know about the security programs and have made the adjustments so I can get in and out at any time."

"Good. After the test is over I will want you to make one final change to the security program—one which no one can be aware of."

"The difficulty will be in physical access to my computer terminal without others present," Yuri said. "And after midnight tomorrow I will not even be able to access the terminal. My clearance will be gone."

"Yes, I know. But the schedule dictates the test will be over by six in the evening. Seven at the latest. Then there will be a large celebration in the dining commons. Is that right?" Dimitry asked.

"Yes, that's right."

"You must go, and you must be seen," Dimitry said. "You must not raise any suspicions or question as to your whereabouts. You must look like you are having a good time and doing a lot of drinking. But you must stay sober. Then, when the party has been going on for some time and the others are drunk, you will be able to slip away unnoticed."

"As usual, father, you have it all thought out."

"We had better hope so. To fail could cost you your life," Dimitry said gently. "I do wish there was another way. I would do it myself if I could."

"Don't worry. I'll be careful," Yuri said. He was trying his best to appear unconcerned.

"Leave the celebration at eleven-thirty. That is enough time before the guard change at midnight. As you say, after that it will be impossible to gain access. The next watch will be informed that the project is completed and that no one should be working."

"I understand. What is it you want me to do?"

"I want you to replace Director Stepovich's code with mine, so that we will be in control, not Boris Stepovich."

Yuri hesitated for a moment at his father's revelation. Alarmed at the risk that they were taking and relieved that Stepovich would be stopped. "That won't be difficult. I'll only need about twenty minutes to do it. I'll have already done it once earlier in the day."

"Good. With the successful completion of the test the project will be over and you can leave the complex. Is that correct?"

"Yes. I will be relieved of my duties and be expected to leave tomorrow."

"Then, in the morning, leave the compound at eight and travel toward Moscow. Exactly two miles from the complex, pull off the road and wait. You will be met by two of my men, who will take you to a safe house. I will meet you there later."

"How will I know they are your men?"

"They will use your sister's name."

His father had been right. With all the other programmers, administrators and even off-duty guards in various states of drunkenness, it had been easy to slip out of the party unnoticed. He was nervous not only about being caught, but because he understood his task was of critical importance.

Yuri had decided not to tell his father about the nightmare he'd had the night before their meeting, when he awoke sweating. The dream was so life-like that it took him a few moments to realize it was not real. In the dream, his enemies were interrogating him to learn his secret. At first he had been strong, but the torture and drugs started to weaken his resolve. So when the opportunity arose, he brought on his own death to prevent revealing his secret.

Though Yuri was not a man who believed in premonitions or superstitions, he couldn't help but think about the dangerous task that lay ahead. These were dangerous times and, if he were caught carrying out his father's plan, he would certainly be put to death, but not before being tortured to find out who else was involved. But Yuri knew his father's plan was important, a plan that could restore Russia to its proper place as a world leader, and had to be completed.

As his mind returned to the task at hand, he thought about how the security was always tight at Kalingstaad. But at eleven-thirty on this night, a night on which the year 2000 test had run without a glitch, there was no one, save a few guards, working. At midnight the new day would start, and the project Yuri had worked on for five years would come to an end—as would his top-level clearance.

Yuri worked furiously to complete his task before the clock struck midnight. He had been able to make adjustments to the security system, granting him unauthorized access, even though someone was always watching, because his talents were far superior to those who monitored him. Still, the system would log his access and leave a trail he could not prevent; he could only hope no one would follow it.

He couldn't help but marvel at the genius of his father. Though Yuri was considered a brilliant computer technician, it was his father who was the master strategist.

At first, he kept turning to see if anyone was coming. But then Yuri's absorption in his work became total and he did not hear the man walk up behind him until he felt a firm hand on his shoulder. Startled, he turned, his pulse racing. He was relieved to see it was one of the guards he knew well. Yuri had put in many long hours getting to this day, and it was not unusual for Antoin to see him at the start of his midnight shift.

"Yuri, you work too hard," Antoin said. A quizzical look replaced his boyish grin as he patted Yuri's shoulder. "But I heard the task was completed and you were all out celebrating. Yet here you are. A good-looking man like you should be making love to a beautiful woman."

"You startled me, Antoin. You're right, but you know I have not had much time to meet women." Unfortunately, Yuri thought, this was all too true.

"Then you should join me tomorrow night. Tasha has a friend who would be just right for you," Antoin said, his boyish grin back. "I promise you will have a good time."

"Perhaps I will take you up on your offer," Yuri said, blushing slightly.

"Good. But now you must go." Once again Antoin put his hand on Yuri's shoulder.

"Please. I just need a few minutes more to finish an adjustment as a result of today's test."

"Ah, Yuri! Always the perfectionist! But I'm afraid you'll have to be satisfied with what you have. It's almost midnight and my orders are to allow no access after midnight."

"OK, Antoin, I understand. But just five minutes more. Then I will go. Please?"

"OK, Yuri, my friend. You have five minutes, but please go then or I will have to make you go. And you must not tell anyone I let you stay this long or I will be in trouble." The smile had gone from his face. "Even though I have not been paid in three months, I must still try to do my job. There is nothing else for me to do."

"I understand. You can count on me not to say a word."

"I know I can trust you, Yuri. I will miss you."

"I will miss you, too, Antoin."

Antoin shook his friend's hand and then continued on his rounds. As Yuri returned to his task he couldn't help but think what would become of Antoin. Once Stepovich discovered that he had been betrayed, and his plan had been sabotaged, he would begin a full investigation. Antoin was certain to be questioned intensely. Surely he would be no match for Stepovich and his men. Once the Director learned Antoin had allowed this breach of security, he would be imprisoned or killed. It pained Yuri to think of this, but he had no time to ponder an alternative. He only had a few minutes to finish.

# CHAPTER 3

▼

# THE PENTAGON, WASHINGTON, D.C. TWO-THIRTY P.M., SATURDAY DECEMBER 18, 1999

## FOURTEEN DAYS TO 0 0

Nick Logan checked his watch for the third time in the last ten minutes. It was just an inexpensive Timex Ironman Triathlon, but he liked it because it was light on his wrist and had an impressive array of functions at a low cost. What he liked most about it was that it was waterproof and kept track of his laps during his morning swim. Now, while he waited for his senior program analyst, he wondered if it, too, would succumb to the Y2K bug. He hadn't thought about it until now. He had been too busy; too consumed by the project. The "Millennium Bug Project" had occupied the better part of the past year and had taken him away from his normal audit supervisory functions at the General Accounting Office.

Logan didn't usually let his mind wander, but he couldn't concentrate while he waited for Kate Peters. It wasn't like her to be late, especially on such an important day. He realized he was letting the pressure get to him, so he leaned back in his big leather chair, took a deep breath and tried to will himself to relax. He let his eyes roam about his temporary office and reflected on how large, comfortable and well appointed it was—that is, except for the mole-like feeling he got having to go up six floors before reaching sunlight. As the project manager, this was his office only until the project was completed. Then it would revert back to the military. There was no arguing that the Millennium Bug Project, housed within the Pentagon, required a high level of security, but he missed seeing the outside world.

His position as a senior field operations manager at the GAO often took him out of his own office and into a temporary location, but it was usually for shorter periods and in aboveground locations. While his own office was smaller and clearly reflected his middle manager status, his view of the small park across the street and of the Potomac in the distance more than made up for what it lacked in size. On a warm, sunny day he would take a break to admire the picture through his window of the park's array of flowers, greenery, birds and, most of all, attractive women. When his workload allowed, he would take his lunch in the park and enjoy the beauty close up. On more than one occasion, he had dated women he met there. And why not. He was still young at thirty-four, handsome, physically fit, and single. The park on a sunny day was an ideal location for starting up a friendly conversation with a pretty stranger.

It was two-thirty p.m. and Kate Peters was already fifteen minutes late. He wanted to go over some last-minute items before the big test at five p.m.—the test they'd spent the last nine months preparing for. Because of the publicity that often resulted from GAO audit findings, he was used to pressure. He thrived on it. But as manager of the Millennium Bug Project, he was nervous about the outcome of today's test. And that was before he'd received the bad news from Paul McGrath, his counterpart and friend at the Social Security Administration.

"Hi, Nick. Sorry I'm late," Kate said, out of breath, as she burst into his office, barely knocking. Nick noticed the perspiration on her forehead and upper lip. She looked flustered. He also noticed the movement of her small, firm breasts as she breathed deeply. There was not much he didn't notice about Kate Peters.

From the very first time he saw her he knew he had to date her. Kate always seemed to be doing her best to appear plain, even girlish. She wore little makeup, with her jet-black hair pulled back from her face, and she dressed conservatively. But she couldn't hide her symmetrical, slightly angular face, cupid lips and ebony black eyes that Nick found strikingly beautiful, even exotic. She had an athletic-looking, firm body with long legs on her tall frame and she moved with a feline grace. He knew from her personnel file that she was thirty-two and single. He also knew that she graduated high in her class from MIT with a computer science major and now worked as a consultant for The Millennium Recovery Co. She was their best technician. This made his decision to accept her as the senior program analyst on the project an easy one. He knew from the beginning that he would enjoy working with her. His only regret was that he would have to wait until the project was complete before he could ask her out. He had a policy never to mix business with pleasure.

"Is something wrong?" Nick asked. It was unlike Kate to show signs of stress. Even under pressure, she was usually calm and controlled. Her file had identified this strength from previous jobs. It was one of the main reasons she'd been assigned the lead spot on the team.

"You haven't heard?"

"Heard what?" Nick didn't think she could already have heard about the Social Security fiasco since McGrath had just called him.

"The Midwest Insurance Co. ran a test of their Y2K programs last night and it blew up."

"Blew up? What do you mean?"

"They've totally shut down their computers. Apparently the security system turned on itself in an attempt at self-defense, unleashing a virus that threatened to destroy their entire file of software programs."

"What kind of virus would do that?" Nick felt his muscles tighten and his stomach turn. First Social Security's failure and now this. He hoped this wasn't an omen of things to come. "Where did it come from? Why didn't they know it existed before they ran the tests? They must have sophisticated virus checkers—how did something like that get through?"

"Nick—slow down. Of course they do." Nick's intensity acted as a catalyst, bringing Kate back to her usual calm demeanor. "I don't have all the details, but it appears the computer's security system developed and unleashed its own virus."

"I've never heard of a system thinking for itself—except in the movies. Is that really possible?" Nick was frustrated because he was not on top of things. He was uncomfortable with these technology geniuses having knowledge he didn't, and he resented how they loved the power it gave them. Kate was not usually like this though, which was another reason he liked her so much.

"It doesn't really think. It reacts. But it wasn't supposed to work like this. They were concerned with their systems security and had determined to make it state-of-the-art. Put simply, their security system was designed to unleash a counterattack on any intruder attempting to penetrate the system. It seems the system worked too well—or else it went completely out of control. It's unclear which." Kate kept her explanation as simple as possible. She had great respect for Nick's intelligence and integrity but a technical guru he was not. Kate was adept at bridging the gap between the technical and non-technical. Another reason she was good at the lead spot.

"That makes what—the fifth major insurance company this year to fail at its Y2K fix?" Nick couldn't help but think that the Year 2000 bug had hit the insurance and banking industries particularly hard. Or maybe they were just the first to admit it. Maybe other industries were actually running further behind than they had disclosed.

"They will be the fifth if they don't have it fixed by Monday. They won't announce anything until then. If you remember, the other four companies whose tests' failed were forced to merge with larger insurance firms or declare bankruptcy."

"How did you find out?"

"I know the woman in charge of their information technology division." Nick wasn't surprised. Kate had made a lot of connections at MIT and as a consultant, though more than he would have expected for a thirty-two year old with not much of an apparent social life.

"She called looking for technical assistance. That's why I was late. She was panicked and I just couldn't cut her off without trying to give her some suggestions. Of course this is confidential. If it were known on the street, the policyholders and stockholders would panic." Kate felt compelled to ask for Nick's secrecy, even though she knew he could be trusted to say nothing. His professionalism was one of the things she admired about him. Unfortunately, she knew it was also what kept him from asking her out. Kate knew Nick was interested by the way he looked at her. On one occasion, he'd also made an awkward attempt at letting her know his policy was not to date women he worked with. She expected he would make a move on her once the project was completed.

The idea was not an unpleasant one. Not only did she respect him for his intelligence, honesty, and directness, but she was also physically attracted. Nick was tall, handsome, physically fit, and personable. He often had a friendly smile on his slightly boyish face and his unusual azure blue eyes were both warm and piercing at the same time. She would very much like to get to know him better. But Kate knew it could never be. Maybe in a different time and place.

"Your secret is safe with me," Nick replied. "Besides, it's nothing compared with what I just learned."

"I'm not sure I want to hear this," Kate said as a shiver went up her spine.

"I wish I hadn't. Just think what will happen that first week after New Years, when millions of checks and direct deposits, totaling tens of billions of dollars, don't go out." Nick pulled on his left earlobe as he gave Kate the bad news.

"Oh my God Nick!" Kate's hands gripped the arms of her chair as her body stiffened and she leaned forward. "That can mean only one thing. Please tell me it's not true."

"I'm afraid it's true. I just got off the phone with Paul." Nick had introduced Kate to McGrath shortly after taking on the project so they could share knowledge and problems. Both held top-level security clearances.

"During our last meeting, Paul said he was in good shape. He doesn't seem the overly optimistic type," Kate said.

"He isn't." Now it was Nick's turn to regain his calm demeanor in the face of Kate's agitation.

"So what happened? What went wrong with the test?" Kate twisted in her chair as she uncrossed and re-crossed her legs.

Nick hesitated a moment, distracted by the movement of Kate's long, silky legs. She had occupied his thoughts more during the last nine months than he cared to admit, her desirability enhanced, no doubt, by her unavailability. It was another reason for wanting today's test to be successful.

"First of all, it wasn't a test. They went live." Nick watched the look of surprise on Kate's face. He thought it was probably much like the look on his face when Paul told him.

"But there's still two weeks to go."

"That's what I said." Nick leaned back in his chair, absently playing with his pen. "Paul said they wanted the extra time to test the agency's interfacing with the Treasury and the state agencies."

"I see. That makes sense." Kate had that studious look on her face that told Nick her mind was racing to process this new information and its possibilities.

The Social Security Administration had been the leader among the government agencies in addressing the Year 2000 problem. In fact, it had been working on the problem for some ten years, though it certainly had its problems along the way in reviewing and correcting more than sixty million lines of code. In December 1998, the President had triumphantly announced that the Social Security system was one hundred percent Year 2000 compliant. What was downplayed was the fact that while the agency's own computers were allegedly in order, Social Security depends on computers outside its control to help issue one trillion dollars in annual payments to forty-five million beneficiaries. The checks are actually issued by the Treasury's Financial Management System, which lagged behind in addressing the Y2K problem. In addition, the states administered the payments to those receiving welfare, Medicaid, food stamps or other types of assistance. The states were in various stages of compliance, with many lagging seriously behind.

"They expected some failures when they went live, right?" Kate asked.

"But they didn't expect any failures in their own programs. And they didn't expect the extent of problems at the Treasury and the states." The serious look on Nick's face made him suddenly look older than his thirty-four years. "Let's get some coffee and I'll fill you in," he said, standing up. "Then I want to talk about *our* test. I know we're ready, but I want to go over a few things. I don't want anything to go wrong. I'd like nothing better than to go out tonight and celebrate."

"Me, too." Kate couldn't help the little gleam in her eye as she got up to join Nick. The gleam quickly went away as the reality of the situation returned.

▼

# CHAPTER 4

# THE WHITE HOUSE, WASHINGTON, D.C. TWO-THIRTY P.M., SATURDAY DECEMBER 18, 1999

## FOURTEEN DAYS TO 0 0

President Justin Stewart called the meeting of his advisors because of the potentially catastrophic Y2K problem that had occurred earlier that morning at the Social Security Administration. The group of advisors assembled in the President's conference room adjacent to the Oval Office. All the top brass were there: Vice President Neil Chandler, Chairman of the Joint Chiefs of Staff General George Armstrong, Ambassador-at-Large Victor Noble, Secretary of State Judith Carlson, Secretary of Defense Paul Donovan, Secretary of the Treasury William Calderon, CIA Director Donald Mathias, FBI Director Darren Alexander, Secret Service Director James Knight, Press Secretary Brent Jones and the man of the hour—White House Year 2000 czar and the chief technical advisor on the President's Year 2000 Conversion Council, Tom Wagner.

The Social Security Administration had been widely recognized as one of the federal government's leading agencies in dealing with the Year 2000 problem. Because of its sensitive nature and high profile, the uninterrupted operation of the agency was critical to the survival of any politician. It was the third rail of politics. Screw it up and you die. That is why President Stewart held a press conference in December 1998 and, amid much fanfare, announced that the Social Security system was one hundred percent Year 2000 compliant. He assured older Americans their payments were secure. Now he'd been informed there were, indeed, some problems and might be disruptions in payments. He wanted answers and he wanted the right ones.

"Judith. Gentlemen. Thank you all for coming on short notice," President Stewart said in a low, deliberate voice as he struggled to remain calm. As he spoke, he tapped his finger lightly on the massive mahogany conference table. "I know you're all dealing with critical issues of your own, and we were scheduled to meet with the Year 2000 Conversion Council on Monday, but this couldn't wait. I'm afraid we've had a national disaster at the Social Security Administration this morning. I want you all to hear about it first-hand so we can get your input. Also, I did not want to discuss it in front of the full council before we've had a chance to analyze the problem and prepare a response." He then turned the meeting over to Tom Wagner, his Year 2000 project chief. "Tom, could you fill us in please."

"Certainly, Mr. President." Wagner stood to address the others. Palms sweaty and throat dry, he was no longer the infinitely confident billionaire. This was a situation he did not relish. He was as used to success as he was unfamiliar with failure. At the age of thirty-six, he was the CEO and majority shareholder of a multi-billion dollar software development corporation. When the President asked him to head the country's Year 2000 Conversion Council, he'd let his ego take precedence over his good sense and said yes. He'd certainly experienced delays and missed deadlines before while developing major software programs. That was the nature of the beast. With a huge, complex program like the one used by Social Security, you could test all you wanted, but you could never be one hundred percent sure it would work until you went live. Wagner had never faced a missed deadline that threatened such catastrophic consequences, though. "Let me start by saying that I don't think we're dealing with a catastrophe here. It is........."

"Excuse me, Tom," interrupted the President in a tense voice, as he leaned toward Wagner. "Didn't we try to process the January payments this morning?"

"Yes, sir. But it wasn't a total failure, and we still have two weeks to fix the problems." Wagner realized how much better he liked being on the other side of the table. He never liked it when one of his subordinates tried to downplay a problem; now he was doing it.

"Two weeks! The agency has been working on this problem for ten years!" The President nearly yelled. "And I'm the one on the record announcing it was one hundred percent compliant."

"I understand, Mr. President. I was just indicating that we still have some time left to recover and to at least reduce any disruptions." Wagner's face flushed as his own anger rose.

"I see, Tom." The President leaned back in his chair. "Why don't you continue with the details."

Wagner cleared his throat and grasped his notes in front of him as he began. "Early this morning the Social Security Administration began what was scheduled to be a live test of its systems to determine that they are, in fact, one hundred percent Year 2000 compliant. As you know, this agency was one of the leading agencies in dealing with the Millennium Bug—or Year 2000 problem—even though it had thirty million lines of code of its own and another thirty-three million lines of code linked to the state agencies."

"Please, Tom," the President interrupted, accompanied by a burst of rapid finger tapping. "We've all heard enough of how difficult the problem is and how *well* the agency was doing. Let's get to the point." It had been seen as a political coup when, with the help of Vice President Chandler, the President was able to get Tom Wagner to head up the council. Now he wasn't so sure. President Stewart was beginning to wonder who was more adept at coming up with excuses: politicians or technology executives.

"Certainly, Mr. President." Wagner glanced at Neil Chandler and tightened the grip on his notes. "There was a major malfunction in the operation of the agency's system when they attempted to operate as if they were cutting the checks due January 1, 2000. Apparently, the base operating functionality failed to recognize the year 2000 protocol and, therefore, many of the built-in control restrictions were outside of the allowed parameters causing the system to initiate pre-programmed security measures. This…"

"Tom—," the President broke in sharply, exasperation filling his voice. "I know this is a complicated issue. But I'm tired. And I've got a headache. I need this in plain English—in Sesame Street terms, if you will." The President looked at Vice President Chandler. "Can you help us here, Neil?"

President Stewart turned to his Vice President as he so often did when it came to technical matters. It's not that he was incapable of understanding technical details; he just didn't like the nuts and bolts level of technology. He was interested in what technology could do, not in how it did it. Fortunately for him the Vice President was enamored by technical details and was a somewhat accomplished—albeit amateur—techie. That and his twenty years as a politician made him adept at bridging the gap between the technical and the "real" worlds. This skill had proven invaluable in dealing with the Y2K problem. In fact, President Stewart would have appointed Chandler to head the project if it had not been too dangerous politically for his friend.

The President was savvy enough about technology to know this Y2K problem represented a no-win situation. At best, it would only cause minor inconveniences, which would prompt his political opponents to question why so much money was spent on a non-issue. At worst, critical services would be disrupted, threatening the economy and the safety of the American people. Vice President Chandler appreciated that the President had kept him out of the direct line of fire.

"I'll try, Mr. President." The Vice President remained seated as he signaled Wagner to take his. A relieved Wagner did so. "Tom has already filled me in on what happened, and I think I understand it well enough to do a reasonably adequate job." He understood the President's frustration but he also understood Tom's. He also felt responsible since it was he who had suggested Wagner as the White House Y2K czar.

"Tom, feel free to correct me if I get off base." Wagner nodded. "As I understand it, when the computer's clock was advanced on the program to the year 2000, all hell broke loose for about twenty percent of the payees. What's made things particularly bad is that it's not just one problem. In some cases it read the '0 0' as 1900 and subtracted one hundred years from people's ages, making a sixty-five year old man minus thirty-five years old. The program was written to ignore the minus sign, but none of these people would be issued a payment because they would be considered too young. This happened in about ten percent of the total payments—or five million people." There was an audible gasp in the room, and the Vice President saw a lot of grim faces around the table. "What happened to the other ten percent was even worse. In those cases the system added one hundred years, turning a sixty-five year old person into a one hundred and sixty-five year old. Since the system has automatic control features to question payments to people older than ninety-nine years, it really hit the fan. At one hundred, the system assumes the recipient is dead and prints out a report that requires the individual to verify they are still alive. This verification must be input into the system before any payments can be reinstated. You can imagine what it was like when the system started to print out more than five million warning notices." The Vice President let out a sigh of his own.

"The thought of ten million people not receiving their checks is frightening," said Victor Noble in his low, raspy voice as he stroked his thin, black mustache, the trace of a sneer apparent.

"Yes it is. But that's not going to happen," the President said firmly, looking intently at Noble. Then he turned to the Vice President. "How bad is it, Neil?"

"It's hard to say, sir," Chandler replied. "The good part is that it's easier to fix the problem once it's broken." The Vice President then looked at Wagner, who was quick to pick up the signal and jump in.

"We already have our best teams working on it and will work around the clock until the problems are resolved," Wagner said with determination.

"What about the eighty percent that made it past these problems?" Noble asked as he leaned back in his chair, peering down his nose at Wagner. "Are you able to process those payments?"

"They were processed properly by Social Security, but there was a problem when the information was transferred to the Treasury Department." Wagner sat straight up in his chair and prepared for additional criticism. "The Treasury actually cuts the checks, and it is a totally separate system. Some of the checks would not process and some of the direct deposits would not link to the banks."

"We also have our best teams on it and won't sleep until it's fixed," Secretary of the Treasury Calderon said, as he dug his fingers into his hand.

"If the problem doesn't get fixed in time, there are going to be forty-five million very upset and frightened people," the President said. His voice was calm, but his look was worried. "Not to mention the serious financial crisis that will develop as a result of the U.S. government's default on payments totaling thirty-two billion dollars."

"We really need to do something quickly before this news leaks out," Press Secretary Brent Jones said, his hand moving to his stomach, drawn by the twinge of pain.

"What are the contingency plans, gentlemen?" President Stewart asked.

"We have already allocated additional programming resources from less critical agencies," Vice President Chandler said. "And, as Tom and Bill have said, everyone will be working around the clock until the problem is resolved."

"And if that doesn't work in time, what is the backup contingency plan?" The room was dead silent. "We do have a contingency plan, don't we?" the President said, eyebrows raised and fingers strumming the table, as he looked from Vice President Chandler to Wagner.

"Yes, sir," answered Wagner. "As I had suggested and was unanimously agreed in the very first council meeting, we determined it would be prudent to develop back-up procedures at all agencies for mission-critical functions. And we strongly encouraged private industry to do the same, even resorting to manual procedures if necessary—and if possible."

"So what is the agency's contingency plan?" the President repeated.

"We will 'trick' the computer into thinking that the checks and direct deposits processed for December were voided and need to be processed again," Wagner answered proudly.

"We'll trick the computer? What will we do, lie to it?"

"Well, actually, yes." Wagner looked sheepishly at the President over his small wire frame glasses.

"Well, Tom. Given that you are in a roomful of politicians we ought to be able to help you with that," the President said with the trace of a smile. "Will it work?"

"We think so, sir."

The President's eyes narrowed with contempt. "We're not even sure that the contingency plan will work? We have only fourteen days until Y2K-Day and all you can give me is an 'I think so'? You're going to have to do better than that."

"What Tom means, Mr. President," interjected the Vice President, "is that we can never be one hundred percent sure until we actually do it. But I'm confident we will get it to work. We may have to make corrections and tweak it some, but it will work."

"Tweak it all you have to. Just make it work," the President ordered as he stabbed the table with his index finger. "I don't want to have to answer to forty-five million elderly and disabled people who don't know where their next meal is coming from because of a stupid computer glitch. Something that most of them—and the rest of us, for that matter—don't understand or at least can't believe is happening."

"We can help by issuing a notice throughout the banking system that we are repeating the December transactions and that banks should honor them," Treasury Secretary Calderon added. "We will make it work, sir. With the expected disruptions of more than a third of the Fortune 500 companies, and God knows how many smaller companies, we have to. The financial markets will already be severely tested, and if that's combined with a lack of confidence in the federal government's ability to function, our whole economic structure could begin to unravel."

"Let's be careful not to exaggerate the problem," Vice President Chandler said. "It's going to be bad enough on its own."

"Yes it is, Neil. But I'm afraid I agree with Bill," said the President. "We have to show the country that we are prepared to deal with the consequences of the Y2K glitches where we have failed to correct them in time. Brent, set up a press conference for first thing Monday morning. We need to deal with this before it explodes in our faces."

"With all due respect, I don't think you should be there, Sir," Chandler said. "I think it will give the announcement too much stature and cause more concern than it allays."

"He's right, sir," Jones agreed.

"Okay, Brent, you hold the press conference. You've had plenty of practice turning turds into tulips during your years with me anyway. Bill and Tom will accompany you to answer technical questions, and each should make a brief statement. Having them there should show we are dealing with this at the highest level without labeling it a Presidential crisis."

"I'll set it up immediately, sir," Jones said.

"Good. But before we break up, I would like to be brought up-to-date on the status of our overall contingency plans. Bill, you've already started, so why don't you finish on the economy."

"Certainly, Sir," the Treasury Secretary replied, taking a deep breath. "I'm sorry to have to report, the additional one hundred billion dollars we ordered printed in September and pumped into the system in mid-November is almost gone."

"You're kidding?" FBI Director Alexander said, his muscles stiffening.

"I wish I were, Darren. We just ordered another fifty billion dollars, but it's unlikely we will get much of it before Y2K-Day. We've also used up most of the paper stock. And believe me all stops are being pulled out to keep enough money available to the system, but I'm afraid people are hoarding dollars at an alarming rate."

"If we run out of funds it will add significantly to the pressures that are building for civil unrest," FBI Director Alexander said. He prided himself on staying calm during crises, but he could not stop the twitch in his left eye.

"We will declare a banking holiday before we let the system run dry," Calderon said.

"We can't do that," Alexander snapped. "If we close the banks we'll just convince people they should be damned worried." The twitch in his eye grew more noticeable. It had developed several months ago, a result of the strain he'd been under for far too long. The infiltration of terrorist groups had been steadily increasing over the last two years. In addition, the collapse of the Russian economy had destabilized that country and, in some respects, made it more dangerous than when the communists were in control. The Director feared it was only a matter of time before some terrorists got their hands on a small nuclear device, compliments of a Russian or former Soviet satellite group, desperate for money. The new millennium, with all of the planned celebrations, was a magnate for these groups. If the Y2K problem brought power failures and disruptions to normal communications, then the chances of an already dangerous situation becoming explosive increased tenfold.

"We may have to close them, Darren," Treasury Secretary Calderon responded. "But then we will 'manage' the system and use the remaining currency as we deem appropriate. I have also spoken with Reserve Chairman Strand, and he is prepared to announce that the Federal Reserve will extend all the credit needed to keep the banking system liquid—much as was done after Black Monday in '87."

"That's good, Bill," said the President. "Keep working closely with Strand and keep me informed. If need be I will go public to appeal for restraint. Darren, since you brought up civil unrest, why don't you go next."

"Certainly, Mr. President. As you know, the bureau has been on full alert since the summer. All agents are on double duty and ninety-five percent of them are working on potential acts of terrorism. We have already infiltrated a half-dozen suspect groups. And we will be prepared to move on them at the appropriate time. But I don't have to tell you that the crises we are facing worldwide are a breeding ground for terrorists. The possibility of power blackouts, lack of communications and disruption in food supplies, combined with financial crises makes this a nightmare."

Everyone in the room was all too aware that the potential breakdown of the country's infrastructure, even for a short time, was an open invitation to those bent on terrorism. The possibility of a banking holiday to prevent a run on the banks would be fodder for the dozen or so militia groups that had already become increasingly more active as Y2K-Day approached. With federal manpower resources stretched thin, the possibility of power failures, the potential for unrest from militia groups taking advantage of the situation, the disruption of medical facilities, and the interference of normal police operations would all serve to encourage the many foreign terrorist groups that harbored hatred for the United States.

"You must continue to concentrate on all potential terrorists," the President said. "The U.S. Marshals will be at your disposal to cover other, less critical, areas. Also remember that the Army's Special Forces are standing by if and when you need them."

"Thank you, Mr. President. I hope we won't need them, but I won't hesitate to use them if we do."

"If I might interject at this time—Sir?" asked James Knight, head of the President's Secret Service, who was sitting next to him, as he always did.

"Of course, Jim," the President sighed. "But I know what you are going to say. And you can save your breath."

"I'm sorry, sir, but I must again strongly urge you to cancel all appearances from now until after Y2K-Day. Given what Director Alexander has just told us I think it is more prudent than ever."

"Forget it, Jim. I know you are only doing your job, but what message does it send if the President of the United States goes into hiding? We'll start a panic for sure. I won't do it."

"Sir—at least cancel your New Year's Eve appearances."

"Again, no. I've already amended them so that by eleven I will be hosting a gala at the White House."

"Yes, Sir, that's a start. I know you didn't want to do it. But it at least assures us that we will have backup generators, communications, an escape route......"

"Good, Jim. I know you've got it covered. And I do appreciate it," the President said as he turned abruptly to CIA Director Mathias. "Donald, bring me up-to-date on foreign developments. What's the CIA's latest assessment?"

"It hasn't improved much since our last meeting, Mr. President," Mathias said in his usual deliberate voice, which still revealed traces of a West Texas drawl. "The rest of the world continues to range from three months to two years behind us in Y2K compliance. Great Britain, Canada, Israel and Australia are in the best shape. They will have disruptions but should be able to weather the storm without catastrophic failures. Asia—including Japan and China—Central and South America and Africa, except for South Africa, are all more than a year behind. Most have concentrated on their emergency services, electrical power supplies and banking systems, so we can hope they will not suffer total collapse—at least not one that will last too long. Western Europe is in the middle, about six to nine months behind us. They might have made the deadline if they weren't trying to reprogram for the Euro at the same damn time."

"So we are still in for serious disruptions worldwide, even if our own systems are operational in time," Ambassador-at-Large Victor Noble said, again stroking his mustache.

"Yes, sir. There is no question about it," Director Mathias said.

"Then we haven't made one iota of progress, have we, Mr. Mathias?" Noble's voice remained low and controlled as his dark brown eyes bore into the CIA director.

"No, Mr. Noble. That's not true at all," Mathias replied angrily, returning the icy stare. "We have........"

"What is the status of the 'Cover the Earth' plan?" the President interjected, as he faced Secretary of Defense Donovan and General Armstrong. He was anxious to cut off any further interchange between Mathias and Noble.

"We're happy to report that the plan has been launched and completed as outlined," Secretary Donovan answered. The General nodded.

The plan, code-named 'Cover the Earth,' was the brainchild of General Armstrong with the support of Secretary Donovan. It called for the U.S. military to have a presence in each area of strategic importance in the world as Y2K-Day dawned, with foreign military bases supplemented by aircraft carriers and their naval escorts. The purpose of the military forces was not to interfere with or prevent any civil unrest that might occur. Indeed, they were not equipped to do so. Cover the Earth's purported mission was to provide evacuation and emergency medical treatment for Americans caught abroad during any catastrophe or civil unrest resulting from the Year 2000 problem. While this was true, it served as a smoke screen for its primary, and more crucial, task of keeping critical communications functioning.

There was much concern among the President and his military advisors that the world's communications systems could be severely compromised if some, or all, of the satellites orbiting the Earth were disrupted as a result of Y2K failures. The problems could become acute if terrorists added sabotage to the mix. The Cover the Earth plan called for each military base and aircraft carrier to have at least one of the experimental "Flying Wing" aircraft currently being developed by the U.S. military. These remote-controlled vehicles have the wingspan of a 747 and solar panels that power their twenty small propellers. The plane flies at an altitude of one to two miles and, because it is unmanned and solar powered, can remain aloft indefinitely. The Flying Wing was designed to supplement or, in some cases, replace communications satellites. One Flying Wing can provide the communications link for a large city or even a small country.

As such, the primary purpose of Project Cover the Earth was to ensure that the President and the U.S. military continued to have essential communications throughout the world. The Flying Wings would also be strategically placed throughout the United States to ensure the operation of critical domestic communications.

"What about Russia and the other former Soviet satellites? What's their Y2K readiness? Have they made any progress?" the President asked.

"Once again, they are a unique situation," Director Mathias responded. "Most of the programs that control their infrastructure will not be ready. In some cases they have still not even started to correct the problem. Their biggest concern is the electrical power grids, so they have concentrated on this area, but we predict they will still experience major blackouts. And there is no telling how long it will take them to fix things once they break because they are so lacking in resources and leadership."

"Yes, the leadership seems to be almost nonexistent," Secretary of State Carlson said.

"That leadership void concerns me, especially considering the crisis they face," the President said. "Please continue, Donald."

"Yes, Sir. As I was saying, the rest of their infrastructure will not be ready for Y2K-Day, but it really won't matter that much. Their services are so poor and unreliable now that most people won't notice much difference. Since the banking system all but collapsed in the summer of '98, they don't count on it very much. They've been operating mostly on a barter system since then. The real concern has to be the nuclear power plants in the region and, of course, their nuclear weapons arsenal."

"We are continuing to monitor these two critical areas closely," General Armstrong said. "We believe it is reasonably well covered."

"I'm not very comforted by terms like 'reasonably well covered' when we are discussing nuclear facilities, General," Noble said.

"By that, Ambassador, I mean we have reviewed the status of their contingency plans in the case of a malfunction of one or all of their nuclear reactors. We believe they can safely shut the reactors down and keep the core properly cooled so that there is no risk of a meltdown. In case of a general power failure, they are prepared with backup diesel generators," the General calmly replied.

"That doesn't answer the question about the state of their nuclear weapons systems. I'd like to know............" The President again interrupted Victor Noble before he could finish.

"Thank you, General. Brent, Bill, Tom, I'll want to review the press release with the three of you before Monday. Please remember that we want to be as honest with the public as we can, without scaring the hell out of them."

"I don't think that is possible or wise, Mr. President," Noble was quick to say. "We should reveal as little as possible."

"I'm afraid I must agree with Victor, Sir," FBI Director Alexander added, although it pained him to agree on anything with Victor Noble. He didn't like him, nor did he like the unholy alliance he had forged with the President. "We could start a real panic if the public knew how critical the situation is. Especially the situation overseas."

"With all due respect, gentlemen, I couldn't disagree more," the President said firmly. "The American people need to believe that we are not hiding information. I believe they will not only be able to handle the truth, but will pick up the ball and run with it. Remember that the American people in this century have led the way in winning two world wars. We've defeated the communists. We've put men on the moon. We've built the most powerful economic and military nation the world has ever known. If we are honest with them and put out the 'call to arms,' they will respond with the 'American Ingenuity' that we are so rightly known for. With their help, we will defeat this damned Millennium Bug. We have to or I'm afraid the world may well be plunged into chaos."

"I agree with you, Mr. President," Secretary of State Carlson said. "But it's a fine line to walk."

"Then we'll walk it, Judith," the President said. "We must walk it or fall off the cliff. I know that all of you are capable of putting your personal careers aside and rising to the level of leadership required if we are going to ask them to win yet another war—against an enemy they can't even see."

"You can count on us, Sir," Vice President Chandler said. There was a chorus of agreement from around the table, though some, most notably Noble, felt the President's comments were out of place—a bit like a campaign speech.

"I know I can," the President said as he folded his hands in front of him. "There's a lot of work to be done before Y2K-Day is upon us. So let's get going."

The Vice President closed the door after ushering the rest of the group out, leaving only himself, General Armstrong and Noble with the President.

"I understand the test of our nuclear weapons control system is scheduled for today," the President said, looking from the Vice President to the General and finally to Noble.

"Yes, Mr. President. It's scheduled for five p.m.," Noble answered.

The computer systems controlling the United States' nuclear weapons arsenal were not immune to the Year 2000 problem, but because of national security issues, the project to correct its Y2K glitches were not open for discussion in the larger group. For that reason, they were also not under the purview of Tom Wagner. Code named "Millennium Bug," the project was overseen by Noble.

This appointment was the result of a report, in November 1998, by the Chairman of the House Subcommittee on Government Management, Information and Technology that gave the twenty-four major federal agencies an overall 'D' grade in their attempts to fix the Year 2000 problem. The grades were based on quarterly reports the agencies were required to file with the Office of Management and Budget, as well as information culled from the General Accounting Office, the federal government's auditor. GAO reports had indicated, in a presentation at a conference in Arlington, Va., that "the mammoth Department of Defense shows insufficient evidence of adequate progress on Y2K compliance issues."

After receiving these disturbing reports, the leaders of the House and Senate established a special joint congressional subcommittee to monitor the Defense Department's progress in dealing with the Y2K problem. The subcommittee strongly recommended that the President appoint them to directly oversee the department's Y2K progress after this editorial appeared in the *New York Post*:

## FAIL-SAFETY-CATCH

To the extent that the general public is thinking about the "Y2K" problem—the fact that many computers can't comprehend dates starting with the year 2000—the worries center around whether Social Security checks will arrive on time and airline reservations will be honored.

Has the public heard about the threat to the American nuclear deterrent?

The Department of Defense has just admitted that its computer people never actually performed tests on three of the five "mission-critical" computer systems they had previously certified as being in Y2K compliance. In addition, no contingency plans were developed in the event any of these computer systems fail due to Y2K.

In other words, there was some big-time lying going on over at the Pentagon.

The President politely refused the subcommittee's request to oversee the DOD's progress, but placated them by agreeing to put a GAO team in charge of the project's day-to-day administration. The Pentagon staff assigned to the project would be responsible to the GAO candidate. He also agreed to appoint a high-level civilian to oversee the Millennium Bug project. As Chairman of the Joint Chiefs of Staff, General Armstrong understood the President's position and helped make it happen, even though he took a lot of heat from his subordinates for putting a civilian in charge of a military project.

What General Armstrong and most others—including the Vice President—did not understand, was the President's appointment of Ambassador-at-Large Victor Noble as that high-level civilian. It was common knowledge that the President had rewarded Noble with the Ambassadorship as payment for his dropping out of the Presidential race in 1996 and supporting him for President. It was just as well known, though, that there was no love lost between them; it was a marriage of convenience. Noble was shrewd enough to realize he couldn't win the Democratic nomination against the popular Stewart, but by supporting him he could gain a position of prestige among Washington's power elite. Stewart knew he wouldn't have enough votes without Noble's backing and supporters. He just hoped he hadn't made a deal with the devil.

Prior to his two terms in the House of Representatives, the Texas Congressman was a successful businessman. As an investment banker, he had earned a reputation as a shrewd and ruthless dealmaker and had amassed a small fortune. But he had also gained a reputation for being very patriotic, with strong opinions on how the country should move forward into the twenty-first century. Even though Victor Noble's ideas were much more conservative than James Stewart's, the President counted on Noble's patriotism to keep their differences in check.

Noble's appointment was well accepted by the congressional subcommittee because he was seen as a strong, independent Congressman. The General and the Vice President understood better when the President explained having him responsible for the project was far better than having him on the sidelines in a position to criticize their progress, or lack of it. As the man in charge of overseeing the project, he would be in the direct line of fire if the project failed. At the same time, though, he was just *overseeing* the project and had no actual authority. All he could do was require that reports were sent back to the President and the Congressional subcommittee. The actual authority rested with the General Accounting Office.

"Is it safe to assume we will not have a repeat of this morning's disaster?" the President asked Noble. The President kept his hands folded in front of him and spoke softly as his eyes met Noble's. The President was angry with Noble for being argumentative during the meeting, but with all the other problems he had to deal with, he did not want to prompt a confrontation.

"Logan has assured me they're ready. The preliminary tests have all gone well. But of course we won't know until we run today's full blown test."

"I read Logan's file. He seems quite competent. He was a good choice, then?" The President never revealed to Noble that he and General Armstrong had reviewed the GAO's personnel file of Nick Logan before he was accepted as the project's field operations manager. His file indicated he was intelligent, resourceful, dedicated, nonpolitical and independent. Just what the President wanted.

"Yes, Sir. He was. He has been dedicated to the completion of the project," Noble said.

"Good." The President then turned to Chandler and Armstrong. "I assume the two of you will be present at the test?"

Of course President Stewart knew that they would. He had already received his report from them that confirmed what Noble had just told him. He was not going to leave the country's most critical project—not to mention the most potentially damaging project to his career—in the hands of the ambitious Victor Noble. These two men were not only his most trusted advisors, but Neil had extensive technical knowledge and the General could command the experience and loyalty of his subordinate, Colonel Henry Clay.

Colonel Clay was the Pentagon's man in charge of the Millennium Bug project before Stewart was forced to bring in the GAO and Noble to appease Congress. It had been a bitter blow for Colonel Clay to have to hand over the project to someone else—especially to a civilian. But he had been hand picked by the General, and he was a loyal soldier, so he did what he was told. He moved to the background, but remained instrumental in moving the project along and keeping the General and the President informed.

They had been pleased when the Colonel informed them that the GAO's Logan was quite competent and appeared to have no hidden agenda. He was committed to completing the project, no matter what it took. Of course this was important because of the critical nature of the U.S. project, but it was made even more important once the President agreed—persuaded by his military and economic advisors—to give financial and technical support to the Russians to ensure they would meet Y2K compliance with *their* nuclear weapons system. Especially since the Russians, for their own security, would not let the American technicians have direct access to their systems.

The risk of an inadvertent nuclear launch from a Y2K glitch was just too great to leave the bankrupt Russians to their own devices. The U.S. people would probably understand this if it ever became known, Stewart believed—and ultimately, news would probably leak out. But how would they accept this support if the Russian system worked and the U.S. system didn't? They wouldn't understand or care that the U.S. system was more difficult to fix because it was more sophisticated and, therefore, included many more lines of code. Just before the meeting, General Armstrong had told the President that the Russians had completed their test successfully. It was imperative that the U.S. test also be successful.

"Actually, if you don't mind Victor, I think I will clear my schedule and attend the test myself. I would very much like to witness the test first-hand and personally congratulate those involved."

"Of course, Mr. President. We would be honored," Noble said calmly. The President had to admire Noble's composure. "He must be one hell of a poker player," the President thought. His expression had not changed for an instant, even though Stewart knew he must be furious at the thought of having his thunder stolen.

Now the damned system had better work, the President thought.

CHAPTER 5

▼

# THE ROAD TO MOSCOW TWELVE-FIFTEEN A.M., SUNDAY DECEMBER 19, 1999

## THIRTEEN DAYS TO <u>0 0</u>

Yuri Petrov wasted no time leaving the command complex once completing his task. Around eleven, he had received an order from Boris Stepovich to report to his office immediately. The messenger had said the Director wanted confirmation of the completion of all phases of the project directly from Yuri and was not willing to wait. He had no choice but to comply. It was not unlike Stepovich to be impatient, and the hour of day meant nothing to him. Yuri delayed his departure only long enough to complete his final task. Unfortunately, he was unable to let his father know that their plan had changed since all of the lines were closely monitored. He decided he would go directly to his father's apartment after meeting with Stepovich.

The road to Moscow was isolated and dark. Yuri drove as rapidly as his old, boxy Moskvich car would allow. It was a typical Russian winter night—snowing and frigid. He knew it was dangerous to travel these roads at this hour, another reason to drive fast. With the fall of communism, life in Russia had become freer but much more dangerous. Gangs of hoodlums roamed Moscow and the outskirts of the city in search of unwitting victims. One could no longer, for instance, take a taxi from the airport to the city and expect to be safe; you had to hire a private car. The gangs usually left private cars alone because they knew the occupants would be armed—as was Yuri—and there was easier prey to be had. But that didn't account for the thugs made braver and more stupid by drink.

What worried Yuri more, though, was the Russian Mafia. They were much more organized, ruthless, and absolutely fearless. He shouldn't have to worry about them for another fifteen kilometers, though; the road was too sparsely traveled this far out for them to bother. And with luck, the snow and the late hour would keep them from bothering at all.

As he drove, Yuri reflected on what had already been a long, tense day. Beginning with the critical test of the nuclear weapons activation system, attended by a score of Russian dignitaries, then making the change to insert Director Stepovich's security code, followed by four excruciating hours of small talk, pretending to enjoy himself, and finally by having less than thirty minutes to carry out his father's latest instructions. And it was not over yet. The most stressful part lay ahead—his meeting with Stepovich.

After last night's meeting with his father, Yuri felt the pressure intensify. It was not only the danger, but also the sense of doubt he felt about this being the right way to accomplish their goal. He understood these last years had been difficult for his father. What hurt the most was not the loss of respect and power that had befallen all members of the Russian intelligence and military communities—though Yuri knew this effected his father deeply—but what the country had become. It cut like a knife into his father's heart. In many ways and in the eyes of many people, his once-powerful country had been relegated to the rolls of third-world nations. This loss of respect for his homeland was shattering.

When Yuri had questioned the harshness of life and the lack of freedom under communism, his father answered that there had never been much freedom in Russia and life had always been harsh. But his father believed communism was an important process that needed to be harsh at first. Later, it would develop and grow and bring prosperity to Russia, as it had brought her military power. To succeed, communism had to change and become more democratic. But the hard-liners had held on too long, and when they fell they fell hard and completely. Instead of making a gradual transition from the tightly controlled communist regime to a freer and more democratic government, with a capitalistic economy, the country was forced to change overnight—a change it was ill prepared to deal with. For most, this newfound freedom had made life less restrictive, but even more harsh. The few that prospered had become painful symbols to the many who had so little.

The longer he drove, the more Yuri grew concerned about the summons from Stepovich. Was this just another example of the Director's disregard for propriety? To hell with the agents; they were only there to serve him anyway. Given the sensitive nature and importance of the task he had just completed, it was not surprising to Yuri that the Director would want to confirm it directly. Still, the timing and urgency of the message left him anxious. Should he ignore the summons and go straight to his father's apartment? He began to realize how much the time he spent behind a desk had left him ill prepared for field assignments.

Buried deep in thought, Yuri never noticed the van that had been following him for the last two miles, its lights out. What he saw—and just in time—was a car, apparently spun out of control, blocking his path. Slamming on the brakes, Yuri managed to stop only several yards from the car, the tires finally catching on the slick road. Now his senses were alert. Eyes searching the car and the heavy woods on the side of the road, he reached for the gun lying on the seat beside him. The hairs on the back of his neck bristled and beads of sweat formed on his forehead, as his hand wrapped around the cold steel of the Glock 17. He had chosen this compact model because it was easier to conceal and use. Never comfortable with guns, he now wished he had practiced more.

A lone man stumbled in front of the disabled car, looking dazed and hurt. Yuri knew it could be a trap, so he put the car in reverse and backed up ten feet. This would allow him room to drive around the car and continue. Then the man stumbled and fell across the road, blocking Yuri's path. He had waited too long to act and now, because of the steep snow banks, he would have to risk running over the man to get away. Moments passed and Yuri made out the blood on the man's face, lit by his headlights. He knew he had to help. The rulebook for any FSS engagement said do not respond to an apparent accident. Yet, he could not leave this man to die.

Gun in hand, eyes scanning both sides of the road, Yuri slowly opened the door. Instantly, he felt cold steel behind his ear. "Be careful, Petrov. We are friends. Or you would already be dead. Give me the gun."

A cold chill ran down his spine. The gunman's words did not lessen his fear.

"Who are you?" Yuri asked, relinquishing his gun.

"We have been sent by your father to bring you safely to him."

"How do I know my father sent you?"

"You are in great danger. Your father fears for your safety. Just like he fears for Katya."

"Katya? What do you know about Katya?" Perhaps his father sent these men after all. They had used the proper code word. Perhaps his father had learned of Stepovich's summons and did not trust him. Few people knew about his sister Katya, especially since she'd been living in the United States for the last twenty years. At the age of sixteen, a year after the death of their mother, it had been determined she would go live in America and become an American citizen. She would join her American family, long time transplanted KGB agents, as an orphaned niece from Poland. But, of course, Stepovich also knew this, as he was a party to the arrangement. Could this be a trap—in case Yuri decided *not* to go directly to the Director's office?

"I know only that your father said her name would get your attention. He was right. Now get out." The man pulled him by the coat collar, keeping the gun to Yuri's head.

"Who are you?" Yuri said as he struggled with what to do as he was yanked from the car. This man's actions seemed more aggressive than necessary, if they were truly sent by his father.

"I am Pasha. That is all you need to know. More would be dangerous to both of us."

"How can I be sure my father sent you?" Yuri was very frightened now.

"You can't. You will come with us because you have no choice." Pasha pressed the gun to Yuri's head and led him to the back of the van. Two other men approached his car, while a fourth very large man, opened the van's back doors from inside and removed Yuri's hat and wallet. The big man then took his things to the pair standing by Yuri's car. He gave the hat to the rougher looking of the two men, he called Valerii, and while Valerii arranged the hat on his head, the big man deftly slipped Yuri's wallet into Valerii's coat pocket. The big man had as deftly removed the rough looking man's own wallet earlier.

The "injured man" had already moved the decoy car behind the van, allowing Valerii to drive off in Yuri's car. As he did so, he felt good about his night's work. For his part in the kidnapping, he received the man's car in payment. Even though it was only a cheap Moskvich, it would bring a decent night's pay for little effort. He would remove the plates when he got to Moscow, and it would be his to sell. Valerii smiled.

"Egor, remember that we need a positive ID." Ivan Malenkov again wished Stepovich had assigned someone else to work with him. He watched Egor put a full clip into his AK47 and then casually stroke the rifle with the back of his hand.

"Ivan, you worry too much. You drive and I'll shoot. You do your job. I'll do mine."

"Just remember what our job is. Stepovich has demanded we have a *confirmed* kill." Ivan didn't want to have to remind Egor that he was the senior agent in charge.

"Yes, Ivan. And I am here because you are incapable of doing it yourself."

Ivan did not reply. He just wanted to complete this distasteful task as quickly as possible and get far away from Egor Skulsky.

As he got within five kilometers of Moscow, the kidnapper in Yuri's car became increasingly alert. He knew he could easily become prey for other criminals like himself. That's when he noticed the headlights rapidly approaching from behind. He pressed the gas pedal to the floor and the engine whined, as the underpowered vehicle gained speed slowly. But it was no match for the powerful Mercedes, which quickly narrowed the gap. With snow banks on both sides of the road, there was no place for the kidnapper to go.

Valerii took aim at the passenger of the Mercedes that drew up beside him, but it was too late. As he prepared to fire, he saw the square-jawed, chiseled face, with lips curled into a cruel smile. The last thing he saw was the flash from the barrel of the AK47, just before the burst of fire blew the side of his head off. Ivan immediately applied the brakes to avoid being hit by the other vehicle as it crashed into the snow bank on the right, then careened across the road, finally lodging in the snow some seventy-five feet down the road.

"Damn it, Egor! You practically blew his fucking head off. You'd have done it with one shot if you knew what you were doing." As soon as the words were out of his mouth, a frustrated Ivan knew his last remark was unwise. Pulling up beside the blood-splattered car, the two men's eyes locked and, for an instant, Ivan thought he might be Egor's next victim. It wasn't smart to confront an animal fresh from the kill. But, damn it! This is exactly why he didn't want Egor along.

Slowly, Skulsky's angry expression changed into a spine-chilling half smile—a smile that said, "never criticize me again or there will be an unfortunate accident." Agents on assignment with Skulsky had died under questionable circumstances before.

His focus regained, Skulsky calmly got out of the car, raised his assault rifle and riddled the wrecked car. After emptying the first magazine, he replaced it and emptied a second one into the driver, followed by a demonic laugh. The laugh—his trademark—had earned him the nickname—"Hyena."

It looked like the type of killing that often took place on these desolate roads by the gangs that now controlled much of Moscow. Skulsky searched the dead man's pockets until he found his wallet, then he checked for Petrov's identification. Petrov's ID would confirm the kill; the body no longer recognizable. Removing the wallet also made it look like a robbery. Just another sloppy job by amateurs.

"It is done. You are too weak for this work, Ivan," Skulsky said as he got into the car. "We know it is Yuri Petrov. The car carried his plates and I have his ID. The fingerprints at the morgue will confirm it."

Ivan looked at Egor with disgust, but said nothing. No good could come from challenging him further. He had known Egor for years, and they had been partners several times, but it amazed Ivan that this man could take *pleasure* in killing, especially a comrade. Ivan was sure Egor would take the same perverse pleasure if his orders were to kill him.

Ivan still wondered what Yuri Petrov had done, or what he knew that was so important that Stepovich couldn't let him live with it. Though Ivan was a committed and loyal FSS agent, the brutality with which his organization often worked distressed him. He wondered if Stepovich was as heartless as Skulsky, just less obvious. It had been easier to believe the end justified the means when Russia was strong and what they did for the FSS seemed necessary for national security. Now that Russia was in many ways a shell of her former self, and so too the FSS, it was more difficult for Ivan to justify his—and the agency's—actions.

As the van made its way to Moscow, Yuri still wondered if he were among friends. There had been very little discussion and no explanation of why they waited thirty minutes in the dark with the lights off before continuing. When they were still several kilometers outside Moscow, the van slowed down and Pasha pulled back the curtain that covered the side window, the only window in the back. That's when Yuri saw his wrecked car, riddled with bullets and the driver with his face blown off.

"Aren't you going to stop?" Yuri gasped.

"Why?" Pasha replied.

"He is your comrade. How can you just leave him like that?"

"That hoodlum was never our comrade. He got what we expected and what he deserved," Pasha said as he looked straight ahead.

"Then, you knew this was going to happen?" Yuri now understood that this man had been sacrificed to protect him.

"Yes. We needed someone to take your place. That punk was easily convinced he had a prize when we offered him your car. I'm surprised he didn't want money too when he saw it was an old Moskvich." His two partners mimicked pasha's snicker. "He was not just an amateur, but also stupid."

"Was my father aware of this?" Yuri asked. He wondered what his father would condone to accomplish his task.

"The details of the plan were left to us," Pasha said. "He has confidence in our abilities."

No one spoke the rest of the trip. Yuri couldn't help thinking about the sacrifice he just witnessed and questioned how many more lives would be forfeited. This man's death made him worry about Antoin. Could his father's plan work? And if it did, was it worth it? Was it worth all of these years without Katya? He knew that men like Stepovich would sacrifice anything and anyone to accomplish their goals. But what about his father?

After they entered the city, the men in the van drove Yuri to what looked to be an apartment complex. He wondered if he had been wrong to trust them. Perhaps he should have tried to escape. Not that he'd had much chance. One of the men slipped out of the van and disappeared inside the building. In a few minutes, he reappeared and signaled his comrades. The driver quickly pulled the car into a secluded spot. He stood guard as Pasha, his gun now concealed in his coat pocket, escorted Yuri into the building.

Yuri was led up three flights of stairs and into a small apartment. As soon as the outside door was locked, an interior door opened and his father stepped out. Yuri breathed a huge sigh of relief as his father enveloped him in a bear hug.

"I wasn't sure if I would see you again," Yuri said. "Your comrades did a good job of getting me here, but they were not so good at convincing me they were friends."

"You were and are in great danger, but not from these brave men," Dimitry said. "They are loyal to me and risked their lives to protect you."

"From Stepovich?" Yuri's body stiffened.

"Yes. He ordered your death earlier today. He now believes this has been accomplished." Dimitry gently squeezed his son's arm.

"Earlier today? Before the test?" A chill went up Yuri's spine as he realized he should never have considered meeting with Stepovich.

"Yes. Before the test. As far as I know, there is no way he could have known about our final adjustment." The realization that Stepovich had ordered him killed without even knowing he had been betrayed made Yuri rock back on his heels.

Dimitry held his son steady. The look of fear on Yuri's face was slowly replaced by puzzlement. Dimitry answered his son's look.

"Boris Stepovich didn't get to be Director by leaving loose ends. You know too much. You could be dangerous to his plans."

"And he would have me killed for carrying out his plan." The coldness of this made Yuri realize he would never understood the brutality of a man like Boris Stepovich.

"Yes. I had thought this a possibility. That is why I arranged for your protection upon leaving the complex tomorrow. I'm afraid Stepovich moved more quickly than I expected. Now we must get you out of the country. It is much too dangerous here."

"What about you? You will be in as much danger as I..."

"I must stay here. And you must go to the United States and join Katya."

"It will be good to see her again, but why not bring her here?" Yuri knew the answer before his father said it. He understood they may need to allow the American nuclear weapons system to be operational, and Katya needed to be there for that. The balance of power had proved itself an efficient deterrent to the use of these weapons. One had to be very careful when this balance was tipped.

"No. You know I need her there. And our manpower is limited. I can protect you both better if you are together. I will send Pasha with you." There was a stern look on Dimitry's face as he clenched and unclenched his fist.

"I don't like leaving you here, but I will do as you wish." Yuri said, clearly pained, hoping his father would not end up like the man on the side of the road.

"Good. These men will get you to Katya safely. Pasha has traveled much in the U.S. so he will be of great value to you. He can also help you with your English. It's been a long time since you attended the English school."

"We should hurry, Dimitry," Pasha said, pointing to the clock. "We've gained some time, but it won't be long before they realize Yuri is not the man they killed. They will be looking for both of you."

"Yes, come, Yuri," said Dimitry, motioning to the bedroom, "so we can go over what you've accomplished tonight and what we must now do."

Yuri hesitated, looking toward Pasha and the others—these men who had risked their lives for him and were going to do it again.

"Don't worry, they are not offended," Dimitry said. "It's safer for all of us not to know any more than necessary to accomplish our goal. A man cannot reveal what he does not know."

Yuri grimaced as he followed his father and the two of them disappeared into the bedroom.

Although well past midnight, Stepovich had not left his office. He had been waiting for the report from Malenkov, who had just arrived.

"So, Ivan, you have been successful?"

"Yes, Comrade Stepovich. We intercepted him as you said. We made it look suitably unprofessional and messy. It was not a problem for Egor."

"That's good, Ivan. You made a positive ID?"

Ivan was not about to tell his boss what he thought. "I told you so. That stupid son-of-a-bitch blew his fucking head off before we could identify him." He had almost made a fatal mistake with Egor and wasn't about to make another.

"It was Yuri Petrov's car and his papers were on him. However—" Ivan hesitated as he looked down at the floor, "we were unable to make visual confirmation because Egor did his job too well. So absolute identification will have to wait until we get fingerprints." Ivan looked up. "I will go to the morgue myself as soon as the body has been retrieved."

"Yes, damn it. Egor can be too aggressive—but he is effective. I want that confirmation as soon as possible, so I know for sure. I'll see the police are alerted and get out there immediately, then have our man at the morgue deliver the prints as soon as Petrov is brought in. I have something *else* for you to do." Stepovich drummed his desk with his short stubby fingers.

"If Egor hadn't been so vicious and trigger happy, we could have made visual confirmation first and still made it look like the gangs got him," Ivan said as he twisted in his chair, unable to contain himself.

The red-faced Stepovich pounded his hand on the desk. "Enough, Ivan, enough! Egor has his value whether you like it or not."

"Of course you are right, as always comrade," Ivan said, again diverting his eyes. He could kick himself for not holding his tongue. He hoped Stepovich did not see his comment as insubordination.

"That's better. Now I have another urgent task for the two of you to complete. You will leave for Washington at once."

"Of course, comrade," Ivan said. He tried very hard not to show his displeasure at hearing he would be teamed with Egor again. "What do you want us to do?"

"This task is of the utmost importance and I want both my smartest and my deadliest agent there to make sure it is completed successfully. Now listen carefully and I will explain what you must do."

# CHAPTER 6

▼

# WASHINGTON, D.C. THREE P.M., SATURDAY DECEMBER 18, 1999

## FOURTEEN DAYS TO 0 0

Kate had left to attend to some final details before the test and Nick, sitting in his office waiting for the dignitaries to arrive, thought back to the previous day's staff meeting.

It was his boss, Charles Grant, who decided that there should be a general meeting to discuss the procedures and protocol for today's all-important test. If it had been Nick's decision he would have spent the time going over the test format and trying to make sure that everything was ready. But Grant was the consummate politician and there was no way that he would let an opportunity to look important in front of the high level individuals that would be there get away.

So at ten yesterday they held a general staff meeting in the main conference room at the end of the hall, two doors down from Nick's office. One of the first in attendance was Colonel Henry Clay and his staff. This was typical of Colonel Clay who was always punctual and expected others to be as well. No doubt a reflection of his military training. A trait that Nick appreciated since he thought that meetings were mostly a waste of time and, at best, worth only about ten percent of the time invested in them. He also knew that Colonel Clay's punctuality also had to do with the fact that he would make sure that he would be occupying the seat at the 'head' of the large conference table.

Colonel Clay was a career officer in his mid-fifties, tall and thin he was always ramrod straight. He had been in charge of this project for some three years now and the pressure had grown in intensity until it was now at a fever pitch. The Colonel was forced to take direct control, and thus direct responsibility, of the project about a year and a half ago. That was when one of the participants in the project had leaked the fact that the project was badly behind schedule to the Congressional Defense Subcommittee, which had oversight responsibility, and that a disaster was in the making.

Until that time the congressional subcommittee hadn't really understood the true nature of the problem. The military in general, and the Colonel in particular, took a great deal of heat for the lack of progress. Captain Auerr, who previously headed it up under Colonel Clay, was demoted and held responsible. This forced Colonel Clay, much to his dismay, to have to step into the direct line of fire, something that he knew could be a strategic mistake, but he had no choice. At the same time, the congressional subcommittee pressured the President to allow the General Accounting Office to come in to oversee the day-to-day operations of the project, a procedure that was rarely ever done. The importance of the project was further emphasized by the assignment of two of the GAO's best individuals: Charles Grant, deputy director, was to oversee the project for the GAO and Nick Logan, senior field operations manager, would directly manage the day to day operations.

Once on the scene, it hadn't taken Nick Logan long to determine that they needed additional help. That was when he reached out to The Millennium Recovery Company, a civilian company that had been formed to deal specifically with the computer date problem brought on by the new millennium. John Hodgers, a man who was smart, talented, and a better politician than he was a computer expert led the company. This was quite evident by the fact that he came with recommendations from very high political places and already had the highest level of clearance ever given to a civilian company by the CIA. To his credit, he understood his technical limitations and had attracted some remarkable talent to his young company.

The best and the brightest was his right hand assistant and the senior technician on the project, Kate Peters, who at thirty-six was young for the position, but that only spoke to her abilities. It was she who had saved all of their asses. While it was Nick's hard-nosed, screw the egos, attitude in administering the project that allowed it to happen, it was her technical expertise that made it happen. Now that the project was reaching it's climax, Nick was hoping that there might be possibilities that he and Kate could see each other socially, something that would have been impossible while they were working on the project and, indeed, Kate had always been more than professional and more than just a little aloof. But beneath that cool business like exterior was a beautiful woman, no matter how hard she tried to cover it up.

In addition to Kate, there were two young men who had also contributed a great deal to the success of the project. Jeremy Johnson was serious, but friendly, slightly built, and wore small wire rimmed glasses. Then there was Waldo Clarke, who was a chubby, jovial man with a big, bushy handle bar mustache that he loved to twist. In many ways they were the exact opposite of each other, but they had the common love of computer programming and were the best of friends.

These were two young men that epitomized the term computer nerd. They had the prerequisite pocket protectors and had been known to get so engrossed with their work they would forget to leave. When the staff came in the next morning, they would see them still working away and would have to force them to take a nap.

It was this kind of dedication and single-mindedness that permeated the entire staff and had allowed them to avoid what could have been a major disaster. While there were many other computer technicians involved in the Millennium Bug project, it was these three individuals that were assigned to the most sensitive area—the final launch command sequence. This also gave them responsibility for and access to the systems highest level of security.

Now that the goal had been accomplished the usual tension of meeting the deadline was replaced by the bitterness that existed among the different groups and the rivalry of Colonel Henry Clay, John Hodgers, and Charles Grant. These three men, as the leaders of their respective groups, would now attempt to take full credit for the success of the project. For the past year they had been dancing around trying to make sure that, if it didn't work, other people would get the blame. Now it was time to do the Ali shuffle and put themselves in a position to take the glory. This would be the part that would upset Nick the most, the part that he couldn't deal with. He loved working with smart people, he loved solving problems, and he loved the pressure. He hated the politics, he hated the backstabbing, and he hated his boss.

The previous day, after making significant progress during the week, Nick Logan had been approached by Colonel Henry Clay and John Hodgers.

"So, Nick, now that all the testing is done, and everything has been tripled checked, I think we can tell Grant that the mission is accomplished, we've done our job and we can report to congress. I think that we can add that it's a job particularly well done and that the A-Team should get special mention." A smiling John Hodgers loved to refer to his group as the A-team.

"I think that you, and everyone else, would do well to remember that it was our military team that laid the foundation, over a three year period of time, that allowed for the success of this mission," Colonel Clay snapped back.

"If the ground work had been so great why were we called in?" Hodgers countered.

"Because it's nothing more than politics," Clay said.

"Boys, lets save that for later. OK?" Nick said. "We're not completely out of the woods yet. We still have the final test to complete, but I'd be happy to report to Charles that we are ready to do that. In the meantime, let's just be civil with each other until we totally wrap this up and then you can do what you want."

"I suppose that you think it's you and your GAO group that are responsible for the success of this mission?" Colonel Clay said. For once he got an agreeable nod from Hodgers.

"I know that without us here the project was in serious trouble and you wouldn't have made it!" Nick thought he caught a glint in Kate's eyes when he set these two straight, which didn't surprise him. She wasn't into this political game and that was one of the many things about her that pleased him. "But enough of this. I'll notify Grant and I'm sure you'll notify your bosses and we'll go from there. But just so that everyone's clear, remember that if it wasn't for Kate, Waldo, and Jeremy we'd all still be knee deep in shit," Nick said getting up to leave. As he did so, he got a half-hearted agreement from Hodgers and Clay, giggles from Waldo, Jeremy hid his head, and just a hint of a smile from the always serious Kate.

Nick was sitting across from Charles Grant after informing him that the project was completed and ready for the final, critical test. It was a large, well appointed office, befitting the position of an assistant director of the GAO and Nick knew that his boss reveled in the status and power that it represented. Nick was always on guard when he was in the presence of his boss and never more so than when he was in the lion's den. He knew that his boss had devoured many others on his way to his position and his strike could be quick and lethal. But, unlike a lion, he would not come at you directly. He was more like a hyena that would nip at your hindquarters from behind, always making sure that he kept out of harms way himself.

Such had been the assignment that Nick had received. When congress had asked the GAO to step in and oversee the project it was almost automatic that the director would assign it to Grant, who embraced it with caution. On the one hand he knew that success could skyrocket his career, but that failure could destroy it. That's why he selected Nick to be the project leader. He knew that Nick was one of the most talented in the agency and was also one of the most dedicated. He would work tirelessly for the success of such a project regardless of the animosity that existed between the two. Grant also had calculated that the fact that he had put aside their known animosity to bring in the right person would make him look good. If the project failed, then Grant would blame it on Nick saying that he did the best he could by bringing in a talented man who failed to come through. Such an event wouldn't help his career but it would keep it from incurring serious harm while Nick's disintegrated. He also had Nick on record as many times saying they were on schedule and that he would make sure that it got done. Now that they were successful, he knew that Nick was not the type that would step to the forefront and take the full credit. Nick did not play that game well, the game that he was so good at.

"Well, Nick, I think that congratulations are in order. We've done it. We've accomplished a great deal here," Charles Grant said, a smug look on his face.

Nick spoke calmly as he sat stiffly in his chair. "There is still the final test, but, otherwise, the project is completed."

"Good, good, I can't wait to go before congress and let them know that the job is done and that they were right for appointing us to oversee it and pull the dumb military's fat out of the fire." Grant was obviously excited.

"I'm sure the military's going to look to take their share of the credit for this, too. They certainly won't sit idly by and let us have it," Nick said. "In fact, Colonel Clay wanted to meet with you tomorrow."

"I will be happy to include Clay and Hodgers in all the meetings and be sure that they get their proper due before congress," Grant said as he leaned back in his chair.

When Grant spoke it sent a chill up Nick's spine. He knew just what Grant meant. He would find a way to cut their legs out from under them. Every time that Nick would start to feel a little respect for his boss he would get new insight into just how cold, calculating and backstabbing he could be when it was in his best interest.

"You can set up a meeting for tomorrow with them. I'll come over to the pentagon around ten."

"I'll set it up," Nick said as he got up to leave.

"Cheer up Nick. Smile. The project's done. There'll be enough credit to go around for the both of us."

"I guess I'm just a little tired," Nick said as he felt the chill go back up his spine and wondered just how much credit he would get and how much his boss would take. Nick then went to the GAO garage where he got his car and headed back to the pentagon where he had spent most of his nights in the last six months. Even though the project was almost complete, this night would be no different. Maybe from habit more than anything else, but he did have some paperwork to finish up. It would take a while to get out of the routine of working twelve to fifteen hour days.

On his way back to the pentagon, Nick couldn't help but think of Kate. One of the good parts of having to spend so much time working these last six months was that he was able to spend a lot of time with her, even if it was under such restricted circumstances. He didn't understand why he couldn't get her out of his mind and why she paid so little attention to him. After all he was young, successful, single and he knew that by most accounts he was considered handsome. He knew that he had developed a reputation as somewhat of a ladies man, but he thought that it was not totally deserved. He had not had a serious relationship with anyone since Heather, his college sweetheart. He didn't know if he ever would again. Yet there was something about Kate that drew him to her. He knew that she didn't have any serious boyfriend. In fact, he didn't think that she had gone out once in the six months he had known her. She didn't have time, she was working too much, and she never mentioned anyone. Of course, he had to wonder if maybe it was just that aloofness and unavailability that drew him to her. He thought that he would have a chance now that things were wrapped up. But first it was back to work to finish up the paperwork that seemed endless. It was more of a struggle going back to work tonight because he didn't expect Kate to be there, after all they indicated that it was all but wrapped up and they expected them all to be out and gone home early. Early by their standards anyway.

As Nick pulled into the underground garage, he stopped to talk to the security guard. "Hello, Ted."

"Another late night, Nick?" Ted said. It had taken Nick two months of insisting to get Ted to stop calling him Mr. Logan and he still would only do it when there was no one else around.

"I'm afraid so, Ted," Nick said as he drove on and took his parking spot after punching in the special code that raised the gate to let him through. Beyond Ted's physical presence, security was extremely tight in the pentagon building. He not only had to punch in his security code, he also had to insert his thumb into a special security device that read his thumbprint. He always felt awkward doing this. He thought that sometime he would get his thumb caught and, since these were throughout the building, he had frequent opportunities to do so. It was impossible to go very far in the building without having to go through this process. At times Nick thought that it was a little too "James Bondish". He was not used to this tight security in his normal functions at the GAO.

As Nick parked his car and started walking to the elevator, he could feel the cameras following him and knew that his picture was being flashed on a bank of television screens, at not one but three separate security stations located throughout the building. This place was so damn secure that they not only had a redundant system, but they had a redundant system for the redundant system. Once he was at the elevator he had to punch in his code, put his thumb in, take it out, and punch in yet another special code before the elevator would open. He would have to go through this process four more times before he could reach his office. Once in the elevator, instead of pressing up he would press down, even though the garage was already two levels underground. He would have to go four more levels down before he would reach his sacrosanct area. This had been the worst part of this past six months—living underground like a mole.

As Nick got off the elevator to head toward his office, the first thing he saw was Sergeant John Morin manning the desk that guards the central hall—both left and right. This is not your typical guard's desk. It is totally enclosed in bulletproof glass, impenetrable even by armor piercing bullets. It is the primary alert station and no one can come or go from this floor without passing by it. The station is self-contained complete with it's own oxygen supply, with a backup system, as well as it's own communication system, with yet another back-up system. It also has a series of controls that can lock the entire building down if need be. It is so state-of-the-art that if the occupant stops breathing for more than three minutes, or if his body temperature drops by more than two degrees, the sensors located in the guard station will sound both remote and local alarms.

On either side of this guard station there is a corridor leading to the inner offices, both protected by bulletproof glass, behind which is a heavily armed guard. These guards wear helmets with full face shields and the latest in bullet-protective clothing that can't be pierced. Lightweight protective gloves cover even their hands. It would take a howitzer to stop them. Access to either corridor is by thumbprint identification, visual scan, by both the computer monitors and the guards, and then a two pass code. And, as was the case in the parking garage, all of this was only secondary to the video cameras hidden in the ceiling and the walls that sent everything that happened back to three security stations that are housed in three separate, unknown, locations in the building. No one person knows all three locations of the monitoring cells and they are all as heavily guarded as this sight.

All this security made Nick feel a little bit uneasy and reminded him how important this place was and the critical nature of their project. So critical was the project that not only was the congressional committee constantly kept apprised of the progress, but so too was the President. Both had been updated on a weekly basis over the past six months and on a daily basis in the last month.

Nick made some small talk with Sergeant Morin as he proceeded to the door leading to his corridor and went through his security routine. As the door swung open, Nick walked through and greeted Corporal Johnson in the same friendly manner and got a reasonably social response. It concerned Nick that these young Marines were wound a little too tight. They were obviously the cream of the crop and always looked like they'd be a little more comfortable if they were out in a jungle somewhere fighting some enemy, any enemy. Nick wanted to foster a light mood so that he wouldn't spook them. He then proceeded to walk purposefully to his office and, bumping into Kate as he did so, nearly knocking her over.

She jumped back and let out a scream. "Oh, Nick, you startled me!"

"I'm sorry, I didn't mean to, but I didn't expect anyone to be here."

"Neither did I. Especially since I had checked your office earlier and saw you were gone."

"I had a meeting with Grant so I had to go all the way across town," Nick said. "Why are you still here? I thought that we agreed in our meeting earlier that all of the pre-testing was done?"

"I just had a few more things to wrap up, a little bit of paperwork to finish and to clean up my office. Things will probably be pretty hectic the next few days so I thought I would do it now. Besides, I've been in such a habit of working at night, I didn't know what else to do," Kate said. She was still recovering from the surprise of the encounter.

"I know what you mean. That's exactly what I was going to do. It looks like you're ready to leave, perhaps we could grab a bite to eat or have a cup of coffee?". The paperwork could wait. Now that this project was all but complete, he felt it was time to put serious effort into his next project—Kate Peters.

"That would be nice, but I'm so tired I'd like to take a rain check if you don't mind?" Kate said. "Besides we have a lot of work to do in final preparation for the big test. And don't we have that meeting tomorrow?"

"Yes, I'm afraid we do. And you have a right to be tired. But I will take you up on the rain check," Nick said, just able to hide the disappointment in his voice. "Are you sure you're all right? You do look a little pale."

"I'm fine. You just startled me and I am tired. I think it's time to go home and get some rest."

"Can I at least give you a ride home then?" Nick asked hopefully.

"No. I have my car. I'll be fine, thanks," Kate said as she turned and left.

# CHAPTER 7

▼

# PENTAGON BUILDING TEN-FIFTEEN A.M., FRIDAY DECEMBER 17, 1999

## FIFTEEN DAYS <u>0</u> <u>0</u>

The meeting to plan the big test finally got started at quarter after ten. Because there were many technical aspects involved in planning this final test, Colonel Henry Clay was accompanied by his top technical team and John Hodgers was accompanied by his A-team. Also there was Nick Logan's secretary to take minutes of the meeting, which was standard operating procedure. With the inclusion of the two technical teams the meeting room was a little crowded.

Charles Grant wasted no time in taking charge of the meeting to make sure that everyone knew who was in control. "Gentlemen. Kate. Let me start the meeting by congratulating all of you on a job well done."

This was not lost on Colonel Clay, as evidenced by the scowl on his face. Once again, he had been the first to arrive to insure that he could take 'his position' at the head of the table. He could kick himself for not being the first to speak. "Yes, let me add my congratulations, too," Colonel Clay was quick to add.

"Thank you both, but let's keep in mind that we have not yet successfully completed the test." Nick wanted to direct the meeting to the technical aspects of the test and away from the jockeying for recognition.

"I thought that you said we were done and ready for the test." There was just a slight trace of panic in Charles Grant's voice.

"We are, but until we successfully complete the final test we won't know for sure."

"Technically, we won't even know for sure then," Jeremy Johnson timidly added. It wasn't that he wanted to speak, he didn't. It's just that he was always very precise and he couldn't let this imprecise statement, however slight, go by without correction.

"What the hell do you mean by that?" Grant was beginning to think that he had been set up. That they weren't really ready and he was getting prepared to pounce on Nick Logan.

"Easy, Charles. All Jeremy means is that you can never be one hundred percent sure." John Hodgers spoke up as he gave Jeremy a dirty look, making him lower his head and slide down into his seat. "But we are as close to one hundred percent positive as is possible."

"I see," Grant said, somewhat appeased.

"Ya, but you never know," Waldo Clarke said, with his characteristic little giggle and a twist of his handle bar mustache, "sometimes shit just happens." He was not going to let his good friend hang out there all alone. Dirty looks from Hodgers or not. Fuck him. He knew that Jeremy couldn't help himself and just wanted to make sure that everyone understood the situation, perfectly. Again, fuck him. And fuck Grant, too.

"I don't like surprises." Grant was getting pissed again.

"All they mean is that you can never know that you have tested for every possibility. That is why we are having the dress rehearsal tomorrow. While it is only a copy of the actual program, this test will be as complete as could possibly be, short of running the live program and actually firing the missiles. Which of course we can't do," Kate Peters said. She wanted to put an end to this before it got out of hand. She knew that Waldo would stand up to Grant if need be and, especially, if he thought that Jeremy was being attacked.

During all of this, Nick couldn't help but chuckle to himself. While he wanted the meeting to be productive, he couldn't help but enjoy seeing Grant get jerked around. "Might I suggest that we get to the heart of the meeting. Remember that we only have two weeks to ground zero."

"Yes, I agree," Hodgers added.

Colonel Clay was just about to speak when Grant beat him to it again and said, "Nick, since you are in charge of the day-to-day operations, why don't you bring us up to date."

Although he didn't like him, Nick had to concede Grant's political abilities. He managed to get himself out of the line of fire and, by throwing the ball to him, reminded everyone that it was the GAO that was in charge. "I'd be happy to." Anything to move this meeting forward. "As you all know, we have called this meeting because we are now at the point to do the final full blown test. The test that is required in order for us to have that ninety-nine plus percent confidence that we have completely adjusted all dates and date references from two digits to four. Thus insuring that the country will still be in charge of its nuclear weapons arsenal when the clock counts down from 1999 to 2000 and we enter the new millennium." Nick emphasized the ninety-nine plus percent as a concession to Jeremy, not only because he liked him, but also because he was right.

"I was a little surprised when you came to me yesterday and indicated that we were ready to have this meeting to discuss the final test," Grant said. "Just last week you indicated that we were as much as two weeks away. Which, if you will remember, I was concerned about because that would leave us with only a one-week cushion. I assume that this had something to do with the acceleration of the timetable?"

Again Nick was both impressed and pissed. Grant not only went on record, as he had done last week, as being concerned that they were running out of time, he was now going on record taking credit for the acceleration. "Yes. And you will remember that we all agreed and indicated we would do everything possible to accelerate the timetable." Nick knew that would piss-off Grant but he didn't care. "In that regard, we can thank Kate and her assistants—Jeremy and Waldo. This past Wednesday they worked through the night without sleep and completed the adjustments on the most critical and sensitive part of the program."

"Yes, the A-Team did a remarkable job and deserves a great deal of credit for it," Hodgers quickly added. Take that Clay and Grant.

"Yes, they do," Nick agreed.

"I agree that they made great progress, but with a serious breach of security, which will be in my weekly report." Colonel Henry Clay was clearly not pleased.

"If we hadn't continued, your very last weekly report would say 'so sorry we didn't make it and we no longer have any nuclear weapons capability, but I am happy to report that we didn't breach security.' This situation called for what we did." Again, it was uncharacteristic of Jeremy to speak up, but he often worked on sensitive information and he knew all about military security from his older brother. Besides, Waldo had come to his defense and that made him bolder.

"That's a boy, Jeremy, give him hell," Waldo said with his usual laugh and his shit-eating grin. He wanted to say 'tell them to go fuck themselves', but he never actually used that word, although he thought about it a lot.

"You civilians may not understand the need for absolutely unbreachable security in such a sensitive area, but I do." The Colonel was not accustomed to what he considered insubordination. He also welcomed the opportunity to emphasize that it was the fault of the GAO and not his. "And I plan on making perfectly clear that this breach of security is a serious issue, was against all of our agreed upon controls, and is the direct responsibility of the GAO."

"Just a moment, Colonel. I'm not sure that I fully understand what took place and that we did anything to be held accountable for." It was now time for Charles Grant to do his dance and make sure that he was not in the direct line of fire.

"What happened was that, while my men were getting some well deserved rest, the 'A'-Team kept on working on the most critical computer code in the key security programs that control the final launch sequence. And, as you well know, we had only agreed to allow anyone access to this area if they had one of my senior level technicians working along with them." The Colonel was enjoying himself.

"It's not our fault if your guys couldn't keep up with us. We......", Waldo said.

"We were at a very critical point and would have lost the edge that we had going for us if we stopped." Kate interrupted Waldo to keep him from getting carried away with himself, as he sometimes did, and to get the meeting back on track. "I'm sure you can understand the need to take advantage of a situation when you are on a roll and the adrenaline is pumping."

"Yes, I can. But you also know that when your men are mentally fatigued the proper course of action is to rest or the results can be disastrous. And that is why my men chose to call for a rest and appealed to Mr. Logan when you refused," the Colonel responded.

"Is that true, Nick?" Grant asked.

"Yes, it is. But...."

"But it is a serious breach of security and of our agreed upon procedures." Grant would always play it by the book. He especially liked this one though, because he could go on record as opposing Nick's breach of security if anything went wrong and enjoy the benefits of the accelerated timetable if it didn't.

"We had already found ten thousand lines of lost code that night. We couldn't stop." Kate was emphatic. "We gave the military team the option to stay with us or get a replacement team. But we couldn't just stop for God's sake. If we did, we would never complete the program fix on time."

"That would seem like a reasonable request, Colonel." Grant loved playing both sides of the fence.

"Not really, Charles. There wasn't a replacement team available at three in the morning and my men were falling asleep at their terminals. So Lieutenant Fulham, the officer in charge, elected to call a halt to the proceedings because they could no longer perform their function of monitoring the civilian team. He then informed Mr. Logan and requested that the system be locked down in compliance with the established procedure. Which Mr. Logan refused to do."

"That's right, I did." Nick was tiring of this bullshit. Put it on record and let's go forward. "I had been there all night as well, and was fully aware of the tremendous progress that was being made, so I suggested that he rest his men in shifts and they could effectively accomplish their task by randomly spot checking the civilian team members. When he refused, I made the decision to suspend the agreed upon control procedures and to keep going forward."

"A decision that, I might add, allows us to be here now planning the final big test," Kate added.

"A decision that, I might add, breached security and may have jeopardized this entire project," Colonel Clay responded.

"If we can ever get around to planning and performing the final test we will know that. Won't we!" Nick's patience had just about run out.

"He's right, Colonel. The breach of security and your objection to it have been duly noted and I suggest that we get on with the discussion of the final test." Grant took the opportunity to take the lead once again, now that he had properly covered himself against this potential problem.

"Let's just remember one thing gentlemen, if we hadn't committed this 'breach of security' we might not be performing this test for as much as a week from now," Kate said firmly.

"And that would leave us only one week before the final countdown," Nick said. "And that might not be enough time to correct any problems that could occur during the final test."

"Yes, gentlemen, we must remember that the program that we are using to perform this final test is an exact duplicate of the now amended program," Kate added. "And, since the entire program is actually a combination of hundreds of programs with a total of some thirty million lines of computer code, it could take the better part of a week, or longer, just to create another exact copy if we needed to test it again."

"All right, you've all made your point," Grant said. "Let's get on with the planning of the test."

The next hour moved quickly as it was spent working out the technical aspects of the test. Then the final two hours dragged on as it was consumed with jockeying for position—who was going to be recognized for what, who was going to lead the test, who was going to sit next to whom, etc.. In short, who was going to get to kiss whose ass first and longest.

# CHAPTER 8

▼

# WASHINGTON, D.C.
# FOUR P.M., SATURDAY
# DECEMBER 18, 1999
## FOURTEEN DAYS TO 0 0

"Nick, sorry to disturb you," Martha apologized for interrupting him. He was obviously in deep thought and she knew that he preferred to be left alone when he was. "We've just been advised that the President's car has just entered the garage and he will be here shortly."

"Thank you, Martha," Nick responded as he was instantly brought back to the present. He had only found out within the last hour that the President was personally going to attend the test. "I'll be right there. Is everyone else there?"

"Just about. Colonel Clay has been there for two hours already."

"I'm not surprised. Remember if you offer to get coffee for the President I can get you introduced."

"You've got it," Martha answered with a smile. Like many secretaries, she had never appreciated having to get coffee for any boss and particularly not for his 'guests'. But Nick had never asked her to wait on him and she liked that. She liked him. She also knew that it pissed off Colonel Clay and Charles Grant that they had to get their own coffee when they came over and Nick liked that.

As Nick made his way to the general computing area, down a short hallway and around to the left from his office, he couldn't help thinking that he hoped his next assignment was above ground. He had spent far too many days in artificial light over the past six months to suit him.

The general computer area was made up of two rooms. The interior room was where Nick Logan and his select group, that was allowed access to the systems security, worked for the last six months. A big rectangular room, about twenty feet wide by forty feet long, with a bank of computer terminals lining the far wall, it was the control room for this test and was a secure room only open to authorized personnel. The near wall was bulletproof glass and separated the control room from the outer room. This adjoining room was about the same size but, instead of computer terminals, it had twenty theater seats that faced the glass wall and was a viewing area to observe the control room. Behind these chairs, in the center of the room, was a huge conference table that served as a general meeting and work area.

By the time Nick arrived, all of the others were there and he got a look from Colonel Clay that said he should take a lesson from him on arriving early. Before he could even say hello the four secret service men, who had been there earlier to check out the room, quickly dispersed among them. They looked everyone over very carefully to make sure that there was no one there they had not already checked out. The agents knew that everyone except them had gone through a metal detector to be checked for weapons as a normal part of their everyday routine. No one except the guards and the secret service were ever allowed to carry weapons in a secure area.

Then another secret service agent appeared in the doorway and quickly surveyed the room. When he got the almost imperceptible nod from the agent that was strategically placed in the back of the room, with everyone else in front of him, he stepped aside and two additional agents stepped through the door followed by the President of the United States—Justin Stewart. Following him was Ambassador-at-Large—Victor Noble, the Chairman of the Joint Chiefs of Staff and Five Star General—George Armstrong and two more secret service agents that remained just inside the door.

As the President and the others were introduced, it was obvious that he was tense and tired. A normally open and friendly individual, this day President Stewart was much more reserved and perfunctory in his greetings. Even though he looked drawn and was showing the affects of his office his good looks were obvious. He was just over six feet tall and solidly built for a man who had just turned fifty. His light brown hair was turning gray at the temples and his steel blue eyes were hypnotic. It was no wonder that, with these good looks combined with the power of his office, he was notorious for having affairs with some the most beautiful women in the world. Since he was a widower, his wife having died some five years ago, these affairs were sometimes less than discrete.

On the other hand, Victor Noble was the epitome of discretion. At fifty-two he was a multi-millionaire business man, a two time United States Senator and a contender for his parties nomination for president, which he lost to the current officeholder. He had been appointed Ambassador-at-Large and was senior aide and confidant to the President as payment for supporting him in the general election. It was widely believed that without this support the President would not have been successful in capturing the White House.

"Mr. Ambassador, this is Nick Logan the project operations manager," Colonel Clay said making the introduction. "I know that you two have talked a number of times."

"Ambassador Noble, it's a pleasure to meet you in person," Nick said. He had spoken with Victor Nobel a number of times recently to update him on the status of the project directly. The ambassador was always very business like in their discussions. Nick believed that they probably had a lot in common relative to the basis of their respective positions. When the GAO was brought in to direct the Millennium Bug project, the President appointed Victor Noble to take direct responsibility for overseeing it for him. This was a no win situation for the ambassador. If the project was successful the congratulations would be very limited since it could not become public knowledge that this problem had ever actually existed. If the project failed he would be the scapegoat.

"Yes, it's a pleasure to finally meet you in person, too, Mr. Logan," Victor Noble responded politely but professionally, as he shook his hand. "I look forward to the successful completion of this test so that we can all proceed with our other duties."

"I couldn't agree more sir," Nick said, feeling strangely chilled by this man.

As the introductions were just about complete, General Armstrong stepped forward and took charge, much to the displeasure of Charles Grant. The general was clearly a step or two ahead of his subordinate, the colonel. "Mr. President, I'm sorry to interrupt but I believe that we should begin the test. You are on a very tight schedule."

"Yes, thank you General," the President said. "It's your show." Because of the importance of the project and the need for as much secrecy as possible, Colonel Clay reported directly to General Armstrong.

"Colonel Clay, will you please gather your team and take your place within the control room to begin the test," the General ordered. "If the rest of you would please take a seat in the viewing area we can get this test underway."

The look on the faces of Charles Grant and John Hodgers did nothing to hide their anger. In their meeting the previous day, it had been agreed that the actual test would be conducted by the military team but that the 'A'-Team and Nick Logan would be present.

"Colonel Clay, we.........." Charles Grant was abruptly cut-off by the General.

"Excuse me Mr. Grant. I am fully aware of the major contributions made by you, Mr. Logan, Mr. Hodgers and his team, but this is a military operation and it will be conducted by the military. It will be handled according to standard military procedures, which do not allow for civilians to be in the control room during a nuclear missile launch sequence. Even a mock launch sequence. So if you will kindly take your seat over here beside me we can begin."

"Certainly General. We've already taken care of the difficult part, anyway." This got a dirty look from the General but Charles Grant couldn't help himself. He was very angry because the Colonel had beaten him at his own game and the smirk on his face didn't help matters.

"Good. Shall we begin then, Colonel," the General ordered as he took his seat beside the President, along with Victor Noble on the other side.

"Yes, sir," Colonel Clay answered as he strode into the control room and gave the order to Lieutenant Fulham to begin. "You may commence the test Lieutenant." He was very pleased with himself for, by putting Grant and Hodgers in their place, he had re-gained some of the respect of his men. He could tell from his response that the lieutenant was happy to have the civilians out of 'his' control room.

"We're ready, sir. The computer clock has been to set to one minute past twelve on January 1, 2000. Start the count down sequence corporal," the Lieutenant's orders were crisp and sharp.

"Yes, sir," the Corporal answered as he and his staff began to throw switches and push buttons with speed and precision. As the count began from twenty on the way to zero, there were lights flashing on the wall in from of them that signaled that everything was proceeding as designed and they were on their way to the launching of the nuclear missiles.

"The first wave of missiles have been successfully launched, sir," Colonel Clay announced as he turned to face the viewers. The country was laid out in a series of grids and the missiles could be launched in waves in any one of four different pre-determined sequences as well as individually or all at once.

"The second wave has been successfully launched, sir." This continued for three minutes until all the missiles were 'launched' under the mock program. "We have successfully launched all of the missiles, sir," Colonel Clay reported with a sharp salute.

"Excellent, gentlemen. Excellent," the President enthusiastically responded. A great weight lifted from him.

There were congratulations for everyone and the President confirmed the General's request to replace the old program with the new one. This would be accomplished in the next twelve hours and would mean that the nuclear missile programs would be year 2000 compliant.

"Now that the test has been successfully completed I would again thank all of you for your invaluable contributions. However, since the test has been successful, I must issue the order to end the project and, with it, all civilian access to the system. Effective immediately, the security clearances for all of the non-military personnel involved in the project will no longer allow access to the system or the control room. And, as soon as the administrative details are wrapped up, access to this level of the Pentagon will be rescinded." General George Armstrong was pleasant, but firm, in his order.

"Please let me add to the General's expression of gratitude. The country owes you all a great deal of thanks and, as its President, I want to tell you how much your contributions are appreciated. Mr. Grant and Mr. Hodgers, the contributions of the GAO and The Millennium Recovery Company have been invaluable in assisting Colonel Clay and his team in successfully completing this project." President Stewart's normally gracious and pleasant manner had returned.

"Thank you, Mr. President," the two men replied in unison. Their egos, damaged by the General, were stroked by the President's praise. This mild euphoria would not last long as it was dashed by what the President did next.

"Kate, I would particularly like to thank you and your team—Waldo Clarke and Jeremy Johnson, I believe. I understand from Colonel Clay that your technical expertise was instrumental in completing the project on time. And Nick, I'm informed that your professionalism and fairness were essential in keeping the operation moving forward. If I can ever be of service to you, please don't hesitate to ask."

With that, the President and his group left leaving Grant and Hodgers steaming, Waldo giggling, Jeremy in awe, and Kate and Nick surprised at the fairness of Colonel Clay. Or was this just another way to put Grant and Hodgers in their place.

# CHAPTER 9

▼

# WASHINGTON, D.C. SIX P.M., SATURDAY DECEMBER 18, 1999

## FOURTEEN DAYS TO 0 0

"There's going to be an impromptu celebration at the Hog Penny Pub nearby. Would you gentlemen like to join us for a drink?" Nick asked as he approached Charles Grant and John Hodgers, who were still standing together licking their wounds.

"I don't know, Nick. It's been a tiring day," Hodgers responded.

"I'd be happy to join you," Grant said. "After all we have successfully completed a difficult task against tough odds and that deserves a little celebration."

Nick had to admire his boss for his resiliency and ability to regroup and bounce back. The Colonel may have gotten the upper hand on the demonstration, but the GAO was instrumental in successfully completing the most critical project on the face of the earth and Grant would get his just reward for leading it. Not to attend this little celebration would just add to the Colonel's victory. "Come on and join us, John. We'll just have a quick drink. You deserve one, too."

"Sure. But just one." John Hodgers was beginning to feel better. He also realized that this was just a small victory for the Colonel. His company was paid very well for their services and their reputation and access to the military and other government agencies was greatly enhanced and would be worth millions.

"That's great. We even got Kate to agree to join us, so now we have everyone." Nick would have been happier if they had said no. But, what the hell, he had to ask. Besides, Kate was going and this would give him an opportunity to get closer to her. "Kate, can I give you a ride to the party?"

"Thanks, Nick. But I want to take my car so that I can leave when I am ready. I'm a little tired and probably won't stay that long," Kate said with a friendly smile. "But I will let you buy me a drink."

"Your on," Nick answered. He would have preferred to drive her but would take what he could get.

It was the typical celebration that often occurred after the completion of a difficult project: a lot of friendly banter back and forth, laughter and patting each other on the back. There was not a lot of heavy drinking. In this day and age that was not as acceptable as it once was and this was not a party group anyway. But everyone was enjoying themselves and it allowed Nick to spend some time with Kate; although he had to share her with many others.

"I think that it's time for me to leave. It's almost eleven and it has been a long day," Kate announced as she was standing with Nick and Colonel Clay.

"Can I give you a ride home?" Nick asked.

"Remember I have my own car, Nick."

"Yes, but I thought that you might be too tired to drive." Nick believed that persistence was a virtue.

"Thank you for being so concerned, Nick, but I'll be fine."

"At least allow me to walk you to your car. I'm ready to leave anyway."

"That would be nice, but don't leave early on my account," Kate said as Nick helped her with her coat. "I'm perfectly capable of taking care of myself."

"You might as well let Nick walk you to your car, or else I will have to," Colonel Clay said with a combination of military authority and a fatherly order. "Call me old fashion, but I can't allow you to go out into that dark parking lot by yourself."

"All right, Colonel, you win. I'll see you at the center tomorrow." Kate was more relaxed than usual.

"First of all, have you forgotten that the project is now complete? And, second, tomorrow is Sunday and any paper work that you have to wrap up can wait until Monday."

"I did forget that tomorrow is Sunday. It's been so long that we've taken a day off that they all just seem to run into one another," Kate admitted.

"It will be good to sleep in for a change," Nick added. "It's been a long time."

"Yes, it will be. Shall we go? Good night, Colonel."

"Good night, Kate. Good night, Nick."

"Good night, Colonel. See you on Monday," Nick said as he followed Kate's lead. They left through the side door that led to the parking lot in the back of the building.

"It's cold tonight," Nick said as he took Kate's arm. "Where's your car?"

They never saw the two men waiting in the shadows at the back of the lot.

"Over here to the left. I think," Kate answered. "I don't remember the parking lot being this dark when I came in."

"Neither do I," Nick agreed. "It looks like only about half of the lights are working."

The light by the side door was more than bright enough for the men to recognize the couple that had just exited. "That is one of our targets, comrade." The agent stationed in Washington informed his companion.

"I know. I have eyes, too. But we must wait for the others. Like the duck hunter, we must not kill the lead bird or the rest will be alerted and scatter. We will kill the last target to emerge and that way this first one will not be aware of it. Make the call and tell them that, as expected, it is the 'alpha' target that has left first and that they must intercept." Egor's partner quietly made the call on his cell phone while he continued to watch the couple search for their car. A search made more difficult because of the lights that they had disabled.

"Here it is over here," Kate said as she activated the button to unlock the car door. "Thank you for walking me to my car and for a nice evening."

"It's certainly been my pleasure. Perhaps, now that the project is complete, we could have dinner together some night?"

"Perhaps. See you on Monday," Kate said smiling as she pulled away.

As Nick turned to find his car he knew she felt something deeper for him too. But she was very good at maintaining a professional approach, or was it just playing hard to get.

The party continued on for the more adventurous of the group, but the rest of the 'A'-Team, Jeremy Johnson and Waldo Clarke, were not included among these. Given that they were not partygoers and were exhausted from the strenuous work that they had been doing, by eleven-thirty the two of them were ready to leave and, as was the usual case, they left together. There was plenty of justification for the frequent comment that these two were joined at the hip. Since he knew he was driving, Jeremy had been careful not to drink too much and was in good shape. His friend Waldo, on the other hand, was not feeling any pain, although he was not drunk. Neither one of them was aware of the eyes that followed them as they looked for their car.

"Where is the car, Jeremy? It's cold and dark out here." Waldo said with a laugh.

"It's in the far back. Remember?"

"I remember that there were places closer to the door and it was a lot lighter."

"It's not my fault, Waldo. I just followed the instructions of the parking attendant."

"I would have just ignored him. Besides. He didn't look like much of a parking attendant to me. Use your control to zap the locks. Then we will see were it is when the lights blink."

"Quit complaining," Jeremy said as he hit the control button and he saw the flash of light to his left. "It's right over hear. Besides, I'm surprised that you can feel the cold."

The two men watched as Jeremy and Waldo rapidly approached. The fact that they were hidden in the shadows just in front of Jeremy's car was no coincidence.

"When they get here, I will take care of this. You will stay here," Egor ordered as he tensed for the kill.

"I will come out if you need me," his companion answered.

"I won't." Egor's senses were now on full alert and he moved quickly forward to intercept the two, before they split up and went to their respective sides of the car.

As Jeremy and Waldo were within five feet of the back of the car, they were confronted by a large man who had, what appeared to be, a gun pointed at them.

"You may stop right there, gentlemen. Leave your hands in your pockets and make a sound and your dead," Egor commanded. His upper lip curled into a snarl.

"Oh, shit!" Waldo said, his smile gone.

"You can have anything you want. Just don't kill us," Jeremy pleaded.

"I know I can. And I will." Egor enjoyed the smell of fear in the air and he would squeeze every second he could from it. "Surely you can beg for your lives better than that."

"Please! Please! Don't kill…" before Jeremy could finish, two bullets ripped through his brain and he was dead before hitting the pavement.

"You bastard! What have you done?" Waldo could speak but he couldn't move.

"You'll have to do better than that, Waldo." Egor's smile was hideous now.

Seeing his best friend lying there bleeding and hearing the killer speak his name made Waldo realize that this was no ordinary robbery. He knew he was dead and wanted to make his last words count so he looked at the face of his killer and said—"FUCK YOU!"

He never felt the two bullets that entered his forehead and exploded out the back of his skull. Neither did he hear the sickening laugh of the 'hyena'.

A short time earlier, Kate was on the way to her Georgetown apartment and was thinking about what would happen next. Her work on the Millennium Bug project was completed. She would miss the people that she worked with so closely for these many months, particularly the two young men that she had come to like very much. Yes they were a little bit nerdy, but they were good friends and brilliant technicians. She had learned a lot from them; both from a technical and a personal nature.

She would miss not working with them any longer, but most of all she would miss not working with Nick. From the beginning she was physically attracted to him and was becoming increasingly fond of him as she grew to know him over these last six months. Underneath that handsome exterior was a strong man who possessed character and principles. These were traits that she admired and that were hard to find. Her father possessed them and any man that she would ever think of living her life with would have to have them. Perhaps in another time and place they could have been lovers, or more.

Unfortunately this could never be; because of who they were and because she was now a woman on the run. Earlier that night, she had informed her superiors that her mission had been completed. Then, separately, she had informed her father that she had performed the additional task he had required of her. She didn't understand why he had her do it, or why he instructed her to the rendez-vous in Boston. All she knew was that he used the secret emergency code that meant that she was now outside the system and at great risk. It was foolish to risk going to the celebration, but who knew what her life would be like now and she wanted to see Nick and her friends one last time.

Her mind was absorbed in these thoughts as she came to Pennsylvania Ave, came to a stop, and then slowly pulled out into the intersection. At this time of night there was very little traffic, but she pulled out slowly anyway, as was her nature, a caution that would save her life.

As she pulled into the intersection, she caught a glint of steel out of the corner of her eye and, instinctively, she turned sharply to the right. She had not actually seen the Mack truck that was bearing down on her and would have hit her broadside, demolishing her small car, if she had not made that quick turn at the last moment. Instead she caught a glancing blow, sending her car careening back across the sidewalk and hitting a telephone pole before it came to rest upside down. The Mack truck never came to a stop; it just kept on going.

Entering the hospital, Nick Logan couldn't believe the events that had taken place in the past two hours. He had just come from the morgue where he identified his two young assistants who had been killed in an apparent robbery. It was just another random act of violence. The two had no weapons, they weren't the type, and there was no evidence of any struggle. They didn't even have a chance to try to run. It was the type of violence that had become all too common in the cities of America and particularly this, its capital. It was so common that Nick got upset with the police at the morgue because of their lack of emotion, which he took as lack of concern. It was while he was there, trying to make sense of what had happened, when the call came on his cell phone that he had better get over to the hospital because Kate had been involved in a serious automobile accident.

At present, the extent of her injuries was still unknown. His emotions were worn thin from witnessing the aftermath of the senseless killings of two young men that he liked a great deal. And now another member of his team, someone he cared for more than he had realized, lay in a hospital with unknown injuries.

He used the time driving from the morgue to the hospital to regain his emotional control. He realized he was in danger of his raw emotions taking over his thought process and he couldn't let that happen. He learned long ago that it was never good to let his emotions get the better of him and rule these situations. He would need that calmness he had always been able to find deep within. This night he was being sorely tested and had to dig deeper than he had ever needed to before.

Nick wasn't sure whether or not he went that deep, but he knew he had to remain calm in order to think clearly, and he had to think clearly because what was happening just didn't make sense. It wasn't adding up. There was something more to this, but what?

The fact that tragedy could simultaneously strike three of the most key people in his project, a project that had just barely been completed, was too much of a coincidence. And he was not a man who believed in coincidences; his life, his thought process, was structured around logic. And this was not logical.

He let that thought process rest for now because he had to see how badly Kate was hurt, both from a professional and a personal concern. Professionally because she was the only one left alive who knew the innermost workings of the project. The other two who knew it nearly as well as she lay dead, stone cold dead, in the morgue. And personally because the attraction that he felt for Kate was different than the typical physical attraction, and need for a conquest, that was all too often the motive. It went much deeper, something he had not felt for a long time.

As Nick entered the hospital and walked toward the emergency ward, Colonel Clay approached him.

"Nick, I'm glad that you're finally here." Relieved Colonel Clay shook Nick's hand firmly.

"How is she, Colonel?" The look of concern on the Colonel's face added to Nick's weariness.

"I'm not sure yet. She's just been here for half an hour or so and they haven't come out to talk to me yet."

"Half an hour? I don't understand. She left the celebration two hours ago," Nick said.

"I know. The wreck was so bad they had to get the Jaws of Life. It took them over an hour to free her from the wreckage. They took their time because she didn't appear to be in immediate danger. There was no major bleeding or anything, but they were very concerned about the position of her neck so they went slowly."

"How is it that you got notified even before I did?" Nick said, not intending any recriminations.

"Again, the wreckage was so bad the contents of her purse were spread everywhere throughout the car and it just happened that my card was the first one they picked up and the officer that found it knows me. More accurately he knows my son, so they called me immediately. As soon as I got here I had them call you. But I must say you look like hell."

"You would too, Colonel, if you saw what I have," Nick said. "And now this."

"What happened?"

"I'm not sure of all the details, but I just came from the morgue where I had to identify the bodies of Jeremy and Waldo. Both of whom had just been shot dead in an apparent robbery," Nick said. His hands clenched into fists so hard that his knuckles turned white.

"My God, I can't believe that," the Colonel said, feeling weak in the knees. "I decided to leave just after you and Kate and they were still there having a good time. It's unbelievable."

"It does seem incredible that, on the very day that we wrapped up the project, they get killed and now this happens with Kate."

"What are you saying?" The Colonel became immediately alert and pulled his mind out of the fog it had drifted into.

"I'm just saying that it's a hell of a coincidence," Nick said.

"Yes, I suppose you're right. But coincidences do happen."

"Perhaps. But I'm not a big believer in them."

"Neither am I," the Colonel said.

Just then one of the emergency room doctors approached them. "Colonel Clay, I'm Dr. Chandler and I've just come from examining Kate Peters. I'm told that you had inquired about her."

"Yes, Dr. Chandler, how is she?"

"Are you family?"

"No. This is Nick Logan and we are associates of Ms. Peters. She doesn't have any family in the area."

"Hello, Dr. Chandler. Please, how is she?" Nick asked, his fists clenched tighter.

"Well, she has a slight concussion and some serious bruises, but I'm happy to tell you that she's going to be fine. From what I understand of the accident, she is a very lucky young lady."

"That's great doctor," Nick said, as he relaxed his hands. "When can she leave?"

"We'll want to keep her at least overnight for observation," Dr. Chandler said. "Perhaps the two of you can talk to her. She is insisting that she is all right and is demanding to leave now."

"Are you sure that she doesn't have any serious injuries?" Nick asked. "I'm certainly not questioning your competence doctor, but Colonel Clay said it took over an hour to get her out of the car, it was so badly mangled. How could she have so few injuries?"

"Like I said, it's a miracle, but these things happen. Apparently, she didn't get hit full force and she had a solid, if small, car. They took such a long time because the doors were jammed shut and her neck was in a precarious position. The medics determined that she didn't appear to have any internal injuries, she was coherent, and they wanted to make sure that she didn't have any neck injuries or that they didn't create any. But again, we would like to keep her over night just to make sure."

"That certainly makes sense. There's no reason not to be cautious," Colonel Clay said, a fatherly tone to his voice.

"I'm glad it does to you, because it doesn't to her. She wants to leave right now and she's insistent upon it."

"I know she can be tough and that she's strong willed. Let me talk to her." A little smile came to Nick's face and then quickly disappeared. "Also doctor, I have some bad news to tell her. Do you think she's up to it?"

"There's never a good time for bad news. Can it wait until morning when she's had a good night's sleep?"

"It could, but I'm afraid she'll hear it from somebody else or even on television. I'd hate for her to hear it that way."

"I see," Dr. Chandler said. "Then I think you should. I would prefer that just one of you go in. This is an emergency department and it's quite close in there. We've given her a mild sedative so she will be a little sleepy."

The Colonel put his hand lightly on Nick's shoulder. "That's okay. You go ahead. Just let her know that I'm here in case there's anything she needs."

"Thanks, Colonel," Nick said as he went into the room.

Standing by the side of her bed, she looked so peaceful that he didn't have the heart to disturb her. Except for a few small cuts and slight bruises on her forehead, you would never know that she had been in an accident. She looked like an angel sent from heaven. He just stood there for the next few minutes admiring how beautiful she was when she began to open her eyes. "Hi, Kate," Nick said softly. "How are you?"

"I'm okay. Sorry they had to drag you back out at this time of the night, but I am glad you are here. It's good to see a friendly face." The combination of the trauma and the sedative had lowered Kate's guard.

"Well, I offered to drive you home," Nick said with a little smile. "I can guarantee it would have been less traumatic than this."

"Next time I'll take you up on it," Kate said as she put her hand on Nick's.

"Good I'm looking forward to it," Nick said. "How's your head?"

"It hurts like hell, but I'll be all right. I have to get up and out of here," Kate said as she tried to get up.

"Now hold on just a minute." Nick put his other hand gently on her shoulder to prevent her from rising. "The doctor wants to keep you here over night for observation and I think that's a smart move. He said you have a slight concussion."

"No! I have to get out of here. I can't stay here," Kate said firmly. The tone of her voice became much more authoritative as her guard returned.

"Easy. This place isn't that bad. You haven't even had the food yet."

"I don't like hospitals and I don't want to stay here," Kate insisted.

"I'm afraid I have some bad news to tell you which might change your mind."

"What is it? Am I really dead and this is just a dream?" She tried to lighten the mood, realizing that she was becoming too agitated and had to calm down. Otherwise she might arouse suspicion.

"No." There was no easy way to tell her, so he just said it. "I'm afraid I have to tell you that Jeremy and Waldo were killed tonight." Nick watched Kate turn pale, her head falling back against the pillow, as she struggled to speak.

"Please tell me you're joking." Kate could feel the tears welling. "And it's a damn bad joke."

"I'm afraid not. They were coming out of the celebration and going to their car when they were shot to death, apparently by a robber."

"That can't be. How could that happen? It must be a mistake," Kate said. As much as she tried to fight it, the tears began to fill her eyes.

"It's no mistake. I've just come from the morgue where I had to identify them. It wasn't pleasant." Nick's voice cracked slightly and he had to hold back his own tears.

Through the tears, she began to see more clearly and her mind raced. Kate was now convinced there was something wrong. She had felt something earlier that night, like someone was watching her. The near death accident had greatly increased her sense of danger and, now, she was absolutely sure of it.

"Tell me more," Kate demanded. Wiping her eyes dry with the tissue Nick gave her.

"I've told you everything I know. The police believe that it was just another random mugging, one of the more violent ones, but not at all unusual in this city."

Kate started to get up, only to be held back by Nick again.

"Hold it. Where do you think you are going? You really have to rest." Nick held her down more firmly.

"No! I really have to get out of here is what I have to do! I can't stay here! I have to get out of here!" Kate appeared to be losing control, but she was not.

"But why do you have to get out of here? There's nothing you can do now for them. The best thing you can do is take care of yourself."

"No, I have to get out of here. I'm not safe here."

"What do you mean you're not safe here?" Nick was confused and afraid that she was becoming hysterical. He was ready to call the doctor to give her a stronger sedative.

"I don't know what I mean. I just know I've got to get out of here." Kate knew that she was appearing irrational and that she had to calm down. "I don't feel comfortable here. I don't want to be alone here."

"Don't worry I'll stay with you," Nick said. "If that will make you feel better." He was embarrassed by the thought that, if he jumped into bed with her, they would both feel better.

"What would make me feel better is to get out of here," Kate insisted.

Again Kate started to get up, but the throbbing in her head and Nick's hand on her shoulder prevented her from doing so. She would have to open up and confide in him, but just a little.

"Nick, you have to listen to me. This accident and the shooting of Jeremy and Waldo are too much of a coincidence. Something's wrong." Kate's eyes pleaded for Nick's compassion, if not understanding.

Nick didn't want to tell Kate that he and Colonel Clay had the same feeling. But there was no substance to it, nothing they could put there hands on, and in her current state he thought it would be better not to agree with her.

"Don't worry. If it will make you feel better, we'll have you moved to another room and we won't have you listed in the registration. And I will stay with you for the rest of the night," Nick said. "I promise that you will be all right."

"I suppose, if I can't get my own way and get out of here, that will have to do," Kate said. It was probably enough for now, and the best she could do.

"Good, that's better. I'll go out and make the arrangements with Colonel Clay." Nick smiled as he patted her shoulder and gently squeezed her hand.

"No, don't do that," Kate ordered. "Don't involve him. Don't involve anyone else. You have to take care of it yourself. You're the only one I can trust, if I can even trust you," Kate said.

"Well, thanks for the vote of confidence. I do think you're being a little bit paranoid. I don't think you have anything to worry about from Colonel Clay," Nick said.

"I don't understand why he's here. How come he heard about this?"

"He explained that. He said his card was the first one found and he knew the policeman that was on the scene. So it was logical for him to call the Colonel; plus I was stuck in the morgue and was harder to get in touch with."

"Still another coincidence that his card was found and his friend was the policeman on the scene. And I don't believe in coincidences."

"I don't believe in coincidences either, but I don't think that this one is that much of a stretch."

"If you want me to stay here you'll have to do as I ask or I'm leaving. You can't keep me here against my will."

"Okay, okay, have it your way. I'll make some excuse and then I'll move you to a private room that nobody knows about." At this point, Nick would do anything to keep her there.

"Good. Thank you," Kate said as she settled back into the bed. "I really mean that. Thank you."

Her sweet voice was music to his ears and he would do anything he could to help her. It wasn't hard to get Colonel Clay to agree to go to the command center to make certain it was secure. He would also assemble his team for their safety.

It wasn't easy, but Nick was finally able to arrange Kate's transfer to a private room and, with the help of Dr. Chandler, without any formal paperwork to leave a trail. Once he had convinced the doctor that this was the only way to keep her here, he was a willing and useful accomplice. He even arranged for Nick to stay in her room all night, to make her feel more secure. This settled Kate down and she was finally asleep on her own; she had refused any medication that would put her to sleep.

The room was on the tenth floor and normally reserved for VIP's. At the far end of a infrequently used corridor, it offered seclusion and anonymity. The room itself was large and well appointed. Nick placed his chair in the corner of the room, in a little alcove, away from the entrance and facing Kate's bed. The serving table also hid him. That way he could see both the door and Kate and, in the semi-darkness provided by a small night-light, he was not easily seen. He saw this in a movie once and thought that it wouldn't hurt to be careful. He was still uncomfortable about the apparent coincidences, but regardless, hard as he tried, he couldn't stay awake. The emotional stress of the evening took its toll on him and he kept drifting off.

It was three in the morning when it happened. The slight click of the door-knob and the additional light coming into the room from the corridor would not have been enough to wake him. But the little clang from the fork that Nick had wedge in the top of the door did. As he saw the door opening slowly he knew that something was wrong. If someone from the hospital staff needed to come in they would just do it. They wouldn't be opening the door cautiously, afraid to alert the occupant of their arrival.

Once the door was open just enough, the intruder slipped inside and quickly closed the door behind him. It had not been very difficult for him to find the room that Kate was in. A simple inquiry or two, about a young woman who was in a serious automobile accident, from a distraught brother was all that it took. A slightly injured patient who was transferred to a VIP room, without the normal paperwork, was the type of gossip that would travel through the hospital, on an otherwise slow night, like a brush fire on a bone dry prairie.

As he slowly moved into the room, Nick's mind raced in an attempt to decide what to do. This hadn't happened in the movie. He did the only thing he could think of. He sprung from his chair and pushed the serving table as hard as he could into the intruder's stomach. But he was more agile than Nick expected and was able to avoid the full force of the attack. At the same time, the intruder swept his leg in a broad arc that caught Nick's ankle with such force that he lost his balance and hit the floor hard.

The intruder then spun around toward the bed, firing two shots into the precise spot where Kate's head had been. From his prone position and to his horror, Nick saw the two flashes and heard the spits as he started to get to his feet. What he didn't know was that Kate, at the sound of Nick crashing the serving table into the intruder, instinctively rolled to her right, out of the bed, and onto the floor. Before he was halfway up he heard two more spits. He didn't see any flashes, the noise had come from behind him in the direction of the door. The intruder pitched backward and lay immobile on the floor.

"Kate, where are you? Are you all right?" Nick was panicked as he couldn't see her in the bed and reached to turn on the lights. "It's all right. He's dead."

The intruder lay in a heap, on his back, with blood poring from his chest. Kate crawled out from under the bed and quickly panned the room to determine the situation. "What happened? Who is that? I told you I should get out of here." Kate fired her questions at Nick as she headed for the closet and her clothes.

"Take it easy, Kate. I don't know who he is. But you're safe now." Nick was trying to gain control of himself as well as the situation. This was something he was not used to dealing with. "If you are looking for your clothes, you are out of luck. They had to cut them off of you after the accident, so there is nothing left. Besides, we are going to have to wait for the police. We have a dead man here."

"The police! Why the police?"

"I don't know what the hell is going on here, Kate. But I do know that we have got to bring the police into this situation. And that's all I want to hear about it."

"I told you that the car accident was no coincidence. I should have left this place then."

"If that was no accident then we should have called the police in earlier. We may have been able to avoid this close call if we had."

"If you didn't have a gun it would have been more than a close call. We would both be dead now." The sarcasm in her voice was harsher than she had intended.

"I don't have a gun."

"Then who shot him?"

"I don't know. I just heard two muted shots come from behind me. I assume from the doorway," Nick said as he started toward the door.

"Don't open that!" Kate ordered, as she rushed over to the dead man and picked up his gun. "Whoever shot him could still be out there." Kate then moved quickly to the door; opening it slowly and peeking out as she did—gun at the ready.

Nick was surprised by the calmness and control Kate showed. He was more than a bit shaken himself. This was the first time that anyone had died in front of him. Never mind the fact that he was shot to death and covered in blood. This man would have killed the both of them if someone else hadn't shot him first; someone who obviously did not want to stick around and be identified. On top of the tragic deaths and Kate's near death just a few hours earlier, it was almost too much for Nick to deal with.

He was certainly having a difficult time processing all of what was happening. Not the least of which was how Kate was handling the situation. He would have expected most people who had two brushes with death within a few hours to be in a panicked, if not hysterical, state. Yet here was Kate taking control of the situation, like she had been trained for it all her life. He had the distinct feeling that anyone found in the corridor would be in trouble.

"Don't go out there, Kate. This is for the police to handle. Not us. And don't tell me not to call them," Nick said forcefully, regaining his composure, as he reached for the phone. So much for any more sleep.

# CHAPTER 10

▼

# STOCKHOLM, SWEDEN EIGHT A.M., SUNDAY DECEMBER 19, 1999

## THIRTEEN DAYS TO 0 0

Sitting in the Stockholm International airport, Yuri reflected on the cat and mouse game being played by his father and Boris Stepovich. With his two protectors, Pasha and Alexei, a direct flight out of Europe, wasn't possible. It would be too easy for Boris' agents to find them. They had a head start, but a small one, and were trying to make the best time that they could. It was no simple task getting from Russia to the United States without getting caught in the process.

The quick way was to go from Moscow to Zurich and catch a flight from there to the States, probably on Swiss Air. However, that was the expected way and Yuri's father had learned over the years that it was safer to do the unexpected. He knew that it was human nature and part of their basic training to play the odds but, in selective situations, he would do the least expected and turn the odds in his favor. So Dimitry sent them to Stockholm through Finland, where they would catch a British Airways flight to Iceland and from there to the United

States. Dimitry knew that there were not enough resources to cover every airport with more than one agent. The major airports in Europe, including Zurich, would be crawling with agents and the outlying airports, like Stockholm, would have none or one at the most. Because the single agent assigned to the Stockholm airport was one of Dimitry's men they would be able to meet with him and get out without detection.

When they arrived at the airport, Pasha knew the agent, Nikolai, assigned to Stockholm and they met in a secluded lounge. Nikolai informed Pasha that it was safe and they could get on the flight without detection. The three men breathed a sigh of relief when they got on the plane and took off without incident.

"Yes, comrade Stepovich. They boarded British Air flight 107 to Iceland ten minutes ago."

The back up agent had done his job well and, as he reported in, Boris smiled, the anger at finding that the dead man was not Yuri subsiding. His old friend Dimitry had learned well, but they were too much alike. Boris knew exactly what Dimitry would do because he was the one that taught him to do the unexpected. Knowing him so well was a great source of strength and at the same time a great weakness. Dimitry also knew him well.

He didn't know what secondary airport it would be so he couldn't have enough agents there to intercept them. But he now knew what flight they were on, and where they were headed, so he could keep them under surveillance and intercept them when the time was right. That would most likely be when they reached New York City; murders there were commonplace and could be successfully carried out and covered up much easier than in Reykjavik, Iceland.

# CHAPTER 11

▼

# POLICE HEADQUARTERS, WASHINGTON, D.C. NINE A.M., SUNDAY DECEMBER 19, 1999

## THIRTEEN DAYS TO 0 0

The next morning, the investigation into the truck accident had taken on new meaning. It was now coupled with the dead man found in Kate's room and the attempt on her life. The police first had suspected that Kate, or even Nick, may have killed the unknown man. Kate had tried vehemently to leave the hospital after the incident and was only kept there by the insistence and physical restraint of Nick and the hospital staff. That and their refusal to give her any clothes.

However, after a short investigation and interrogating witnesses that had seen another man leave Kate's room, the police had determined that neither Nick nor Kate were viable suspects. They decided that it was best to let Kate get some sleep. She had had a very difficult night and was nearly hysterical with her demands to leave. They had sedated her, against her will and then put her into a new room, under heavy guard, while they investigated the crime scene. Nick had refused to leave and slept outside her room.

Kate had been sedated so heavily that she was still groggy when they took her to the police station for further questioning. She was quite placid and, even though she indicated that she wanted to leave, she was only in a mild state of agitation. Lieutenant John Thomas, who headed up the investigation, met Kate and Nick at the police station. Nick had met him for the first time the night before regarding the killings of Jeremy and Waldo. He liked him.

"Kate, this is Lieutenant John Thomas. Lieutenant, this is Kate Peters." Nick hoped to keep everything moving as quickly and as friendly as possible. He just wanted to get the hell out of there.

"Hello, Miss Peters. I appreciate your coming down here so quickly after what you have been through. And please let me extend my condolences for the loss of your friends. I understand that you were close."

"Thank you, Lieutenant. We were close on a professional level. I really didn't know them very well on a social level," Kate responded in a deliberate and weary voice. She knew this was a situation that required great caution. Especially since she was still groggy from the sedative that they had given her. "Can we get started? I know that you need to do this, but I am exhausted. I don't know how long I can remain coherent."

"I sympathize, Miss Peters, if you will go with Detective Carlton we will wrap this up as quickly as we can. But we did have three murders last night so you can appreciate that we need to get to the bottom of this," Lieutenant Thomas said.

"Yes, I do understand and I want to help you as much as possible. But I really have no idea what is going on either and I'm afraid I can't tell you anything more than I have already told your officers at the hospital!."

"Often people will remember more the next day and sometimes know things that may turn out to be significant and don't even know it. That's why they pay us to be investigators."

"Yes, Lieutenant, I guess I can understand that," Kate said as she was escorted into the interview room.

"Lieutenant, go easy on her please. She's had a very difficult night, as you know, and she is the victim here," Nick said, the concern written all over his face.

"Don't worry, Mr. Logan. We gave up the rubber hoses a long time ago." The lieutenant smiled.

The Colonel put his hand lightly on Nick's shoulder. "Thanks and please call me Nick." He returned the smile.

"Okay, Nick. If you will follow me we can get through the questions that we have for you."

Detectives Jamie Carlton and Bobby Jones went into one of the interrogation rooms with Kate Peters and, when they started out, were very cordial to her.

"Are you all right, Miss Peters? I know you had a rough night," Detective Carlton said.

"Yes, I have and I'd feel a lot better in my own bed, in my own apartment, resting," Kate said. She was still fighting off the affects of the sedative.

"You seem a little nervous," Detective Jones said.

"You'd seem that way, too, if you were almost killed and then shot full of sedatives and forced to stay where you didn't want to stay and didn't feel safe," Kate replied.

"I guess I can understand that," Detective Jones said.

"Do you know the man that tried to kill you in the hospital?" Detective Carlton asked.

"No, I've never seen him before in my life," Kate answered.

"You have absolutely no idea?" Detective Jones added.

"I've never seen the man before in my entire life, I told you," Kate was more empathetic.

"Do you know of any reason why someone would want to kill you?" Detective Carlton said in a soothing tone.

"No, I can't think of a single reason."

"You don't have any enemies?" Detective Jones barked. "None at all?"

"I don't exactly live a hard, fast life. I spend most of my time working and I have a very limited social life." Kate remained calm. If these two were going to play good cop, bad cop it would take a lot more than what Detective Bobby Jones had to phase her.

"I see," Detective Jones said.

"Can you tell me who he is?" Kate asked looking straight at Jones.

"We're working on that. He seems to be a man with a very limited past," Detective Carlton said.

"I see detective." Her face revealed nothing, but Kate knew that the lack of any past probably meant that he was an assassin for one of the intelligence agencies. The question was—which one?

When he first met John Thomas Nick had liked him immediately. He was a no nonsense detective who showed a sincere compassion for the death's of his two friends.

"I can't say that I'm happy to see you again, Lieutenant."

"I certainly can understand that," Lieutenant Thomas replied. He observed how drawn and tired looking Nick looked this morning.

"I don't spend a lot of time in police stations and now I've been here twice in the past twelve hours. Fortunately, this time it's only with a potential victim."

"Lucky for her that you and her white knight were around or else she would have been the third dead body," Lieutenant Thomas said. "What do you suppose that's all about?" There wasn't any hint of accusation.

"I have no idea," Nick shook his head slowly. "We were working on a very high profile project, but we concluded that yesterday. We're not exactly in the cloak and dagger part of the defense business. The three of them are computer geniuses. I can't imagine them ever hurting anyone or causing anyone to try to kill them."

"From what we can determine, I'd have to agree with you," Lieutenant Thomas said leaning forward in his chair. "You do think that these were related instances then. Don't you, Nick?"

"I have no specific reason to believe that they are, except for the fact that I don't believe in coincidences. Not this kind." Nick was being straight forward with the lieutenant; he had no reason not to be.

"Did they spend a lot of time together?"

"They spent a lot of time together at work. And we worked long days so, yes, they spent a lot of time together. But they didn't socialize. The two young men did a lot of socializing and were very close, but, as far as I can tell, Kate didn't do any socializing at all." There was a very slight, almost imperceptible brightening in Nick's eyes that wasn't missed by the Lieutenant.

"Don't you think that's a little odd. After all she's a very attractive woman."

"Yes, she is. And she's also quite dedicated to her work. We've been working on a very sensitive and demanding project and she was the key to its success."

"I see. That doesn't help us much."

"It sounds to me like you also think that the murders and the attempt on Kate's life are related."

"Let's just say that I don't believe in coincidences either."

"It sounds a little more than that to me." "And I think I have a right to know if it is. I'm still in charge of an extremely important project and I'm sure you've already checked how high up my clearance goes."

"I know how high up your clearance goes, but this isn't a federal issue. This is the jurisdiction of the Washington, D.C. police."

"Yes, I know. But I can make it a federal issue. I can get the feds involved if I have too," Nick said firmly, but with no hint of a threat. "You seem like a nice guy, Lieutenant, and I don't want to step on any toes, but this project is important enough that I'll do whatever I have to do, to whoever I have to do it, to make sure that it's not compromised in any way."

Lieutenant Thomas took a long hard look at Nick. He never liked being strong-armed, particularly by the feds, but with Nick it was something different. What it was, was sincerity. So he decided to take him into his confidence. He also knew he could probably back up what he had said.

"Apparently one of your young friends liked to record things. We found a small recorder in his jacket pocket. He had had the presence of mind to turn it on," Lieutenant Thomas said.

"That would be Waldo," Nick said. "He was always recording everything. It was sort of a hobby of his and he hated taking notes."

"We've recovered the tape and it's given us some new insight into the case."

"What's that?" Nick's senses were alert. The adrenaline was overcoming the weariness.

"Here. I'll show you." Lieutenant Thomas opened his drawer and pulled out a tape player and put in a cassette tape. "We could use your help with the voices. But I warn you, Nick. It isn't pretty."

"Play it," Nick said as his body stiffened.

Lieutenant Thomas then fast-forwarded it to the spot he wanted. It took him a couple of starts and stops to get it right where he wanted.

"Oh, shit!" Then Lieutenant Thomas stopped the tape.

"That's Waldo," Nick focused on the tape recorder.

"You can have anything you want, but please don't kill us." Again, Lieutenant Thomas stopped the tape.

"That's Jeremy," Nick stiffened further disturbed by the fear in Jeremy's voice.

"I know I can. And I will. But surely you can beg for your lives better than that."

"I don't recognize that voice. The killer?" Nick asked as he turned to Thomas.

"We presume so," the Lieutenant said. He watched Nick's reaction closely. A lot could be learned when a person was under stress, or was suppose to be.

"Please! Please! Don't kill..." Then they heard two spits. Nick cringed when he heard Jeremy's plea for life cut short.

"You bastard! What have you done?"

"That's Waldo, again." Nick could hear the anger mixed with disbelief in his friend's voice. He felt sick.

"You'll have to do better than that, Waldo."

"FUCK YOU!" They heard Waldo's words just before hearing two more spits.

For a moment, Nick thought he was going to be sick to his stomach. He had never heard anything so terrible in his life. The words of one friend's plea for life and another's act of defiance, just before they were executed, were all too vivid in his mind. Two young lives snuffed out in an instant.

"Are you all right, Nick?" Lieutenant Thomas asked. Nick was pale and the Lieutenant knew his surprise and pain were real.

Nick struggled to gain control. "Ya, I think so. You were right. It wasn't easy."

"I'm sorry you had to hear that. I know that you'll have to live with it for a long time."

"But why, why shoot them? They were going to give them their money."

"Unfortunately, Nick, that happens all to often. And their money was gone so it looks like it was a robbery."

"You say that like you really don't believe it."

"Well, I have severe doubts. Even in this town we don't get many robberies and murders where the perp uses a silencer."

It now struck Nick that they were awfully quiet shots. He wouldn't have even recognized them as shots if he hadn't already seen their bodies, including the bullet holes. He didn't realize that he hadn't really heard shots because he was so distressed by the terror in Jeremy's voice.

"In fact, in this town, I've concluded that the louder the better. It tends to keep the bystanders at a distance, but this one wanted be sure he was neither seen nor heard.

And he only took their wallets, even though they were both wearing expensive watches. He probably didn't bother with them because that would have slowed him down."

"This new revelation doesn't make me feel any better," Nick informed Thomas.

"No, I didn't think it would. There is something else."

"I'm afraid to ask."

"Listen," the Lieutenant said as he rewound the tape slightly and let it play again.

"You'll have to do better than that, Waldo."

"My God! The fucking bastard knew his name. How?"

"It's possible that he was casing people inside the restaurant and he overheard his name." The tone of the Lieutenant's voice said that he thought this possible, but unlikely.

"It's also possible that the killer knew Waldo. Or both of them. And it's not a robbery at all." Nick was getting angry.

"Yes. That's very possible," the Lieutenant said. "That is why we need all of the information that you and Miss Peters can give us."

"I'm afraid to ask. Was that the end of the tape?" Nick was hoping that Thomas would be merciful and say yes. This was enough. No, it was too much.

"No. There's one last thing. I didn't play it because I didn't think you needed to hear anymore."

"I don't want to hear anymore. But you'd better play it. I think that I should have all the information available. My gut tells me that there is something much bigger here."

"What? Don't hold anything back from me, Nick." Lieutenant Thomas' voice was firm. "I'm the professional here. The best thing that you can do for your dead friends is to let me do my job. What is it?"

"I don't know. It just doesn't add up. It just feels bad. Play the tape."

The Lieutenant then played the last bit of the tape and they both heard the hideous laugh of the killer after he had completed his gruesome task.

"What kind of man gets that kind of pleasure out of killing another human being. It doesn't even sound human. It sounds like, like..." Nick couldn't even think anymore. He felt like he had aged ten years in the last twelve hours.

"Like a hyena?" the Lieutenant offered.

"Yes. He has a laugh like an animal, a hyena. What kind of sick bastard are we dealing with?"

"Possibly a psychotic. We are looking into that possibility."

"Do you have any other information?" Nick said.

"No, not yet," the Lieutenant said.

"Given the situation, I expect that you will keep me informed with whatever you find." Nick was trying like hell to get on top of the situation.

"Under these circumstances, you can count on it. But remember that this is my jurisdiction and I will inform you as I deem appropriate," the Lieutenant said.

"Thank you. It really is a matter of national security and I am not just trying to sound important. Believe me, I wish it wasn't," Nick said. "Do you think it's time to release Kate, she's had a long night. So haven't I. It would be good if we could get out of here."

"I'll have them wrap it up for now. I'll arrange for a police detail for Kate and for you, too, if you'd like," the Lieutenant said.

"Thanks, but that won't be necessary. I've already arranged for two US Marshals to meet us here and to get around the clock protection from them," Nick said. It wasn't lost on the Lieutenant that Nick had chosen to use the US Marshals rather than the FBI.

"Suit yourself. My budget's tight anyway," the Lieutenant said. "But be careful. I don't know who he or they are yet, but I do know that we're playing with some pretty tough people here."

"Thanks, Lieutenant, and I really do appreciate your help on this. Now we should go. I see the marshals are here and I really want to get Kate to her apartment to pick up some stuff and then get her to a safe place."

# CHAPTER 12

▼

# REYKJAVIK, ICELAND ONE P.M., SUNDAY DECEMBER 19, 1999

## THIRTEEN DAYS TO 0 0

While Yuri and his associates were on their way to Reykjavik, Iceland, Boris had sent Ivan and Egor on to Washington, D.C. to take care of matters there. Once their mission was complete they would go on to New York City and take charge of the interception and removal of Yuri Petrov.

There was plenty of time to accomplish this because of the length of the flight from Sweden to Iceland to New York, including a long layover in Reykjavik. There were only two agents in Reykjavik and they were ordered not to approach the target. Their responsibility was to make sure he got back on the plane to New York. Boris did not want another failure, like what happened outside of Moscow, for fear that Yuri would go so deep underground they might never find him in time.

When British Air flight 107 arrived in Reykjavik the three men, to the surprise of the FSS agents, got off the plane. Even though they had a three-hour wait, they were not changing planes so the agents felt they would remain on board; that would be the safest thing to do. They knew that it was Yuri getting off the plane, even though he was wearing a black trench coat with the collar turned up and a gray felt hat with the brim pulled down. They could see him clearly enough to recognize him from his photo.

"That's him, Stephan" said Leonid, the senior agent. "His poor excuse at a disguise has done little to cover his face. He looks just like his photo."

"You would think that he would have worn dark glasses or not shaved, or something," Stephan responded. "It doesn't seem right. It is very sloppy. And now they are getting off the plane and increasing the chances of being seen."

"Perhaps they have become careless because they believe that they have been successful in deceiving us. Or perhaps it is because they know that they are relatively safe in Iceland. There are no guns allowed in the country," Leonid said. "Or maybe it is just because they are hungry. Look there."

When Stephan turned to look, he saw that they went into the restaurant and took a booth in the back corner. Apparently they hadn't eaten in some time and felt they were safe enough to chance it since they were taking the roundabout route to get to the United States.

"If it were me, I would have had one of my guards get the food and bring it back. Or gone hungry," Stephan said. "I would not risk exposing myself like this."

"For one thing, they know that nothing will happen to them in the airport. The worst that can happen is that they are discovered and their destination is learned."

"That would be bad enough," Stephan said. "In New York we would be able to kill them. Even in the airport."

"Yes, that's true," Leonid responded. "Perhaps they are over confident. But can you blame them. We are not the powerful and feared force that we once were. They know that there are fewer of us than there used to be. And that, if caught, some of us are more subject to bribes."

"Some of us," Stephan answered.

"Yes. Some of us," Leonid said looking coldly into the eyes of his younger comrade. "When is the last time that you were paid?"

"Six months ago," Stephan answered.

"Me, too. I work because my savings and pension were wiped out by the financial crises in the summer of '98. And still I have to wait six months to get paid."

"The financial collapse last year was very unfortunate for many people. But in the end it may be a very good thing. The old communists regained some power and it made a lot of others question this move to capitalism. Another such crisis and who knows. Hunger is a powerful force."

"Perhaps. We'll see. But now we had better do our jobs, pay or not," Leonid said as he looked in the direction of the restaurant and nodded. "The target is on the move."

Having finished their light meal, Yuri and his escorts emerged from the restaurant and made only a half-hearted attempt to conceal themselves. Further infuriating Stephan, who took it as a personal affront. Then they proceeded to go into the men's room.

The FSS agents stayed, inconspicuously, outside just to observe and make sure they got back on the plane. Once out of the men's room the three men walked quickly, with their backs to the agents, toward the gate to board the plane. The two escorts, on either side of the man in the black trench coat and gray hat, were obviously protectors of the man in the middle.

It was Leonid who took up the more comfortable position watching the gate while Stephan took a position standing near the window so he could see the plane. They weren't taking any chances. As the plane started taxiing away from the loading platform, Stephan stayed there so he could constantly keep his eye on the plane. Once the plane took off they relaxed. The plane was on its way to New York and it was no longer their responsibility. However, they would continue to stay at the airport until it actually arrived in New York to make sure that it did not return to Reykjavik for any reason.

Earlier, as the Concorde flight made it's approach to the Washington International airport, Egor's comments brought Ivan out of his deep thoughts.

"Isn't it marvelous what these capitalists spend so much money on," Egor said.

"Yes, allowing us to travel at such great speed certainly makes our job easier," Ivan answered.

"I wonder if they have any idea just how useful to us these supersonic planes can be?"

"I'm sure they've been just as useful to them."

"At least it will give us plenty of time to do what we have to and still get to New York to intercept this traitor, Yuri. This time he won't get away from us," Egor said.

"This time, let's be professional about it so that we can make a positive identification and know that we have done our job right," Ivan said, giving Egor a cold stare.

"Ivan, my friend, you must learn to take more pleasure in your work," Egor said laughing.

Egor's statement made chills run up and down Ivan's spine, as he didn't know what upset him more, being called friend by this barbarian or knowing that, friend or not, he would kill him in an instant, if ordered to. Indeed, men like Egor and men like Boris made him wonder if what he was doing was truly in the best interest of Russia. He had long ago recognized the benefits of using whatever means are available to achieve a desired end. The question now was, what end would really be attained.

# CHAPTER 13

▼

# NEW YORK CITY—JFK AIRPORT
# FIVE P.M., SUNDAY
# DECEMBER 19, 1999
## THIRTEEN DAYS TO 0 0

FSS agents Malenkov and Skulsky had arrived at the JFK airport from Washington only minutes earlier when they were met by four New York based FSS agents. These agents had been assigned to assist them in intercepting Yuri Petrov on his arrival from Iceland. If the flight from Reykjavik had arrived before Malenkov and Skulsky then they were to put Petrov under surveillance until those agents could join them. Agent Malenkov quickly took control of the operation and ordered the two New York agents to take up a position north of Petrov's arrival gate and two would take up a position south of the gate. Malenkov and Skulsky had to stay back, well out of the way. They wanted to make sure Petrov and his bodyguards, who might recognize them, didn't spot them. He was pleased that they arrived in time so that they could accomplish what they failed to do in Moscow.

As if he could read his mind, Egor Skulsky said, "It is good that comrade Stepovich ordered us here to finish with this Petrov. It shows that he still has confidence in us and that this mission is extremely important. If it wasn't he wouldn't have had us racing to Washington from Moscow to take care of business there and then up here in New York to take care of Petrov." Skulsky then gave Malenkov a little grin to let him know that, even though Malenkov had told him nothing, the significance of this operation was not lost on him.

"Yes, Egor. And we had better be careful. We have failed him twice already," Ivan said. "I would not like to fail him a third time."

"Moscow was not our failure. He already knew that his life was in danger. And that was not our leak. That was Stepovich's problem," Egor said angrily.

"Perhaps. But if his head hadn't been blown away we would have immediately know it wasn't Yuri Petrov that much sooner."

There was dead silence and the icy stare from Egor made Ivan's neck hairs stand on end. Then Egor added, "And Washington was not my failure. I got my two. It was your target that got away."

"You're right, Egor," Malenkov conceded. "That is why I wish we were still in Washington. So that I could correct that."

"She's underground now, so you wouldn't find her. And when she does surface, our regular Washington comrades have the knowledge and local experience to find her even quicker than we do. Then we can correct that mistake. Just like tonight will correct the Moscow mistake. Then we can go back to Moscow in triumph and face Comrade Stepovich without fear."

"Yes, Egor, that is what I expect to happen. So tonight, when Petrov and his bodyguards arrive, we first must wait for them to exit the airport. There are too many people and too much security to do anything inside. But, before we do anything, we must confirm that it is Yuri Petrov and not another impostor. Is that clear?"

"Perfectly clear..... Comrade Ivan."

The flight from Iceland had landed and was now unloading at it's assigned gate. The four New York agents were in position to check the incoming passengers from the flight. These men would not recognize Yuri, having spent the last twenty years in the United States, but they had been provided with a picture to assist them. Besides, it would not be difficult to pick out the three men traveling together, trying to look inconspicuous and constantly checking their surroundings for danger. It wasn't long before they spotted them waiting to come through the customs gate. The lead agent radioed Ivan on his small portable walkie-talkie that they had set on a frequency careful to avoid the airport security and the local police channels.

"We have spotted them, comrade. They will be coming through the customs gate shortly."

"Are you certain it's them?"

"Yes, sir. It's obvious the three men are traveling together. We can't positively identify Petrov. The man in the middle of the other two has his hat pulled down and his collar up, as if he was still out in the cold. But, of what we can see of his face from this distance, it certainly could be Petrov."

"Could be is a lot less sure than *is*, comrade. Make sure you stay back and they don't see you," Ivan Malenkov instructed. He thought for a moment and then asked, "And you said the three of them are traveling together? Standing in a group?"

"Yes, sir."

Ivan thought that this was strange. The proper procedure was to have only one of the bodyguards close to Yuri. The other one should be at least fifteen to twenty feet away. It would be less obvious that he was with them and he could observe other people better. And he would be much freer to move if he saw something happening. These men were guarding him like amateurs. And it was very unlike Dimitry Petrov to work with amateurs. Perhaps he had no choice and limited resources to work with. Ivan thought it was almost as if they wanted to make sure that it was known they were together and were protecting the man in the middle. Another cold chill went up Ivan's back and this time it wasn't from Egor's look. He began to feel very uneasy.

"Stay close to them," Malenkov ordered. "They probably only have carry on luggage so they won't be stopping at the luggage carousel."

Ivan Malenkov was right. They each had a large carry on bag and headed immediately for the exit.

"You're right, comrade Malenkov, they're heading for the main exit. We will be right behind them."

Ivan then radioed the driver that they would be at the main entrance and to be ready to leave. They would meet them at the rendezvous point that they had originally set up which would give them time to get lost in the crowd and then get to the car without being noticed. Ivan then radioed the others.

"Remember, it's only on my signal that we will take them out. If I wave you off, I want no gun fire."

Ivan didn't like the setup. If it was Yuri it was going to be very messy, but they had no choice. If they let him get away into the crowd and into a safe house, they might not find him again in time. So they chose to make it look like a Russian 'Mafia' hit. The Russian gangs had earned a reputation for extreme cruelty and were not above assassinating an enemy in a crowd of people, not worrying if anyone else got hurt in the process.

Ivan Malenkov wanted to make sure it was Yuri Petrov before they started killing people; more concerned about giving another false report back to Boris Stepovich than the hell that would break loose here. Ivan and Egor had positioned themselves in the shadows outside the main exit. The spot gave them the opportunity to see the men as they came through the brightly lit exit. They would be able to approach rapidly and open fire before their victims knew what was happening. The agents following them would block any retreat. When the firing began, this would be the one time that Ivan would be glad he had Egor with him. He knew he was deadly with the Uzi, so easily concealed beneath his coat. The plan was for Egor to take out Yuri and the man to his right. Ivan would take out the man to Yuri's left and then make sure that Yuri was dead. As Ivan got the word that the men were almost at the doorway he nodded to Egor. He could feel the tension growing in his body. It was as much from the thought that he might soon take another life as it was any concern that he might be killed. He looked at Egor and saw an ice cold stare in his eyes and an almost expressionless stone face, but he also saw the slightly curled up lip of a smile—the hunter waiting for its prey.

Then the double doors pushed out towards them and the three men emerged from the building. Egor Skulsky was already preparing to open his coat and raise his weapon, but had to wait for the doors to swing shut behind them closing off any avenue of escape. In the moment it took to do this, the three men stepped into the light and Ivan could immediately recognize that the man in the middle was not Yuri Petrov. He immediately radioed the others to abort as he saw the barrel of Egor's gun emerge from his coat. Ivan instinctively and quickly grabbed it and pushed it back down, only to receive a deathly cold stare from Egor.

"Egor, no. It's not him," Ivan said.

"We should eliminate them anyway. They're the enemy," Egor said.

"The risk is much too great for so little value," Ivan said as he looked into Egor's eyes. It was only for a short moment, but Ivan was not sure that Egor could back away after having prepared himself for the kill. Then Egor's eyes seemed to refocus and he returned his gun to its hiding place as they slipped into the darkness. They met the others at the rendezvous point and sped away. Ivan Malenkov was very upset. It appeared that Dimitry Petrov had won another round. His respect for him went up another notch.

"There's no way he could have gotten by us, comrade Malenkov."

"No. He didn't get by us. He was never on the plane," Ivan said calmly. "I want you to immediately contact our agents in Iceland and have them start tracking how he got out of Iceland. It wasn't by plane, at least not a plane to New York."

"Yes, sir."

Ivan Malenkov dreaded the call he was going to have to make to Boris Stepovich.

# CHAPTER 14

▼

# WASHINGTON, D.C. ELEVEN A.M., MONDAY DECEMBER 20

## TWELVE DAYS TO <u>00</u>

The body of Waldo Clarke was being taken back to his family's home in Minnesota for the funeral and burial. His mother and father were thankful to Eric Johnson, Jeremy's brother, for having the required autopsies performed on a Sunday and then the bodies released. They couldn't get out of Washington quickly enough. They had pleaded with Waldo practically begging him, not to go to one of those dangerous cities in the East. But their son had said that he wanted to go were the excitement was. And now he was dead.

In contrast, Jeremy Johnson was to be buried in Washington, where he and his brother lived with his aunt and uncle. Their parents had been killed in a terrible automobile accident early in their lives. His brother, Eric, had brought up Jeremy, to a large extent.

The funeral was very sad, which was not unusual for a young man who was so well liked and who had died a violent death. No one who knew him could imagine him ever harming anyone.

A large number of those attending the funeral accepted his aunt and uncle's invitation to go back to their home after the funeral. They had adopted the two boys when their parents had died; Eric was seventeen and Jeremy was only twelve. They were kind people and had done their best to provide a good home for the boys. The boys loved them deeply, but they couldn't replace their parents so there was always an extremely strong bond between Jeremy and Eric. It was not only a strong brotherly bond, but almost a father-son bond. When Eric had made his decision of what college to go to he chose Georgetown University so that he could remain living at home and be with his brother.

As Nick and Kate were standing in a corner of the living room drinking a cup of coffee, the US Marshals close by, Eric approached them.

"Mr. Logan, Miss Peters, I'm Eric Johnson. I want to thank you for coming. My brother told me a lot about you. He liked the both of you," Eric said. His voice was controlled and measured, but the pain just below the surface was obvious. It showed in his eyes.

"We're terribly sorry about your brother. He was a wonderful young man and we'll miss him," Nick said.

"Yes. He was. I will miss him, too," Eric said with tears evident in his eyes. "I will miss him a lot." He had wished that he had not said this. He was close to losing control in front of these people and he couldn't do that. His training had prepared him to deal with adversity, but it was on the verge of failing him. The depth of his pain, of his emptiness, was almost beyond bearing. All that kept him going, that would keep him going, was the anger and hatred that he felt for his brother's killer. There was nothing left in his life but to find the killer and to kill him.

"Your brother often spoke of you. It was quite clear that he not only loved you, he worshipped you," Kate said.

"Not as much as I worshipped him," Eric quickly answered. "Mr. Logan, can I see you alone for a moment, please?"

"Certainly, but please call me Nick."

"All right, Nick. We can go in here," Eric said and he led Nick into a small room off of the living room and closed the door. Once inside, Eric spoke first.

"Please tell me everything you know."

"I'm not sure I'm at liberty to do that," Nick responded.

"I'm his brother, I have a right to know," Eric demanded. "I have a need to know."

"I understand, but I've used my position to get some classified police information which I'm really not at liberty to divulge."

"Okay, Nick, let me tell you what I know that you know. You know some common street mugger didn't kill them. You know somebody who used a silencer killed them and that somebody knew Waldo's name. I know that you know, or at least suspect, that there is some kind of relationship between their murders and the attempts on Kate Peters' life. That's what I know you know," Eric said. "I also know that son-of-a-bitch made Jeremy, my beautiful Jeremy, beg for his life. I know that he has a sickening laugh—like a hyena. Now I want to know everything else that you know."

"How did you get that information?" Nick was amazed. "Did you talk to Lieutenant Thomas? I can't believe that he would release that information."

"No, he wouldn't tell me much of anything," Eric said angrily. "I have resources."

"What the hell kind of resources could you have? Who the hell are you?"

"The kind of resources that can get me a copy of Waldo's tape. I heard my brother's voice when he begged for his life. I heard the muffled shots that took his life. I heard the hyena's laugh," Eric said coldly. "And, as for who the hell I am, I'm that hyena's worst fucking nightmare and for anyone associated with him or who gets in my way."

"Look, Eric, I know that your in some kind of Special Forces. Your brother was very proud of that; as he should be. And I know you feel a strong need to avenge his death, but this is police business and it's best left to the professionals. I'm certain that all the resources necessary are going to be put into this, in fact, I'll guarantee that," Nick said.

"I appreciate that, Mr. Logan, but I have resources at my disposal that you don't; a lot of resources. I am going to be a part of this investigation. And, yes, I am out to avenge my brother's death; and I will. Make no mistake about that," Eric said firmly. "What I want to know is why someone would want to kill him and Waldo and why someone tried to kill Kate."

"That I don't know. I wish that I did. All I can tell you is we were working on an extremely sensitive, important project, but I don't know how it's related to them at all," Nick said.

"If the 'Millennium Bug' project was so important a project, so secretive, then tell me why there wasn't security for these key people?" Eric demanded.

"What do you know about the project?" Nick asked, but did not get a response. He paused for a moment. "That's the part that really hurts, Eric. Up until that night they were under surveillance and had security protection, but we had finished the project that day and they had all asked for the surveillance to be stopped. They wanted to go out that night and let their hair down a little and not feel like they were under a magnifying glass. Since the project was complete, and they were no longer technically under my control, I agreed. That's a decision I'll regret for the rest of my life," Nick said. "I will do everything I can to help find their killers. I promise you that."

"I believe that, because I understand it. After all, their deaths were related to your project and they were killed on your watch. You can also rest assured that I won't stop until I get their killers. So I suggest that, if you have nothing to hide, we work together. And if you have something to hide, rest assured I'll find out," Eric said. "And I won't let politics or anything else get in the way of getting at the truth."

"Neither will I," Nick said. "But you can also believe that you, or anyone else, threatening me won't work."

"Understand one thing, Nick, I never threaten—I act," Eric said in a calm, quite voice that made it clear that this was not bravado but merely the cold, hard truth. Then there was a knock at the door. "Think about what I said. I strongly suggest that we work together and you keep nothing from me, because I'm going to be there anyway." He then opened the door and answered his aunt's call.

As Eric left, Nick felt the hairs on the back of his neck stand up. There was definitely something special about this man. He was capable and confident and wasn't a man to make idle threats. Any man whose life had just been shattered was a dangerous man. But a man with a dead heart, trained in the art of killing, was lethal. Nick silently hoped that Eric would realize they were on the same side.

# CHAPTER 15

▼

# VIRGINIA COUNTRYSIDE ELEVEN A.M., MONDAY DECEMBER 20

## TWELVE DAYS TO 0 0

Victor Noble had summoned the stern faced David Ford to his mansion in Virginia. The fifty-eight year old Ford was an intense man and the Deputy Director of the Central Intelligence Agency.

The Noble estate was one of the largest in the county, as befitted a man of stature and wealth. At least that was what Victor Noble had told himself when he spent seven million dollars for it ten years earlier. A purchase he had never regretted. It had become his refuge from the rigors and unrelenting pace of Washington, was a marvelous place to entertain, and offered all the facilities and privacy one needed for a well equipped command center.

"Christ, David, how the hell could you let that happen," Victor Noble demanded. His gunmetal black, piercing eyes seemed to penetrate through Ford.

"Regular surveillance had been pulled. I had to put two of my own men on it who had to be a lot more inconspicuous. And damn if those two little jerks didn't sneak out the back door," David Ford responded firmly.

"It's a damn good thing your man got to the hospital in time to save Peters' ass or this whole thing would be up in smoke." Victor Noble's criticism could be particularly biting when he was angry. And right now he was furious. His limp made more acute by his efforts to quickly cross the large, mahogany paneled room and confront Ford. "This isn't the first mistake you've made as far as she is concerned."

"We've been through this before, Victor. I still don't know how she was able to get the level of security clearance she needed for the project." David Ford had to bite his lip to keep from screaming at Victor Noble. It was just this kind of arrogant, know it all, sons-of-bitch that had kept him from being named the Director of the agency. He couldn't forget the fact that he had been passed over three times. Passed over for lesser men. Men who were better politicians and, thus, better connected.

"Perhaps she had assistance from the mole that is buried deep within the agency." Victor Noble needled the Deputy Director.

"There has never been any proof that there is a mole within the agency," Ford said, restraining himself from saying more.

"Then did your department just do a bad job? It is your department's responsibility, isn't it?"

"You know it is." Ford thought what an arrogant ass Noble could be. Some day he would kick that ass—hard.

"If it weren't for my resources we would never have known about it. And we would never have had this opportunity." Victor Noble would never be accused of being humble.

"So perhaps we should be thankful for it."

"Yes. We should. With this power I will be able to control the President. Once I control the fate of the country he will have to agree to following my agenda. He will be like a puppet on a string." Noble smiled, pleased with himself.

"I'm concerned that, once we are past the crisis, we will no longer have any control over him. And he will still be the President. With all of its inherent power."

"You have to learn to see the big picture, David; especially if you are going to be my CIA director. When faced with the possibility of this country being turned into an inferno, Justin Stewart will have to agree with my conditions. Conditions that will insure us that he will have to dance to my tune after the crisis is over."

"How can we be sure of that?" Ford asked.

"For one thing, our illustrious President is notorious for his love of beautiful women."

"That's true. But he is a single man since his wife died. And there is no evidence of him ever having an affair on her."

"Yes. But now it is like an obsession with him. Like it is the only way that he can get his late wife out of his mind. And it is a weakness to be exploited."

"I still don't see how that will work once the immediate crisis is over. After all, his appetite for women is well known and he was still re-elected for a second term," Ford pointed out.

"Ah, my good, David, you do lack vision. But that is all right because I have all that we need." As he said this, Victor Noble gave David Ford that all knowing half smile, made more biting by his thin, black mustache, which made Ford want to kick his ass right then and there. Then he continued: "How accepting do you think the American people would be if they find out that their President was having a tryst with a beautiful woman, who had past 'connections' with the hard line communists. The same men that brought this country to the brink of nuclear annihilation?"

"I see. He will have to continue to follow your direction," Ford said. "He will have no choice. As long as you can prove it."

"Don't worry. I will be able to prove it. Enough so that he will not only have to follow my directions for the rest of his Presidency, but he will have to support me in the next election."

"You are a man of vision." Ford knew that Noble loved to have his ego stroked and that it would also help to keep him thinking that he was his obedient puppy dog.

"Yes. And that is why we must not fail. We are putting the country in great jeopardy by allowing this to happen. We must have Kate Peters to be in control of the situation. It is a risk, but history is full of great men who had to use whatever means necessary to achieve great ends. Without the immediate threat of communism we have taken our military superiority for granted. The Russian bear is still a formidable animal with the ability to destroy the world many times over. And she is a wounded animal and wounded animals are the most dangerous. We need strong leadership for the difficult years ahead. Not a pretty boy who chases everything in a skirt."

"Of course you are right, Victor," Ford said.

"Where is she now?" Noble asked.

"At the moment, she's at the funeral of Jeremy Johnson."

"I hope you have her under an extreme amount of protection," Noble said. His tone was accusatory.

"I have two of my men on her at all times and she is also being guarded by two US Marshals," Ford answered.

"US Marshals! Why US Marshals? Why not the DC police or, more likely, the FBI?" Noble asked.

"Apparently, this Logan has a long standing relationship with people in the US Marshals office and he trusts them more. After the events of the last couple of days, he is being extra cautious."

"I see. Perhaps I've underestimated this Logan. I wouldn't have expected this of a bean counter. I thought that he was a weakness we could manipulate. Possibly he is someone we should eliminate," Noble thought out loud.

"Give the word and I can have that done immediately."

"No. Not yet. There's already too much attention focused on the group who led this project. Besides, he may still be the weak link and right now he's our best lead to Kate Peters. He is also helping to protect her. And, we need all the help we can get. So let him live—for now," Noble said. "Once we get control of her, then he'd better not get in our way."

"You're right of course, Victor. I'll put another team on Peters right away. And a separate team on Logan."

"Yes, David, please do. That should have been done already. We can't afford any more failures."

"I'm on it," Ford said as he put on his overcoat.

After Ford left, Victor Noble sat assessing the situation. He could understand why Ford had not made it past Deputy Director. While he was extremely competent and dedicated, he lacked the ability to see the total picture and to be able to put things into perspective. He realized that very few people could see past the details, really see past the details, and he was confident and took pleasure in the fact that he could. He was what the country needed as its leader.

# CHAPTER 16

▼

# HOTEL SUITE— WASHINGTON, D.C. ELEVEN A.M., TUESDAY DECEMBER 21

## ELEVEN DAYS TO 0 0

Nick Logan secretly took Kate Peters to a hotel located on the outskirts of Washington. Out of the mainstream of the Washington activity. It also provided suites of rooms with two bedrooms off of a center living room. The general operating procedures called for one of the two marshals to be in the central living room at all times. This meant that there would always be one of them with Kate if she were in the living room or between her and the outside door if she were in her room.

"I have to check in with Grant," Nick informed Kate.

"No. Please. I don't want anyone to know where I am," Kate pleaded with Nick.

"Don't worry, I don't have to tell him where you are. Only the four of us know and it will stay that way," Nick said as he looked at her and nodded to the two US Marshals on the other side of the sitting room.

"Do you have to call him?" Kate continued. "His phone line could be monitored."

"Yes, Kate I do. He's my boss and I have to let him know you are safe. Then we have to discuss what our next step should be. I'll use the phone in the bedroom and call him on his direct, secure line. You can listen in if you want."

"If you don't mind, I would be more comfortable if I did," Kate said.

They both went into the bedroom and closed the door. Nick then dialed the private number of Charles Grant.

"Hello, Charles. Nick Logan here."

"Where are you? Is Kate with you?" The tension in his voice was high.

"Yes, she's with me and she's safe."

"Safe where?"

"No disrespect, Charles, but right now I think the fewer people that know that the better until we can sort this out," Nick said, getting satisfaction out of telling his boss no.

"I want the two of you in my office now," Grant demanded.

"I'm not sure it's a smart thing to go to your office."

"No, I won't go, so forget it," Kate said loud enough for Grant to hear her.

"That's an order," Grant said angrily.

"You can order me and I'll be there, Charles. But Kate refuses to leave. I'm not sure we have the authority to order her to. Even if we do, I don't think we have the moral right to risk her life that way. Right now she's safe and under the protection of two U.S. Marshals, whom I trust completely."

"Then tell me where you are and I'll come there," a frustrated Grant said.

"Sorry, Charles. But you could be followed." Nick couldn't help being pleased.

"If you tell him where we are, I'm out of here," Kate said.

"I think it's best if I come to your office alone and we can discuss the next steps together," Nick offered.

"Okay, but get your ass over here right away. And, if anything happens to Miss Peters, remember she is under your protection so she is your responsibility," Grant said as he slammed the phone down.

"Why does Grant want me there?" Kate wanted to know, as she began to pace the floor.

"I'm sure he's just trying to determine if the program has been jeopardized. I can understand it. I have a lot of the same questions." Nick wanted to calm Kate down if he could.

"He just wants to cover his butt. He doesn't know enough about the project to know if it has been corrupted," Kate said sarcastically.

"You may be right, but he is my boss and I'll have to go."

"I understand. But he no longer has any authority over me. And neither do you. So I'm staying right here. I don't feel that safe even here and I would be a hell of a lot more exposed going to Grant's office. I might as well wave a red flag," Kate said, still pacing and looking very worried. "We may have already done that by calling him."

"I told you that I called him on his direct, secure line." Nick had the urge to grab her and hold her to make her feel safe.

"How do you know that it is secure? Any security can be breached." She didn't want to be unkind but she knew Nick was out of his element.

"I think that you are getting a little too paranoid."

"Do you really think so?"

"Okay. You win. I'll go over myself and clear it with Grant," Nick said.

Nick knew that he could force her to go, because the nature of the project and his status as the project manager gave him the authority to have her arrested by the military police. But that was something he didn't want to do. He didn't want them involved and he didn't totally disagree with her. He also didn't know whom to trust, either. Nick finally had agreed to let her stay there with the marshals, but under strict orders not to leave the room until he came back. Kate agreed because she was tired and wanted to get some sleep anyway.

"Promise you won't tell him where I am," Kate pleaded as she stopped pacing. "I don't trust him. I don't trust anybody."

"I won't tell him, but you're going to have to trust somebody. You can trust me. If I had wanted you dead I'd have had ample opportunity to have had it done by now," Nick said as he took her by the hand.

"You're right, I'm sorry."

"You'll be safe here until I get back."

"My life is in your hands," Kate said, looking at Nick and lightly squeezing his hand.

"You can count on me." At that moment Nick realized, no matter what, he had committed himself to protecting her life at all cost. Grant was right, she was now his responsibility.

"I have to leave for a little while," Nick said to the marshals as he entered the sitting room and grabbed his jacket. "I'll be back as soon as I can. Don't let anyone in but me."

As he pulled out of the hotel's underground garage, Nick's mind was racing in an effort to process everything that was happening and how he was going to handle his boss. He knew Grant was not at all happy about being told that Kate wouldn't come to his office to meet with him. He certainly would feel slighted that Kate felt safer with him. It would be one more thing he would hold against him, but that didn't bother Nick, in fact he got a perverse pleasure out of getting Grant upset, although it could hurt his career. But at this point it didn't matter. He was involved in something much more serious than where his career was going and, if it weren't resolved, he wouldn't have much of a career anyway.

It was five o'clock, and the middle of rush hour, so it would take him approximately forty minutes to get across town to the General Accounting Office building. When he arrived he used his GAO pass to gain access to the underground parking. He then went to the first floor and through the minimum-security check that everyone had to pass through in government buildings these days. He took the elevator to the fourteenth floor, turned right out of the elevator and headed for the corner office. It had not really surprised him, when he'd first seen Grant's office, that he was able to manipulate himself into a corner office ahead of others of equal rank and with more seniority. He gave him credit for that. Nick first entered the outer office occupied by Grant's secretary, Linda, but, since it was almost six o'clock, she had left for the day. He knew that she would have turned on the monitoring system and, as soon as he opened the door, a buzzer would go off in Grant's office and Nick would appear on his monitor. Grant kept his office locked at all times. He could either hit the button to unlock the door and let his visitor in or hit the alarm alerting security that there was trouble in his office.

Nick had thought this a bit paranoid. After all they were members of the GAO, not the CIA. As Nick approached the inner door, he could hear the buzzer unlocking the door. He opened it and went in.

"Hello, Nick, come in and sit down," Grant said as he pointed to a chair in front of his desk. He didn't bother getting up to shake his hand.

"Hello, Charles. How are you?" Nick said, immediately wishing he hadn't.

"I'd feel a hell of a lot better if Kate Peters was here. And I knew what the hell was going on," Grant said angrily.

"Kate's being here wouldn't help us." Nick responded as he took his seat.

"Maybe not. But I'd rather be the judge of that."

"Understood, Charles. But I didn't think it was my place to cuff her and drag her over here."

"Okay, I understand that, but why is she so reluctant to come here?"

"Come on. She has almost been killed twice. The poor girl is afraid to stick her head out the door."

"You're a smart guy, Nick, what do you think is going on?"

"I don't know. All I know is that someone is trying to eliminate the key technical people on my team and they've succeeded with two thirds of it. And I'll be damned if I'll let them succeed with the last third."

"No, we can't let that happen. Why would they want to kill them; especially now that the program is completed and the test was successful. I could have understood if this happened before it was completed. That's why the security was so tight on everyone," Grant said.

"I know. I wish we hadn't relaxed the security so quickly."

"Hindsight is great, but we had no way of knowing that once the project was complete their lives would be in danger."

"I know, but I still feel responsible. They were part of my team and were key to the successful completion of our project."

"I know. Doesn't it make you wonder why they were murdered after completion of the project?" Grant asked.

"Yes. It does. I ran it through my mind and I only have one logical conclusion as to why," Nick answered.

"And that would be?" Grant said.

Nick knew that Grant had come to the same conclusion he had. He might not have liked Grant for the way he played politics and looked for the personal gain in everything he did, but he never said he wasn't smart. For Nick to try to avoid the conclusion at this point would be senseless and stupid.

"The only conclusion that makes any sense. The project was sabotaged after the successful test and the person, or persons, who did it is now trying to eliminate the very people who could possibly fix it in time." Nick saw the knowing look on Grant's face. "But it doesn't make sense because after they completed the test, they shut the project down. Security has been so tight, I can't believe it's been breached. So, who would have had an opportunity to sabotage it?"

"I agree. Except for one thing. I looked at the logs of the day of the test. It seems odd to me that, after the test was completed, Kate came back and logged back onto the system. Before it was totally secured and off limits even to her—and to you."

"I'm aware of that. In fact, I was back there myself and asked her what she was doing. But she had a logical explanation and I thought nothing more of it. Besides, if she did do anything to the system why would she be trying to have herself killed?"

"I don't know. Maybe there's been some kind of a falling out; some kind of a double cross. Maybe she got herself in with some people that are beyond her capabilities. Or maybe they weren't even legitimate attempts on her life." Grant emphasized this last statement and leaned back in his chair waiting for Nick's reaction.

"I can't believe any of that, especially the part of the attempts on her life. They came much too close to be anything but real." Nick knew that Grant was trying to get more of a reaction from him.

"That may be true. The fact remains that she was the last person to have access to the programs before they were fully secure and before we started having these problems. Now she's trying to go into hiding," Grant said firmly.

"Charles, for God's sake. She's going into hiding because someone is trying to kill her," Nick said emphatically. He didn't like this line of thinking.

"Perhaps, perhaps not," Grant replied. "Regardless, we must do another test."

"I'm not sure I agree. Another test, in itself, has it's own dangers and difficulties."

"Well, if you had closed down access upon completion of the test we wouldn't be in this position. Since you didn't, and since Kate had access and is acting suspicious, we have no choice," Grant said as he put his hands together in the form of a steeple and put them to his lips.

So, that's what it was, Nick thought. It's not just the suspicion that there could have been some sabotage that Grant's concerned about. This was an opportunity to show a critical management mistake on Nick's part and for Grant to cover his ass and get a pat on the back at the same time. No wonder he had the corner office, the son of a bitch.

Nick did not accept Grant's reasoning. "But it was always secure to everyone but a few of us. And those technical people could have sabotaged the project at any time. So why would they complete the project and then sabotage it?"

"Perhaps that's the very point. If they sabotaged it before they completed it, we would have kept on working and maybe would have caught them or would have still been successful in spite of them. What better way than to have a successfully completed project, have it put to bed and, just before it's totally secured, sabotage it," Grant said thoughtfully. "In any event, the test is set up for three o'clock tomorrow. And this time make sure you have Kate there, in handcuffs if necessary."

"Thanks for discussing it ahead of time," Nick said. He realized Grant was attaining a new level of being a prick.

"Nick, you were out of touch until you called me. And I couldn't wait. It's scheduled for tomorrow at three. Be there. The both of you."

"I think it's a mistake, Charles. But I'll be there and I'll have Kate there, too." Nick wasn't pleased. Just then his cellular phone rang and he immediately got a knot in his stomach as he answered it. "What do you mean gone?" Nick said as he stood up. "Where has she gone? How long has she been gone? Begin the search, I'm on my way."

"What the hell is going on?" Grant demanded.

"Kate's missing."

Grant sat up straight now. "How the hell could she be missing? I thought that you had two U.S. Marshals with here at all times."

"I did. One was getting some sleep in the second bedroom and the other one just went to make a quick trip to the bathroom. He didn't think that there would be any problem. The door to the hallway was well secured."

"That means that she left on her own."

"It looks that way." Nick knew this looked bad as he put his cellular phone in his pocket.

"What other way could it be? I told you that you should have put her under the protective custody of the FBI instead of taking on the responsibility yourself," Grant said coldly. "I think that it's time to call the FBI and have an all points bulletin put out on her and have her picked up."

"Couldn't you hold off on that for a while. I'd like to try to find her and see what happened."

"You're too close to this. I know you have a loyalty to your staff, but this goes beyond that." Grant paused "Maybe there's something else between you and her?"

"There's been nothing between us," Nick said calmly. It was the truth and he didn't want to give any other impression.

"But I have the feeling you would like there to be. I'm sorry, but I'm calling the FBI and, if we find her or not, you had better be there at three tomorrow."

"I'll be there. It's too important to leave to anyone else as long as it's my project. It is still my project, isn't it?" Nick asked as he stood before Grant.

"For now," Grant said, as he looked up at Nick, the slightest trace of a smile on his face.

Kate had not hesitated to seize the opportunity she had been waiting for. She had told the marshal, in the living room, she was going to her room to get some rest. All she had to do was wait for him to have to relieve himself and she would sneak out. Kate knew that this could get Nick into trouble, but there was no choice. She trusted Nick, but he was in over his head. Although smart, he had no experience in the world of clandestine operations. He proved that when he made the call to Charles Grant, believing his line was secure. Kate knew better and now she had to get out of here.

As she left the hotel room there were two escape routes. She could take the elevator or use the stairs. While the stairs offered her the least chance of being seen, they also would take longer. She was concerned that the marshals might discover her gone before she could get away and catch her on the stairs or down in the lobby. And, if Grant's line was tapped, there could be others waiting for her in the stairway. So she made a quick decision to take the elevator. Once in the elevator she had another decision to make—would she get out in the lobby or go down to the parking garage. The lobby would be the safest, but the most obvious. That's why she wouldn't do that. It would be too easy for someone to spot her coming out. It was the logical place for someone to be waiting for her. So she pushed the button for the parking garage, hoping that she could get out without being spotted. The drawback was that there would be fewer people there and less safety. It helped that there were four levels to the garage; putting the odds in her favor. At the worst, there would likely only be one person watching each level. When she arrived at the first parking garage level she quickly left the elevator and headed for the street exit. Where she hoped to mingle with the crowd, find a cab, and get away.

Kate had been partially right about the lobby. It was under surveillance and required that the teams be split. So there was only one agent in the garage. Although there were four levels to the garage, the CIA agent had set up on the first level. This level had direct access to the street and anyone leaving would have to go by him. As soon as he saw Kate exit the elevator he radioed his two partners, who were in the hotel lobby. One was watching the elevators and the other was trying to find out what room she was in. The phone tap on Charles Grant's line had provided them with the hotel where Kate was located, but it didn't tell them what room she was in. The orders from Assistant Director Ford were to locate her and put her under surveillance. They were to take her only if they could do so without harming her. This situation presented that opportunity. She was unprotected and the location was perfect; there was no one else around. He notified his partners of his intentions and directed them to head for the parking garage entrance to cut her off if, somehow, she reached it before he could get to her.

As Kate hurried toward the exit, she heard the car's engine turn over and she broke into a run without hesitation. This forced the surprised agent to floor the gas pedal and the squeal of the tires only made Kate run faster, but she wasn't going to beat the car to the exit.

"Captain. The subject is racing towards the exit. There's a car chasing her and it appears it will catch her before she can reach it. Shall I take it out," Corporal Semanski asked as he drew his weapon.

"Yes, Corporal," Eric Johnson ordered. "But not critically."

"Yes, sir," Corporal Semanski said, as he raised his pistol, went to one knee, and fired two silent shots in rapid succession. The passenger side front tire was blown out and the car veered sharply to the right; smashing into the wall. The air bag exploded upon impact, dazing the driver.

Kate hesitated only briefly at the sound of the car's impact. Then she quickly made her way to the exit. Reaching the street, another car came to a screeching halt in front of her and the passenger door flew open immediately. Eric Johnson had been waiting in the parking lot of a convenience store diagonally across from the hotel.

It had been an easy task to trace Kate and Nick here and keep them under surveillance since he had tagged both of them at the funeral. The technology at the disposal of MicroForce, along with the intense physical and mental training of each man and woman, made them the most powerful fighting force, person for person, in the world—bar none. First, they had all been recruited from the world's elite fighting forces—the Green Berets, the Special Forces and the Navy Seals. They were the best of the best. Then they were given, and thoroughly trained in, the most advanced array of technology and fighting power that had ever been developed; making a James Bond movie look like the dark ages. It multiplied their fighting power a hundred fold. The tiny, flesh-colored microdot, which he had placed at the back of the neck of Kate and Nick during the funeral, would stay in place unnoticed for more than a month; regardless of how many times it had been washed. Each dot had its own unique identification code and could be tracked up to a mile away by a small, hand held, combination transmitter and receiver. It worked much on the concept of radar by sending out its own low-frequency signal that would be reflected by the microdot and transmitted back to the unit. The sensitivity of the unit was so great that someone could be wearing a scarf around their neck under a heavy, hooded parka, enclosed in a coffin, and it would still detect them.

When Nick, Kate, and the U.S. Marshals had registered at the hotel, Eric had sent Corporal Semanski to wait and monitor them in the lobby. He knew that he could be recognized so he took the position outside in the first car; with Private First Class Brad Wilson in a second car.

When Nick left, Eric sent Private Wilson to follow him. Believing Kate was the key he stayed with her. When he saw her movement on his monitor, he could tell that she was using the elevator and not the stairs because of the speed she was descending. Johnson alerted Corporal Semanski who used the stairs to the garage when the elevator didn't stop at the lobby.

"Eric!" Kate was momentarily frozen.

"Get in," Eric Johnson ordered, as he opened the passenger side door.

"Thank God it's you," Kate blurted out as she followed his command. Almost before she was in the car, Eric sped away leaving the other two agents, who had come out the main entrance, scrambling to get out of the way.

"I have her Corporal. Stay and observe the area. See what information you can gather. I'll meet you back at the house in two hours," Eric said as he put his two fingers to his throat.

"Who the hell are you talking to?" Kate asked with a quizzical look.

Eric ignored her question. "It looks like we almost got here a little too late, judging by the look on your face, when I pulled up. What happened?"

"Someone was chasing me in a car."

"Who was he?"

"I don't know,"

"You have no idea?"

Kate was emphatic as she looked back at her would be captors or assassins. "I told you I don't know. I'm just a damn computer programmer. I have no idea why people are trying to kill me."

"Where are the U.S. Marshals?" Eric asked. "Why aren't they with you?"

"I left them in the hotel room," Kate said calmly.

"Left them? Why would you leave them?" Eric looked at Kate with surprise.

"I didn't feel safe. I thought that I would be better off if no one knew where I was." It was a weak explanation but she had nothing else to offer.

"It looks like you have at least two different groups after you, one trying to kill you and one trying to prevent it, lucky for that or you wouldn't be here," Eric said. He looked at her to see her reaction as well as hear it.

"I have no idea who is doing what or why, but I don't mind telling you I'm damn scared. I've got to get out of this city." He was smart and he was testing her, Kate thought. She would have to be careful.

"Is that why you were sneaking out from the U.S. Marshals?" Eric continued.

"Yes. I can't trust anyone. Not even the marshals because I think they are in over their heads," Kate said.

"You can trust me."

"Can I?"

"Think about it. Do you think I would have had my own brother killed?" the pain on Eric's face obvious as he said this.

"No. You wouldn't. But how come you were here right now? How did you know I was there? Or do you just ride around the city looking for women to save?" Now Kate was the aggressor.

"No. Nothing is random. But I'll explain that on a need to know basis and right now you don't need to know," Eric said firmly. "Where were you heading?"

"I was just trying to get to safety, away from all of this."

"Come on, you must have had something more specific in mind than that. You weren't going to just wander the city. And, know one thing, you're not going anywhere if I don't agree," Eric said as he gave Kate a look that convinced her of that.

"I have to get to Boston. I'll be safe there." Kate gave Eric a sincere look as she decided she would have to work with him, for now anyway.

"What's in Boston? Why will you be safe there?"

"I'll tell you that on a need to know basis and now you don't need to know," Kate said.

"That's not good enough, Kate," Eric informed her. "I can get away with it but you are not exactly in the drivers seat."

"It will have to be. That's all you're getting. You'll have to trust me, too."

"Okay, for now. I'll trust you because you've almost been killed three times and I don't have any reason not too. But if you lie to me, or I find out that you had anything to do with the death of my brother or in any way stop me from finding out who did, you'll regret it. I won't let anything or anyone stop me from finding my brother's killer."

Kate had no doubt of that, and was not about to challenge him. "Where are you taking me."

"We have a safe house where we can go for now. Before we start our trip to Boston we have to contact Nick Logan," Eric said.

Kate twisted in her seat to face Johnson more directly. "No, he'll try to make me go in and I won't go in."

"I know. We've already talked about that. I won't let him take you in, but we can use his help and I think we can trust him. You must trust him or you wouldn't have let him take you to the hotel. Besides, someone has to be with you at all times on the way to Boston and I can't be. And I can't spare a man either."

"I don't need a baby-sitter," Kate said as she turned and faced forward again.

"You do if you expect me to let you go anywhere. Besides, do you know your way around Boston? Have you ever been there?" Eric questioned her.

"No, I haven't."

"You know that Logan is from Boston. He can help us get around."

"Okay, if he agrees to take me to Boston, then I'll go with him," Kate agreed. She knew that Nick had feelings for her and that could be useful. She felt guilty for this thought.

"He'll agree."

# CHAPTER 17

▼

# PENTAGON COMPLEX, WASHINGTON, D.C. THREE P.M., MONDAY DECEMBER 20, 1999

## TWELVE DAYS TO <u>0</u> <u>0</u>

Nick's mind raced in two different directions as he anxiously waited for the test to begin. Where the hell was Kate and why did she leave the protection of the marshals. How was he going to explain this; there was going to be hell to pay. In attendance was not only Charles Grant, John Hodgers, and Colonel Clay, but also General George Armstrong, and Victor Noble.

"Gentlemen, Charles Grant and I have brought you here in a matter of utmost urgency," Colonel Clay said. Turning to the General and Victor Noble he added, "Gentlemen, thank you for taking the time to join us today."

"Thank you, but you can skip the pleasantries, Colonel," Noble said. "We're here because the President is very upset at the chain of events in the last two days. When he left here after the successful test two days ago he understood that the

'Millennium Bug Project' was completed and put to bed. Since then two of the three most key software engineers have been murdered and an attempt was made on the life of the third one. And now we are informed that this Kate Peters is missing under very unusual circumstances. The President wants an update on the status of this project as soon as possible. Has there been any word on the where-abouts of this Ms. Peters?"

"No, sir, we're still looking for her," Colonel Clay said.

"I understand that she was under your protection last, Mr. Logan," Noble said as he turned to Nick. "What happened?"

Nick stood straight and still, trying not appear nervous. "Yes, sir, she was. I had her in a safe hotel, protected by two U.S. Marshals. Then, it appears, she left on her own."

"And where were you when she left?" Noble asked with an edge to his voice.

"I was in the office of my boss, Charles Grant."

"I had called him and Kate Peters to my office because of the events that had taken place. I wanted to take control of the situation," Grant interjected.

This was the kind of situation that was made for men like Grant. If something did go wrong, he could take credit for stepping in and uncovering it and laying the blame at Nick's feet; which would accomplish his goal of ruining Nick's career. If nothing were wrong with the test, he still had planted the seeds that Nick had screwed up and there could have been a problem and it was only luck that there wasn't.

"I see," Noble said. "Why didn't you follow your bosses order and bring Miss Peters with you, Mr. Logan?"

"I tried to but she refused to go. She was deathly afraid that she was going to be killed and she felt safe there." Nick thought that Noble and Grant were a lot alike; something he didn't need.

"Apparently not safe enough. It's too bad you didn't try harder, Mr. Logan," Noble criticized. "As soon as she is found, I want to be notified."

"Yes, sir," Colonel Clay answered.

"Enough of that for now," Noble said as he turned to Colonel Clay. "Bring us up to date on the status of the project."

"As you know, we successfully conducted the initial tests of the system by sim-ulating the year 2000 and everything worked perfectly. That was two days ago. Upon completion of the test we closed the project and secured the systems so that no one could make any alterations to them," Colonel Clay answered.

"So then we have a viable system," General Armstrong said.

"To the best of our knowledge," Colonel Clay said.

"But there's a hesitation in your voice," Noble observed.

"Based on the events that have occurred since that time, we feel that it is prudent to do another test," Grant said. He welcomed the opportunity to step in, again.

"I see. Do you agree with him, Colonel Clay?" Noble asked.

"Yes sir, I do. Even though these three engineers past all the clearance tests, there is no telling what or who they may have been involved with. Under the circumstances, we have to assume the worst. I would rather be safe than sorry."

"I agree," General Armstrong said.

"Gentlemen, I understand the concern, but I think we're taking an unnecessary risk of opening up the system again. I would feel a lot more comfortable if Kate Peters was here. After all, she was brought into the project because we had problems with it before," Nick had to speak up even though he knew she was already on soft ground.

"My men are perfectly capable of monitoring this test. Just as they were perfectly capable of completing this program," an angry Colonel Clay responded.

"All right gentlemen, that's enough," General Armstrong ordered. "Mr. Logan, I don't think we have time to wait to find Kate Peters and I believe that another test is warranted under these circumstances."

"I couldn't agree more," Noble added. "When can we do it?"

"We can do it within the hour," Colonel Clay informed them. "That's why I have my senior software engineers here; they have also been involved with this program for a long time. Longer than Kate Peters."

"Gentlemen," Nick began and then stopped. It wasn't the dirty look that he got from Charles Grant and Colonel Clay that stopped him, but the realization that he was on the wrong side of this issue and his protests wouldn't help. There wasn't anyone in the room that would back him.

"Yes, Mr. Logan," the General said.

"I still think it's a mistake and we should wait for Kate Peters," Nick finally said.

"As I said, we don't have the luxury to wait and I don't see the need," General Armstrong said. "Proceed with the test."

It would take the next hour to set up for the simulated test. The General had offered to show Victor Noble the facility and, of course, Grant and Colonel Clay tagged along. Hodgers and Logan excused themselves to go to their respective offices to finish up some paperwork while a special team, under the control of Colonel Clay's men, prepared for the simulation.

When Nick got to his office, he had a message from Eric Johnson. He picked up the phone and dialed the number he had left. After a long moment there was a voice at the other end.

"Hello, Nick," Eric said.

"Good guess."

"I never guess," Eric said. "What more do you know about the murder of my brother and Waldo?"

"I don't know anything more. I haven't talked to the lieutenant today. The only thing I know more is that Kate's gone," Nick said.

"I know," Eric said. "I want you to meet me tonight after you talk to the Lieutenant Thomas and fill me in on everything you know."

"But, I may not know anything else."

"Meet me tonight."

"Okay. When and where?"

"Call me tonight at eight and I'll tell you when and where," Eric said and hung up.

"Eric? Eric?" There was no reply so Nick hung up frustrated. He then picked up the phone and dialed Lieutenant Thomas; using the direct line that the lieutenant had given him.

"Thomas here."

"Hello, Lieutenant. Nick Logan here. I was calling to see if there was any new information."

"I'm sorry, Nick, but there is nothing new since I talked to you last," the lieutenant answered.

"I'm sorry to bother you but it's very important that I be kept up to date on anything that you find."

"No problem. I understand. Like I said before, if there is anything worth discussing, that I can discuss, I'll call you immediately," the Lieutenant said.

"Thank you, Lieutenant," Nick said and hung up.

He did a little more work but couldn't concentrate for very long so, after a half hour, he went to check the progress on the test. When he got there, Colonel Clay and Grant were already there observing the status of the test. He wondered how Noble and the General had pried themselves free from these two. He learned that Noble and the General asked for a secure room to have there own meeting and they were in there now with the head of the complex security, Captain Peter Fuller.

"Your report, Captain," the General ordered.

"Yes, sir. Mr. Logan made two calls. One to an 'Eric' who was inquiring about the murder of his brother. Mr. Logan had no information, but agreed to call a Lieutenant Thomas to get an update. The man named Eric then asked him to meet him tonight with any information he had," Captain Fuller said.

"Where did they say they would meet, Captain?" Noble asked.

"They didn't, sir. All that this Eric said was to call back later on the same number at eight this evening," the Captain answered.

"I see," Victor said. "And where was that call placed from?"

The Captain nervously shifted his weight from one foot to the other. "Well, sir, that's a problem. We don't know exactly."

His look was intense and his words were biting. "What do you mean you don't know exactly?" Noble demanded. "You were ordered to trace the call. You did trace the call, didn't you?"

"Yes, sir, we did. But it seems it was placed using some very sophisticated jamming equipment. We had a great deal of difficulty being able to trace it," the Captain continued.

"You were able to trace it, weren't you?" Victor said irritably.

"Well, yes sir. Sort of, sir."

"What do you mean 'sort of, sir'. You either traced it or you didn't trace it. Which is it?"

"We traced the call, sir."

"Good. So where was it placed to?"

There was perspiration on the Captain's upper lip. "Well, sir, that's the problem. We traced the call to a spot in the middle of the Pacific Ocean," the Captain said.

"The middle of the Pacific Ocean?" Victor was surprised. "Are you sure your equipment is working properly?"

"Yes, sir. Quite sure, sir. We believe this is a piece of sophisticated equipment beyond anything we've ever seen."

"I see, Captain," Victor said. "And the second call?"

"The second call was made to Lieutenant Thomas at the Washington D.C. police department."

"Yes, I know who he is," Noble snapped.

"Mr. Logan was just inquiring as to any new information on the murders. The Lieutenant indicated that he had no new information, but he would keep him informed," the Captain said.

"Is that it?" Victor Noble asked.

"Yes, sir, those are the only two calls that he made. And he received no others?"

"Thank you, Captain, that will be all."

The Captain hesitated.

"You're dismissed, Captain," the General said.

The Captain saluted and left.

"Who is this Eric?" Noble asked.

"He's Eric Johnson, brother of Jeremy Johnson, one of the slain software engineers," the General informed Noble.

"Oh yes, that's right. I do believe I've heard the name," Victor said. "Didn't I also hear he's in the military, Special Forces or something like that?"

"Yes, I believe that may be correct," the General said. You will never know the truth about this man, the General thought.

"Would you please find out everything you can about this man as quickly as you can?" Noble ordered.

"I'll do it right away, Victor," the General said. "I'm also going to have Nick Logan detained."

"No, don't do that," Noble said.

"But Victor, I think we should. After all, he ignored an order by his boss to bring Kate Peters in and then she disappears. He gets a call by Eric Johnson on a line that is totally untraceable and he doesn't want us to conduct another test. I think we have some questions for Mr. Logan," the General said. He knew the more that he pushed this, the more Noble would resist.

"Your points are well taken, but I don't want Logan detained for now."

"I do think we should take the opportunity to question him," the General said. "It's too risky to let him go. We may lose him."

"General, you were there when the President put me in charge of the operation, therefore, I want you to let Logan leave. I will take responsibility for him."

"Yes, Victor, as you wish," the General said.

"Good," Noble said. "Now I think it must be time for the test. Let's go and see. And please let me have that information on Johnson as soon as you get it."

"Gentlemen, I'm glad that you're here. We are just about ready to conduct the test," Colonel Clay said with enthusiasm.

"Good. We are anxious for the results," Noble said.

"If you'll kindly take your seats over there, we'll begin," Colonel Clay said as he took his seat beside the General. "You may proceed Lieutenant Walsh."

"Yes, sir," the Lieutenant said. "All right gentlemen, we will simulate the year 2000 in ten seconds, at which time we will attempt to fire missiles in the Nevada desert that are aimed at the Soviet Union, excuse me, Russia. Three, two, one—arm the missiles."

The Lieutenant gave the order to a Private Richards who was at the console controls.

"The missiles are not arming, sir," Private Richards said.

"Try it again, Private," the Lieutenant said.

"I have, sir. They won't arm. They won't respond," the Lieutenant said.

"Try arming missiles in another part of the country," General Armstrong ordered.

"Yes, sir," the Lieutenant said.

"Okay, let's arm the missiles in Alaska," the Lieutenant said.

"Yes, sir."

Again they had the countdown. "Three, two, one—arm the missiles," the Lieutenant ordered. His tension was obvious.

"Yes, sir," Private Richards said as he tried to arm the missiles to be ready for firing. "Nothing, sir."

"Try it again!" the Lieutenant ordered.

"Yes, sir," Private Richards said as he attempted to arm the missiles again. Then red lights started flashing, buzzers started going off all over the place and the warning lights came on. The message read: 'ILLEGAL ENTRY ATTEMPTED ABORT, ABORT.'

"What's happening Colonel?" General Armstrong demanded to know.

"I'm not sure, sir."

"Lieutenant Walsh, what is happening?" Colonel Clay asked.

"The system has indicated that we made an iliegal entry and is warning us that, if we don't shut down immediately, it will take over and shut it down—permanently," the Lieutenant said.

"I recommend that we shut down our test immediately, sir," Private Richards said. "There is no telling what damage may be caused if we let the system take over."

"Do it before the whole damn system blows up," the General ordered.

"How could this happen, Colonel?" Victor Noble demanded to know.

"I don't know, sir. It worked perfectly the other day."

"Why not try the override code and see if that works," Nick said.

"Yes, I was just going to suggest that," Colonel Clay said. "Lieutenant Wilson, you know what to do. Please proceed."

"Yes, sir."

The override system was a backup fail-safe system that would allow the computer's internal security to be overridden if the proper codes were entered at the same time that the proper keys were inserted. For the real system the override code and the keys are a closely guarded secret and require the cooperation of the President and the Chairman of the Joint Chiefs of Staff. Each had a part of the puzzle and it could only be activated with their combined efforts. For the simulation this security was not necessary. So Lieutenant Walsh and Private Richards each inserted their keys and simultaneously punched in their portion of the code to override the security system. As soon as they had completed this task, the alarm stopped and the computer seemed to go back to normal and it appeared that the security had been overridden.

"It looks like that worked, sir," the lieutenant said. "Shall we continue?"

"Yes, Lieutenant. Please do," Colonel Clay responded.

So Lieutenant Walsh proceeded to give the order again to go into red alert and to arm all of the nations land based nuclear warheads. But, when this was completed, the computer did not respond. After a few seconds, the screens went blank and then came back on and displayed 'ACCESS DENIED'. The computer then activated its own voice capability and eerily announced to the stunned onlookers—"illegal access has been attempted. If you persist, I will close the system in ten seconds. Repeat.. illegal access has been attempted.. sign off and close down the system 10, 9, 8,7,6,....."

"Hurry, turn it off Lieutenant!" Nick ordered.

The lieutenant quickly shut the system down before the computer reached ground zero.

"What the hell's going on, Colonel?" demanded General Armstrong.

"Yes, please tell us," Noble ordered.

"I'm not sure," the Colonel said, now wishing that he had left the program under Logan's control. He was obviously searching for what to say when Nick Logan came to his aid. Nick thought about letting him hang out there and swing on his own, but he wasn't that kind of guy and this project was to important to play politics or try to cover his own ass.

"I'm afraid our system has been breached," Nick said.

"What the hell do you mean breached," General Armstrong said.

"Yes, I think you had better explain," Grant said.

"I can't exactly say without having the technicians fully review the program."

"And how long will that take?" The General asked.

"It could take a day or days," Nick responded. "It is hard to tell. It depends on what it is."

"What do you think, Lieutenant Walsh?" Colonel Clay asked.

"I think Mr. Logan is right," the lieutenant said.

"We don't have days, gentlemen," General Armstrong reminded everyone.

"If we go forward we could destroy the test program. And let me remind you that this is the only test program that we have and it would take weeks to prepare another one from the actual control program," Nick said.

"We have no choice but to go forward, Mr. Logan. We have to know if we have a viable nuclear weapons system or not," General Armstrong said.

"Then give us at least half an hour to make sure that they've properly duplicated the most recent programs to include everything that may have changed up to the time it was totally closed down."

"What do you mean? Why isn't it the same program we tested the other day?" Victor Noble asked.

"Please gentlemen, give us a little time. Go have a cup of coffee and just give us half an hour" Nick said.

"Okay, Mr. Logan," General Armstrong said. "Come on gentlemen, let's grab some coffee and hope that's just a minor screw-up."

Nick went down to work with Lieutenant Walsh and the rest of his staff, who were now almost in a panic situation.

"I have no idea what happened. I've never seen it like this."

"Take it easy, Lieutenant. Go slow and take a deep breath. Everyone just relax," Nick said in the calmest voice he had.

"Relax, how the hell can we relax. Everything we've done, all of this work, we thought we had it fixed and now it's going to blow up in our face," Private Richards said.

"It's not going to help any if we panic and stop thinking. So come on, think about it. Did we copy everything properly? Did we screw anything up? We've got half an hour to retrace our steps and double check everything."

"Okay, you're right," Lieutenant Walsh said. "Come on people. Let's get the procedural manual out and go step by step to make sure we haven't forgotten anything."

"That's good, Lieutenant," Nick said.

The panic subsided with the help of Nick's calm attitude. They wouldn't have blamed him if he was all over them, up one side and down the other. After all, he had been cut out of the process at the end, but then they remembered that that wasn't Nick's style. They wouldn't have blamed him if he stayed on the sidelines and let them swing, this had the making of an absolute disaster.

The nervousness continued to subside as they concentrated on the task at hand. Things moved along swiftly and could find nothing wrong with the simulated program—to their dismay.

"Well that's it, Nick. We checked everything out and we can't find anything. This is as complete a replica of the system as we can possibly make it and certainly the same as it was the other day when it was successful."

"Okay, we'll start the test again. But what ever happens, if it starts the countdown again, don't wait for me to signal you to shut it down. The last thing that I want to do now is destroy this simulation module without having the opportunity to check it over thoroughly. To put it through an autopsy, so to speak, if we have to," Nick said.

"I understand," Lieutenant Walsh said. "Thanks Nick."

"Good luck," Nick said as he went to join the others.

"Are we ready to go again?" Colonel Clay asked.

"Yes, we are," Lieutenant Walsh said. "Or at least as ready as we can be in a half an hour."

Again, the initial logging on went smoothly. This time they were going to try to establish a red alert sector by sector but, as they did so, all hell broke loose again. The alarms were going off worse than before.

"Shit, here we go again," the lieutenant said.

"Use the override again," Nick ordered.

So they immediately went through the same procedure to override the security. When they did so, the alarm stopped but immediately the monitors flashed 'access denied' and the computer's voice activated again. "You have again activated the system without proper authorization. I have taken control. Good Bye."

"What the hell do you mean it has taken control?" General Armstrong said to Colonel Clay.

"I don't know, sir. Lieutenant, what's going on?"

"I'm not sure, sir. But I think the computer is thinking."

"Oh shit. Intelligent security," Nick gasped. "Kate was right." Nick immediately wished he hadn't said this. It was not like him to speak before he thought.

"What do you mean Kate was right? She knew about this?" Noble asked.

"She knew about intelligent security, as did others. We were working on it here but we hadn't installed it yet. At least I thought we hadn't," Nick said.

"Is this some kind of sick joke, Colonel?" Noble said. Because, if it is, I'm not laughing.

"It's no joke, Mr. Noble. Lieutenant, what's going on? I didn't think we'd installed the intelligent security. I didn't think that it was ready?"

"I didn't think we had either, sir, but it appears to be operating and it's in complete control. I can't do anything."

"You can't shut the system down, even with the emergency shut down?"

"No, I can't. I can't do anything. It won't respond at all."

"Come on Lieutenant, we've got to get this shut down. I don't want this system to be destroyed," Nick said.

"What do you mean destroyed? What do you mean you can't shut it down?" Grant said. "You have to be able to shut it down. Pull the plug for Christ sake."

"You can't just pull the plug. Remember when we described the backup systems to the mainframe computer? This is tied in to the same thing. You don't just pull the plug. There's built in battery backups upon built in battery back ups."

"Oh shit, look at this," Lieutenant Walsh said.

"What is it?"

"The system is starting to eat up the program."

"What do you mean eat it up?"

"It's unleashed some kind of virus. A virus that our built in security can't, or won't, stop. It's going to destroy the program."

"We can't let it do that. It would take weeks to put another simulated program together for us to test again. We'll be left with only the main system."

"I can't stop it, Nick. It's gone."

"Son of a bitch," Nick said.

"This isn't good, is it Nick?" Colonel Clay said, his battle hardness showing through as he fought to remain calm.

"No, Colonel, it isn't. We apparently just destroyed the simulator so we can't test it any more."

"But we do have a complete back up system to our regular system—don't we?" General Armstrong hesitatingly asked. "We're not totally at the mercy of one system?"

"No, Sir, that's true. We have a complete back up but, if we test it on that back up and it fails, then we would be left with only one system. Security procedures, and good sense, doesn't allow us to touch either of them at this point," Colonel Clay said.

"What do you suggest that we do, Colonel?" General Armstrong asked.

"I suggest that we proceed with a two pronged approach. One is to try to put together another test program as quickly as possible. The other is to very carefully analyze the back up system and try to find out how this intelligent security system works and gain control of it."

"Do you agree, Mr. Logan?" The General asked.

"Yes, sir. I do. I think that we should begin immediately."

"Do it then. Use all the resources you need and don't sleep until it's done," Victor Noble commanded.

"Yes, sir." a frustrated and embarrassed Colonel Clay said.

"Mr. Logan, I suggest that you find Kate Peters and get her in here as quickly as possible," Victor Noble said.

"I would do that if I knew where she was," Nick responded.

"Well, you had better find her. She trusts you. You may be the only one who can get her in here," Victor Noble said. "In the meantime, I will have the FBI put out an all points bulletin for her. This breach of security has cost us dearly."

"But there's no hard evidence that she has anything to do with this. After all there have been two attempts on her life in the last two days," Nick offered.

"Nick, I know this is not your area, but there's been two 'apparent' attempts on her life in the past two days. Maybe the fact that they haven't been successful tells us more than we've been seeing. In any event, she will soon become the country's number one most wanted person so if you know where she is, you'd better get her in. We need her alive, but you can never tell what's going to happen once we set the hounds on her," Victor Noble said.

"Yes, Sir, I'll try to find her as quickly as I can."

"If you have any leads, you'd better keep us informed," Grant added.

"Yes, you had better," Victor Noble said. "And it would be wise if you let us know your whereabouts at all times."

"Are you saying that you think I had something to do with it?" Nick confronted Noble directly. He had had enough of this bullshit.

"No, Mr. Logan, I'm not," Noble answered. "But others might and it's prudent to suspect any and all of us. Now gentlemen you've got work to do and I've got bad news to relay to the President."

# CHAPTER 18

▼

# WASHINGTON, D.C. SIX P.M., MONDAY DECEMBER 20, 1999

## TWELVE DAYS TO 0 0

The recent turn of events had Nick Logan stunned. Just the other day he was on top of the world, having completed the most difficult project of his life and receiving a personal thank you and handshake from the President of the United States. Now the project was in turmoil; the live program was corrupted and the test program was completely destroyed.

Nick had just spent the last hour huddled with Charles Grant, John Hodgers, and Lieutenant Walsh to put a plan of action together to present to Colonel Clay. They had concluded that they should first try to perform the equivalent of an autopsy on the test program, to see what they could learn. That is if the virus hadn't completely destroyed all traces of it, which is what they feared. Even then there were detailed recordings of what had taken place and a careful analysis might shed some light on just what happened. Simultaneously, they would have a crew working on analyzing the back up program to see if they could detect if and where the program was corrupted. They would have to do this off line, reading the code line by line, because they couldn't risk turning it on and possibly losing the back-up system; leaving them with only the primary system.

Once they had agreed upon the plan, Grant indicated that he and Hodgers would take it to Colonel Clay and Lieutenant Walsh should begin to organize the staff to implement it. Nick would have to follow Victor Noble's order and find Kate.

"You'd best find her and bring her in. For her sake as well as ours. She would be much smarter and safer to let us bring her in rather than the FBI or CIA. There's no telling what might happen then," Grant said.

"Who brought in the CIA? I thought the FBI was the only one in on this," Nick said surprised.

"Get real. Everyone's going to be in on this, the FBI, the CIA, the Washington police, the Secret Service, you name it. It will be a lot easier on her to come in voluntarily. And it will be a lot better for us if we're the ones she comes in with."

"I hear you. I'll do my best. But I don't know if she'll listen to me either."

Grant's tone and look were both serious and threatening. "She had better."

By the time that the meeting was over it was almost eight o'clock and time for Nick to make his call to Eric Johnson. He went to his office and placed the call. Again, it seemed to take a little longer than usual.

"Hello, Nick. I'm glad to see that you are punctual," Eric Johnson said.

"Hello, Eric."

"Have you spoken to Lieutenant Thomas? Do you have any new information for me?"

"Yes. I have spoken to him. And, no. I don't have any new information for you."

"I see." A slight trace of disappointment in his voice.

"I'm sorry. I really wish I had some information for you. But I'm afraid that I don't. And I have another problem that will have to take precedence for now."

"I know. Go home. I'll contact you."

"What do you know?"

"I know your problem. Trust me. Now go home."

"Again, what do you know? Eric. Eric. Damn it." Nick put the phone down hard. Eric had hung up on him again. This day wasn't getting any better, but it was late and he needed to go to his apartment to get some rest anyway.

Eric Johnson was already in Nick Logan's apartment when he received Nick's call. The fact that he had called from his office was one indication that Nick was an amateur in the world of law enforcement or espionage. Any professional would have assumed that the call was being traced. This was consistent with the complete background check he had ordered and received on Nick.

The report showed Nick was just what he appeared to be. He received his undergraduate and graduate degrees in business from the University of Massachusetts—Amherst; where he also starred in the decathlon for the track team. He graduated with honors and he went to work for a prestigious national accounting firm and obtained his CPA certificate from the state of Massachusetts. He then went to work for the General Accounting Office where he earned a reputation for being bright, fair, a hard worker, and non-political.

Except for his fondness for beautiful women, he didn't have outside interests or vices. There certainly wasn't anything in his background to link him in any way to the killings. The bug Eric found in his apartment and the surveillance in the hall outside only spoke to the fact that he was also a potential victim. The report he'd just received from Private Wilson, that Nick was now being followed by two men and was absolutely unaware of it, convinced Eric that Nick had no idea of what was going on.

What was even more interesting was that the men following him were CIA agents. It didn't surprise Eric that the CIA was following Nick, even though they were not supposed to be involved in affairs within the country. This had international implications and, besides, the so-called restrictions on their actions had never stopped them before. There was no mistaking who they were. The iris identification made by Private Wilson was fool proof. He had used the ultra miniature and powerful infrared binoculars built directly into a pair of thick-framed eyeglasses. Standard issue to every member of MicroForce.

These binoculars are so powerful that they can focus on a person's iris, in the dark, with enough clarity to make a positive identification from three hundred yards away. The reading would then be transmitted back to the main computer at MF central command center, identified, and transmitted back to MF field operative in a matter of seconds. The beauty of the iris identification was that it was even more reliable than fingerprints and were much easier to obtain. Even the wearing of sunglasses and contact lenses had no affect as long as the scanning device was of high quality and powerful enough.

Ever since the bombing of the government building in Oklahoma City, there had been a concerted effort to build a massive database to be used for iris identification. The federal government has used every opportunity to add to the base. And, since the technology allows extremely sensitive optical scanning devices, combined with high—speed computers, to 'tag' an individual from a simple photograph, it has been able to build a comprehensive 'tag file'. The state motor vehicles license application files have been a major resource.

Of course, all government employees were required to be photographed for their identification badges and these were simultaneously fed into the data bank. Employees with high security clearances, such as those in the FBI, Secret Service, and CIA were maintained in a highly classified section of the data bank and only accessible to those with the highest level of security clearance. Of course, MicroForce had access to the very highest level of security. But, since it did not officially exist and was known only to a few people, MicroForce unit members were identified as regular army personnel.

All government offices, military installations, airport, train, and bus terminals, and many other public locations have been or are in the process of being equipped with scanning devices that will feed the iris readings into a vast bank of computers that can identify any 'tagged' individual in a matter of seconds.

While he waited for Nick to return, Eric couldn't help but think about the technology, which was beyond the cutting edge, and the vast resources available to MicroForce. This combined with dedicated and highly trained men and women to make MF, pound for pound, the most deadly fighting force in the world. And what he had learned earlier had increased their fierceness and effectiveness and put it all at his disposal. He had had no idea what awaited him when he was ordered to report to General Armstrong's office earlier in the day.

When Eric reported to the General's office, the General's aide immediately announced him and then instructed him to go in.

"Come in Lieutenant," General Armstrong said as he returned the salute.

"Yes, sir."

"At ease, Lieutenant. Please have a seat," the General said as he pointed to a large leather chair and then took a seat in a matching chair opposite him. There was a small coffee table between them.

"Thank you, sir," Eric said as he took his seat. Eric sat very erect and all of his senses were on full alert.

The General spoke with compassion. "I'm terribly sorry about your brother. Please accept my condolences."

"Thank you, sir."

"I understand that you were very close."

"Yes, sir. We are...I mean were." Eric wondered how long it would be before he could speak of Jeremy without getting a lump in his throat.

"I also understand that you are thinking of resigning so that you can devote full time to finding his killer."

"How did you know that?" Eric was surprised and the tone of his voice showed it. "Excuse me, sir, but only one person knew that I was thinking of resigning. And he knew it was in strict confidence."

"Yes. Corporal Semanski informed me of it. But, before you get upset with him any further, please hear me out."

"Of course sir," Eric said. His mind was racing to try to understand why Corporal Semanski would report this to Chairman of the Joint Chiefs of Staff. He didn't even know that Dick knew General Armstrong and he had known Corporal. Semanski for three years; ever since they went through the 'Force's' special training together. He confided in Dick partly because of their friendship and partly because he knew that he would understand his feelings. Dick had lost his older brother to a terrorist attack in the Middle East. That was six months before he had joined MicroForce.

"Before you make any decision, I would like you to meet someone. Someone who can help you direct your anger and attain your goal."

"Who is he? And why would he want to help me?" Eric knew that there was always a price to pay. He had learned early that nothing ever came without a cost attached to it.

"He wants to help you because he understands your pain. But, more importantly, because you can be of great value to the country in dealing with a dangerous situation." The general knew that Eric Johnson was fiercely loyal and had calculated that he would respond to his country's crisis. "For now we will refer to him by his code name—Silver Fox."

"You know that I have pledged my life for my country, General," Eric said. "But I swore on my brother's grave that I would get his killer. And I won't, I can't stop until I do." The lump was back in his throat.

"I understand, Lieutenant. But it would appear that the crisis that we are facing and the death of your brother are somehow related. Although we don't really understand how or why." The General shifted in his chair for the first time.

"I see. But how can I be sure?" Eric asked. "I have to be sure. I have to kill the bastard who took Jeremy's life. Excuse my language, sir. But I have to."

"I won't lie to you, Eric. We can't guarantee it. But what we can guarantee is that we can put the full resources of MicroForce at your disposal. What we can guarantee is that, if you do not survive the mission and fail to avenge your brother's death, we will commit sufficient resources until that is accomplished. You have my word on it. You will also have the word of The Silver Fox."

"Your word means a great deal to me," Eric assured the General. "But the word of The Silver Fox means nothing."

"Once you meet him, it will," General Armstrong said rising from his chair. "If you are prepared to say yes, subject to his making a believer out of you, then I will arrange for you to meet him."

"In that case, sir, I think that I should meet him," Eric said as he also got up. "When can we do it?"

"Now. We don't have any time to waste," the General said. "My car is waiting for us."

"I'm ready, sir."

"You do understand, Lieutenant, that, for the record, this meeting and the one that you are about to have never took place.

"Yes, sir, I do."


The General's limousine was armor plated, the glass was bullet proof, and the interior fitted with Teflon shades. The Teflon shades provided additional protection in the case of an attack and when pulled down, as they were now, provided a complete black out. From both inside and out.

Besides being designed to protect its occupants, it was obviously well equipped to serve as a mobile command center.

A computer screen and keyboard were built into the back of the front seat. There was a mobile telephone with a secure satellite link. Another red telephone was locked in place and could only be released by punching the proper code into the keypad directly below the phone.

"Do you usually travel with the shades down, sir?" Eric Johnson asked. "Or is it that I'm not suppose to know where I am going?"

"No and yes," the General responded. "You have to admit that it is better than a blindfold."

"Yes. It is."

They continued to drive on with little further discussion as the General spent most of the time on the telephone with his subordinates. The Lieutenant did learn that the General knew The Silver Fox very well and trusted him completely. But he knew very little of the secret society that The Silver Fox had founded; other than it contained only the most highly trained fighters who were nothing short of fanatical in their loyalty.

After a little more than an hour the limousine came to a stop. At that point, the General apologized as he slipped a blindfold over the Lieutenant's head. It was an indication of the trust shared among them that his hands remained free and he was simply asked to leave the blindfold in place until instructed to remove it.

The General then held him by the elbow and led him into the rambling country house, through a large foyer and then into an interior room with no windows. The Lieutenant was then instructed to remove his blindfold. It didn't take long for his eyes to adjust to the light; there was very little in the room. It was richly appointed with solid mahogany paneling, overstuffed leather furniture, a stone fireplace that dominated one entire wall, and a huge mahogany desk that occupied most of the wall opposite the fireplace. It was definitely a man's room.

General Armstrong and Lieutenant Johnson stood facing the desk, looking at the back of a large leather chair behind the desk. As the chair swung around to face them it revealed a man in his early sixties, with thinning gray hair and a short, well trimmed gray beard. He was a handsome, distinguished looking man who was, at the same time, a rugged looking individual.

"Gentlemen, thank you for coming. Please have a seat," The Silver Fox said, his voice was deep and strong. He offered neither a handshake nor a salute.

He pointed to the two chairs that were in front of his desk and the two men took their seats. "General, it's good to see you again."

"It's good to see you again, too," the General responded. "As you know, this is Lieutenant Eric Johnson."

"How are you, Lieutenant? I'm very sorry to hear about the loss of your brother."

"Thank you, sir. As you know, I'm not very well."

"Yes. I'm afraid I know only too well."

"Gentlemen, I think I should leave you now," the General said. "Lieutenant, once again I would trust this man with my life. And I think that you should too." Then the General turned to face The Silver Fox and said, "The Lieutenant knows the basic ground rules. The rest is up to you."

"Thank you, General. I'll take it from here. Give my best to the President."

"I will. Lieutenant, your transportation back has been arranged, no matter what your decision. Good luck. I'm afraid that we shall probably never met again. My thoughts and prayers will go with you." The General shook the Lieutenant's hand and then the hand of the Silver Fox and abruptly left the room.

"So! You've suffered a loss and now you want to quit your special force. Your very special force," the Silver Fox wasted no time getting to the point. He had never been one to beat around the bush. The direct approach always seemed to work the best for him.

"I've suffered more than a 'loss'. I've lost the only person in this world that I loved. That I would do anything for. That I would die for." The Lieutenant surprised himself with his uncharacteristic display of emotion. "I will avenge his death. I will find and eliminate his killer."

"Believe me, I understand how you feel. I'm sorry to say that I have been there myself."

"Please don't tell me that time will heal my grief."

"I wish that I could say that time would heal it all. But it won't. It will take some of the sharp edges off of the pain. And it will allow you to think more rationally about how best to avenge your brother. But it won't make it go away. It hasn't for me and for many others that I know who have suffered such severe losses."

"Yes, I know that you suffered a terrible loss as well. General Armstrong told me that your wife and daughter were killed in an attempt on your life. I'm sorry," the Lieutenant said. Again regretful for his emotional outbreak with someone who has also known such suffering.

"Thank you. But I'm not looking for your pity. Just like you are not looking for mine. I just wanted to make sure you realize I am not just using hollow words."

"Then you understand why I have to do this," Eric said.

"I understand that you have to dedicate yourself to avenging your brother. But it is how you go about it that I take exception to."

"I need to resign so that I will have the freedom to do what I must."

"What you must do is use all the resources at your disposal to accomplish your goal. It is my understanding that there is a strong connection between the death of your brother and this Kate Peters disappearance."

"Yes, from what I've seen, that's a real possibility."

"Then why not stay with your MicroForce unit and use all those fantastic resources to help you get your killer. And at the same time serve your country, as you have sworn to do." The Silver Fox was clearly making a statement and not asking a question. He was also appealing to the Lieutenant's strong sense of patriotism. He had done his homework well. He knew that there were two things that Eric Johnson loved deeply: one was his late brother and the other was his country."

"That would be great except that I would still be under the control of the military and not free to pursue my goal or Kate Peters."

"That could be changed." The Silver Fox spoke with authority.

"Changed how?" Eric asked.

"You could be assigned to me. It is unofficial of course. Neither I nor my group have any official standing."

"Then how could I be 'assigned' to you?" The Lieutenant asked. "Who would 'assign' me? And what is your group?"

"Easy Lieutenant. One question at a time," The Silver Fox responded. "General Armstrong, with the blessing of the President, will assign you to general light duty in respect of your recent tragedy. You will officially be going through training exercises to get acclimated to your knew crew members."

"What new crew members?" The Lieutenant could feel himself being pulled further and further into this man's world. It was due in no small part to his direct approach and the strength that emanated from him.

"I'll explain that later. If you choose to join us."

"Who is us?"

"Not yet. Do you trust General Armstrong?"

"Yes, I do."

"Do you want to help your country in what may be its most critical hour?" The Silver Fox's voice rose.

"Yes, I do!"

"Do you want to avenge your brother?" His voice louder still.

"You fucking know I do!"

"No, I don't." The Silver Fox's voice was now low and calm. "I know you want to kill his killer. But do you want to really avenge him by stopping the men who gave the order to kill your beautiful, your sweet, Jeremy?"

"YES!"

"Then you trust me?" His voice again loud.

"Yes."

"With your life?" Louder still

"Yes."

"Then you are ready to join our society?" He commanded.

"Yes, sir. I am." Eric Johnson was almost out of his chair and on his feet.

"Good. Because your country needs you and I honestly believe it is your best chance to truly avenge Jeremy." The Silver Fox was now as calm as if he were soothing a young child.

Eric fell back in his chair. "So now tell me about your society and my new crew."

"We are a group of men and women who have all known the pain that you now feel. A pain so deep and hurts so bad that you can feel nothing else. Not only your heart but also your soul is dead. If it were not for this pain you would feel nothing at all." The Silver Fox spoke with compassion.

"Yes, you know the pain."

"That is why we call ourselves the 'Brethren of Dead Souls', or BODS. But, rest assured, that this is not some over hyped fraternal organization. Like you, each and every member is prepared to give his or her life on command. What is truly unique about BODS is our members would gladly die to advance the cause against evil. Partly because of their belief in good, but more so because death is the only thing that will relieve this pain. We hope."

"I understand."

"I know you do. That's why you're here. You also understand that the combination of this willingness to die, with intense military training and the resources of MicroForce can combine to create the most lethal fighting force on earth."

"Yes, it would be lethal as all hell. Wouldn't it," the Lieutenant agreed.

"Very. More than you can imagine. But you will see it. It is truly unbelievable. You will see when we assemble your crew."

"I am anxious to find out more about my crew."

"Two of your members are already in place.

"They are! Who?"

"Corporal Semanski and Private Wilson." The Silver Fox was pleased to see the surprise on Eric's face. "Each of the six MicroForce units has at least one BODS member."

"But I've known Dick Semanski for three years and he never even hinted at anything like this," a bewildered Johnson said.

"If he had it would have meant that I made a serious mistake in allowing him to become a member of BODS. I can't afford to make those kinds of mistakes. Our operations are crucial and our effectiveness relies on our secrecy and an absolute total dedication to BODS."

"But if they are dedicated to BODS what does that mean about their commitment to the military and their units? Are they being subversive?"

"No. They are not being subversive. The President and General Armstrong are fully aware of their presence and their reporting relationship to me. It is intended to strengthen the units. Not subvert them. They would never undermine or disobey their unit commander's orders. But they may feed me information that will determine the orders given to those unit commanders."

"I see. So Corporal Semanski and Private Wilson have been reporting back to you."

"Yes, they have. And that is why you are here. No one gets the opportunity to join us that we haven't observed in action and that we don't know intimately."

"So what about my new crew members? And why are we adding more BODS members?"

"The critical nature of this operation justifies taking members from other units to create a MicroForce unit made up entirely of BODS. And because it is an entirely BODS unit it can then report directly to me. Which will give us a freedom that is not available to the President and the General."

"So you are saying that we will be rogue element," Lieutenant Johnson said.

"That's right. You will be on your own. The government will not acknowledge you at all if your activities should become public knowledge. You will report directly to me. Your communications will be through the normal channels but will then be diverted to my communications center. Just like your normal communications, this diversion will be untraceable-even to the MicroForce command center."

"Are you still prepared to go forward and become a member of BODS?"

"Yes. So tell me about my new crew members," Eric was getting anxious.

"I will shortly. But first, there is one more thing."

"What's that?"

"You've seen both Semanski and Wilson without their shirts on I'm sure."

"Yes, of course I have. Why?"

"Then I'm sure that you noticed they both have similar and somewhat unusual scares on their chests. On their left breasts to be more exact."

"Now that you mention it, yes I have. But neither of them wanted to discuss it, so I dropped it."

"That's because it is the mark of the BODS. The mark of the X that dissects the left breast at the nipple symbolizes a dead heart. We all carry it." Having said this the Silver Fox opened his shirt to display the X that dissected his left breast. "There are no members without it. Are you prepared for this?"

"Yes, I am," Lieutenant Eric Johnson said. He was a man more than willing to be a part of such an elite and committed society that would help him to attain his goal.

"Good. Because it is more than just a symbol of your commitment, it is a test of your commitment and your strength."

"You will not find me wanting," Eric responded. "Now can I hear about my new crew?"

"Your crew will be a compliment of seven members of the BODS. Joining you, Corporal Semanski and Private Wilson will be Corporal John Anderson, and Privates First Class—Pete Peterson, Kurt Kincaid and Martha—'Marty'—Nelson. You will meet them as soon as we complete your initiation and then they will accompany you back to Washington."

"Good. Then let's do it," Eric was ready.

# CHAPTER 19

▼

# NICK LOGAN'S APARTMENT NINE P.M., MONDAY DECEMBER 20, 1999

## TWELVE DAYS TO 0 0

Entering his apartment, Nick immediately sensed he was not alone. He quickly turned on the light, muscles tensed, ready for action. Though prepared, he jumped back and let out a little gasp startled by the presence of Eric Johnson casually sitting in Nick's favorite chair.

"Don't worry, I'm not here to harm you. Quite the contrary, we've actually been following you to make sure that no harm comes to you," Eric said, as he remained motionless.

"What are you doing here? How did you get in? Breaking and entering *is* against the law you know, Eric. And, besides, why should any harm come to me?" Nick's anger was apparent as he moved towards Eric.

"Harm might come to you because of your project. *Your* project that got my brother killed. *Your* project that's caused at least two attempts on Kate Peters' life. *Your* project is involved somehow in all of this," Eric said as he raised his hand, palm out, in a stopping gesture. "But I would stop right there until we've finished our discussion. Then if you want to throw me out.... well, you can give it a try."

Nick stopped, his anger subsiding a little. "I told you before. I had nothing to do with your brother's death. I liked your brother. And I don't kill people. It's not who or what I am."

"I know that. I didn't say you were responsible. I said you were involved. You're a major player in the project, so that makes you a major player in my brother's death and in the attempts on Kate's life, whether you like it or not."

"That may be. But I don't like it. And I don't like people breaking into my apartment."

"I can understand that. But better me than them," Eric informed him.

"What do you mean them? Who are they?" Nick demanded, as he took a seat opposite Eric.

"Take a look." Eric felt the pain, from the cuts in his chest, as he pointed to the small screen sitting in a little case on the table next to him. It looked like a personal organizer with a small screen and keypad, but it also had a small toggle switch. Inside contained a row of three tiny, almost see-through, marble sized objects. They had a small speck in the middle that reminded Nick of a cat's-eye marble, like he used to play with as a kid. There were also two empty slots, so it could carry five in all.

Looking at the screen, Nick was amazed at the quality, even though the screen couldn't have been more than four inches across. What he saw was a man standing in the stairwell, with the door slightly open, and looking down towards Nick's apartment.

Nick couldn't believe what he saw. "What have you got, cameras in my stairwell?"

"Sort of," Eric said as he smiled for the first time. "But much, much better."

"When did you do that? How did you do that?" Nick sat back down, wondering what was going to happen next.

"I don't know. This is highly classified information."

"Remember. I have about as high a level of clearance there is."

"Not this high. But you have already seen it. And you may even have to learn how to use it, after you agree to go with us," Eric said as he reached over to the table and pushed a button.

"I haven't agreed to go anywhere with anybody," Nick responded.

"You will," Eric said with confidence. "Watch the box."

Nick could see one of the 'marbles' rise from its slot and then disappear. All that was left was the empty slot and Eric moving the toggle switch.

"Where the hell did it go?" A surprised Nick asked.

Eric moved the toggle switch, pushed a key and then responded to Nick. "Look at the screen."

As he followed Eric's direction, Nick saw himself from behind and above. He quickly turned and looked up, but saw nothing. "I know it's small, but I know what to look for and I still can't see anything."

"That's because it's not just see through, it's like a chameleon. It can take on the color of its immediate background." Eric explained as he pushed another key and the marble seemed to glow. "Now you can see it."

Nick looked up at the ceiling and saw the small glowing object. "Yes, I can. Does it have its own light?"

"No. But it can reflect any available light, no matter how slight, and appear to glow when we want to be able to follow it. It also uses the available light source for its power. Although it does have the ability to store enough energy to operate for three to four hours in complete darkness."

"How far can the marbles travel from the home base?"

"They have a range of up to a mile. And they are not marbles. They are 'PIP's'—Personal Information Probes. And we nicknamed the home base—'Gladys'." Eric determined Nick might as well be totally informed.

"As in the singing group?" Nick was happy to find out that these very serious, and dangerous, men had a little sense of humor.

"Yes. And speaking of singing groups, the PIP's provide us with audio as well as visual." Eric reached over and pushed another key. Then he clapped his hands and it could be heard through a speaker located in the home base. Eric then reached over and pushed the audio key again to turn off the sound.

"Here, look down the hall," Eric said as he hit a button and the picture switched from the stairwell to outside the apartment two doors down and across the hall. "When I came in, a man we identified as CIA was being let into this apartment. The chances are they've been living here for quite some time. My guess is at least ever since you've been working on the Millennium Bug Project."

"I don't believe it. Why? I have absolute top security." Nick said as he got up and started looking around his apartment.

"In this city, information is absolute power and no one trusts anyone," "Eric said as he watched him with amusement. He was impressed that Nick was catching on.

"Well, how do I know they haven't bugged my apartment too? They're probably listening to us right now?" Nick began to pace the floor looking all around. He was getting angry, again.

"Good guess," Eric said as he threw the four miniature cameras to the floor at Nick's feet. "I hope you've been a good boy. Because I'm sure everything that you've been doing for the last six months is on a tape somewhere."

"Everything has been taped?" Nick picked up one of the cameras and then sat back down. Things weren't getting any better. He didn't even want to think what might be next.

"Yes. You have four rooms and you have four cameras equipped with microphones."

"But I only have three rooms. A living room, a bedroom and a kitchenette," Nick said.

"What? You don't think they're going to have privacy in the bathroom, do ya?" Eric said with a small laugh.

"You're kidding." Nick was a little embarrassed and a lot angrier.

"No, I'm not kidding. I said everything that you've done for the last six months is on tape somewhere. And I mean everything."

"Son of a bitch," Nick said as he moved toward the door. But Eric was at his side, his hand on Nick's wrist, with amazing quickness.

"And just where the hell do you think you're going?" Eric held him firmly, but non-threatening. He was not trying to test Nick, although he would do whatever was necessary to stop him.

"I'm going to kick somebody's ass for that." A red-faced Nick was furious that his privacy had been violated. And by his own government, the same government that he worked for and was dedicated to.

"First of all, there are two of them in there. And I'm sure that they are well armed. But, even if you were successful in kicking their ass, what good would that do. Except to let them know that you're on to them. Right now all they know is that a masked man came in and dismantled their surveillance equipment; probably the same person that interfered with their attempts to snatch Kate this afternoon." Eric released Nick's arm as he spoke. He expected Nick would listen to reason. He also knew that his interest would be easily shifted to Kate.

"What about Kate? What do you know about Kate? You say attempts. Does that mean they didn't get her? Where is she?" Nick's attention was now fully focused on Eric and, as usual when it was important, he wanted information faster than it could be given.

"Take it easy. She's all right," Eric said as he patted Nick's arm. "They didn't get to her, but only because my team and I were there to prevent it."

"Where is she? I have to talk to her. She has to come in. The test failed today. I need to speak to her. Take me to her." Nick demanded as he stared intensely at Eric.

"I think it would be better if you just spoke to her on the phone," Eric said and then paused for a moment. "Besides. That's the agreement I have with her."

"Agreement. What agreement?" Nick asked. He was fully concentrating on Eric now, not knowing what to expect.

"I've agreed not to force her to come in," Eric said. He then, looking directly at Nick, said firmly, "I've also agreed not to let anyone else take her in. For now anyway."

"How could you agree to that? Why would you agree to that?" Nick knew it was time to control the emotions that Kate aroused in him and to think, and act, calmly and clearly.

"For one, she is afraid for her life. With good reason. Wouldn't you agree?"

"Yes. But we can give her protection," Nick responded weakly. Not fully believing it himself.

"Protection from who? By whom?" Eric said firmly. "It was the CIA that was after her earlier today."

"I'm still comfortable with the US Marshals. And with today's test failure she has got to come in and clear herself."

"If she comes in you won't be in control of who protects her. And what if she can't clear herself?" Eric paused to let the thought sink in. "Are you prepared for that?"

"I believe that she can." Nick thought to himself that he wasn't sure if he really believed this, or just hoped for it to be true.

"But if she can't, wouldn't you want to find out how and why she is involved?"

"Yes. I would." Nick could feel himself being pulled into something against his better judgment.

"Then come with us to Boston," Eric continued. "I don't know why, but Kate is determined to go there. And I know that you're very familiar with the area."

"Yes. I'm from the Boston area," Nick said. Then he paused for a moment and added sarcastically, "But I'm sure that you know all about that."

"Yes. I know all about it."

"If I do agree with this, how will we be able to get her there? Besides the people after her to kill her, we have the CIA spying on us and there is now an all points bulletin out for her. Every police agency on the east coast will be on the alert for her. And, if that's not enough, I'm sure that she will be number one on the FBI's unofficial most wanted list." By the time he finished, Nick had convinced himself, if not Eric, that this was an impossible plan.

"That is all true," Eric admitted. Then quickly added, "But I have been given significant resources and freedom to deal with the situation. I have also been instructed to allow Kate to go to Boston."

"Who could allow you to do that?" Nick carefully watched and listened to Eric and believed that he wasn't just being boastful or trying to bluff him. "And does that mean the APB will be called off?"

"Let's just say that my authority comes from as high up as possible for anyone in the military. But this is an unofficial assignment and we are on our own. If the APB were called off it would cause alarm bells to go off in too many places."

"That makes sense, if you are trying to keep your involvement a secret. But what you said, or at least implied, is that your authority comes from the Chairman of the Joint Chiefs of Staff—General Armstrong," Nick said. Then, as it dawned on him, he was wide eyed as he blurted out, "Or, hell! If I take it to its logical conclusion, the President himself."

"You can take it anywhere you want. But it is all unofficial and I would deny anything. And so wouldn't they," Eric said firmly. "If you choose to join us it will be in an unofficial capacity."

"I can understand why they couldn't call off the APB if they wanted to remain 'out of it'. But I don't understand why they would want to stay out of it. And I don't understand why they would allow her to remain on the loose."

"I can't answer that. Not because I'm not allowed to, but because I don't know." The intensity in Eric's eyes increased as he continued, "What I do know is that it meets my current needs. And I'm a military man. I don't need to know the motives of my superiors."

"I see. But if I do agree to go with you, I'm afraid an APB will be put out for me also. In fact, I'm sure that my boss would get great enjoyment from it." Nick winced at the thought of giving Grant the opportunity to nail him and further his own career in the process.

"That's the good news." Eric's intensity was replaced with a little smirk. "If you agree to join us, Charles Grant will be put on special assignment; a lousy special assignment in Alaska." Eric pause as he watched Nick's smile grow. "You will be temporarily assigned to Colonel Clay, with express orders to do nothing else but to find Kate Peters and deal with the situation in your best judgment."

"You could do that?"

"Not me. But it will be done."

"As pleasing as the thought of Grant in Alaska in the middle of winter is, I'm afraid I have a lot of trouble agreeing to this on your word alone. After all, you do have a personal motive."

"I'm afraid you have no choice," Eric replied firmly.

"That's not good enough, Eric," Nick also spoke firmly. "I'm not about to risk my career and probably my life, and Kate's life, without some confirmation from the highest level."

Eric had anticipated that Nick was much too smart and careful to accept Eric on face value. Not when so much was at stake. That's why he had obtained the agreement of General Armstrong to speak with Nick. The only caveat was that Nick had to agree to go with them only subject to unofficial confirmation by the General. "If you agree to go with us, then General Armstrong will confirm it."

Nick thought for a moment and then realized that the only way to be with Kate was to agree. "If General Armstrong unofficially confirms what you've told me, I'll go. But I have to be given one chance to talk Kate into coming in."

"And if you can't talk her into it, then you'll commit to coming with us?" Eric asked.

"Yes. If you will commit to protecting Kate with all of your resources," Nick replied.

"As long as she has no direct connection to the death of my brother, then you have my word on it," Eric answered.

Nick nodded and then moved to pick up the phone. "What's the number?"

Eric just looked at him with a big grin on his face and shook his head. "You have to be kidding me. I know that it's not part of your training, but will you start using that brain of yours. I'm told you're supposed to be smart; a very good strategic thinker. So start thinking strategically, will you."

Nick felt a little foolish. "Yes, I guess you're right. It's probably bugged."

"More likely it's tapped somewhere in the basement. I don't think these guys are leaving any stone unturned. Plus I'm pretty sure right now they probably have a directional microphone, somewhere in the building across the street, pointed at your window right now trying to pick up our conversation."

"So why the hell have we been talking like this," Nick asked.

Again, Eric grinned and nodded to his personal unit on the table. "Gladys also contains an ultra sonic impulse that interferes with any attempt to eavesdrop on anything within a fifty foot radius. I'm sure right now they must be pretty upset with the failures of their equipment; not knowing if the equipment just had a mechanical failure or they were involved with something that they hadn't faced before."

Then Eric pulled out a small, two inch square metallic object, flipped up a wafer thin top, slid the bottom cover down, and revealed one of the smallest and thinnest cellular phones Nick had ever seen. The top slid up to be the earphone, the bottom slid down to be the speaker, and the middle revealed a tiny LED screen, but there was no key pad on which to dial.

"Now who needs to use their intelligence," Nick said. "You're not planning on calling her on a cell phone? They're certainly not secure."

"Normally that would be true," Eric said holding the phone so that Nick could see it better. "But, as you might expect, this phone is anything but normal. It's equipped with a built in scrambling device. And it is absolutely untraceable."

"How can you be so certain?" Nick said, a worried look on his face. "It would be very dangerous to Kate if the call were intercepted and traced."

"Trust me. Like all of our equipment, this phone is beyond the state of the art." Eric looked straight at Nick and spoke in a low, sincere tone. There was no hint of bragging in his voice or manner. "Kate Peters is in danger, but she won't be put at further risks because of our inability to do our job."

"I didn't mean to imply anything like that. And the more I see, the more of a believer I am becoming."

"Good. And you haven't seen anything yet," Eric said, as he then held the phone to his ear and spoke. "On. Safe house." Then, after a short pause, "Private Peterson. Lieutenant Johnson. Put Ms. Peters on." Then Eric pushed a switch and placed the phone on the table beside him. It was now in speaker mode and Nick heard Kate's voice and was relieved.

"Hello, Lieutenant."

"Hello, Ms. Peters. I'm here with Nick Logan."

"Hello, Kate. Are you all right?"

"Yes, I'm all right." Kate sounded tired. "Thanks to the Lieutenant and his men."

"So I heard. Why did you try to get away from the US Marshals? They were there to protect you. I understand you almost got kidnapped or, even worse, killed." A concerned Nick said.

"That's true. I'm sorry I ran, but I had to do it. I know you don't understand, but I can't be sure that even the US Marshals are safe. Ask yourself. How did they know I was there? Why were they waiting for me?"

"I don't know, but you have to come in. We can protect you if you come in. Plus you've got some questions to answer. You've got to get the suspicions off of you or I'm afraid there will be even more people looking for you."

"I can't come in. I can't trust anybody. I have to go where I can find the answers myself."

"And that's Boston?" Nick asked. "What's in Boston?"

"I can't tell you right now."

"You've got to come in," Nick pleaded. "We ran another test today. It was a disaster."

"Why another test? We were successful before. They can't do that." Kate was surprised and upset. She had not expected them to run another test after completing a successful one.

"They can and they did. With everything that's happened, your disappearance, the murders, the attempts on your life, they were afraid that there might have been some sabotage since the first test."

"But how could it be sabotaged. It was secured."

Nick hesitated, "Not totally secured. You were logged in for ten minutes on the system after the test was completed."

"You were there. I explained I just had to put a few finishing touches on it."

"You had better come in and explain that. I tried to, but I'm afraid I wasn't very successful. You can help us fix it. If we have a successful test, everything will be okay."

"I can't. I can't risk it." Kate hesitated, and then added, "It's better if you cut your losses and forget about me. I'm sorry."

"I'm sorry, too. I was hoping I could talk you out of this. But, since I can't, I guess I'm in for the ride."

"Please, I don't want you involved in this any further. Stay out of it. Salvage what you can of the rest of your life."

"Thanks, Kate. But I think that's what I'm doing," Nick said. Then he turned to Eric and asked, "Where do we go from here?"

"I'll make arrangements for you to be taken to the safe house. Then you and Kate will head for Boston under our protection. All right Kate?"

"I wish you would reconsider, Nick. But, if not, all right," Kate answered.

"I'll see you soon," Nick said as Eric ended the call.

# CHAPTER 20

▼

# THE WHITE HOUSE— OVAL OFFICE ELEVEN A.M., TUESDAY DECEMBER 21, 1999

## ELEVEN DAYS TO 0 0

General George Armstrong had completed his brief meeting with Nick Logan and was updating the President on the outcome. The General had refused to answer most of Nick's questions. He would only confirm that Eric had the unofficial authority to utilize his military team and equipment in a training exercise; an exercise in which he would be given broad discretion as to its implementation. The General also emphasized he had the utmost confidence in Lieutenant Johnson and his commitment to the country.

"So then, he agreed to go with Kate Peters," President Stewart said, as he sipped his coffee and absently patted the head of his golden retriever, Trixie.

"Yes, sir. He wasn't happy with the fact that I wouldn't answer most of his questions. But he was satisfied that Lieutenant Johnson had not become a renegade bent on revenge." The General leaned forward in his chair, "He was particularly interested in why we would allow her to remain free. Considering the test failure and the significance of the problem."

"Can you say that you are absolutely sure that we should let her go?" The President asked.

"From your tone, I can see that you are still concerned with it yourself."

"I have my doubts, General. There is a hell of a lot at stake," the President answered. "And you?"

The General sat back in his chair, hands folded on his lap. "In any military operation there are risks involved. But there are risks involved in bringing her in. There is no guarantee she can or will fix it."

"But at least we would have her under our control and would probably have a better chance at fixing the system," the President said. He stopped petting Trixie, to her dismay, and started tapping his fingers on his desks.

"That's assuming that she had something to do with the sabotaging of the system. There's no guarantee that she did," the General responded calmly.

"The fact that she is running, and that she has to get to Boston, are good reasons to think that she is involved."

"Yes. But remember that there have been two attempts on her life. Which is also a pretty good reason to run."

"Yes it is," the President agreed, but was no less nervous.

"We have confirmed that the assailant at the hospital is a Russian with the FSS. And we learned from Lieutenant Johnson that the man in the parking garage was CIA," the General reminded President Stewart.

"So what the hell is going on here? Who the hell is this Kate Peters? Why the hell is the FSS trying to kill her? If she did sabotage the project and is one of them, you would think that they would be trying to get her out. Not trying to kill her. And why the hell is the CIA involved? This is a domestic issue." A frustrated President looked at the General and gave him a sarcastic smile, "Hell! Hell! Hell! General. It's a hell of a damn situation."

"Yes, sir, it is." The General paused and then said firmly, "We don't know who the enemy is. We know the Russians have something to do with it all. But what? How? We have good reason to believe there is a mole deep within the CIA. And the agent in the garage may be a link."

"So, if we bring Ms. Peters in, we damn well may be signing her death certificate. I would not want that to happen. And it wouldn't solve our problem."

"No, sir. It wouldn't. And we can't even trust everyone on our own team."

"I assume you are referring to Victor Noble," the President said a little angrily. "I know that creating the special cabinet level position of 'Ambassador-at-large' is like having a loose canon on board. But if I didn't, neither one of us would be here now."

"I'm sorry, sir," the General said apologetically. "I know that you had no choice. But it does create additional problems, and it does tie our hands. It's another reason why we should let Ms. Peters stay free. We can learn a lot more by not bringing her in and I honestly believe that she is safer out there, under the protection of Lieutenant Johnson and his elite MicroForce unit. Especially now that it is an entirely BOD's team."

"Yes. How is the Silver Fox anyway?"

"He's fine. He sends his best."

"You're probably right about her being safer with them." The President paused then asked, "They do have everything at their disposal?"

"Yes, sir. They have the entire array of equipment available to them."

"All unofficial of course?"

"Of course."

"Then I guess that we are committed to this," the President said as he began to tap his fingers again. "But, in case it doesn't work, are we ready with operation 'Red Sky'?"

"As much as we can be sure. But, like a man never knows if he will rise to the challenge when called upon, one never knows if a complicated weapons system will work until it is put to the test."

The President wondered if that was a reference to him. He didn't think it was. Not from the General, he wasn't like that. He knew that a number of people questioned whether he had what it took to lead the most powerful country in the world. He had been accused of being just a surface politician, of not having any depth. But deep inside he knew he had what it took to meet the challenge of the presidency during this critical time. He would rise to the occasion just as others had done before him.

# CHAPTER 21

▼

# WASHINGTON, D.C.
# TWELVE P.M.,
# TUESDAY
# DECEMBER 21, 1999
## ELEVEN DAYS TO 0 0

Immediately after his meeting with General Armstrong, Nick Logan spoke with Lieutenant Johnson and informed him that he was prepared to agree to his terms. The Lieutenant then instructed him to return to his apartment and get what he needed for the trip. Private Kurt Kincaid would meet him in front of his building at one o'clock. Nick put a few things into a small overnight bag. He would travel light, as instructed. He wished now that he had a gun. But, unlike many of his colleagues, he had decided against it. He really didn't like the fact so many people now owned, and often carried, handguns. He felt it made a bad situation worse.

Nick was waiting outside his building when, precisely at one, Private Kincaid, the blonde haired, blue eyed man in his mid-twenties described by Lieutenant Johnson, pulled up. He was also driving the Ford Bronco with the license number that the Lieutenant had indicated. "Hello, Mr. Logan. I'm Private Kurt

Kincaid." The Private smiled and extended his hand, giving Nick a firm handshake.

"Hello, Private Kincaid." Nick returned the smile as he settled into the passenger seat. "So where are we off to? Where are Eric and Kate?"

"Please don't use their names again until I give you clearance, Mr. Logan. The first thing we must do is lose your tail."

"We've already had to lose them once today. I'm surprised that I was allowed to come back."

"Not a problem, Mr. Logan. We will easily lose them again."

"I'm sure you will. And please, call me Nick."

"Yes, sir," Private Kincaid said, and then put his hand to the side of his neck. "Lieutenant Johnson. This is Private Kincaid. I have the subject and we're proceeding as planned."

"Who the hell are you talking to?" Nick asked.

"Lieutenant Johnson, sir," Private Kincaid said matter-of-factly.

"How the hell are you talking to him?"

"Sorry, Lieutenant. Could you repeat that? The subject was talking to me, asking me how we are communicating. Yes, sir. I will. The Lieutenant says to please not interrupt, Mr. Logan. He'll explain it to you later."

Nick began to speak and then thought, what the hell there must be some kind of communication device hidden on his body. He would be patient and find out later. What he didn't understand was how Private Kincaid could hear Lieutenant Johnson and he couldn't. There were no visible signs of an earphone on the private.

"Yes, Lieutenant. I see them behind us."

"So which car is following us?" Nick asked.

"Well, sir, if you promise not to turn around and just view it through your side view mirror, it's the red Chrysler about three cars back"

"Yes, I see. The one with two men in it."

"That's right, sir."

"I assume you're going to tell me when the high speed maneuvers to lose them are going to start," Nick said as he checked his seat belt.

"We won't be needing any evasive maneuvers to lose them."

"Oh! How are you going to get them to stop following us?"

"That's not really a problem. At the next stoplight, they will be disabled. We will proceed through the light and get on the beltway to see if there is anyone else following us."

"What do you mean they'll be disabled? Are you going to bomb them?" Nick thought that a little levity might loosen the private up.

"No, sir. That won't be necessary," Private Kincaid responded as serious as ever.

Nick was beginning to wonder what kind of crackpots he was getting into bed with. He decided it would be better not to ask any more questions and to just observe for a while. Sure enough, after they had stopped at the next light and proceeded through it, he could see in the mirror that the red Chrysler didn't follow. He kept watching as the occupants of the car got out and started lifting the hood.

Nick couldn't help it, he had to ask, "How the hell did you do that?"

"It's not really difficult, sir. But it's up to the Lieutenant if he wants to divulge that information."

"I see, and when do I get to see the Lieutenant?"

"Soon, sir"

What Private Kincaid couldn't tell him was that all of the new government vehicles were equipped with the Telstar communication control system. This allowed a car so equipped to be started up or turned off via satellite communications. Seen as a security feature, the FBI, CIA, and Secret Service all controlled their vehicles through their computer systems. MicroForce had the ability, once they identified the car through the license plate, to access the appropriate agency's computer and to override it and send a signal to turn off the engine.

In this case it was the CIA's computer that MicroForce overrode. Once they did, it could only be turned on again via the computer. An ignition key wouldn't work. But MF was now jamming the signals and even the CIA's computer wouldn't be able to turn it back on. MF didn't want to keep the jamming going on for too long or to totally disable the car. They wanted them to think there was some malfunction in their own system and not that their security had been breached. If there were a second car following them, they would have to use an alternative tactic.

After approximately three miles on the highway, Private Kincaid said, "Copy, sir. There doesn't seem to be anyone else following us, Mr. Logan. We'll get off at the next exit ramp and see if anyone follows us off."

"There could be any number of cars getting off with us, Private."

"Of course. But then we're going to get right back on. Anyone else who gets right back on again will continue to be observed. It's unlikely that they would also have made the same 'mistake' that we did."

"I see," Nick said. He was more determined now to keep his mouth shut. He was obviously dealing with people who were good at their job.

At the next exit ramp, they got off and then right back on. Within minutes, Nick heard the private say, "Roger. Copy. Mr. Logan, it appears that we weren't followed so we will proceed to the next step."

Nick didn't even bother to ask. He wasn't sure he wanted to know. They got off at the next exit ramp, went down four blocks and then pulled into a private garage. Once inside the garage, the private immediately sped up to put distance between them and anyone else who might be entering the garage. Once they reached the third floor, he stopped quickly and ordered Nick out. Before Nick knew what was happening, the door was opened and another man was waiting to get in and pointing to another car with Lieutenant Johnson in the driver's seat. Nick got out as Lieutenant Johnson signaled him to come over; he was assisted by the strong arm of the man waiting to take his place. The car then immediately continued to go up to the next level as Nick quickly took the passenger seat beside Lieutenant Johnson.

"Crouch down so no one can see you," Lieutenant Johnson commanded.

"You like giving orders, don't you?" Nick answered firmly. He didn't like receiving orders.

"When it's necessary," Eric responded, he was used to receiving and giving orders. "Now do it!"

Nick reluctantly crouched down in an uncomfortable position.

"This isn't exactly comfortable."

"Don't worry, it will only be for a few minutes. And it is necessary."

They then proceeded to exit the garage onto a street opposite from where they had entered. About five minutes had gone by when Nick heard, "Anything, Private? Good. Proceed to the rendezvous point. Okay, you can get up now. It's all clear."

"You know, I'm beginning to think you are all a bunch of fruitcakes. Talking into thin air and then acting like someone's talking back, when you can't hear anything, it is a bit unsettling. I'm beginning to wonder if I should be with you guys."

"Do you want to see Kate?"

"Yes. Of course I do."

"Then you want to be with us."

"When do I get to see her?"

"Soon. But remember, you can talk to her but you can't force her to come in."

"I remember, but I still don't agree. For Christ sake, Eric, we've just had a disaster at the test sight and she's the prime suspect. Besides, she's probably the only one that can fix it, even if she didn't do it, which I don't think she did. Every FBI and CIA agent, half the district police and God knows who else is out looking for her. And, while it's been made clear that she's wanted alive, not to be harmed, who the hell knows what will happen if she's found by some over zealous jerk that wants to make a name for himself."

"That's just the point. Who the hell knows what will happen once she's in custody."

"But she's a lot safer coming in with us. We can protect her."

"No. That's where you're wrong. We can't protect her once she is brought into the system. We'll have no power there. The system will be in control and it will be out of our hands. And I don't trust it. Do you?"

Nick wanted to scream with frustration. He wanted to get Kate back so they could fix the problem, but he also knew that Eric Johnson was right. Once she was brought back in, they would have no control. And, no, he didn't trust the system either. There were too many damned politicians involved, too many people trying to make a name for themselves, and not really giving a damn who they hurt along the way.

"No. I don't. I don't like it, but I've given you and the General my word that I won't try to force her to come in. But I still want to find a way to get her back to the project and yet not out of our control. Maybe we can work something out."

"I doubt it. But you can try as long as I have your word you won't try to force her in."

"You have it."

They continued to drive for another half hour. There was more talking into the air and then they finally turned into the driveway of a modest house and pulled into the attached garage. They went directly into the kitchen from the garage. Then into the living room, where Kate was guarded by two military personnel—one male and one female.

"Hello, Nick," Kate said sheepishly as she twisted nervously in her chair.

"Hi, Kate." He wanted to say more. To scold her. But he was too happy to see her to do it.

"What happened to the test?" Kate asked breaking the silence.

"It was an absolute disaster. But perhaps you already know that," Nick was over his initial pleasure of seeing her and angry about the situation.

"I'm not what you, or they, think I am. Exactly what happened at the test?"

Nick hoped what she said was true. He carefully watched her reaction, as he told her about the test failure, but he couldn't get any reading, as Kate was her typical analytical self.

"I see," Kate said.

"Why did you run?" Nick had to hear her explanation first hand.

"I ran because I wasn't safe. That's why."

"You had two US Marshals to protect you. You didn't need to run."

"First of all, I didn't think two US Marshals would be enough. Second, I wasn't sure I could trust them and, third, I couldn't be sure that you wouldn't force me to come in."

"I wouldn't force you to do anything," Nick said sincerely.

"Maybe not. But your boss would. Wouldn't he?" Kate paused, as she looked hard at Nick, then continued, "Wouldn't he? He cares more about his job than he cares about my life. Or your life for that matter."

"You're right. I can't argue with that. But you could have confided in me. Trying to escape alone could have gotten you killed."

"Yes, I know. But staying where I was could have got me killed, also. And I didn't want to put you in danger, so I waited until I could go alone. Has Eric told you that he identified the man in the garage as CIA?"

"Yes, he did."

"How did he find me?"

"I don't know."

"They probably had Grant's phone tapped."

"Come on Kate, he has top level security. They couldn't tap his phone. Not without a lot of high level people knowing about it."

"I have to agree with Kate," Eric interjected.

"Is that just a guess Eric?"

"No. It's not just a guess. It's a fact."

"How the hell do you know these things? Or is it just a bunch of bullshit?" Nick was more frustrated than angry.

"I know," Eric Johnson spoke firmly. "I never bullshit."

Nick wanted to pursue this, but it would have to wait until later. He turned his attention back to Kate, "You have to come in."

"No, I don't. I'm a dead woman if I do."

Nick sat down beside Kate, held her hand, and tried to reason with her, "You have to come in and help us understand what happened. And you have to help us fix the program or we will have a catastrophe on our hands."

"Right now the only place I feel safe is with Lieutenant Johnson and his squad."

"Okay. I can understand why you're feeling safe with them, but they can come in with you."

"That's not possible," Eric said immediately. "First of all, I'm on an official leave of absence for thirty days because of my brother's death and I have no official capacity to go in and protect Kate."

"Maybe I can work something out that you can be her official bodyguard," Nick said.

"I doubt it. Besides, it will be much tougher for me to protect her inside the lion's den than being able to roam free out here. And, in there, my chances of finding my brother's killer are greatly reduced, if not eliminated"

"And I won't go. Not willingly anyway," Kate said. "You keep trying to trust the system, and I don't trust the system."

Nick couldn't really blame her at this point. From the very beginning his attempts to bring her in were only half-hearted. He knew there was a lot of truth to what she said. He also knew that going along with her was probably going to be the end of his career, and maybe worse. But he also knew that she and Eric were right, it was the best way to keep her safe. And, who knew, maybe it was the best chance of averting a disaster. After all, General Armstrong was in agreement with letting Kate remain free, under the protection of Lieutenant Johnson and himself.

"Do you have a plan, or are you just going to stay in hiding?" Nick said.

"I have to get to Boston. I have reason to believe that we'll find our answers there," Kate answered as she took her hand back from Nick and got up and moved to the window, even though the blinds were closed.

"All of our answers?" Eric asked.

"Possibly. I don't know," Kate said.

"Why do you think that? What do you know?"

"I don't know anything. Call it intuition."

"You want us to defy the US government and become fugitives based on intuition?" Nick said.

"I don't know about us. But that's what I'm doing. And I don't really expect you to do that." Kate was resolved to do it her way.

Eric's senses told him it was a hell of a lot more than intuition but, even if it were just that, he would take her anyway. She was the center of forces trying to kidnap or eliminate her, as they had done his brother. It was clearly his best lead to finding his brother's killers.

"It doesn't look like I have very much choice. I'm going with you."

"I'm not sure that's a very good idea," Kate said. She came back over and sat beside him. "It's already proven to be a very dangerous situation. There's really no need of you risking your life, too."

"I'm already into this up to my eyeballs. There's no backing out now."

"He's right, Kate. It would probably be more dangerous if he didn't come with us. The forces looking for you would certainly expect him to know where you are. And that wouldn't be good for him."

"Okay, you win. We should leave first thing in the morning," Kate said.

"I'll make the arrangements," Eric said.

"This ought to be good," Nick remarked.

"You don't know the half of it," Eric responded.

# CHAPTER 22

▼

# MOSCOW
# EIGHT A.M.,
# WEDNESDAY
# DECEMBER 22, 1999

## TEN DAYS TO 0 0

In the dark, dank sub-basement of the FSS building was an isolated complex of cells and interrogation rooms. It was a place most only knew of by rumor for those unfortunate ones who were brought there for questioning rarely left alive. And those who worked there were afraid of saying anything lest they, too, become victims. Director Stepovich and his First Deputy, Vladimir Kosloff, were there to supervise this interrogation personally. This was highly unusual and emphasized its importance.

When Boris Stepovich had learned the man agents Malenkov and Skulsky had killed was not Yuri Petrov, he knew that Dimitry had discovered his plan to kill his son. It also proved that the listening device discovered in his office had been planted by Dimitry, who hadn't cared about it being found because he was going underground, which made the director suspect that it went deeper than discovering the plot to kill Yuri. There was something more. As soon as he had learned that his office had been bugged, he ordered his undercover agent at the Kaling-staad nuclear facility to investigate Yuri Petrov's activities on the day of the test. The last day he had access to the system and what should have been his last day alive.

The agent learned that Yuri had not been seen at the celebration after eleven, and that he was friendly with the guard on duty in the computer complex that evening. That's why Director Stepovich ordered the guard brought in. It was his interrogation the Director and his deputy were on their way to observe.

"What do you expect to learn from this guard?" Deputy Kosloff asked as they proceeded down the cold, gray corridor to the interrogation room..

"I don't know. But I'm sure that there is something more. Why did Dimitry bug my office? How did he move so quickly to save his son and get him safely out of the country?" Boris Stepovich stabbed the air in front of him with his finger as he spoke.

"Petrov has always been a resourceful man, comrade."

"True, Vladimir. But there is something else. I'm sure of it," Stepovich said as they reached the interrogation room and prepared to enter. "Now we must find out whatever this guard knows."

As he followed his boss into the room, Vladimir Kosloff felt a twinge of pity toward the young man for Boris Stepovich would be certain he learned everything.

The interrogation had already been going on for almost two hours and it showed on Antoin's bruised and bloody face.

"Tell me, Vassily, what have we learned from our friend?" Stepovich asked of the agent in charge of the interrogation.

"He has revealed that he discovered Yuri Petrov working at his computer just before midnight, Director Stepovich." Vassily was pleased he had something positive to tell his superior, even though it didn't seem like much.

"So Petrov was working after the project was completed and while the others celebrated," Stepovich said. Standing beside Antoin, he grabbed a hand full of hair and pulled his slumping head back forcefully. "Didn't you think that was strange?"

"No, sir. Yuri often worked late." Antoin managed to say through the pain.

"So Petrov is a friend of yours?" When the answer did not come quickly enough, Stepovich pulled harder and repeated his question. "Do not lie to me. He is your friend? Isn't he?"

"Yes." Antoin struggled to remain conscious.

"So you and he were working together."

"No. Please stop. I know nothing more," Antoin pleaded.

"Why was he there?" Stepovich demanded. "The project was closed. No one was supposed to be there."

"He said he just had a few thing to clean up."

"So you let him. Even though you were not suppose to," Stepovich said calmly as he released his grip.

"Yes, sir."

"And you were afraid to say anything because you had not done your job."

"Yes, sir. I thought it would be all right."

"I can understand. He was a friend. Someone you trusted." Stepovich then took a chair and sat in front of Antoin. "But he is an enemy of Russia and you must tell me what else you know."

"Please. Believe me. I know nothing else." Antoin looked at Boris Stepovich with eyes that begged for mercy. "I swear I would tell you if I did."

"I know you would." Again Stepovich spoke calmly. "It would be in your best interest to do so."

"I know nothing else. Please believe me," Antoin again pleaded.

"I believe you," Stepovich said as he patted Antoin's knee. "These men will give you something to make you feel better."

Boris Stepovich signaled for Vladimir and Vassily to follow him as he left the room. Once outside he turned to Vassily, "He knows nothing, but use the drugs anyway. If he reveals anything call me. If he doesn't—kill him. I want no trace left of him."

"Yes, Director Stepovich. I will take care of everything," Vassily said as he went back into the room.

"Get word to Ivan immediately. He is not to kill Yuri," Stepovich commanded as he turned to Deputy Kosloff. "We must have him alive."

"As you order, Director," the Deputy responded. "But why?"

"Why would Yuri Petrov go back to work on the program after he had already accomplished what we asked and it was off limits?"

"I don't know," Kosloff said as he thought about it. "Perhaps to sabotage our plan."

"Precisely. And that would be bad enough, we would lose our ability to control the country's missiles," Stepovich said as he paused and took a deep breath. "But I am afraid it could be worse."

"What would be worse? Our plan would be ruined and all the risks we took would be for nothing."

"He could have substituted his own code for ours." Stepovich spoke solemnly as they made their way back down the dark corridor. "That's what I would have done. I just didn't expect Dimitry to do it."

As they continued down the corridor, Deputy Kosloff didn't ask the obvious question, 'If it's what you would have done, why the hell did you put him in a position to take control?' This was not a time to question Stepovich's plan, not even for Kosloff who had been with him for over twenty years.

From his silence, Stepovich knew the question that Kosloff wanted to ask but wouldn't. "Remember, we had to have Yuri's expertise to be able to put our own plan into action and we had our own man observing all of his work." Stepovich paused for a moment, thinking about the failure of this agent. "We must punish him when this is over."

"I didn't think that Dimitry would be 'disloyal' to the agency." Boris Stepovich continued. "I knew that he was capable of conceiving it, but not of doing it."

"Maybe he didn't," Kosloff offered. "But I don't see how we can test it again."

"We can't. We have no way to justify it," Stepovich responded. "Besides, the more I think about it the more sure I am that's what he did. That's the reason why he left the bug in my office after he found out I ordered Yuri's death. He was sending me a message that he was now in control."

"It also made his son more valuable to us alive than dead," Kosloff added.

"Yes, it did." Stepovich responded and then added, "It also made Katya more valuable to us alive. We can use her as bait to get to Yuri."

"But, Boris, that is very dangerous. If she gets into the hands of the Americans they may be able to get the code from her and regain control of their missile system."

"We will have to take that chance. We must have control of our missiles. Maybe it has been fortunate that our assassins have failed with Yuri and Katya. Give the order not to kill Katya as well as Yuri. Now!"

In the northwest corner of Moscow, in an old abandoned warehouse, Dimitry Petrov was being briefed by his key aid, Stephan. He was pleased to hear that Yuri and Pasha had made it to Iceland and then had successfully eluded the FSS, who thought they were on their way to New York, and were now heading toward Boston by car. He had been distressed to hear that two attempts had already been made on Katya's life. Boris Stepovich had indeed moved quickly but, fortunately, had been unsuccessful.

When Stephan informed Dimitry that the guard, Antoin, was taken into custody by the FSS he knew that Stepovich would soon understand what happened.

While he would be surprised and furious at what Dimitry had done, it would mean that Yuri and Katya would be more valuable alive than dead.

"Stephan, get word to Yuri and Katya that the pressure to find them will be intensified, but it will be with the intent to capture rather than to kill them. They will understand the difference that will make."

"Right away, Dimitry," Stephan said and then left to follow his superior's order.

Dimitry Petrov knew that Boris Stepovich would give anything to be able to conduct another test to see if he were still in control or if his worst fears were confirmed—Dimitry was now in control. But Petrov knew another test was impossible. The test would fail as planned and then Stepovich would have to reveal his code to see if it worked or if it had been changed. In either case he would expose himself and lose control of the missile system. Dimitry also knew the pressure to find him would be intensified.

# CHAPTER 23

▼

# ROAD NORTH TO BOSTON ELEVEN A.M., THURSDAY DECEMBER 23, 1999

## NINE DAYS TO 0 0

Traveling north on interstate 95 in the black Ford Explorer XLT, Nick could feel the difference the extra weight made in the ride of the large vehicle. Lieutenant Johnson explained its choice as typical of the large number of SUVs on the road, so it easily blended in. However, this vehicle was anything but typical. The steel plate in the doors added another thousand pounds and combined with the bullet-proof glass to make the interior impregnable to anything less than armor piercing bullets or an anti-tank missile. An eight cylinder, three hundred and fifty horse-power, powered it, turbo charged engine designed to accommodate the extra weight and still make it one of the fastest vehicles on the road. The forty-gallon gas tank made up for the engine's fuel performance of just nine miles per gallon and the tires were capable of traveling another fifty miles at high speed after being severely punctured. Under other circumstances, Nick doubted he would have been able to overcome the urge to turn on the 'police' siren and floor it. But one look over at Kate in the passenger seat brought him back to reality. She was quiet and looked tired as she starred straight ahead. Having started at six in the morning, they had already been on the road for five hours and were just north of Trenton, New Jersey.

Nick had protested to Lieutenant Johnson when he learned he and Kate would be traveling alone. He demanded that they have at least two of Eric's team with them. He wasn't at all satisfied with the Lieutenant's explanation that, with his limited resources, it was better to have two of his people in a vehicle behind them. This way they could better observe who might be following Nick and Kate, and be in a position to take the assailants out rather than be caught up in the middle of an attack.

Nick protested that they should have both the protection of a car following them and of guards with them. He hadn't realized when he signed on that they would not have adequate resources to do the job right. It had surprised Nick when Kate didn't join in his protest. In fact, she had been surprisingly quick to agree with Eric Johnson and to suggest to Nick it was all right and he should let it go.

The vehicle following them was an identical black Ford Explorer, occupied by Privates Kurt Kincaid and Martha 'Marty' Nelson. The two privates were dressed in civilian clothes, also identical to what Kate and Nick were wearing. It was obviously not a coincidence, they were prepared to take their place, or at least cause confusion, if the situation required. Nick liked this idea and could readily imagine the advantages it might provide. He still would have preferred a guard or two in the car with them, especially since neither he nor Kate were armed. He couldn't help feeling exposed, a little like live bait.

What Nick didn't know was that there was more protection in the immediate area than he could ever have imagined. Directly above them, at two thousand feet, was Lieutenant Johnson and the rest of his MicroForce team in their top-secret aircraft. Like a typical helicopter, they could go as slow or as fast as required to stay with the Ford Explorer. But that is where the resemblance ended, this was anything but a typical helicopter. The first, and most obvious, difference was the noise level. Or more precisely, the lack of it. Even while hovering, with the rotors at peak performance, it was whisper quiet. The engines used an advanced baffling system that significantly 'hid' the noise they produced, and the rotors were only one third the standard size, also significantly reducing the noise. The remaining noise was then eliminated by the sound waves that were deliberately created by the aircraft for this purpose. In its simplest definition, it was competing sound waves canceling each other out.

Powered by two large jet engines on the wings, that could rotate ninety degrees, and a third engine on the tail it was part helicopter and part jet plane with a top speed of over six hundred mph. Its combination of speed and agility was easily beyond anything else in the sky. Fueled by its own self contained, ultra small, nuclear capsule it could stay aloft almost indefinitely. The aircraft's ability to hide in plane sight earned it the nickname of 'Casper', the ghost ship. Its stealthy shape enabled the aircraft to avoid detection by enemy radar and it used visual stealth to blend into the sky through sensors that measure the sky's brightness and hue, and electrochromic coatings applied over a white skin that changes shade to match the background. In addition, when operating at low speed, Casper had the capability of creating its own 'cloud' by using the heat from the jet engines to create a mist that develops an artificial cloud surrounding the aircraft.

Little was said as they continued driving north. Nick was anxious to question Kate further, but he expected that the SUV was bugged. Eric Johnson and who knew who else would hear everything they said. And neither of them was in the mood to make small talk. The tension had been high since they started and five hours on the road only served to increase it.

Unknown to any of them was the large gray sedan following the second SUV. The two CIA agents were having no difficulty staying with the vehicle carrying Nick and Kate, even though they were well behind and out of sight of them. Rounding out the caravan were the two FSS agents who were following the CIA car.

"I don't know about you, but I'm getting pretty hungry," Nick said breaking the silence. "I could use a break and some food."

"That sounds good. I could eat something," Kate replied as she smiled for the first time today.

"Good. I'll pull off the highway and we can find a place for lunch."

"Not yet, Nick." The sudden sound of Eric Johnson's voice, as if he were in the back seat, startled both of them. Kate's muscles tensed as she whipped her head around to look into the back seat and Nick had to fight his initial reflex to slam on the brakes. Both of them had suspected that Eric was listening to them, but they didn't expect to hear his voice.

"Christ, Eric. You scared the hell out of us," Nick responded angrily. Feeling a little foolish speaking into the air.

"I'm sorry. Perhaps I should have explained that we were monitoring you," Lieutenant Johnson said apologetically. Seating in the co-pilot's seat, peering down from Casper, Eric could easily see their vehicle on the monitor in front of him. Using the toggle control in his right hand, he was able to direct the high-powered telescope to its target as he sat comfortably in the large cabin of the aircraft. It was almost eerily quiet as Corporal Semanski, in the pilot's seat to Eric's left, concentrated on keeping Casper moving slowly above the Explorer. Private Brad Wilson was in the navigator's seat to his right and Corporal John Anderson and Private Pete Peterson were in the rear of the cabin observing their monitors and able to control their individual telescopes. These two were already dressed in light battle gear, and would be the first to be ejected in case of an emergency on the ground. "I just assumed you would understand that we would do it. For security."

"Of course we did," Kate spoke calmly. "We just didn't expect to hear your voice like you were seating in the back seat."

"I understand. And I am sorry, but don't get off here. Go up to the next exit and get off going north on route 31. There will be a small sandwich shop a mile up on the left. You can eat there, but don't get out of the car until Privates Kincaid and Nelson get there."

"Anything else," Nick said sarcastically.

"Yes. Let Private Nelson go in first. Then I'll let you know when it is clear for you to go in."

"You really do like to be in control. Don't you?" Nick shot back.

"He's just doing his job," Kate said. "He is responsible for our safety. It's good to see that he's good at it."

"Thank you, Kate," Eric said. Again carrying on a conversation as if he were in the SUV with them. "I know your not use to getting instructions so directly, Nick, but you will appreciate the need for this when we get into a crisis situation."

"We'll see," Nick responded.

Less than a minute passed, after they got to the sandwich shop, when the black Ford Explorer XLT, driven by Private Kincaid, pulled into the parking lot of the little strip mall and parked as far away from Nick and Kate as possible. They didn't want to draw possible attention to two identical vehicles driven by two similarly dressed couples. As soon as Private Kincaid backed into his parking spot, Private Nelson got out and made a slow and indirect approach to the restaurant. She appeared to be heading for the convenience store next door before she drifted to her left and disappeared into the restaurant. This gave her a better opportunity to view the area before she went inside. Once inside, she secretly released two P.I.P.'s to help monitor the small dining room.

Private Kincaid remained in the vehicle with the engine running. Already facing out, he was prepared to move in an instant. He had immediately put on the special eyeglasses that allowed him to take an iris reading of everyone who came into the area, without drawing attention to himself. The readings were transmitted to Casper and, from there, to the MicroForce super computer and the results of the search relayed back to Casper in a matter of two to three seconds. If there were any positive 'hits' these would be immediately communicated back to Private Kincaid.

There had been no hits of interest and no one suspicious arrived in a time frame that would have suggested that they could have been following them. They had been there for ten minutes already and Private Nelson had indicated that the inside of the restaurant was clear, so Lieutenant Johnson gave Nick and Kate the signal to go in. They wasted no time getting into the restaurant, they were hungry.

That's when the gray sedan, with two men dressed in dark suits, pulled in and parked to the right of the pharmacy. Private Kincaid was alert as soon as they had entered the lot and was able to get an iris scan before they parked with their backs to him. His instincts had told him to expect something, but he was surprised when he was informed they were CIA. The passenger got out and went into the convenience store.

Lieutenant Johnson had rejected the suggestion it could just be a coincidence. He ordered Private Kincaid to move with the man in the car. If he got out he wanted Kincaid close to him. He alerted Private Nelson to the situation and would have liked to alert Nick and Kate but, of course, they were not equipped with the transmitter implants. Normally Eric would not have been so concerned about the CIA but, in this operation, everyone was a potential enemy. Then a dark blue Mercury Marquis, also with two men in suits, pulled into the lot and parked opposite the restaurant. The iris scan had revealed nothing, they were not in the computers files. This troubled the Lieutenant because almost everyone with a driver's license was in the iris files. It meant that the odds were they had some form of special or illegal license, although it was possible that it meant nothing. He alerted Private Kincaid to observe them, as well, and be prepared to move quickly. Once again, he updated Private Nelson on the situation and put the Casper team on full alert to make a rapid descent if the situation turned hot.

Inside the restaurant Nick and Kate were oblivious to what was going on outside. Freed from the monitoring devices of their protectors, they broke their silence and carried on some small talk. It was too public to have any serious discussion, Nick would have to continue to wait. Instead he used the time to familiarize Kate with the city of Boston. He enjoyed talking about his city, with its rich culture and historic landmarks. They ate light and were finished and back in the SUV in less than forty minutes.

As soon as they had closed the doors they heard from Lieutenant Johnson. "I'm glad that you are back. We have a possible situation developing." He quickly went on to explain about the two CIA agents and the two other suspicious men they couldn't identify. "I want you to go north on route 206 instead of getting back onto route 95."

"But isn't that a small back road? Pretty isolated at this time of the year?" Nick questioned Eric's decision.

"Yes, it is. And that's precisely why I want you to take it. We can get a better idea if anyone is following you and we will also be in a better position to do something about it. Now get out of there," the Lieutenant ordered. "I don't want to have an engagement in a public parking lot."

"Neither do I," Nick snapped as he put the Explorer in gear and pulled out of the parking lot quicker than he should have. "The difference between us is I don't want to have an engagement anywhere."

"Don't drive so fast. We aren't trying to lose them and we don't need to get stopped by the police."

As the Explorer proceeded north, Lieutenant Johnson and his crew carefully observed the agents and the other vehicle to see if they followed. Privates Kincaid and Nelson had been ordered to wait for movement from one or both of these vehicles before they moved. That way they would be behind the target and able to move in quickly if necessary.

Five minutes had passed and Lieutenant Johnson was about to give the order for Privates Kincaid and Nelson to leave when the CIA agents pulled out of the parking lot and headed north on route 206. Almost immediately, the Mercury Marquis followed the gray sedan. The Lieutenant and his team were confused. The agents had left much too late to insure that they could effectively follow Nick and Kate, but that is exactly what they were doing. It was as if the Explorer was bugged and they knew where it was even though they couldn't see it. But that was impossible, the SUV had been thoroughly scanned that morning and under constant surveillance ever since. The vehicle was also equipped with ultra sensitive sensors that could detect any foreign objects attached to it and, when the remote control was used to deactivate the security system it would blink and sound a small warning alarm. Nothing had sounded either in the morning or when it was activated in the parking lot.

In addition to the SUV, both Nick and Kate had been thoroughly scanned and the only thing on them was the MicroForce tracer that Lieutenant Johnson had placed on their necks. Still it was clear that the CIA agents were following the SUV and it appeared the unidentified men were following them, but at a normal, visual distance. The Lieutenant had seen enough and determined his course of action. He ordered Corporal Anderson to initialize the computer control system and to immobilize the agent's gray sedan. Lieutenant Johnson didn't need the CIA getting in his way and he wanted to see how the unidentified men responded.

Corporal Anderson had locked onto the gray sedan's computer within five seconds of the order and was just waiting for an appropriate location to safely disable it. He didn't have to wait long on the lightly traveled road, within two miles was a steep grade with a truck-passing lane. This was ideal so the Corporal activated the system, shutting off the engine, and watched as the gray sedan slowly pulled over into the truck lane and came to a stop. The black Mercury also pulled over a safe distance away and waited. When the agents couldn't get the car started, with the help of their computer control staff, they got out of the car and raised the hood to see if something had broken.

As soon as the other men saw this they quickly pulled out and continued north at a high rate of speed for the narrow road. If there were some form of tracking device on the Explorer these men lost the benefit of it when the CIA vehicle was disabled and were now in an obvious effort to close the gap between them and the Explorer. As soon as the gap had been closed, and they had the Explorer in view, they slowed down and maintained the same speed as the SUV.

Lieutenant Johnson had seen enough to know he wanted to find out who these men were and why they were following Nick and Kate. "Private Kincaid, bring your vehicle to within fifty yards of the target and be prepared to move in."

"Yes, sir," Private Kincaid said as he accelerated the vehicle and the powerful engine immediately responded.

"Corporal Semanski, position Casper directly over the target and be prepared for a rapid descent."

"Yes, sir."

"Private Wilson, look for a wide spot where we can force them off the road without killing them." Eric Johnson then turned to Corporal John Anderson, "John, as soon as Brad finds an acceptable location I'm going to jam their computer and cause it to stall. They'll lose their power steering and I want you to use the .50-caliber machine gun to blowout their right front tire, causing them to veer off of the road to the right. At the same time I'll hit the front end with a small concussion rocket that will cause the air bags to deploy, temporarily disabling them and then we will move in."

"Got it, Lieutenant."

Within two minutes Private Wilson had located a grassy opening in the thickly treed landscape and notified the lieutenant. As soon as the target approached ground zero, the MicroForce team moved into action with the precision and high tech weaponry that made them such a formidable force. On his command, Lieutenant Johnson activated Casper's jamming device aimed at the Mercury and disabled the car's computer making it stall. As it slowed, Corporal Anderson blew out the tire, with one fifty caliber round, causing the driver to lose control as the car was pulled onto the grass. The driver was forced to slam on the brakes and, as he did so, the small concussion missile, fired by Lieutenant Johnson, hit the front end. The impact activated the air bags stunning the occupants for just a few seconds, but it was long enough.

On orders, Private Kincaid closed the gap to within fifteen yards before the target was disabled so he and Private Nelson were already at the rear of the car while the occupants were still slightly dazed. Simultaneously, Corporal Semanski, upon the firing of the concussion missile, had made a rapid descent to twenty feet above and slightly to the front of the target. Immediately, Corporal Anderson and Private Peterson leaped from either side of Casper. They no longer used repelling ropes, as that was much too slow, instead they leaped free form. They were able to do this from heights as high as seventy-five feet with the aid of rocket belts that used small, short bursts to slow the descent as they approached the ground. Sensors in the rocket automatically control the firing of the micro miniature rockets and tiny gyroscopes built into the belt help the free faller land upright. This allows the MF commando to fire his or her weapon as they are rapidly descending.

By the time the occupants of the vehicle were alert enough to reach for their weapons they were surrounded by four MF commandos, with weapons aimed at their heads, and thought better of it. The MF team quickly secured the two men, put them in the SUV, and vacated the scene heading for the rendezvous point. There was a safe house in a secluded location outside of Flagtown, about an hour further north. After dark, Casper could be landed without being noticed and there was a large barn where it could be housed out of sight. This location had been chosen for its proximity to New York City. At top speed, Casper could be over the city in fifteen minutes. There were ten such safe houses throughout the country. It was often easier than landing at the closest air force base for, while at a distance the MF jet copters looked enough like a normal helicopter to go relatively unnoticed, up close the aircraft were anything but normal. But, more importantly, these safe houses had been set up so that MF could operate outside of the normal military channels, as it was doing now.

When Lieutenant Johnson had informed Nick and Kate that they would be stopping for the night they both strongly protested.

"But we can be in Boston in another four or five hours and then we can rest," Nick said.

"I don't want to stop," Kate added sharply.

"I'm afraid it's not a request." Eric had caught himself before he used the word order. Why couldn't they be like the rest of his MF team—follow orders with no questions asked.

"There you go with the orders again," Nick said.

"You do like to give orders," Kate added. "But we don't have to follow them."

"Yes, you do." Eric Johnson didn't wait for a response before he reminded Nick of who was in control. "I'll shut your vehicle down, if I have to."

Kate turned and asked Nick "Can he do that?"

Nick nodded as he conceded control to Eric, "Tell us where you want us to go."

The Lieutenant gave him directions as needed and less than an hour later they were pulling onto a gravel road that ended a quarter of a mile later in front of a moderate farmhouse with a large barn, both in need of a coat of paint. They were instructed to park the SUV in front of the house and take their suitcases and go into the house. The Explorer would be parked in the barn for them. Nick protested that he could park it himself and Lieutenant Johnson ordered him to park it out front. When Nick insisted that he could park it himself, the Lieutenant had Private Wilson turn the engine off, disabling the vehicle and angering Nick.

Once inside, the array of high tech communication and computer equipment seen, through the open door of a large room on their right, revealed it was something more than a dilapidated old farmhouse. A young man, who introduced himself as Private Crawford, emerged from the room and hastily closed the door behind him. He escorted Kate and Nick to a small room opposite the main room and informed them that Lieutenant Johnson would be with them shortly. He then excused himself and left; closing and locking the door as he did. Nick immediately tried the door and was not at all pleased when he confirmed that it was locked. Kate sat patiently, as if she had expected as much.

Less than fifteen minutes had gone by when Lieutenant Johnson entered the room and immediately was confronted by Nick's angry protest. "We're not your prisoners, Lieutenant. I resent being locked in this room."

Eric Johnson remained calm as he responded, "I apologize for that. Private Crawford was just following standard operating procedures. We have some very sensitive equipment here and no one without the proper security clearance is allowed to be left unattended. He had something else he had to take care of so he followed procedure and made sure that you were secured."

"How long are we going to continue to be 'secured'? How long are we going to be here? And how the hell did you get here?"

"You will no longer be secured if I have your word that you will confine yourselves to this room, the kitchen and the upstairs bedrooms."

"Fine. We should be leaving first thing in the morning, anyway."

"There may be some delay in that. We may have to be here through tomorrow."

On hearing this, Kate was no longer content to remain silent, "We can't do that! We have to get to Boston as soon as possible. We should have been there today."

"I agree. If we left now we could be there by ten."

"I'm sorry but we can't. For one, it's to dangerous to travel at night."

"Then I agree with Nick. We should leave first thing in the morning," Kate insisted.

"I'm sorry but I have my orders," Lieutenant Johnson said firmly. "We will leave first thing the day after tomorrow. And please remain only in the designated areas, or I will have to have you secured." He then turned and left before they could have much of a chance to protest. He wasn't about to explain to them that he wanted the extra time to interrogate his captives, absorb what he learned, and adjust his plans as necessary. He would learn everything that the two men knew. The modern drugs would insure that. The only drawback was that they took about twelve hours in total to administer safely. And, while he suspected that they were FSS agents, he did not know who they were so he had to proceed slowly.

"I'm getting awfully tired of being ordered around by him. Maybe we should just get the car and go on without him and his team."

"I would be happy to do that, Nick. But he has already shown he is in control of the car. And he is in control of us, too. At least for the time being. Like it or not."

"I'm afraid you're right. And I don't like it. It's a hell of a place to spend Christmas Eve."

------- ▼ -------

# OVAL OFFICE, WHITE HOUSE
# FOUR P.M., FRIDAY
# DECEMBER 24, 1999

## EIGHT DAYS TO 0 0

President Stewart had called an emergency meeting of his two most trusted advisors, Vice President Chandler and General Armstrong. He hated to call them away from their families Christmas Eve celebrations. He was scheduled to be at a gala event shortly himself, but it couldn't be helped. Their was a serious leak to the press that the Social Security Administration had not fixed the Y2K problem, as he had previously announced, and was not going to be ready to produce all of the payments due on January 1. Those payments due to federal welfare recipients were in big trouble. They included fifteen billion dollars of payments to families with over eight million children administered by the Administration for Children and Families.

The Administration was doing its best to dispel the story, but with little success. One of the major networks indicated they had an impeccable source and would have a special segment on the evening news. When Press Secretary Jones informed the President he was livid and knew that he would have to pre-empt them. He only hoped that he would have the ammunition he needed to do it. That's why he had called this emergency meeting.

"Neil. George. I'm sorry that I had to take you away from your families on Christmas Eve," the President said as he got up to greet the two men.

"We certainly understand, Mr. President," Neil Chandler responded. "Brent filled us in while we were waiting."

General Armstrong wasted no time. "It seems there has been a serious leak. Do we know who?"

"No concrete evidence. But I don't need any. I know who it was."

"Victor Noble?" The General offered.

"No doubt in my mind."

"I can't believe that he would use this for his own benefit. It's too critical to the good of the country. And, as self-absorbed as he is, he is loyal to the country."

"Yes he is, Neil. But what you're missing is that a man with an ego as big as his can easily justify the country's need for him badly enough to take a risk, a big risk."

"Perhaps you're right, sir. Regardless of who or why, we're in trouble if this gets out on the six o'clock news. The country is already jumpy as a result of the forced business mergers and bankruptcies resulting from some organizations failure to solve the Y2K problem."

"Not to mention the bad news coming from overseas," the General added. "We can expect most of Asia, with the possible exception of Japan, to experience serious problems, beginning with power blackouts. Russia and the rest of Eastern Europe will be much the same. We're still not sure about Western Europe, but there is no doubt there will be some serious problems. South and Central America could be a disaster. The bright spots remain Australia, Great Britain, Canada, and us."

"It gets worse, gentlemen," the President said. He got up and started to pace around the room. "The reason I had kept you waiting was because I was on the phone with the Japanese Prime Minister. He informed me that Japan would be announcing a 'banking holiday'. Beginning December 31 there will be an indefinite moratorium on all business and non-essential government activities."

"Great. The second largest economy in the world is shut down. We have to get the network to put a hold on their news story. At the very least we have to get them to tone it down," Vice President Chandler insisted.

"We have to do more than that," General Armstrong commanded. "We have to attack. We have to meet it head on and show the country that we are in control. That we have a back up plan."

"I agree, General" the President said. "We have to be honest and straight forward with the American people. We have a back up plan and we have to announce it."

"But we still have a week to fix it. And the contingency plan is less than perfect,." Nick reminded them.

"Then that is what we will tell them. If they believe us, they'll support us. If we lose their confidence we will be inviting chaos." The President stopped pacing. "I've asked Bill Calderon to standby for a conference call."

The President picked up his desk phone and instructed his secretary to put the call through. Within a minute the Secretary of the Treasury was on the line.

"Good afternoon, Mr. President," came the serious voice on the other end of the line.

"Hello, Bill. I'm here with General Armstrong and the Vice President. I trust that Brent has brought you up to date on the current crisis?"

"Yes, sir, he has."

"Good. I would like to have your comments and then I need you to bring us up to date on our contingency plan."

"We are in relatively good shape on the primary social security payments. We've made a lot of progress in the last few days. There may be a few glitches, but we are prepared for these. There may be a few ripples, but no big waves."

"Then what I told the country months ago is still true."

"Yes, sir. It is."

"You're sure?"

"I'm sure."

"Good. Now for the bad news."

"The bad news is in the payments of aid to dependent children, food stamps and other welfare payments. As you know. As we've discussed before. It has been much more difficult to make this area Y2K compliant because, while they are funded by the federal government, the actual payments are administered by the states. That means that we had to coordinate with fifty states and the hundreds of vendors that they use to help them maintain their systems."

"I know. And," the President was becoming impatient.

"And clearly a number of states won't make it at all and others will have spotty problems."

"How many won't make it, Bill?"

"It's hard to be sure, sir. Possibly as many as half."

"That's consistent with the information that was leaked," Neil Chandler said.

A defensive Secretary of the Treasury quickly responded. "The leak didn't come from my office."

The President was now sitting at his desk with his hands folded in front of him as he spoke calmly. "We know that Bill. The problem is, the leak is accurate. It has too much substance. We can't create a smoke screen by denying it. In a week they'll know we were lying and then won't believe anything we say. That means we are going to have to respond. Can you please fill us in on the status of the contingency plan."

Secretary Calderon cleared his throat as he began. "I'm pleased to report that we have had a great deal of cooperation from the financial and business community. I have to agree with you, Mr. President, that if we are honest and direct with the American people they will respond. If they believe they are being told the truth and no one is trying to take advantage of the situation, they will respond in the interest of the country."

"Perhaps they realize it is in their own self-interest as well."

"Perhaps, General. But I think it's more than that. All of the major retail grocery store chains in the country have agreed to work off of a voucher list system. It is a bit complicated and I won't bore you with the details, but it will guarantee that everyone who doesn't receive their checks will have food to eat. This can also be expanded to include all benefit recipients if needed."

"So, if the Treasury does have some problems in paying the country's retired workers they will be able to be added to the list?"

"That's correct, sir. We have worked closely with the General's special emergency team to be able to utilize the 'flying wing' system for communications if the normal channels are unavailable."

"That's excellent, Bill. What else?"

"The country's major banks have agreed to support us in the event a short term moratorium has to be placed on mortgage and loan payments. In general, I have met with the heads of the country's leading financial institutions and we can count on their support and cooperation."

"I have had the same level of cooperation from the heads of the country's leading corporations. For example, the chemical industry has agreed to voluntarily cooperate and to temporarily shutdown any chemical plants that have not been certified as compliant by the GAO," the Vice President added. "It is obvious that you are right about getting the support of the American people in a time of national crisis."

"Thanks, Neil," the President said with a smile. Then he looked at General Armstrong and turned somber. "General are the troops ready?"

"Yes, sir. My team has worked with the state's governor's councils and the National Guards have already quietly been put on alert and will be able to be placed at strategic locations with food, water, and emergency shelter as needed. Of course, they will also be in a position to help enforce marshal law if that becomes necessary. In that regard, we have canceled all military leaves until further notice. We have our entire armed forces on standby alert and will be prepared to move wherever we are needed at a moments notice."

"Good. Now I think it's time to call for an immediate press conference. Bill, of course I'll want you to be there along with the rest of the cabinet, but I'll want you to be right beside me. You may have to help with some of the details if I find that necessary."

"Certainly, sir. I will be pleased to do whatever I can."

"I know. You had better get ready. And, Bill."

"Yes, Sir?"

"Please don't mention the press conference to anyone. Not anyone at all. Just come on over as quickly as you can."

"Certainly, Mr. President," the Treasury Secretary said as the President severed the connection.

"Neil, will you organize getting the rest of the Cabinet here. Don't tell them why. Tell them not to discuss it with anyone else or each other. And don't notify Victor Noble." The President spoke firmly.

"But why the secrecy. And what do we say to Noble when he finds out? He'll be furious."

"The secrecy gives us the element of surprise. And the element of surprise gives us power. The power to keep our opponents and critics off guard," the President said as he glanced at the General who nodded slightly. "As for Noble, I'm sure he will be furious. He'll be damned furious."

"What will we tell him after he sees the press conference with all the other cabinet members there?"

"We'll make a lame excuse about a slip up and it falling through the cracks because of the short time frame involved."

"With all do respect, Mr. President, he'll see right through that."

"I'm sure he will. But two can play at his game. Anyway, when this is over, one of us won't be here any more."

"Let's make sure its him, Mr. President."

"Thanks, Neil. I plan on it. Now I would appreciate it if you would go and notify the rest of the cabinet and then work with Brent to make sure that we're ready on time."

"Yes, sir. I'll see the two of you at the press conference."

He waited for his Vice President to leave before Justin Stewart turned to General Armstrong, "What's the current status on the Millennium Project, George?"

"I'm sorry to say that it still isn't operational, sir."

"We're running out of time, General."

"I know, sir." The General hesitated to tell him the rest of the news. He had had enough surprises to deal with for one day, but this was too important to wait.

The President sensed there was something more his friend had to say, but was reluctant to give him more bad news. So he helped him along, "Go ahead, General. Tell me the rest of it."

"The subjects are temporarily delayed going north."

The little smile that had returned to the handsome face of Justin Stewart quickly disappeared. "What happened? Are they all right? Are they still under our control?"

The confidence returned to George Armstrong's voice as he answered. "Yes they are all right and yes we have them under our control. Two separate vehicles were following them and Lieutenant Johnson elected to take defensive action. The lead car was CIA and they were able to disable it by over riding its computer system."

The President angrily pounded his fist into his opened hand. "What the hell is the damn CIA doing following them. I'll get Mathias' sorry ass over here to explain."

The President had fire in his belly when challenged and was one of the reasons why the General liked him. Though he was primarily a man of peace, he would have made a good military leader. But now was not the time to unleash that fire. "Remember, sir, we don't know if Director Mathias knows anything about it. It could be a rogue element within the agency. We're in the middle of dealing with a serious information leak that you believe came from one of your own cabinet members. The problem still is we have enemies within and we don't know who they are."

A weary President sank heavily into the large chair behind his desk. "Yes, there are very few we can trust completely and that saddens me. You said there were two cars. Who was in the second."

"At this point we don't know. They couldn't identify the car so they couldn't override its computer. So they took more aggressive action to disable it and capture the occupants for interrogation. That is why they are now at a safe house in New Jersey."

"Who do you think they are?"

"I think they are probably Russian. So doesn't Johnson."

"Jesus. And you think that we should still leave Kate Peters out there. I don't mean to sound cold hearted, but she is much too valuable to let her get killed. Or, worse yet, fall into the wrong hands."

"That's exactly why I think we should leave her where she is. I know I can trust Lieutenant Johnson and his team. They are dedicated to protecting her. They are the best, and have the most sophisticated resources at their disposal to protect her. I think our best chance is to go with what we know and let this play out while we continue to try to de-bug the program with our own team."

"Okay, General. I'll defer to your judgment. You're much more experienced at this sort of thing than I."

"Thank you, sir. I also feel good about this Logan. My gut tells me he is the kind of guy you would want next to you in a tight spot. He could be our ace in the whole."

"Good. Now tell me, how is project 'Red Sky'? We might need it more than ever if the Millennium Project remains non-functional."

"It's not ready to be fully operational, but it will be ready for limited use if necessary."

"I'm afraid it may have to be."

# CHAPTER 25

▼

# ESTATE OF VICTOR NOBLE
# FIVE P.M., FRIDAY
# DECEMBER 24, 1999
## EIGHT DAYS TO 0 0

He glanced at the expensive antique grandfather clock, located prominently against the opposite wall, for the third time in ten minutes. Victor Noble was waiting anxiously for David Ford, now five minutes late. He didn't like it when people were late for meetings. Especially when they had some explaining to do. And Ford had some explaining to do. Noble had on the flat screen television set that was usually concealed in a combination communications and entertainment wall unit to the left and slightly behind him. The set was on but the volume was down and he wasn't paying attention to it. He wanted to make sure he didn't miss the six o'clock news.

Finally there was a wrap on the door before it was opened by Hans, his 'assistant', who ushered David Ford into the office. No one got in to see Noble without going through Hans. "As you instructed, sir. Here is Mr. Ford." He then waited at the door until receiving the signal it was all right to leave them alone.

A harried David Ford offered his greeting and his hand, "Hello, Victor. I'm sorry that I'm late, but I wanted to get as much information as I could before we met."

An irritated Victor Noble didn't rise from his seat or offer his hand in return. "I see. And what have you found out?"

Ford let the insult pass as he had done many times before. "We lost the subjects because of a mechanical failure of our agent's vehicle."

"What type of mechanical failure?"

"Apparently their car's computer system either failed or was deliberately shut down."

Victor Noble's impatience continued to grow as he began to stroke his mustache with the tip of the index finger of his left hand. "Which is it? Did it fail or was it deliberately shut down?"

"We're not completely sure. But it looks like it was deliberately shut down to disable the car."

"If I understand you correctly, you're telling me that someone accompanying the subjects was able to override the CIA computer and take and keep control of the vehicle."

"Yes, except we don't know if they were with the subjects or following them like us."

"Either way, we are dealing with some highly sophisticated people. Aren't we?"

"Yes. I think we are."

"Then we can't wait any longer. We have to take her now."

"I'm not sure I agree, but right now that doesn't really matter."

"Oh! Why not?"

"Because we haven't been able to find them yet."

"Why not? You should be able to zero in on the transmitter."

"That's the problem. We haven't. That area of New Jersey is pretty rural and the range of the transmitter is limited to a half mile radius."

"How many teams do you have on it?"

"Two."

"Only two. How the hell do you expect to find him with only two teams looking for them?"

"I wasn't really so concerned because we know they are headed for Boston and I have a unit at each of the major routes leaving New Jersey and heading in the direction of Boston. I knew we could just wait and they would eventually come to us."

"I see. Well that's really not good enough. Is it, David!"

David Ford wasn't in the mood for another one of Noble's lectures on his shortcomings and how he would show him how it should be done. When he turned away from Noble's cold stare the picture on the large, silent screen surprised him. The President was taking the podium at what appeared to be the start of a press conference.

"David! Are you with me?"

Angrily, Victor Noble followed the fixed stare of his companion and was equally shocked at what he saw. He immediately turned up the volume. It was too early for the six o'clock news, yet here was the President discussing the problems related to the federal welfare payments administered to by the states. He was already addressing the problem that wasn't suppose to be made public until the nightly news according to the sources he used to leak the information. The two men looked at each other, but neither said a word. They waited and watched in silence as the President addressed the problem and then outlined the back up procedures being put in place to alleviate any inconvenience this Y2K failure might have caused.

As much as he disliked him, Victor Noble had to admire the President on his ability to address and control an audience. No matter how difficult that audience may be. He handled most questions personally and effectively brought in Treasury Secretary Calderon, and other members of the cabinet, to add some details. More importantly, having the full cabinet there and ready to participate demonstrated the support that the President enjoyed among them. It also was not lost on Victor Noble that his public exclusion from the group had escalated their war. It was winner take all.

When the press conference was over, the Deputy CIA Director turned back to Noble and struggled to just barely keep the smirk off his face and out of his voice. "Well, I guess that knocks the shit out of that leak undermining his authority," he said. He thought about asking him if he was invited but thought better of it, wishing now he had said nothing at all.

Noble took his time shutting off the television and turning slowly to stare at Ford with an icy glare. Absently stroking his mustache, he used this time to regain his composure. "Yes it does, David. And it is one more reason to take her now. Not later. I don't want to argue with you about it. I want you to put enough resources on it to find them. Tonight. Is that understood."

"I understand."

helicopters to circle the area. Use as many as you have to."

A frustrated David Ford almost bit his tongue as he replied, "I understand, Victor."

"Good. Then do it."

Noble then swiveled in his chair until his back was to Ford and, as if on cue, Hans came in to usher the Deputy Director out. That was fine with Ford, he wasn't going to offer him his hand this time, either. Screw Victor Noble and all the other higher ups in his career that were just like him. He knew how to do his job better than they did. After all, hadn't he located the subjects an hour ago.

▼

# CHAPTER 26

# SAFE HOUSE, RURAL NEW JERSEY FIVE P.M., FRIDAY DECEMBER 24, 1999

## EIGHT DAYS TO 0 0

In the large central room of the old farmhouse sat Nick Logan, Kate Peters, Lieutenant Eric Johnson, and several other members of his crew. The remainder of his crew, as well as the security team, was occupied with their duties. It had been a long and frustrating day for Nick and Kate and they were trying to relax and enjoy what they could of the Christmas spirit. Not going anywhere, they accepted the drinks Eric offered. Nick a scotch and Kate a vodka tonic. The others joined them with various soft drinks, Eric with ice water. They were obviously still on duty and not ready to completely relax.

The conversation was light and the tension level declining when a private entered from the kitchen and announced that the President was about to hold a special press conference. An unscheduled presidential press conference always generated a lot of interest, but on Christmas Eve it was electric. Everyone was immediately alert as the private put on the television. The President was just entering the room and taking the podium. No words were spoken but the looks shared by Nick, Kate and Eric expressed their deep concern as the President began to speak.

The President was his usual calm and confident self as he deftly explained the current problem that existed with the federal governments welfare payments as a result of the Year 2000 computer problem. He went on to briefly outline the back up procedures that were in place if the problem wasn't resolved in the next week. He also took advantage of the opportunity to assure the country that the primary social security payment system was not affected and was Y2K compliant. He went on to emphasize that this was a good indication of how the administration and the financial, business, and other leaders of the country worked together to avert any potential crisis, and how they would do so for any of the other Y2K related problems that might arise.

The President then opened the floor for questions. He adeptly handled most of them himself, but strategically involved members of his cabinet to answer in more detail when appropriate. The press corps was obviously pleased with the candor with which their questions were answered. After thirty minutes total, the President was able to conclude what appeared to be a very successful press conference. Once again, he had showed himself to be a master of the podium.

When he was done and the television turned off, Kate was puzzled and had to ask Nick, "Why would he pick Christmas Eve to hold such a press conference?"

He thought for a long moment and then responded, "He must have been forced to."

Kate was a little surprised at the response. "Who can force the President of the United States?"

"The press," Nick answered. "They must have been going to announce it on the six o'clock news. Otherwise he would have waited until after Christmas to announce it."

Eric was impressed with Nick's observation and gave a little smile as he agreed. "He obviously went on the offensive to steal the thunder and short circuit whoever leaked the information to the media. That's good. I like that. It shows strength."

Nick took notice of the little smile but couldn't have been more serious when he added, "He certainly is very effective. You would never guess the tremendous pressure he must be under right now."

Both Kate and Eric knew that Nick was referring to the failure of the missile system programs, but neither responded. There were others present who were not aware of the situation and there was nothing new to add at this point anyway. It had not gone unnoticed by them that there were no questions at the press conference concerning the military's preparedness for the dawn of the new millennium. The President had long ago declared that any such discussion was off limits in the interest of national security. Besides, it was Christmas Eve and no one wanted to deal with Y2K any further this night.

The security staff had prepared quite an impressive dinner, by military standards, and had taken their seats at a long, rustic dining table. It was during dinner that Lieutenant Johnson introduced Kate and Nick to Corporal Ed Maxwell. He was in charge of the six-member Special Forces team that was their host and provided the security for the small compound. Eric informed them they were confined to the large common room or their sleeping quarters. A guard would accompany them or be outside of their rooms at all times. They were not to attempt to go anywhere else without his or Corporal Maxwell's consent.

Once again, Nick didn't like the military style of the orders and strongly suggested that he and Kate should be armed if they were in such danger. His suggestion was ignored as Eric Johnson finished his dinner and excused himself. He needed to check in with the rest of his men. Corporal Maxwell having already abruptly taken his leave a few minutes earlier. It was only eight o'clock, but it had been a long day and they were tired, so Nick and Kate retired to their respective bedrooms. As promised, there was a guard outside in the hall. Nick was disappointed with the arrangements. He would have loved to be able to get out and find out what was so interesting in the barn.

The compound was closely watched from the woods, some fifty yards away, as Lieutenant Johnson opened the door and prepared to cross the open yard from the farmhouse to the barn. This was the only activity seen since the surveillance started ten minutes earlier. He also observed there were no guards posted outside of either building and that troubled Egor Skulsky. There should be guards posted. They had captured two of his fellow agents and should be on the alert for the possibility of others. But they weren't. Or at least they didn't appear to be.

Perhaps he had missed them. The infrared binoculars were very effective, but they didn't turn night into day. There was very little light coming from the house or the barn, and there was only a quarter moon with slightly overcast skies, without the field glasses visibility was limited to a just few yards. He slowly scanned the entire open area around the buildings. The area was heavily wooded, but had been cleared of all trees for at least fifty yards in every direction, creating a buffer zone between the woods and the buildings that would be difficult to cross without being seen. That is if anyone was watching, and they had to be watching.

The subtle signal had gone unnoticed by the others at the dinner table, but it brought Corporal Maxwell to a stage one alert. Coming from Private Stapleton, his subordinate in charge of monitoring the surveillance system, meant there were possible intruders. As soon as they were alone, in the state of the art control room, the Private briefed his superior on the situation. The heat seeking sensors had detected the presence of six large life forms, located in the woods in front of the farmhouse. They were too deep in the woods to be seen by infrared. At first, it was thought they could be some of the many deer in the area, which frequently set off the alarms, but the behavior of these forms was not that of deer.

The Private went on to inform Corporal Maxwell that the six forms had initially appeared moving as a group towards the front entrance of the house until, within twenty yards of the edge of the woods, they stopped and two moved off to the right, two to the left, and the remaining two moving forward to within ten yards of the clearing. The two groups moving left and right stopped approximately thirty yards on either side of the center group. This meant, whoever it was out there, they had a clear view of the front and both sides of the farmhouse.

Almost as soon as the heat sensors had indicated the presence of possible intruders, Private Stapleton had seen the signal from Alpha 1, a red light on the board in sector A—the front of the house. The presence of the light, without a verbal communication, meant that there were intruders too close to risk radio contact. The control center's response was transmitted to Alpha 1 via the receiver in his wristwatch, the three short vibrations felt in his wrist told him that his message was received, they also observed the intruders, and to make verbal communication when possible. Simultaneously transmissions were sent to Alpha's 2 and 3 alerting them as to activity in sector A, to remain where they were, and to await further instructions. Then Private Stapleton quickly stepped from the control center, took three steps down the hall, saw Corporal Maxwell observe him, and quickly returned to his post. It was not by accident that the Corporal sat with his back to the wall. This had taken less than two minutes from the first detection of the intruders.

Ivan Malenkov watched his comrade closely, amazed at his display of control. Not normally a patient man, he was stocking his prey like a big, hungry cat. It began when they first arrived and took up the current position. Though pressed for time, he worked quietly and cautiously, making sure they didn't walk into a trap. He quickly dispersed the other four agents that accompanied them, sending two to the left flank and two to the right, with detailed instructions of what to watch for, and to wait for word from him before moving from the assigned posi-tions.

It was Malenkov who was getting impatient, knowing they were running out of time. "What do you think, Egor?" He whispered.

"There doesn't appear to be many of them. There are no guards anywhere on the perimeter," Skulsky whispered back as he continued to scan the area. He low-ered his field glasses and looked at Malenkov, "There's something wrong."

"What?"

"I don't know," he said, hesitating for a moment. "It's too easy."

Once Corporal Maxwell entered the surveillance room, it took less than a minute for Private Stapleton to summarize the situation and display the six intruders on a second, larger monitor. The infrared still showed nothing, meaning they proba-bly wore camouflage, as well as staying concealed. The woods were thick, but not that thick. Anyone simply walking in the woods would show up as they moved between the trees. The monitors of the other two sectors showed nothing, but what was expected, Alpha's 2 and 3. Because of the limited manpower there were only three sectors, but placed in a triangle, with Alpha 1 in the front and Alpha's 2 and 3 at each side towards the rear, they were able to get complete visible cover-age of the perimeter of the farmhouse.

Quickly assessing the situation, Corporal Maxwell immediately confirmed there was no activity in the other sectors and ordered Alpha's 2 and 3 to reposi-tion themselves to the front corners of the house, and prepare to repel a frontal assault. He then stepped from the control room just in time to stop Lieutenant Johnson, before he closed the door and descended the stairs. The Lieutenant didn't hesitate to respond to the Corporal's urgent request to close the door and join him in the control room.

Once there, no time was wasted in bringing him up to date on the situation. No sooner had the Corporal finished than a transmission came through from Alpha 1. "Control. Alpha 1." The transmission was clear and crisp, even though the tone of voice clearly indicated he was whispering. The security force was equipped with MicroForce personal communicators, linked through the MF secure satellite and extremely sensitive.

"Alpha 1. This is leader," Corporal Maxwell responded, as he pushed the but-ton that would tie in Alpha's 2 and 3. "Status report on intruders."

"Confirm six intruders, heavily armed, dressed in black with black ski masks." Alpha 1 didn't waste time indicating their position, they would already know this, he supplied them with information they wouldn't have.

"No markings on them?" Corporal Maxwell asked, as he looked at Eric Johnson The Lieutenant had informed him that any number of agencies, the FBI, state and local police, US Marshals, even the D.E.A., could be looking for the subjects in his protection. All of these agencies would wear markings that clearly identified them, it was standard operating procedure to prevent accidental shootings.

"None, sir. Solid black."

The Corporal paused for a moment, still looking at Eric Johnson, then continued with the orders he had to give. "This is leader one to all personnel. We are now on full alert for operation—Defend. Repeat. Operation Defend." This told everyone that it was to be a purely defensive operation. The targets would be allowed to leave the area if they made no attempt to approach the house or the barn. Once they entered the clearing it would be considered an assault on the house and dealt with accordingly. They would be allowed to proceed approximately halfway across the clearing, about twenty-five yards, when the high intensity floodlights, concealed at the peak of the house and the barn, would turn night into day. If they did not immediately respond to the command to lower their weapons, they would be fired upon with deadly force; caught in crossfire from the farmhouse and the soldiers in the field they would face almost certain death.

The Corporal's hesitation came from the information that Eric Johnson had provided upon arrival. The two men that had been captured earlier that day were most probably Russian, the Lieutenant was ninety-five percent sure of it, and he would have no trouble defending his subjects from such a clear enemy. Young and eager, he would welcome the opportunity, but he did not relish the thought of firing upon fellow Americans who were carrying out orders. The men in the disabled car were CIA and it would be very much like them to carry out a clandestine operation, especially after the embarrassment earlier in the day.

The general alert was a signal for the guard in the hall to move the subjects down stairs, into the central room, where they could be better protected and quickly moved to the basement, if need be. He directed Nick and Kate to the back corner of the room, away from any windows or doors, instructed them to stay there, and took his place at the left front window. Corporal Maxwell had already taken his position at the right front window. Both were armed with M-16's and 9-millimeter side arms, as were the soldiers in the field. These firearms were a good combination of mobility and firepower. The heavy artillery came from two .50-caliber machine guns, one each located on the roofs of the farmhouse and the barn. Operated by remote control from the surveillance room, they were currently manned by Private Stapleton and could be locked on to the heat seeking sensors if desired.

Lieutenant Johnson had immediately notified the MF team of the situation. They already had the barn secured, but they needed to be alert to the need to assist in the defense of the farmhouse. He didn't expect they would be needed to defend against only six intruders. However, things could change quickly in battle, his team, and Casper, had to be ready to move rapidly.

When they were hurried downstairs, still arranging their clothing, Nick again protested they should be armed and able to protect themselves, if necessary. Once again, he was refused and not pleased. As they took a seat on the floor, in the corner of the room, Nick clearly positioned himself in front of Kate as her protector. It was a futile move, he wasn't even armed, but his concern for her and his bravery was not lost on Kate, as she looked around for an avenue of escape, she also wished they were armed. She appreciated the professionalism and commitment of the men around her, but she preferred to defend herself. She was more than capable of doing so.

Although he was the senior agent in charge, Ivan Malenkov would defer to the judgment of his comrade when he was displaying caution in a combat situation. Egor Skulsky was always ready to fight, but he was not suicidal. Still time was running out and they would have to move shortly or abort the mission. "The helicopters will soon be here. We are going to have to move now or call it off." When informed earlier of the location of their target they were told they would have a small head start on the CIA, who would be using helicopters to move in quickly. Their plan was to be into position near the farmhouse and use the helicopters as a distraction to get in, get their target, and get out. It was a daring plan and counted heavily on the element of surprise for its success.

"We'll go," Egor Skulsky answered. He brought the small radio to his mouth to signal the other agents. "Get ready. We go in ten seconds."

The agents checked their weapons, AK-47 assault rifles, and moved to the edge of the clearing, ready to bolt across the opening as soon as the helicopters were directly over the farmhouse.

When the alert came from Private Stapleton, Corporal Maxwell rushed to the control room, followed closely by Lieutenant Johnson. The Private informed them that he had just picked up the sound of aircraft close by and then they saw them on the monitor, picked up by the infrared scanners, three helicopters, just above the tree tops, coming fast.

Prepared for this possibility, they immediately knew what to do without saying a word. Corporal Maxwell ordered the aerial spotlights turned on, to blind the pilots as much as to illuminate the helicopters, and Lieutenant Johnson went to the central room and ordered Kate and Nick to follow him. The firmness of his command and the tension in his voice removed any thought of resistance on their part; they followed his orders without protest.

He led them down the narrow stairs to a musty, dirt floor basement and through a small doorway, bringing them into a narrow passage. It was dark, the only light coming from Eric's flashlight, with a low ceiling; not even Kate could stand erect. Fortunately it only took a few minutes to cover the one hundred foot length of the tunnel and they quickly found themselves in the middle of another dark basement. They immediately recognized Private Kincaid who was guarding the tunnel entrance and then stayed behind, covering their backs, as Lieutenant Johnson led them up the stairs.

When they entered the large, open room it looked more like the inside of an airplane hangar than the old barn it appeared to be from the outside. In the middle of the room was an aircraft that looked like a hybrid between a helicopter and plane, as Kate and Nick saw Casper for the first time; they stopped where they were to look at the craft before them. It was almost as big as a Huey transport, yet it was as sleek as an Apache helicopter. While it had a main rotor blade, like a typical helicopter, it was much smaller and, unlike any helicopter they had ever seen, it had short stubby wings with small jet engines at the end of each wing. It also had a larger jet engine at the tail of the craft, where the anti-torque tail rotor would normally be.

Nick couldn't contain himself any longer as he yelled to Eric Johnson, "What the hell is that?"

The Lieutenant turned to face Nick, the uncharacteristic trace of a smile on his face, and answered like a proud father answered, "That, sir, is Casper. Our friendly ghost ship."

A puzzled and very curious Kate asked, "Is it a helicopter or a plane?"

Eric knew they didn't have time for this so he answered quickly, "Neither and both. For lack of a better description we call it our jet-copter." He then motioned for them to come with him. "But come. We don't have time for this now. Later."

Both Nick and Kate hesitated, as Nick asked, "Aren't those helicopters I hear outside? Isn't it dangerous to try to take off? Won't they shoot us down before we can even get airborne?"

Then Kate, looking hard at Eric, spoke, "I would feel much safer on the ground. Especially if I was armed with one of those." She pointed to the unusual, and lethal looking, assault rifle carried by Private Nelson.

The thought that she could probably handle one was a little unsettling to Eric, as he responded, "No they won't shoot us down. No it isn't safer on the ground. No you can't have one of those." He was running out of patience, as he pointed to the aircraft and said, "On the ground Casper can't do much to protect us, but in the air she is the best protection you will ever have. Now get in."

Believing him, and also expecting to be forced if they refused, Nick took Kate by the arm and led her into the aircraft. They were quickly led to two seats at the rear of the cabin and strapped in by Private Peterson, who then took his naviga-tor's seat just in front of them. Lieutenant Johnson took his place in the co-pilot's seat, as Corporal Semanski already occupied the pilot's seat. Corporal Anderson and Private Wilson manned the fire stations on either side of the cabin. Each fire station had a .50-caliber machine gun and a battery of rockets; this was in addi-tion to the fire station at the front of the craft that could be operated by either pilot. A fourth gun and battery of rockets, complete with an infrared camera, was located at the rear of the aircraft and could be operated by remote control from any of the other fire stations

The sound of the helicopters intensified, as they approached the rear of the farm-house, and his men began to move forward. That's when it hit him, and he immediately located the agents on his right, scanning the woods behind them he saw the movement. Approximately twenty yards behind them was a soldier with his rifle positioned to fire. That was it. There were no guards because they didn't need any. They knew they were there, which meant they had sophisticated sur-veillance equipment, and would allow them to enter the clearing, catching them in a deadly crossfire.

Egor Skulsky grabbed Malenkov's arm, stopping him from entering the clear-ing, as he radioed the other agents and aborted the operation seconds before they stepped into the open. He quickly instructed them of the enemy behind them and the possibility of more in the area. They were to head for the pre-arranged meeting location, but not directly. They should make a wide swing to avoid the enemy directly behind them and to make sure they weren't followed. That's when they heard the gunfire and turned to see the action at the farmhouse.

Casper was equipped with retractable wheels, lowered from the landing skid, allowing the craft to maneuver on the ground, like an airplane. As Private's

Kincaid and Nelson opened the large barn doors, Corporal Semanski pushed the throttle forward and Casper roared from the barn and streaked down the road under heavy fire from the helicopters overhead. Though hit a number of times, there was no damage done to Casper's multi-layered 'skin'; it was capable of withstanding much heavier fire.

Certain there was nothing above them, Corporal Semanski pulled back sharply on the stick, the wing mounted jet engines automatically tilting to a ninety degree angle, and the aircraft leaped straight into the air. Rapidly climbing to three hundred feet, the altitude of the other helicopters, Lieutenant Johnson fired a warning burst from his machine gun to alert the other aircraft they were heavily armed and were more than capable of defending themselves, as well as withstanding any attack from them.

The weapons on Casper were extremely accurate, guided as they were by a laser beam that fed information back to the aircraft's computer. The special helmets each of the crew wore contained a computer chip capable of sending and receiving information from the main computer and, using the controls on the arms of their seats, they could direct their fire to precisely where they were looking. This allowed Eric to put his fire just to the left of the pilot, hoping to scare him off.

Unfortunately, when one of the enemy helicopters fired a rocket at Casper and another fired one that hit the barn, causing heavy damage and possibly injuring or killing members of his team, Eric Johnson was left with no choice but to fire to disable or kill. He knew that Casper could evade the rockets, as it had done with this one, and even survive a direct hit, but he had ordered his men and Corporal Maxwell's security team to fire only to warn them off, which left those on the ground very vulnerable. Before another rocket could be fired, he released a short, deadly burst and turned the helicopter firing on the barn into a ball of flames, lighting up the night sky, before it plummeted to the ground.

As the two pilots watched their fellow pilot and his crew crash and die, Corporal Semanski had brought Casper to a position directly behind the remaining two helicopters. They had only hesitated for a few seconds and were shocked to find that their target had already maneuvered behind them. When the burst of fire all but tore off their landing skids the pilots called off the attack, took evasive action and flew off in different directions.

Private Peterson manned the radar and had the precise locations of both retreating helicopters. With the jet engines at only half throttle, Casper's vastly superior speed allowed Corporal Semanski to chase one, break off, and then the other; both pilots thought he was after them. When it was clear they would not be returning, he broke the chase off completely and returned to the farmhouse. Lieutenant Johnson had already confirmed that no one on the ground was hurt, even though the barn had been heavily damaged.

He also learned from Corporal Maxwell that the intruders on the ground had retreated and were no longer in the area. A few passes over the perimeter, using Casper's heat seeking and infrared sensors, confirmed that the area was clear. Of course, they would not be able to stay at the compound now. The fireball in the sky, the noise of the crash, and the gunfire were sure to draw attention; they were not that isolated. Corporal Maxwell and his squad would cordon off the area and place it under military control. It was an unfortunate accident of a military helicopter on a routine training mission and was off-limits to all civilians, including the local and state police. A complete media black out of the incident would be ordered in the name of national security. It would be weeks before the paper work caught up with the fact Corporal Maxwell had no authority to issue such an order. By then it wouldn't matter and Corporal Maxwell didn't exist as far as the military was concerned.

Lieutenant Johnson ordered privates Kincaid and Nelson to immediately get the two vehicles out of there and met them at Hanscom Air Force Base in Massachusetts. He then ordered Corporal Semanski to head northeast for the base. Eric had also determined not to report this incident to his superiors, neither General Armstrong nor the Silver Fox, for he was certain they would order him to bring Kate Peters in. Eric still didn't fully understand why he was being allowed to use her as bait. He was sure there was more he didn't know, but if he knew how much danger she was in the President would never leave her out here.

# CHAPTER 27

▼

# ABANDONED WAREHOUSE— MOSCOW THREE P.M., SATURDAY DECEMBER 25, 1999

## SEVEN DAYS TO 0 0

The barren office in the old warehouse was cold and the small wood stove, fighting the minus thirty-degree outside air, struggled to keep the temperature inside above freezing. Dimitry Petrov sat in one of the old wooden chairs and shared a bottle of vodka with his comrade, Stephan, who sat in the other; both huddled close to the warm metal to get all of its meager heat. Neither had spoken in the last half-hour, each lost in their own thoughts.

It was Christmas day and he missed his children. Not that this day had much meaning in the Russia of his time, but he would always manage to be with at least one of his children. It saddened him to think of how long it had been since he saw his little Katya and now Yuri too was gone. There was little comfort in knowing they were probably much warmer than he; after all, he had put their lives at great risk. And for what?

What he had just learned from Stephan troubled him deeply. His comrade was a trusted aide of Prime Minister—Sergei Ivanov and, as such, was privy to a great deal of sensitive information. Especially since President Sokolov, as a result of his failing health, had taken to including the Prime Minister in all of his important meetings. And the Prime Minister liked to share his thoughts with his aide. It made Dimitry wonder if so many years of forced silence now worked to make some of his countrymen too talkative. In any event, it worked to his benefit.

There had been a meeting earlier in the day between Boris Stepovich, President Sokolov, and, at the President's insistence, Prime Minister Ivanov. The subject of the meeting was the approaching new millennium and the impending crisis the dawn of 2000 would bring. The President didn't need to be reminded Russia was not in good shape for the Year 2000 problem. Not the least of his concerns was the country's power grid; widespread power failures were expected

The Director's statement generated the negative effect he had expected, and would make President Sokolov more receptive to his plan. He waited a moment, letting the President fully reflect on the situation, before he spoke again. He then informed President Sokolov the United States nuclear missile system would not be operable once the year 2000 dawned. He assured the President his information was from the highest sources and could be relied upon.

Given all of the problems he had to deal with in the poverty-stricken Russia, he was pleased to hear the United States was having some serious problems of its own, but he didn't see how this could be of help to them. The President was shocked when Director Stepovich proposed taking advantage of the situation by holding the threat of a nuclear attack over their head; an attack they could not respond to. He reminded the President their system had been tested and would function properly when the year turned to 2000, and they should take advantage of the situation. Specifically, the Americans should pay substantial sums of money, dissolve NATO, and not oppose the return of the Communists to power—among other things.

Dimitry expected Stepovich knew of Yuri's late night, last minute adjustment to the program, and that neither he nor the President was in control of the Russian missiles anymore. He did have to respect the Director's boldness in trying to pull off a bluff of this magnitude. That was until he heard the rest of the plan.

Because he was bluffing, not even able to fire a single missile to demonstrate he could, he proposed using the North Koreans to send the warning. Their nuclear missile capability was limited, but it was enough. Since it was a relatively new and simple system, it was Year 2000 compliant. The North Koreans had the ability to launch two medium range missiles. The targets—Tokyo and Taiwan.

The initial reaction of President Sokolov was one of shock. How could they get away with such a thing? How could they get the North Koreans to risk annihilation? But Boris Stepovich had expected the reaction, and the questions, so he continued on in a calm and rational tone; one belying the fact he was suggesting a course of action that could result in bringing on Armageddon.

The President was a tired man with failing health; he had dealt with one too many problems and was desperate for some light at the end of the tunnel. What at first sounded irrational started to take on the aspect of the possible and became more rational as the Director continued. It would be perfect, as one missile destroyed Tokyo, causing severe damage to the world's second leading economy; the second would destroy Taiwan, pleasing the Chinese very much.

The destruction of Tokyo would hurt the western economies, and would show the United States could not, or would not, protect one of its most important allies. The Chinese would officially condemn the North Koreans, but unofficially would be very pleased. They would also officially oppose any nuclear retaliation so close to their borders.

The North Koreans would count on this 'protection' from the Chinese, especially since it was an unfortunate accident. A malfunction in the early warning system caused by the Millennium Bug, and setting off a chain of events, out of the control of the North Koreans, leading to the tragedy. But how could they be blamed? The CIA had been advising of the very real possibility of an early warning system malfunction in the Russian system for over two years. They never thought it would automatically cause the missiles to fire, but they really had no way of knowing how inter-related the North Korean system was. The Chinese would not only secretly welcome the destruction of Taiwan, but it would remove a sticky political issue for the rest of the world, most particularly the United States. And years of hatred of the Japanese by the Koreans would be avenged by the destruction of Tokyo.

In any event, the communist leaders of North Korea were desperate to remain in control. And, with their economy in shambles and most of their population starving, they were prepared to take drastic measures.

By the time Boris Stepovich was through, President Sokolov was giving serious consideration to his proposal. He ordered the Director to continue with these plans under the utmost secrecy, but he was not to implement any of it; he needed more time to think it through and would get back to him in a day or two.

Dimitry was stunned by the time Stephan was finished with his report. He couldn't believe even Boris Stepovich would propose a plan that would kill millions of people and threaten the world with a devastating war. It was lunacy; he was crazy. The thought haunted him; maybe they were all a bunch of crazy, power hungry, old men who had little to lose and were willing to risk the future of the world in the name of some dream that was never to be.

He had to stop Boris Stepovich at all costs. He would go to President Sokolov and convince him that Director Stepovich was a madman, whose plan would destroy Russia. And that it was he who had the control of the nuclear missiles and not Stepovich, or the military, or the President. It was a dangerous move because he would risk exposing himself and being caught by Stepovich's men or being arrested by the President for treason.

In either case, he could not let them take him alive. No matter how strong he might be, he knew they would ultimately get the code. If things did go badly, and he couldn't convince President Sokolov, then he would get a message to Yuri to have Katya fix the US system so they would again have the missiles as a deterrent; a deterrent that had worked so effectively for so many years before he tampered with it.

What a foolish old man he was, he thought.

# CHAPTER 28

▼

# THE WHITE HOUSE— OVAL OFFICE ONE P.M., SUNDAY DECEMBER 26, 1999

## SIX DAYS TO 0 0

The General waited impatiently for the President to come down from his living quarters. He would rather have had more time to investigate and had this meeting tomorrow, but he knew the President wanted to be directly involved after hearing the preliminary report.

Earlier a senior aide had notified General Armstrong of a military training accident. Normally this wouldn't be brought to his attention on a Sunday; he would be briefed with the details first thing Monday morning. But this incident had the markings of something more than an unfortunate training accident. For starters, it was unlikely there would be any training exercises on Christmas Eve in the area, second, there were reports of gunfire, and, third, the military personnel on the ground were Special Forces; which was quite unusual. The General's extensive staff routinely scanned reports from many sources; information was important and the General never relied solely on others for his. If a staff member thought something didn't add up, or there appeared to be more to the story, they were authorized, and expected, to dig deeper. After completing a preliminary review, they would make a decision that it didn't warrant any further investigation or bump it up to the next level.

This incident had been bumped up to the next level, and the next, until it got to the desk of one of the General's senior aides. He was immediately aware the incident took place at a safe house for a top level operation, reporting directly to the General, and standard operating procedure was to notify General Armstrong on a high priority basis. The information was already a day old; that it occurred on Christmas Eve was no excuse.

Upon the President's arrival, the General placed a secure call to The Silver Fox; the incident took place at an MF safe house most recently used by his 'rogue' BODS unit.

Indeed the Silver Fox had received a call from Corporal Maxwell, just before midnight on Christmas Eve, informing him of the attempt on the safe house. The incident was of great concern to him, but of greater concern was Lieutenant Johnson's decision to go silent until late afternoon on Christmas Day. All attempts to communicate with the MF unit went unacknowledged; even those directly from the Silver Fox. This could only mean they were unable to communicate as a result of physical damage or capture; or they had become a real rogue unit. Given the report of Corporal Maxwell, it was very unlikely there was any physical damage to the aircraft or that they were captured.

The Silver Fox was angry and relieved when he received the transmission from Lieutenant Johnson. He was relieved to learn everyone and the aircraft were safe and currently at a remote hangar at Hanscom Field, and he was angry at the breach of procedures by the Lieutenant. He had to find out if the cover of being a rogue unit had become a reality. Had he and the General miscalculated Lieutenant Johnson? Was he so bent on avenging his brother he could no longer be trusted? The Silver Fox had to find out; he would have to see him in person. The Lieutenant's protest that it would delay their efforts and put Ms. Peters at greater risk was to no avail. He was to come in. The Silver Fox did allow him to leave Peters and Logan at the base with three of his men. They would be safe there for now. It would only take a half-day for the Lieutenant, and the rest of his crew to get here, have the meeting, and get back. Besides, it was one thing to attack a remote safe house and quite another to attack an air force base. Even if it was just a small Air Force contingent located there now; the rest of the base being turned over to civilian use. He was pleased the Lieutenant agreed to come in with his aircraft; it meant he had not become a rogue unit—not yet anyway. And he would not have to order Corporal Semanski to take command of the unit.

He had been meeting with Lieutenant Johnson and Corporal Semanski for the last hour when the call came. He wanted to be unavailable for the General, to have more time to question the Lieutenant, but he couldn't; he knew the call originated from the oval office and the President would be there. The Silver Fox went into a small inner office, steeling himself for what was to come and then spoke firmly, but calmly, "Good morning, General. You had a good holiday I trust?"

The General let a small smile come to his face, as always The Silver Fox was calm and in control, "Yes, thank you." Then the smile disappeared, "Until about an hour ago, anyway." Before he could respond, the General spoke again, "I'm here with the President and I'm putting you on the speaker phone."

"Hello, Mr. President. Merry Christmas."

The President's intensity level dropped slightly, "Thank you. Merry Christmas to you, too." Before this could continue any further, the President spoke, "What the hell happened the other night? Is everyone safe? And why wasn't I informed before this."

The Silver Fox stared at the empty seat across from him, as if the President were sitting there, before he responded. "Yes, Mr. President, everyone is perfectly safe. As to what happened, we're not totally sure at the moment. What we do know is there was an attack on the safe house, in an apparent attempt to capture or kill Ms. Peters. Of course this was quickly repelled by our people; she was never in any real danger."

"Not in any real danger!" The President said, as he turned to look at the General.

Before The Silver Fox could respond, the General added, "Our preliminary reports indicate there was heavy automatic weapons fire and one, maybe two, possible explosions. The report also indicates there was one helicopter downed, resulting in the loss of three lives."

The Silver Fox was impressed; the General's sources were good, so there was no sense in trying to deny it. "That's reasonably accurate."

"And you still think they were not in any real danger?"

"Yes. That's correct, Mr. President." He wasn't lying; he was confident it was true. "The result speaks for itself. None of our people were hurt and the enemy lost three of theirs and one of their aircraft."

A surprised President demanded, "One of their aircraft? How many were there?"

The Silver Fox was upset with himself for creating such an opening. Now he had to be careful, not knowing how good their information was, he couldn't lie. "My report indicates there were three helicopters."

"Three! Christ! That's it! I want them brought in now!" President Stewart ordered as he stabbed the desk in front of him.

"But, sir, she is much safer with us than if she is brought in," the Silver Fox stated. "We haven't made a positive identification of the helicopter and it's occupants, but the indications are it may be a rogue element of the CIA." He paused before giving him the next bit of news, information he was sure the General didn't have. "We also have proof the Russians were following them and were probably on the scene at the time of the incident." The two men captured hours before the attack had been identified.

"I have to agree with him, sir," the General said. "We know we have a serious leak in our internal security."

"General, are you telling me that even you don't have the resources to protect her?"

"No, I'm not. What I'm saying is MicroForce is the very best we have. They are the best equipped, the best manned, and the most mobile." The General hesitated before he spoke, he knew he had to remind the President of one of the main reasons they had allowed Kate Peters to remain out there under MF control. "They also have the ability to find out everything she knows, and we don't." General Armstrong paused again, before adding, "Time is running out."

Both the President and The Silver Fox knew what he was speaking of, but no one would say the words. Among the many chemical weapons the government was constantly adding to its arsenal was a new strain of drugs to add to its family of 'truth serums'. This strain, referred to as 'Know All', was particularly powerful, but also volatile. In the tests done on prison volunteers, the ability of the drug to reveal everything the subject knew was remarkable. The problem was, fifty percent of the test subjects had developed irreparable brain damage and were little more than vegetables. It was determined to be safest when it was slowly introduced into the body over a minimum of twelve, and preferably twenty-four, hours. Know All would produce results in as quickly as an hour, but the affect on the subject was always catastrophic when done this quickly.

"Yes, it is," agreed the President. Then he addressed the Silver Fox, "So let's compromise. We'll bring her in, but leave her under MF control at your estate. Hell damn few people know where you live. I don't. Then we can begin to slowly learn what she knows; hopefully it will be what we need to know."

Kate Peters would remain in the control of MF because it would be much harder for anyone to discover what they had done; since very few people knew they existed. They all regretted the use of Know All on someone like Kate Peters, who just might be an innocent person in the wrong place at the wrong time. But this was an issue of national security of the highest level and they would have to take that chance. However, it could never be linked back to the President or his administration in any way. His enemies, particularly Victor Noble, would have a field day with it. The President of the United States linked to the use of an illegal drug that could have, or did, destroy the brain of a young woman, innocent or not, would be devastating. How could he have let things get this far out of control?

"With all do respect, sir. We can do that without bringing her in and risking her discovery." The Silver Fox found himself repeating much the same argument that he had just received from Lieutenant Johnson. "The attack on the safe house shows us how desperate these forces are to get to her, and the intelligence resources available to them."

"Then why have you left Ms. Peters and Mr. Logan at Hanscom Field with only three of the MF crew and no aircraft?" The General asked and then added, "And where is Lieutenant Johnson and Casper now?"

"They have been left there temporarily while I had Lieutenant Johnson fly up to my estate. I wanted a first hand report of the incident. They would be safe at the base for the few hours it would take the Lieutenant to come down here with the rest of his crew and the aircraft."

"And where are they now?" The President asked.

"I was satisfied with his report and comfortable he is in control of the situation. Therefore, I ordered him back to Hanscom Field to pick up the subjects and move them before they are discovered."

"That's a good idea," the General said. "I'll make sure they get additional protection and don't leave the base until Lieutenant Johnson arrives."

The Silver Fox interpreted it to mean they were under 'house' arrest. "That would seem prudent until the Lieutenant can pick them up and move them to another safe house."

The President then ordered, "Once they arrive I want them to contact you and wait for your orders before they leave. The three of us will then discuss whether they should be allowed to remain out there or to come in. Is that understood?"

"Yes, Mr. President."

"Good. We'll speak then. Thank you."

The three men exchanged good-byes and the call was disconnected.

The Silver Fox hung up and returned to his study, taking his seat at his large desk with Lieutenant Johnson and Corporal Semanski still seated opposite him. He lightly stroked his short gray beard, lost in thought for a long moment before speaking. "The subjects, Peters and Logan, as well as the three MF crew members, are no longer free to leave the base. They are under protective custody until you return to pick them up."

"That doesn't present any problem," Lieutenant Johnson responded. "They shouldn't be leaving the base anyway."

"The problem is I then have to call the President and General Armstrong to discuss the next step." The Silver Fox leaned forward as he continued. "The President is going to order me to bring you in. At best, I will be able to bring you here. At worse he will confine you to Hanscom Field."

"He can't do that; you can't do that," exploded the Lieutenant. "That will put her at more risk and won't get us the information any of us want."

"He can and I will. If the President orders me to recall you I will have no choice. I won't ignore a direct order from the President. If I do I will be through and there is too much at stake for me to leave right now."

"You're too important to lose, but I'm not."

"Are you saying you would ignore my order and become a real rogue element?" He wasn't surprised by the Lieutenant's reaction; he counted on it.

"Yes, sir. I am."

"You realize your career will be through. And that's if you are successful; if not you probably will end up in jail."

"I understand. But if I fail it won't matter, and if I succeed I will at least be able to live with myself."

"You will be in it on your own. Your crew will just be following your orders; Corporal Semanski has never heard this conversation. Understood?"

"Understood," said Lieutenant Johnson.

"Understood," said Corporal Semanski.

"Good. But you can't take Casper back to Hanscom Field. If the President orders you to stay there we will have no choice. I can't condone the use of force against our own military."

"Neither could we," the Lieutenant said and the Corporal nodded agreement.

"You will have to contact your people and have them escape from the base. Then you can recover them and take them to a special safe house near the Quabbin Reservoir in western Massachusetts."

"Why there?" Eric Johnson asked. "Why not nearer to Boston where Kate wants to be?"

"For three reasons. One it is difficult to fully utilize the abilities of Casper in Boston, and it's now apparent we need all its capabilities. Two we need to start to introduce the drugs through her food. This will begin to get her ready and better prepared for a booster shot if it has to be done quickly. This will help the drug work better and give Ms. Peters a better chance of survival. This can be done over a period of a few days."

"But we're running out of time and we could add it to her food anywhere we are," Eric said. "Why spend two days hiding there?"

"That's the third reason. Time is our enemy, but we can turn it to our advantage. If we show patience we can let Ms. Peters and those who are after her get anxious, because time is running out, and they will make a mistake."

Eric Johnson wasn't sure he agreed, but wanted to keep the hunt alive so was willing to follow the directive. His muscles tensed as he spoke, "It's risky, sir, but whatever you think is best."

"Good," the Silver Fox said. As the Lieutenant and corporal started to get up to leave, he added, "There's one more thing." He waited for them to settle back in their seats. "You have to promise me you won't wait until the last minute to administer the booster shot. You will need a minimum of twelve hours, and preferably twenty-four, to give Ms. Peters a reasonable chance of not suffering brain damage. Let's remember there is no concrete evidence she knows anything at all. She just may be an innocent bystander."

A skeptical Eric Johnson asked. "Then why are people trying to kill her?"

"It could be because she is so knowledgeable about the system, or maybe because she knows something she is not even aware of. Regardless, she deserves the benefit of the doubt from us. Agreed?"

"Agreed."

"Good. Then you had better go."

After the phone conversation ended the President turned to General Armstrong and asked, "Do you think it worked?"

"Yes. I think it did."

"So Lieutenant Johnson and his crew will never show up at Hanscom Field?"

"That's right. They know you would order them in, and they would not be prepared to fight fellow soldiers."

"By not coming in he will become a true rogue, and his actions will be further removed from any link to the administration."

"And left on his own, Lieutenant Johnson will push it to the limit. He will do whatever is necessary, including as large a dose of Know All as required."

A very solemn President Stewart added, "Yes, General, the stakes are very high, and we have to use whatever means available. But it is unfortunate Ms. Peters may have to be sacrificed."

# CHAPTER 29

▼

# HANSCOM FIELD— BEDFORD, MASSACHUSETTS THREE P.M., SUNDAY DECEMBER 26, 1999

## SIX DAYS TO 0 0

It was just after three p.m. when Private Kincaid received the secure call from Lieutenant Johnson over the MF telecommunications system. The private quickly confirmed they had just been ordered by the base commander not to allow Ms. Peters or Mr. Logan to leave the base without his permission. The Lieutenant and the Private hastily formulated a plan. It was to be put into effect immediately, before the Commander decided to put them in a locked, guarded facility.

The plan was simple and Private Kincaid quickly explained it to the others. First Private Peterson would take one of the Explorers and leave it parked a short distance from the base. Then Privates Kincaid and Nelson would pose as Kate and Nick and attempt to leave the base in the other SUV. This would occupy the base security and the commander long enough for Kate and Nick to escape through the hole in the fence made by Private Peterson after he left the SUV and made his way back into the base. He would then take up a position opposite this escape route so that he could create another diversion if necessary.

It wasn't. The plan worked perfectly. The base, or what remained of it, was a low security facility and it was easy; almost too easy. The only hitch came when the base commander decided to detain Privates Nelson, Kincaid, and Peterson until he received further orders.

Nick and Kate had been instructed to wait a short period and then, if not joined by the MF team, to proceed toward Boston on their own. The MF team would catch up with them. They were only too happy to be free of their guardians and their orders, at least for a short while. Especially since they had each been given a 9mm Smith & Wesson in the event they were temporarily split up from the MF team.

As pre-arranged, Nick drove down route 93 towards Boston and Kate used the SUV's phone to get a room at the Marriott Long Wharf Hotel. They were to wait there until contacted by Eric Johnson. There were no adjoining rooms available, or even two rooms close together, so they settled for a room with two queen size beds.

Nick had often stayed there on his periodic trips back to Boston and used his personal organizer to get the Marriott's number. As he did so, he unknowingly activated the signal, and was picked up on the scanner of the CIA team covering the routes north of the city. They were easily followed on the screen as they crossed the Charles River, went south on Atlantic Avenue, and then pulled into the Marriott Long Wharf. The other two teams, who were covering the roads from the south and west, were immediately alerted and were now also converging on the hotel.

It was almost five o'clock when Lieutenant Johnson and his team hovered over Fenway Park. It was the home of the Boston Red Sox baseball team located within the heart of the city. Since it was winter there was not even security inside the park. It was an ideal place within the crowded city to land; running whisper quiet, using infrared without any lights, and in full anti-radar stealth mode it could do so unnoticed.

The base commander had detained his team members for a short time and then released them; indicating he had no real basis to hold them. They were now waiting outside the park in the Explorer. Once Casper landed, Lieutenant Johnson and Corporal John Anderson quickly disembarked and made their way out of the park; joining Privates Kincaid, Nelson, and Peterson on Lansdowne Street. Once in the vehicles, they immediately headed for the Marriott Long Wharf to find Kate and Nick. Eric had given Private Kincaid authority to do whatever necessary, short of attacking any of the Hanscom personnel, but he was very concerned that Kate and Nick were now out on there own. He could only hope they made it to the hotel so he could get a fix on them. The neck tracers had a limited range and they were not yet within it.

Nick had parked the Explorer in the hotel garage, not wanting to put it in the hands of a valet, and then checked in. Their room was on the second floor so they wouldn't have to worry about intruders getting in from outside the hotel. It was the first time they were really alone since the beginning of this journey, and the first time they had ever been alone in a hotel room together.

Nick was trying to relieve some of the tension in the room and the small courtesy bar in the corner seemed just the right thing. "How about a drink and something to snack on?"

"That sounds great. I'm starved," Kate said, as she kicked off her shoes and relaxed on the couch in the small sitting area. They hadn't eaten for hours and Kate needed to relax for a little while. More importantly she needed to get Nick to relax. "I'll have a glass of Chablis and all the snacks they have in there."

Nick grabbed a couple of small bottles of Chablis, two glasses, an arm full of snacks and dumped it all on the coffee table in front of them as he sat beside Kate. For a long while they said nothing as they ravaged the individual little bags of food in front of them: potato chips, nachos, mixed nuts, pretzels, corn chips, nothing was safe. Only after they ate everything did they lean back and sip their wine.

"Not exactly a gourmet meal by candle light," Nick observed.

Kate rewarded him with one of her warm, but rare smiles, and a gleam in her eye he had never seen before, as she responded, "No, but I enjoyed it." She then lightly touched his hand and added, "Especially since there is no one else here to see what pigs we made of ourselves."

Nick then gently took her hand in his and spoke softly, "As much as I want to be alone with you, I'm concerned we don't have any of the MF team with us. I hate to think of what might have happened to you at the safe house if they weren't there."

"But you were my knight in shining armor, there to protect me," Kate said only half jokingly. Then added more seriously, "I do appreciate that, Nick."

Nick held her hand more firmly, but still gently. "Then let me help you. I want to help you." He took her hand in both of his. "I know there is more to this than you are saying. Why are we here in Boston? Why do these people want to kill you?"

Kate put the fingertips of her other hand to his lips, and he instinctively kissed them. "Slow down, Nick. Things are not always so easily explained."

"Okay. I'm listening."

She hesitated for a moment as she lightly stroked his cheek. "My dear, sweet Nick, you're so intelligent and yet so naïve. With you everything is black or white, right or wrong."

"I've found things are usually that way; people simply create smoke screens to confuse and cover up."

"I'm afraid in my world there are many shades of gray."

Nick stroked Kate's cheek. "Tell me about your world. I want to understand."

Kate then leaned forward and kissed him lightly on the lips. "I need to shower. Then we'll talk."

As Kate started to get up, Nick pulled her close and kissed her deeply and she kissed him back. Kate wanted to stay in his arms and let him make love to her, but she knew she couldn't. She gathered herself and pulled back before she lost control, "Please, before we go any further I have to take a shower, it has been a long day."

"I know. Me too," Nick agreed. "You take yours first, but hurry.

Kate got up and headed for the bathroom, and Nick couldn't take his eyes off of her. The way the fabric of her slacks clung to her tight backside was mesmerizing. After she disappeared into the bathroom, Nick got up and went to his trench coat hanging in the closet. He retrieved the gun and cell phone given to him by Private Kincaid, his personnel organizer and another slim, metal box. He put the gun, phone, and organizer on the towel he had spread on the couch. Before adding the slim, metal box he opened it, took out a small round ball and gently tossed it into the air. He then added the box to the towel, wrapped everything up and waited for his turn to use the shower.

The hot water warmed her body and made her skin feel clean as the soap smelled fresh and sweet. She would have stayed there much longer; as it was, she stayed longer than she should have. When she finished, she dried herself off, wrapped one towel around her body and another around her head, although her hair wasn't wet. Gathering her clothes in a bunch she left the bathroom.

"It's all yours."

"Thanks. That was quick," Nick said. Adding, "I'll be out shortly"

"Take your time. It will take me awhile to dry my hair anyway," Kate responded. "I prefer to dry it with a towel rather than a blow dryer, so I can do it out here."

Nick closed and locked the door behind him, turned on the shower, and unwrapped his towel. Taking the slim, metal box he opened it and punched a few buttons. The small screen immediately lit up and displayed the entire bedroom. Kate was in the middle of the room as she removed the body towel and stood there naked. Nick felt guilty for not turning away, but he couldn't. For one, he had to observe everything she did, not knowing what might be important later. More importantly he found her intoxicatingly beautiful, and he felt something he knew went deeper than lust.

He felt guilty for spying on her at all; naked or clothed. When Eric Johnson had given him his own set of PIP's, and stated he might have to use them in this type of situation, he wanted to refuse to take them. But he had to concede it was his responsibility to keep an open mind and to help keep her under surveillance; no matter how distasteful he found it. Besides it could also help to keep her safe and to prove she was just an innocent victim, so he took them.

After she had slipped on her panties and bra, she removed the towel around her head and revealed her perfectly dry hair. She then quickly put on her black wool slacks, slid her sweater over her head, and put on her trench coat. Reaching into her right pocket she pulled out a plain, black scarf and put it over her head; pulling it close around her face. From her left pocket she pulled out the pistol and expertly checked the clip, it was the sixteen round version, illegal in this country. She put it in her right pocket, without removing her hand, and opened the outside door slightly. She checked the hallway, looked back in the direction of the bathroom, and then disappeared as she quickly closed the door behind her.

What was she doing? Was she leaving? Was she meeting someone? Nick was confused and disappointed as he watched her progress. Since the PIP was programmed to lock onto her, it automatically followed Kate down the hall. She was moving cautiously toward the main lobby. Nick put on his trench coat, checked his gun before putting it in his pocket, and followed Kate at a safe distance as he observed her on his control screen.

Kate constantly scanned the hotel lobby as she made her way across it to the bank of pay phones near the small gift shop. There was no one else using the phones so she had her choice and elected the one furthest from the gift shop and, therefore, the most secluded. Nick released another PIP and stationed it in the lobby opposite Kate so he could see the entire lobby, even though he was well out of the way and had the appearance of someone busy using a personal organizer. He then released a third PIP and sent it outside to scan the front entrance.

Whoever Kate was calling she obviously didn't want Nick or Eric Johnson to know about it. Otherwise she would have used the personal communicator Eric had given them when he took away their cell phones. He explained their cell phones used the commercial transmission network and could easily be traced. The personal communicator, on the other hand, was untraceable.

As Kate dialed the special number, she turned her back to the lobby to shield the keypad and prevent anyone from copying it. Anyone that is except Nick who was observing the number dialed on his screen as it was transmitted by the PIP that was above and slightly behind Kate's right shoulder. He wished he could remember how to turn on the sound.

It was a number that connected her to a cell phone through a network which was difficult, but not impossible, to trace. It rang twice before it was answered.

Security dictated that Pasha answer the phone to prevent the recognition of Yuri's voice by any unfriendly caller who somehow obtained the number. "Hello. Who is this?"

There was a pre-determined script to follow.

"This is an old friend," Kate responded.

"An old friend of whom?"

"An old friend of Yuri's."

"Does this old friend have a name?"

"Yes."

"And what is that name?"

"That name is—Katya."

"And who is Katya?"

"Katya is the sister of Yuri and the daughter of Dimitry."

There was a pause and then an excited voice, "Katya, it is so good to talk to you again. It has been too long since we last spoke."

Kate had to brush away a tear as she felt the emotion, so long restrained, begin to well up from deep within her. "It's so good to hear your voice, Yuri." She took a deep breath and continued, "It has been much too long. How have you been? How is father?"

Yuri's voice now sounded tired, the excitement gone. "Father was good when I last saw him. And I am good; at least as good as can be expected in this difficult time."

"I know. It has been difficult and dangerous, but it will be over soon. And we can all be together again."

"Yes, it will be over soon. But how it will end, and that we will be together again, is not certain."

"But father has planned very carefully. We must trust his decision." Kate decided not to tell Yuri there had already been three attempts on her life.

"I'm not so sure, Katya. We need to talk. And then maybe we need to talk to father. We are playing with more than fire here; forces much more powerful than us."

"But father's plan has temporarily given us this power. The codes are the power to affect change; the changes father dreams of."

"But dreams are not reality, and maybe shouldn't be."

Kate didn't want to believe what she was hearing. All they had risked getting to this point and now Yuri seriously questioned what they were doing. She understood his concerns; she had them herself. What they were attempting was unthinkable and, yet, they were on the brink of pulling it off. They had to trust in their father; they always had and he had always been right.

She scanned the lobby as she continued, "Where are you now?"

"We're north of you; in southern Maine. We can be there in two hours."

"No! Don't do that. It's too dangerous here. I'll have to get away and get to you."

"Get away. Get away from whom? Are you all right?"

"I'll tell you all about it when we meet, but I'm all right for now," Kate said. Then she saw him. He was standing near the elevators to the parking garage. She caught him looking at her and he turned away a little too quickly. "I have to go, Yuri."

"Wait, Katya. You don't know where to meet us. We're in......"

"No! Don't tell me! I'll call you when I can. Good-bye," Kate said and abruptly hung up. She fought the urge to run and acted as if she were making another call; giving her a chance to find the others. Slowly scanning the lobby it wasn't long before she saw another suspicious man standing by the elevators and a third near the main entrance. They had covered all of her options. She would have to get by the man at the entrance. She didn't want to get trapped in the hotel and she certainly didn't want to get trapped in the garage. She completed her call and began moving slowly toward the main entrance; the men moved with her.

Watching Kate on the monitor Nick knew something was wrong. It wasn't long before he saw the three men. They were almost too obvious; as if they wanted her to know they were there so she would panic and make a mistake. He watched her hang up the phone and head for the main entrance. It's what he had expected, and hoped, she would do. They would have more options out there and the PIP had not picked up any sign of other enemies. But he would have to gain a little time to give them a chance to escape. The restaurant entrance was to the right of the main entrance and on the same side as Nick. There were small groups of people constantly coming and going from the restaurant as Nick made his way along the right side of the lobby and towards them. The large palms and other potted vegetation along the lobby wall helped him stay out of sight. He stopped behind one of these large palms to focus on his monitor. He hoped he remembered how to operate the other functions Eric had shown him better than he had the sound function.

Kate was about twenty feet from the entrance door, the man near the entrance had backed away to the left side of the lobby, the other two men were still some fifty feet behind her, and a group of diners were leaving the restaurant. He had to do it now. The two PIP's inside the lobby were in place above the men and all that was needed now was the proper command. He hoped for the best as he sent them on their way. The first one exploded in a small ball of flames a few feet in front of the two men closing in on Kate. The second exploded near the man at the entrance. The effect of the two small explosions and resulting fires caused the men to believe they were under attack and seek cover. It also caused the group leaving the restaurant to panic and hurry for the hotel entrance. Nick took the opportunity to join them and grab a stunned Kate as they swept by her.

Within seconds they were on the street in front of the hotel. Kate was happy to see it was Nick who grabbed her, as she relaxed her trigger finger on the gun in her pocket. Kate started to survey her environment to determine a direction to flee when Nick pulled her abruptly to the right.

"This way Nick ordered." There was no hesitation in his decision: he knew to the left was Boston Harbor and the Atlantic Ocean, straight ahead was an apartment building, and to the right was the heart of the city. As they sprinted the fifty yards to Atlantic Avenue, they turned to see the three men exiting from the hotel and starting after them.

Nick and Kate dodged the traffic as they made their way across the street. The traffic was light, but it still had to move slowly because of all the construction and detours caused by the suppression of the central artery project, commonly known as the 'Big Dig'. In the middle of the divided avenue were various mounds of dirt and construction equipment that offered numerous places to hide. Beginning to tire, they took refuge behind a huge crane. It was better to face their pursuers than to catch a bullet in the back.

The three men quickly crossed Atlantic Avenue and spread out as they approached the location of the crane.

"I don't understand it. They zeroed in on us like we had a beacon," Nick said.

This time Kate gave the order, "We can't stay here. If one of them gets behind us, we're dead."

Nick agreed, "Okay. Let's try to slowly get the rest of the way across the street. Then maybe we can get lost in the crowds at Fanneul Hall Marketplace."

Moving from their hiding place they were spotted by one of the men who took careful aim at Nick's head, but the silent bullet ripped through his shoulder and sent him sprawling to the ground before he could pull the trigger. Nick and Kate turned at the sound of the anguished voice to see one of their pursuers crawling for cover. They immediately took refuge behind a large bulldozer, and none too soon as a torrent of bullets ripped through the ground behind them and ricochet off of the heavy metal.

No sooner had the firing stopped when Kate reached around the bulldozer and fired three shots in the general direction of their pursuers.

"I don't think you're going to hit anyone that way," Nick said.

"No kidding," Kate answered. "But at least they know we are armed, and it might slow down their pursuit." Then she added, "Who the hell shot the other guy?"

"Good question, but I'll be damned if I know."

Just then Nick's MF cell phone rang.

A startled Nick answered, "Hello."

"Nick, it's Eric."

"Where the hell are you?"

"We're right behind you. Don't worry we have you well covered."

Nick looked around behind him but could see nothing. "'Where are you? I don't see you?"

"That's the point," Eric responded and then continued. "Now listen. We can't get the SUV down to you, so you are going to have to come to us."

"I don't think I like the sounds of that," Nick said. "Can't you just swoop down with Casper and pick us up?"

"I could if I had her here, but I don't."

A disappointed Nick responded, "Oh. That's too bad."

"Yes it is. But don't worry we have plenty of firepower to protect you. Just do as I say and the two of you will be fine."

"What choice do we have?"

"None. So listen to me. When I count to three you'll see the flashes of light coming from our gunfire, but you won't hear anything. That's when I want the two of you to run like hell and meet us at the corner of State Street. Do you know where that is?"

"Yes. It's only about a hundred yards from us."

"Good. Now get ready. One, two, three."

They saw the flashes of gunfire coming from three different spots: left, right, and center of the direction they were headed. They both took a deep breath, Nick grabbed Kate's hand, and they started running for all they were worth. They could see the constant flashes of gunfire and hear the pinging of bullets hitting metal behind them.

What they couldn't see were the bullets hitting all around their pursuers; giving them no chance at all to fire at Nick and Kate. They almost stopped running and dove for cover when they heard the explosions behind them, but managed to keep their heads and continue towards State Street. Privates Kincaid and Nelson and Corporal John Andersen provided the cover fire for their escape.

Although there were only three of them that was more than enough, because they were equipped with advance production prototypes of the new military rifle. Scheduled for general use by 2005, the Objective Individual Combat Weapon may be the most lethal gun ever developed. Accurate to one thousand meters, it has twice the range and is smaller and lighter than the M-16. It uses two types of ammunition controlled by a single trigger: a standard 5.56mm NATO bullet, with a 30-round magazine clip, and a new 20mm high explosive air-bursting round that can be set to detonate at any range in front of, behind, or above targets hidden behind barricades or dug into trenches. The real effectiveness of the gun comes from its computerized firing system built into the sight, a laser rangefinder, an infrared night vision mode, and a video camera with a 6x zoom lens. Wired to a helmet-mounted video display, the camera allows a soldier to accurately fire around a corner without exposure to hostile return fire.

The MF team was easily and effectively keeping the three pursuers pinned down and unable to return fire. The night vision infrared mode allowed them to fire extremely close without hitting any of them. To make sure none of them got off a lucky shot, they fired a series of concussion grenades that detonated over their heads. They didn't use regular explosive grenades since they did not want to seriously injure or kill anyone unless they absolutely had to.

Nick and Kate emerged from the construction sight near State Street and were immediately intercepted by Eric Johnson. He led them to the Explorer waiting nearby, and driven by Private Peterson. They entered the SUV as the remaining

MF team made a controlled retreat until they were all in the vehicle and heading for the Southeast Expressway. They had managed to get away before the police arrived, and were now heading west on the Massachusetts Turnpike.

# CHAPTER 30

▼

# ESTATE OF VICTOR NOBLE
# ONE P.M., MONDAY
# DECEMBER 27, 1999

## FIVE DAYS TO 0 0

Victor Noble paced the floor of his study as he impatiently listened to the report of David Ford. He had been informed of the incident the previous night involving the Boston Police, and now wanted the complete details directly from the Deputy Director. He cringed at the thought of an actual confrontation between the two. A dead Boston cop and/or CIA agent would be a field day for the media. They would be all over this kind of story and force a widespread government investigation. If there was ever even a hint of Deputy Director Ford or himself being involved with a clandestine element of the CIA their carriers would be finished.

The Deputy Director had not completed his report, but Victor Noble couldn't wait any longer. "What the hell were your men thinking? Having an open gunfight in the heart of the city of Boston."

He wasn't going to tell Noble his men were out for revenge; furious at the loss of three of their own and the embarrassment they suffered on Christmas Eve. "They had them trapped and alone. They didn't want them to get away."

Victor Noble stopped pacing directly in front of Ford, his face inches away from the Deputy Director's, his black eyes staring into Ford's, as he growled, "But they did get away. Didn't they?"

David Ford did his best not to blink, "Yes. They did."

Still inches away and staring hard, he growled again, "And they weren't alone. Were they?"

He felt like the black eyes were piercing through him and he wanted to grab him and make him stop, but he didn't. "They were at first. My men were sure of that."

"But then, just like the other night, they soon had more protection than your men could handle. Didn't they?"

Ford struggled to maintain control. He had lost three good men and wanted to kill this son-of-a-bitch for implying they deserved it. "We would have had her before her protectors could have helped her if it wasn't for that bastard Logan. She was heading right into our trap when he interfered."

A slight smile, more like a sneer, came to Nobel's face as he patted Ford on the cheek and said, "This Logan has gotten in the way once too often and has out-lived any usefulness he may have once had. He should be eliminated at the first possibility." Then Noble turned his back to Ford, showing no fear of him, and walked to his desk.

Ford wanted to tell him that order had already been given, and for the girl too, but he couldn't. Instead he took the opportunity to get back at his tormentor, if only a little. "I told you we should have done that from the beginning."

The same little smile on his face, Victor Noble responded, "Yes, you did suggest that, didn't you. Occasionally you are right." The smile disappeared when he asked, "Now tell me, are we in trouble with this incident?"

Ford would have somehow loved to implicate Noble in the incident and watch him squirm, but he couldn't without implicating himself. Besides, he needed Noble. "We'll be all right there. No Boston cop was hurt, and no one was killed, so we managed to squash any further investigation. It was just a couple of drunks using the construction equipment for target practice."

"And if someone in the Boston Police Department tries to follow-up on the identity of the three agents involved?"

Ford was going to tell him it was covered and beyond Noble's need to know, but he let his ego get the best of him and told him more than was necessary.

"Again, that's no problem. When my men are on unofficial business they use false identities. In this case the Boston Police will be chasing down three non-existent FBI agents. When the FBI denies any knowledge of them, the Boston police will just think it's another run around. Like the one they got in the Whitey Bulger case."

"Good. Now where do we stand on capturing the girl?"

"I'm afraid we don't know where they are right now. We're quite sure they aren't in the city of Boston or we would have gotten a signal by now."

"Is the signal still working and with them?"

"It was as of last night."

"Have you made any progress in finding out who it is that is giving her this protection?"

"Only that they are heavily armed and I'm certain they are a secret military unit. The guards at the safe house in New Jersey were a legitimate unit of the Army Special Forces that has now all but vanished. I've brought in additional, more heavily armed men."

"Well, pull out all of the stops. We have got to find them. We have got to get the girl. Time is running out."

"What about the other Y2K problems that are cropping up?" Ford asked, referring to the report that at least one third of the nations 911 emergency systems were not Y2K compliant and the Senate report that there would likely be local, regional, and possibly even national power blackouts of unknown duration. This was in addition to the persistent rumors that currency was in short supply and the banking system was in danger of running out.

"That's not enough. Unfortunately President Stewart and his team are very adept at developing contingency plans and convincing the public that everything will be all right; no matter how inadequate the plans are." Noble twisted the end of his mustache, the sneering smile returning to his lips, as he added, "I need the girl. I have to expose the crises in our nuclear weapons system. But I have to be in control of fixing it or else I will have to let the opportunity pass. The risk to the country of exposing the problem without offering a cure would be much too great."

# CHAPTER 31

▼

# OVAL OFFICE
# TWO-THIRTY P.M.,
# MONDAY
# DECEMBER 27, 1999

## FIVE DAYS TO 0 0

President Justin Stewart was meeting with General George Armstrong, who had become his almost constant companion of late. The General had just brought the President up to date on the incident in Boston the night before. They both were very concerned at such a close call and, again, the President questioned the decision to leave Kate Peters out in the field.

Their discussions included a telephone call to the Silver Fox, who reminded them the only reason there was a close call was because the MF unit had been summoned to Washington. Again it was the MF unit that rescued them and now had them under deep cover; which meant they were on their own. The Silver Fox also assured them that whatever Kate Peters knew, they would know before midnight December 31. But he also reminded them that what she knew might not be the key to unlocking the nuclear weapons system and freeing it from the Millennium Bug.

The President didn't need to be reminded not to put all his eggs in the Kate Peter's basket. Indeed, under Colonel Clay's direction, there were three teams of software technicians working around the clock to resolve the problem, and with some notable progress. The General was pleased to report they were almost ninety-eight percent sure the system was currently operable and would be until the year 2000 dawned; then the system would succumb to the Millennium Bug sabotage and destroy itself if access was attempted.

"So you're telling me we currently have a nuclear missile capability," the President said. "But we won't have one after midnight on Friday."

"That's right, sir."

"It's great that we've made progress, but I wouldn't want the hawks among us to know the current situation. Would you?"

The General understood all too readily what the President meant; the extreme hawks might push for a pre-emptive strike before our nuclear capability was crippled. "No sir, I wouldn't. The information has been designated as top secret and only a few people are aware of the status."

The President was comfortable the General felt the same way he did about this threat and would do everything possible to keep this information secret. "Good. Now, what about our other Y2K problems?"

"We've contacted all of the localities whose 911 systems are not Y2K compliant, and we will have military units there by tomorrow to set up portable communication facilities and manpower to assist the local police and fire departments deal with any problems. As for any power outages, we already have large units positioned just outside the major cities for possible crowd control, and these are equipped with a number of generators and portable floodlights. We also have mobile units strategically placed around the country to go to other areas that need help or to reinforce any of the larger city units."

"Good, General. We need to show the public we are ready and able to respond to whatever crises occurs. And, if I have to declare marshal law, we have to be able to demonstrate we are in control. Now, what about our friends overseas?"

The General let out a little sigh of exasperation before he answered, "The Russians are certain to have failures of their power grid. This will require the cores of their nuclear reactors at their twenty-six power plants to be cooled using standby generators. It is very unclear what shape their generators are in, but we have to assume that many of them have been cannibalized for parts or stolen and sold. They are not exactly forthcoming in their discussions with us."

"I assume we have standby units with portable generators ready to respond?" The President asked.

"Yes, we do. The problem is we need to be able to respond to the rest of Eastern Europe, the Middle East, Asia, South America, and even Western Europe. So we are stretched pretty thin. What concerns me most is the Russians, either because of distrust or pride, waiting too long before they call for help."

"I'll have Secretary Carlson talk to the ambassador to see if we can convince them of the potential crisis and our desire to help."

"Unfortunately our mutual distrust for one another goes back a long way and works to the benefit of hawks and hardliners on both sides."

"Some prayers couldn't hurt either. We are going to need all the help we can get."

# CHAPTER 32

▼

# MOSCOW—OFFICE OF THE PRESIDENT ELEVEN P.M., TUESDAY DECEMBER 28, 1999

## THREE DAYS TO <u>O</u> <u>O</u>

President Leonid Sokolov had reluctantly agreed to a secret meeting with Dimitry Petrov. The urgent request had come from Prime Minister Ivanov, whose persistence finally overcame the President's concerns. Normally he would have granted the request without hesitation. He knew Dimitry Petrov, though they weren't friends, and respected his long dedication to Russia. He was known as a man of principle, something rare in Russia these days. He was also known as a man wanted by Director Stepovich, although for what reason was not known. But Boris Stepovich was a dangerous man and even President Sokolov was careful not to give him any reason to be his enemy. Not unless it was very worthwhile.

It took a little while for the Prime Minister to convince him, especially since he didn't know what it was that Petrov wanted to discuss. He only knew that his aid, Stephan, assured him it was in the interest of national security and Dimitry Petrov would not expose himself to potential capture if it were not critical. So the President finally agreed to a late night meeting that would include only the four of them: the President, the Prime Minister, Stephan and Dimitry Petrov. Of course they would be unarmed and the President's personal security would be just outside the door.

The greetings were cordial but brief. The President offered them some vodka, which they accepted. It would have been impolite not to do so. The Prime Minister did the pouring and they all drained their glasses in one gulp. Then it was time for business.

The stress was beginning to show on Dimitry, his face looked tired and drawn, as he spoke, "Thank you for seeing me, Mr. President. I'll get right to the point."

President Sokolov folded his thick fingers and rested them on his large stomach. "Please do. It is late and meeting with you is not exactly without its risks."

"I understand. That is exactly why I requested this meeting." Dimitry leaned forward as he continued, "You must not listen to Boris Stepovich. This plan to have North Korea launch two……."

Red faced and furious, the President bolted upright and pointed a meaty finger at Petrov and spoke loudly, "What the hell do you know about that?" He was angry for losing his temper; now he couldn't deny such a plan.

Dimitry was not upset at being interrupted, but he was concerned and saddened to see the leader of the country succumbing to the pressures of the office. There was no doubting the problems the country faced were enormous. The economy was in shambles, food was in short supply, the military hadn't been paid in months, and the dawn of the new millennium loomed as a disaster. "I know that Stepovich has proposed a plan to have North Korea launch a nuclear missile strike against Tokyo and Taiwan. It is a desperate plan, and one that he devised because he knows the nuclear missile system is not operational."

The President almost choked on his words, "What do you mean it's not operational. I was there for the test. It worked perfectly."

"Yes, it did. But it doesn't now."

"How do you know?"

"Because I had it changed. I am in control of the country's nuclear missiles."

"Are you saying you sabotaged the system?" Asked Vice President Ivanov.

"I took control of the system. It will still work, but only with the proper code. And only I know the code."

"If that's true, then you are a traitor." The word traitor was spat from the President's mouth and cut deep into Dimitry.

"It is true and I am not a traitor. I did it because I love this country. But I won't go into the details."

"Why are you coming forward now?"

"Because things are out of control. This North Korean plan is crazy. It has to be stopped."

"Perhaps. That is what I thought at first. But there is something to be said for creating tension between the Chinese and the Americans. Then we can play one against the other," President Sokolov said. "We will show the Americans that we don't need their assistance." The President's words were exactly what Dimitry did not want to hear. They were all just a bunch of crazy old men. "How do I know you are telling me the truth?"

"Schedule another test and you will see."

"I see. You really leave me no choice," the President said, as he signaled for his security guards. "You will be my guest until the test is completed."

Dimitry had expected this. He hoped that the President would be smart enough not to involve Director Stepovich. "I understand, but I trust my whereabouts will be kept secret?"

"Do not be concerned about Boris Stepovich. If you are lying you will be shot. And if you are telling the truth you will tell me the code. I am not like Stepovich, but I am the President and I will be in control of our nuclear weapons."

# CHAPTER 33

▼

# QUABBIN RESERVOIR— WESTERN MASSACHUSETTS TWELVE P.M., WEDNESDAY DECEMBER 29, 1999

## TWO DAYS TO <u>O</u> <u>O</u>

The rustic old lodge was solidly built and tight to the weather. While it was cold and snowing outside, the big open area, which served as the central meeting room, was warm and dry. Located in a very remote area of forest surrounding the Quabbin Reservoir in western Massachusetts, it could only be reached by hiking in or by helicopter. It was noon and with military precision, just like the previous two days, they gathered for lunch. All but the three who were on guard duty.

Lieutenant Eric Johnson wished he had the foresight to put himself on guard duty to avoid sitting down with Kate and Nick. As each day dragged on the tension grew, and he knew he couldn't delay much longer. The excuse for delaying wasn't very good the first day he used it and it wasn't getting any better.

They barely sat down and began eating when Kate started, "This is the third day we have been stuck here sitting on our hands. Are we ever going to move or are we going to usher in the new millennium from our castle in the woods?"

Eric had hoped he might get to swallow a few bites before he had to get into this, "We've been trying to find out who it is that is after you. We had a close call in Boston and we don't want to have another one."

Kate's frustration neared the exploding point and she fought for control. "But that's because you weren't with us, and now you are. We need to go to southern Maine and we will be all right."

"That's what you said about Boston," Eric said more sarcastically than he had planned. He hesitated and backed off a notch before continuing, "And where in southern Maine? We need a specific destination before we can go. I have to be able to check it out for security."

"I don't know. I won't know until we get there." She needed to get somewhere she could make a call, but certainly couldn't tell them that.

Nick cleared his throat to get their attention before he spoke, "I agree with Kate. We need to get out of here. We're running out of time and I know a place in southern Maine that would be perfect for security."

Eric knew he was going to have to move forward, he had delayed here as long as he could and time was running out. He was anxious to move on himself. "Tell me about it."

"It's a first class hotel located in Ogunquit. It's called The Cliff House because it is located high on the cliffs overlooking the ocean. The rocks below the cliffs make it impossible to land a boat. The one road in is the only access; except by helicopter, of course."

"It sounds like it has possibilities. Does it look straight out to the ocean? No beaches, boat docks or islands nearby."

"None. The hotel is located close to the edge of the cliffs and looks straight down to the rocks that roll into the ocean; appearing and disappearing with the tides."

"Are you sure it is in southern Maine?" Kate asked.

"It is about as southern Maine as it gets; it is only twenty to thirty minutes up the Maine Turnpike."

"It sounds as if it just might be perfect. I'll take Casper and part of the crew to check it out this afternoon. Are you sure it is open at this time of year?"

"Quite sure. I'm on their mailing list. They close a few weeks before Christmas and then re-open for Christmas and stay open through New Years."

"Good. Now let's finish our lunch so I can get ready to go and check it out," Eric said. He then changed the subject, "You haven't eaten very much, Kate. If you don't like it I can have the cook prepare something else."

Kate had finished half of her meal and put the fork down. "No thank you. I've had enough."

"I know it's not a gourmet meal, but it's really not that bad," Eric said. "I hate to see you go hungry."

"I've really had enough." Kate paused and then put her manners aside and added, "Besides everything I eat here leaves a funny after taste in my mouth. Does the cook have some secret seasoning?"

Nick could see the pressure getting to Kate; sarcasm was not like her. But he understood; sitting around was getting to him too. "Perhaps we can go with Eric to check out the Cliff House. It would give us a break in the boredom around here." Nick turned to Eric as he finished.

"I don't see why not," Eric responded.

"As much as I would like to get out of here, I don't enjoy flying in the helicopter as much as you apparently do," Kate said stifling a yawn. "Besides, this food seems to make me sleepy as well as leaving a bitter taste in my mouth. I think I will just take a nap."

"Suit yourself," Eric said. "I will leave most of the team here anyway. It will be perfectly safe." Eric was comfortable to leave Kate without the protection of Casper because their location was so remote and heavily monitored with both ground equipment and satellite surveillance. In addition, there was a safe room made of concrete and steel buried beneath the lodge that could withstand any attack long enough for them to return with Casper.

"Perhaps I'd better stay," Nick said.

"There's no need. You heard Eric, I will be perfectly safe while you two get to play with your little toy." Kate smiled as she spoke, the sarcasm gone from her voice. "Now, if you'll excuse me, I'm going upstairs to take a nap."

"Come on," Eric said. "Your knowledge of the hotel and the area may be of use to us."

Within a half hour they made the final preparations and were in the air silently streaking towards the southern Maine coast. At an altitude of ten thousand feet they were cruising at five hundred mph and would be over the Maine coast in less than a half hour. Corporal Dick Semanski was at the controls with Lieutenant Johnson as the backup and Private Peterson as the navigator. There would be no problem in locating the hotel. If it had an address it had coordinates and could easily be located using the aircrafts computer and the satellite system.

While this was the third time Nick had flown in the craft, it was the first time Eric Johnson had really had the opportunity to show off Casper. Since Nick had already seen some of what it could do, had top-level clearance, it could mean his life, and he was firing questions at him in rapid succession, he thought it was appropriate to let Nick in on some of Casper's advanced technology.

When Eric told him to slow down and he would answer his questions Nick was pleased. "I know we took some direct hits the other night at the safe house, but it didn't seem to have any affect on Casper. How come?"

"Because there wasn't any," Eric said as he brought a three-dimensional image up on his computer screen. "This is a picture of the skin of the aircraft. As you can see it is multi-layered with a honeycomb weave between each layer. The key to its strength is each layer is made out of advanced polymers coated with Kevlar."

"Do you mean to tell me we are flying along at five hundred miles an hour in a plastic plane?"

Eric smiled as he answered Nick, "Very special plastics, yes. There are six layers of skin, which would be far to heavy if it were made out of the typical metals. These are very advanced polymers that are not yet available commercially. They were developed for us by your alma mater I believe—the University of Massachusetts. They apparently have a very strong engineering school and are the world's leader in polymer science. In case you didn't know."

Nick felt a sense of pride, "Yes, I did know something about that. Although I graduated from the School of Management and didn't get on the other side of the campus very much."

"I understand that's highly rated as well."

"Yes it is, thank you. How much of a hit can Casper take?"

"It can handle any caliber machine gun in existence. It can also withstand small missile fire. Besides the layers that I showed you, if you look closely at top layer of skin you will see that there really is no flat surface. Instead it is a series of dimples of different depths and patterns that helps to deflect and diffuse the force of any direct hit."

"What about armor piercing bullets?"

"Absolutely no affect. As for our own weapons, we have seven .50-caliber machine guns: Three in front, one on each side, and two in the back. They can all be operated by each one of the seven stations, either individually or all at the same time."

"That's impressive."

"That's the least of it. We have the ability to fire multiple rockets forward and aft. We can even fire missiles with tactical nuclear warheads, although we don't have any on board at present. But the most potent weapon we have is our laser."

"You have a laser?"

"Yes, we have a laser. And it is capable of hitting a target up to five miles away in less than a second. It has the power to obliterate anything that flies, to sink a battleship, or to destroy the better part of city block. It also can be adjusted to hit a single individual in a crowd without hurting anyone else."

Nick shook his head from side to side slowly, "This aircraft is amazing. What else does it have?"

Eric smiled like a proud father, "A lot more, but I'm afraid it will have to wait." Eric then pointed at his screen, "I believe that's your Cliff House below."

Nick looked at the screen and saw the hotel as clearly as if he were standing next to it, although they were still five thousand feet above it. "Yes, that's the Cliff House. Pretty secure, don't you think?"

Eric didn't respond immediately, he was busy watching the screen as Corporal Semanski made slow, ever-widening circles around the three story main building and the smaller out buildings. The passes showed that the hotel was virtually surrounded on three sides by steep cliffs that fell straight into the sea. It was high tide now, but it was obvious that even at low tide a landing on the rocks and attempt to scale the cliffs would be nearly impossible and easily observed from Casper.

Heavy woods broken only by the access road that led to the rural Shore Road between York and Ogunquit about half a mile away bordered the fourth side. The area was fairly rural, with a golf course on the other side of the public road, a small number of expensive looking homes overlooking the sea, and no place to land a boat for a good mile on either side of the hotel.

Finally, Eric answered Nick, "Yes, it looks good from here. I would have preferred if the woods had been open fields, but that can be handled with some monitoring devices and a few men on the ground."

Nick was pleased his selection had met with Eric's approval. "So we'll do it then?"

"Not just yet, Nick," Eric said as he turned to Corporal Semanski. "Corporal, generate a cloud and bring it down to two thousand feet so that I can release some PIP's."

"Yes, sir." The Corporal pushed some buttons on his control panel and within seconds they became engulfed in a cloud on what had been a clear day.

Nick could hardly believe his eyes as he looked out the window and saw nothing but a white puffy cloud. "Did you just create a cloud?"

"Yes. It's part of our stealth capabilities," Eric said as he smiled. "We can even make a gray cloud if the weather calls for it."

He then pushed a button and a series of ten small screens, which wrapped around the cockpit, lit up. The PIP's were in action. One raced down the access road, two others were systematically scouring the woods on either side of the road, and the remaining seven were headed for the hotel and its out buildings. Besides the main hotel there was the original small motel off to the right, two houses near the parking lots, and a large maintenance building partially hidden by the woods. The main building received three PIP's and the out buildings one each.

They all quietly observed the screens as each building and the surrounding area was thoroughly searched. After an hour of this Eric was prepared to announce his decision, "Okay, I've seen enough. It will do. Lets go back and get ready to come here tomorrow."

The PIP's were left in place, to be used when they returned, as Corporal Semanski returned to five thousand feet and headed back to western Massachusetts.

# CHAPTER 34

▼

# MOSCOW—OFFICE OF THE PRESIDENT FOUR P.M., THURSDAY DECEMBER 30, 1999

## TWO DAYS TO 0 0

A furious President Sokolov clenched his fists and paced the floor as he waited for Dimitry Petrov to be brought to his office. The test had been completed that morning and the results were disastrous. Prime Minister Ivanov, accompanied by Stephan, had attended the test on his behalf and had just finished their report. The short of it was Dimitry had told them the truth; they currently had an operational missile system, but that would end at midnight tomorrow. Then they would be left defenseless against a nuclear attack. And it was not just the United States that he was concerned about; China, the giant on their southern border was an old enemy and might seize the opportunity.

Dimitry was brought into the room under heavy guard and placed in a chair in the center of the room. President Sokolov's anger took control and he wasted no time in getting to the point, "Let me congratulate you Dimitry. You were right. The test of our ability to fire our missiles as we enter the new millennium has failed." The President stood directly in front of him as he continued, "Thanks to you our country will enter the new millennium defenseless against our enemies. We will be a sitting duck against a nuclear attack."

Dimitry raised his head but not his voice, "You have completed the test I see."

"Yes, we have completed the test and proved you to be a traitor," the angry President said. "Do you hear me, Dimitry? A traitor!"

"No matter what you think, Mr. President, I am no traitor," a defiant Dimitry Petrov responded.

"What do you call leaving your country defenseless." President Sokolov didn't wait for a response as he continued, "This changes everything, we need to consider a first strike before we lose our capabilities." the President directed this last statement at the Prime Minister more than anyone else.

Prime Minister Ivanov took a deep breath, to give him an opportunity to recover from this statement, before he responded, "But Mr. President, that would be absolute suicide."

The President waited for a long moment, taking his seat before continuing, "Yes, it would. And I'm not suicidal. So we will just have to work on our friend, Dimitry, to get the code that will give us our power and respect back. Regardless of whether we do or not, we will privately support the implementation of Director Stepovich's plan to use the North Koreans. Those crazy bastards will do our dirty work for us."

"The code may give you back your power, but never your respect. This North Korean plan is proof of that. And that is why I will never give you the code," a determined Dimitry said as he gave the signal to Stephan. He knew it was over; his plan had failed and maybe it should have. It was the plan of an old man trying to recover what once was. But his country could never be what it once was, and maybe it never was quite what he thought it to be. In any event he should have left the balance of power as it was. It had worked that way for some four decades and now it was out of whack. He hated to admit it, but if only one country could have the bomb he felt it should be America and not his Russia. Now he can only hope he hadn't helped bring on a global disaster and his children would be safe.

"Your sense of duty to your country may not be enough to get you to tell me the code, Dimitry," the President spat out his name as he leaned forward, "but you will tell Director Stepovich." He let it sink in for a moment before continuing, "I will give you a little more time to think about it. But time is running out. Although I have been informed the United States will be in a similar situation when midnight strikes there, I cannot be sure of this. And, even if it is true, our time zone is ahead of theirs, which will leave and eight-hour gap when they have a system and we don't. I won't let that happen; if you don't tell me you will be given to Boris well before that."

"You can't let Boris Stepovich have the code," Dimitry warned.

"Then give it to me."

"Call off the North Korean attack."

"You are not dictating how this country will be run. Now tell me the code."

"No. You are too dangerous."

"Take him away," The President ordered his guards. "You only have a little while to change your mind, Dimitry."

As the guards led him away he briefly made eye contact with Stephan to make sure he knew what to do.

It was two excruciating hours before Stephan could excuse himself from Prime Minister Ivanov and get to, what he hoped, was a secure telephone and make his call. He quickly briefed Yuri and Pasha on what had happened and the order to abort. Stephan had all of the correct answers to a series of questions given to Yuri by his father; so Yuri agreed to abort the mission as soon as Katya contacted him. He was not unhappy to stop this desperate plan, but he was saddened and terrified for his father. Stephan promised to do whatever he could to free him.

Director Stepovich was very pleased when his deputy gave him the good news. A few hours earlier, their undercover FSS agent in President Sokolov's personal security force had reported the meeting between the President and Dimitry Petrov. They had hoped this would require a communication from Dimitry to Yuri. Stephan was suspected of having ties to Petrov so it was an easy step to follow him and trace his call.

"Excellent, Comrade Vladimir. Excellent," a smiling Boris Stepovich said. "We have the exact location in this southern Maine?"

Deputy Kosloff was always happy to give his superior information that pleased him, "Yes, Director Stepovich. We have an exact location."

"Good. You have already notified agent Malenkov to move in?"

"Yes, sir. He and Skulsky and their supporting agents are on the way as we speak."

"Good. If I can't have Dimitry then I'll have his son. I'll find out what I want to know. You reminded agent Skulsky that I want Yuri Petrov alive? If he let's himself get carried away, I will cut of his balls and feed them to him?"

"I used those words exactly, sir."

"Good. And our friends in North Korea?"

"They are ready to go. Just as you have planned."

"They really are fucking crazy bastards. You have to love them."

# CHAPTER 35

▼

# WASHINGTON, D.C.— OFFICE OF THE PRESIDENT ONE P.M., THURSDAY DECEMBER 30, 1999

## ONE DAY TO 0 0

President Stewart hung up the red telephone that was a direct link to Moscow; his face was ashen. The discussion he just had with President Sokolov left him deeply concerned about the Russian President's stability. The red line was only to be used in the most severe crisis situations; such as the use or possible use of nuclear weapons. But he went on about not needing any help from the United States to deal with matters of internal security, that Russia was still a major nuclear power, the new millennium would restore his country to her former status, and the United States had better be prepared to recognize this.

He tried to assure the Russian President that he and the United States government held him and his country in the highest esteem. But it soon became obvious President Sokolov wasn't listening to him, as he kept babbling on about the Y2K problem and the new millennium bringing America back to earth. President Stewart couldn't determine if President Sokolov had gone mad or was simply terribly drunk. He hoped the latter, as dangerous as that was.

As soon as he gathered himself, he called the Secretary of State and the Chairman of the Joint Chiefs of Staff and relayed what had happened. They all agreed a full cabinet meeting was called for. This call had only added to the growing concern over the Y2K problem as the new millennium approached. They would meet in an hour, which would be no problem. At the beginning of the week the President had informed all the cabinet members to stay in Washington and be ready to meet on short notice. All New Years Eve celebrations were on hold.

In exactly one hour, President Justin Stewart entered his conference room filled with the cabinet members. In addition, he asked the Directors of the CIA, FBI, and Secret Service to attend. He wasted no time in giving them the full details of his disturbing conversation with President Sokolov. In addition, he brought them all up to date on the current status of the readiness, or lack of it, of the US nuclear missile system to deal with Y2K. For those cabinet members who were not involved in any aspect of national defense they were hearing about this for the first time and were shocked. He then addressed CIA Director Mathias. "Donald, can you shed any light on what might have triggered this outburst?"

"I don't have anything concrete, but we've just started to hear some rumors their nuclear weapons system will not be Y2K compliant by the new millennium."

A somewhat confused and angry Victor Noble leaned forward and demanded, "Didn't you just tell us last week that they tested their system for compliance and it passed with flying colors?"

"Yes, Victor, I did." Donald Mathias was not affected by Noble's cold stare; he had suffered too much in Vietnam to be affected by this man. "But apparently it is a fluid situation. The rumor has it there has been some form of sabotage. They retested the system and it failed miserably."

The President spoke before Noble could. "How good is your information?"

"We are still trying to verify it, but the source has been reliable in the past. The satellite photos have not revealed any unusual activity at their nuclear command center. But….."

The President was getting impatient. "Keep trying, Donald. I don't have to tell you how important that information is."

"Yes, sir, we will. And no, sir, you don't. As I was saying……."

This time it was Victor Noble's turn to interrupt. "If they are facing the loss of their nuclear capabilities that certainly could cause Moscow to act irrationally.

They may even be tempted to launch a preemptive strike. Isn't that true Mathias?"

The Central Intelligence Agency Director was trying to remain calm; like most military men he got frustrated when political maneuvering got in the way of intelligent analysis of a potentially explosive situation. "That's certainly possible, but I don't think its true. I certainly don't have any specific intelligence to suggest it."

"I don't think they are going to send you a written notice," Noble quipped. "As the President has informed us, the current status of our nuclear capability is precarious and may not exist as 2000 dawns. If the Russians are aware of this, or suspect it, they may feel additional pressure to strike while they still can."

President Stewart thought of stopping this lime of discussion, but then decided to let it play out a little longer. It was always good to know where your enemies stood.

"I don't follow that line of thought," Director Mathias responded. "If they did know, and I doubt they do, they would have to be happy and relieved we were going to be in the same boat as them."

"First of all, I suspect strongly that they already know about our problem." Noble was obviously referring to the rumors there was a mole buried deep in Mathias' organization that was responsible for some embarrassing and serious information leaks. "Second, they might think the sabotage of the system went even further and we are already without a system and, therefore, they should strike before they lose theirs. Finally, even if they are not sure about the current functioning of our system, there is an eight-hour time difference and they know they will lose their system eight hours before we do. They may well believe we will use this gap to take advantage of them by making demands on them or by initiating a crippling nuclear attack since we know they cannot respond in kind. Something I think we should seriously consider."

The President wasn't surprised by the statement, but knew it was time to take control. "I want to discuss how we keep this situation from escalating. Not how we take advantage of the it. Judith, what are your thoughts?"

The Secretary of State had patiently waited for her turn. "While President Sokolov's outburst is more than a little concerning it's also somewhat understandable. He lost a great deal of support in the Duma in the elections just completed, and he faces a presidential election next July."

"There's no question he is under an extreme amount of pressure," the President added. "The economy is in a shambles, his people are going hungry, he can't pay his soldiers, he's losing his control of the Duma, he has had four prime ministers in the last seventeen months, and he is facing Y2K failures of God only knows what proportions."

"Yes, sir. It's hard to imagine being in his position and not being desperate," added Secretary Carlson. "That's what makes him so dangerous. And we can't forget the war that is raging in Dagestan. This is a land of two million Muslims who fiercely want their independence, as their Chechneyan neighbors did a few years ago. And we all know how bloody that war was. Now the Chechneyan rebels are helping Dagestan, and the stakes are extremely high. Dagestan represents seventy percent of Russia's frontage on the oil rich Caspian Sea. They won't let it go. Period."

"I would think that would only serve to occupy them and give them something else to focus on instead of creating a crisis with us," the President said.

"Yes, to an extent, that's true. But combine the critical war in Dagestan and a crisis with the United States and President Sokolov has a perfect excuse to cancel the July presidential elections and clamp a state of emergency on the country."

"I see. So you think he is creating a crisis for show and his own political agenda?"

"Yes, Mr. President, I do. But that's not to say things can't get out of control and create a real crisis," Judith Carlson responded.

"Yes it's a dangerous game he is playing," the President agreed.

"If it is a game," Victor Noble added. "I think it is much more than that, and we should discuss our options."

Speaking quickly and loudly a determined Director Mathias got the floor. "Please, if I may, Mr. President, there may be something else happening of equal or more importance."

The President tensed, he didn't need another problem, "Certainly, Donald. Let's hear it."

"Just before this meeting, I received word there is some unusual activity in North Korea."

"What kind of unusual activity?"

"Our satellite photos show a lot of activity at their nuclear missile sites. It looks like they are preparing for a launch."

"Are you certain?" the President asked.

General Armstrong had wanted to get more information before reviewing it with the President, alone, but now he couldn't wait. "I've also received a similar report from our intelligence. We're trying to get some confirmation, but we haven't had an opportunity yet."

"We're trying to confirm it, too, but we also haven't had time. I wouldn't have brought it to your attention yet, if not for this meeting."

"I understand, Donald. Under the circumstances, Judith, we should inquire through diplomatic channels immediately. The language should be strong but not threatening."

Victor Noble would not let this opportunity slip by, "The North Koreans are more unstable than the Russians have ever been. Do we know what their status is on the Y2K issue as it relates to their nuclear missiles?"

"Of course we can't be positive since they have such a closed society, but we believe they are compliant. Their systems are so new they probably never had the problem." Director Mathias responded as the President shot him a look that said he wished he hadn't.

"That's the strongest evidence yet for considering a pre-emptive strike," Noble observed.

The President wasn't ready to discuss this any further, "What we need to do right now is for Director Mathias and General Armstrong to check with their staffs to get a further update, Judith needs to send that message requesting an urgent response, and the rest of us need to make whatever arrangements are necessary to be back here in an hour. While your staffs should be available to you twenty-four hours a day for the next two days, they should not know where you are. They can call you on your secure lines, which will be routed here. There is to be a complete media blackout. We are going to the War Room until this crisis is over. One way or the other."

# CHAPTER 36

▼

# CLIFF HOUSE— OGUNQUIT, MAINE TWO P.M., THURSDAY DECEMBER 30, 1999

## ONE DAY TO 0 0

The drive from western Massachusetts to southern Maine was uneventful. Nick drove the SUV along the country roads, leading from the reservoir to the Mass Pike, while Kate took in the scenery. A light snow fell and covered the woods, meadows, and old barns of western Massachusetts with a blanket of white. As before, Privates Kincaid and Nelson followed in the other SUV and Lieutenant Johnson and the rest of the MicroForce team hovered above them in Casper.

They had called the hotel from the safe house the night before for a reservation, and were told they were lucky to get the one room with two queen-size beds. Two rooms adjoining were out of the question; the one room was only available because of a last minute cancellation. But they could check back today if they wanted to; who knows there could be another cancellation. That's just what Nick was going to do, as he opened his personal organizer and turned it on, while he exited the Mass Pike and turned north on route 495.

That's when Lieutenant Johnson's voice boomed at them, as if he were in the back seat. "What the hell did you just do?"

A startled Nick responded, "What do you mean?"

"I mean—what did you just do." An unusually excited Eric Johnson repeated. "We just picked up a signal coming from your vehicle, and it sure as hell wasn't there when we scanned the truck this morning. So one more time—what did you just do?"

Nick thought for a moment and then answered him, "I just turned on my personal organizer to...."

"What damn personal organizer! You were supposed to leave everything behind. That's why we issued you one of our cellular phones."

"I'd be lost without my organizer. Besides, it has never been out of my sight."

"Turn it off."

"What?"

"Turn it off!"

Nick decided to appease him and turned it off, "Okay. It's off."

Eric watched his monitor closely, "Now turn it back on." Nick did as instructed and confirmed what Eric thought. "Your damn organizer is bugged."

Nick was surprised and embarrassed, "It can't be."

"It can be and it is. There's no denying the signals I'm reading on my monitor."

"But why didn't your scans pick it up before this?"

"Because it is only transmitting when your organizer is on. We would have to be scanning it when it was on. It works off of the battery in your organizer. My guess is that, when they are in range, they can also send a signal and get a short, quick response even when the organizer is off. That way they can make sure they haven't lost you."

"Well they can track it on the side of the road," Nick said as he prepared to throw it out the window.

"No! Don't throw it out," Eric ordered. "Pull off into the rest area that is coming up and wait for Privates Kincaid and Nelson. When you see them pulling in, leave it on the side of the road. They will take it from there."

"What are you going to do with it?" Nick asked.

"They'll pick it up and it will eventually find itself on a vehicle heading south towards Rhode Island and away from us." Eric was careful to keep any anger or incrimination out of his voice. Nick was not trained for this; it was an easy mistake for him to make. "Now why don't you make that call to the hotel to see if they have another room."

Nick did as Eric suggested and was told there were no more cancellations and they could only give them the one room. Eric, listening in to the conversation on his console, didn't like it but would allow the plan to continue. He still felt certain he could provide more than adequate protection.

The rest of the trip was uneventful and the scenery was boring until they left the Maine Turnpike at the town of York. From here, Nick took the Shore Road he was familiar with. He and Kate were soon absorbed in the beauty of the cold Atlantic Ocean crashing against the rocks as they drove along the winding road. For the moment they were typical awe struck tourists.

# CHAPTER 37

▼

# SANFORD, MAINE FOUR P.M., THURSDAY DECEMBER 30, 1999

## ONE DAY TO 0 0

It was chilly inside the little cabin nestled in the woods; the December winds blew through it and overwhelmed the small kerosene stove struggling to keep them warm. Yuri and Pasha had been here for days, too many days, and were getting anxious as time was running out. The phone call from Stephan had come as a shock to both of them. Dimitry was a prisoner and in extreme danger, the plan they had all risked their lives for was to be aborted, and they had no way of contacting Katya.

The news distressed Pasha, crushing his dream of his country's return to power, but this was a Russian's life and he would follow his new orders. Yuri was both distraught and pleased. Distraught that his father's life was in great jeopardy, and pleased the ill-conceived plan was being aborted. He had never felt comfortable with it, but who was he to question his father. Now all they could do was to wait for Katya's call; for some reason she no longer had her secure cell phone so he couldn't call her.

The waiting had been hard in the isolated, old cabin. It was located on a lake in the small town of Sanford in southern Maine. Primarily a summer cottage, it was one of ten set in a semi-circle among the woods, and a short distance from the lake's shore. All of the other cabins were unoccupied; the only other inhabitants were the elderly couple who owned the resort and lived in the main house. The old man was pleased to accept the generous sum of money these crazy foreigners were willing to pay to be isolated and cold in the cabin furthest from the road and house. His wife had wondered if they wanted the isolation because they were still in the closet and needed privacy. He agreed she might be right, but who cared the money was good and it was their business what they did.

Pasha was pacing the floor ever since they had received the phone call from Stephan. He went from the front window to the rear window; pausing at each long enough to scan the grounds outside. Although it was difficult to see anything as the darkness, made worse by the tall pine trees surrounding the cabins, approached. This time he remained at the front window longer than usual, and then raised his hand for silence when Yuri started to ask if he saw anything.

He watched and listened a little while longer, wishing again that the cabin had side windows, before speaking. "Something is wrong. Put on your coat and get your Glock ready," Pasha said as he checked his own pistol and turned off the one small light that illuminated the cabin.

"What is it Pasha?" Yuri asked as he did as instructed.

"The storm door on the main house is open and banging in the wind. The old man should have come out by now to close it."

"Perhaps he is asleep."

"Maybe. But the old woman would wake him or come out herself. If I can hear the door banging against the railing from here, then they can hear it for sure." Pasha then moved to the side of the door as he opened it slowly. When nothing happened he announced, "I'm going to see what is wrong. If anything happens leave by the back door immediately. Do not hesitate for anything. Is that clear, Yuri?"

"Yes, but be careful."

Pasha stepped quickly through the door and started to move to his right; hoping the darkness would conceal him. But before he could take another step the bullet he never heard shattered his skull and sent him sprawling backwards into the room. He was dead before he hit the floor and never heard the hideous laugh of the man who shot him with the help of his infrared riflescope.

For a moment, Yuri was stunned by the sight of his friend lying on the floor in a pool of blood, his face unrecognizable in the beam of his flashlight. Then Yuri remembered Pasha's instructions and quickly headed for the rear door. He opened the door only to have a gun thrust in his face by one man and his own gun hand grabbed and immobilized by another.

The man holding the gun to his face spoke firmly but quietly, "Don't be foolish, Yuri. Resistance can only get you hurt or killed. And we really don't want to do that." Besides the order to take him alive from Director Stepovich, Ivan Malenkov had no desire to kill this young man. He would have preferred to allow Pasha to live also, but he couldn't argue against Egor. He would have been much too dangerous to try to take alive.

They took Yuri's gun and then forced him back into the cabin. The light was now on and there was another large, muscular man with a rifle standing over Pasha's body admiring his work as if he had just shot a twelve-point buck. "How's that Ivan? I told you I would take him out with one clean shot. All we had to do was be patient and wait for him to make his fatal mistake. I knew he would have to check out the banging door."

Ivan Malenkov could not share the joy his comrade took from the death of another. "The important thing, Egor, is that we have Petrov alive. Now please remove his body. We don't need to look at it any longer." They had determined to use the cabin as the site for the interrogation. Pasha had chosen a well isolated location and, if not for the tracing of the call from Russia to the cell phone, they would not have been found. The old couple would no longer be of concern as they too were counted among Egor's victims.

Egor smiled as he approached Yuri, grabbed him by the hair, and forced him to look at grotesque face of his friend, "On the contrary. I think it is perfect for young Yuri to look at as he decides whether to tell us what we want to know or not." Yuri struggled to turn away, but Egor forced him to look. The pain caused by his tormentor's strong hand causing his eyes to open. "Look at your friend, Yuri. You are all alone now and what we will do to you will be worse if you don't cooperate."

"All right, Egor. You've made your point. Now let him go and seat him in that chair." Malenkov then turned to the third man and ordered, "I've seen enough of him. Now take him out back." Egor pushed a trembling Yuri down hard into the straight-backed wooden chair and the third man removed Pasha from the cabin.

The interrogation then began. Ivan Malenkov asked the questions and Egor Skulsky inflicted the punishment when they didn't get an acceptable answer, which they never did. As they explained, what they wanted to know was simple.

Where was Katya? And how could he contact her? But Yuri was strong willed and endured the blows to his head and body stoically. It was not until they had broken all of the fingers on his left hand did he confirm that she was somewhere in southern Maine. By the time they had broken all of the fingers on his right hand, Malenkov was convinced he had no way of contacting her and that he was waiting here for her to call him. And that's what they would do now.

To continue the torture could result in Yuri's death, which would not get them the code or Katya. Besides, Director Stepovich had ordered them to keep Yuri alive at all costs. If they could get the code from him that was a bonus, if not he was the hostage that would get them the code. If they could also get Katya all the better, but if not then better that she were dead.

# CHAPTER 38

▼

# CLIFF HOUSE—
# OGUNQUIT, MAINE
# SEVEN P.M.,
# THURSDAY
# DECEMBER 30, 1999
## ONE DAY TO 0 0

The afternoon had been uneventful and even relaxing. After checking in, Kate and Nick went to their room to freshen up and Kate was immediately taken by the beautiful view. There was a large picture window that looked straight out to the Atlantic Ocean as far as the eye could see. To the left of the window was a glass door leading to a small balcony. Without hesitating, Kate went out onto the balcony where Nick quickly joined her.

"I told you it was beautiful, didn't I?" Nick said as he moved close to her and almost put his arm around her.

Kate nestled into Nick for warmth as she looked down at the icy water crashing against the rocks a hundred feet below. "I thought you were exaggerating, but you weren't. If anything, it is even more beautiful than you described."

Nick put his arm around her to help keep her warm. "I think the ocean is even more beautiful, more wild in the winter."

"I think your right." Kate said as she snuggled a little closer. She knew she couldn't try to contact Yuri until everyone else was asleep so she decided to try to steal a little time to be with Nick. Who knew what tomorrow would bring; she might never see him again or even be alive. She was in a beautiful place with a man she was falling in love with and she would simply be just Kate for a little while.

They stayed there for over a half-hour enjoying the ocean, saying nothing, until they realized how cold they were getting. When Nick suggested they go to the hotel pool and exercise area and take a sauna to warm up he was a more than a little surprised, and certainly pleased, when she agreed. They managed to have a relaxing afternoon together as they struggled to keep the real world at bay for a little while.

That evening they were sitting in the large, well appointed dining room ready to have an intimate dinner. The dinning room was on the corner of the building and had two walls of solid glass providing a perfect view of the cliffs and the ocean crashing rocks below. Nick managed to get a table next to one of the corner windows with a breathtaking view of the light snow, illuminated by spotlights, blowing sideways.

The atmosphere was ideal for temporarily denying any thoughts of a world on the brink of crashing down upon them like the ocean on the rocks below. Like all new lovers, they were alone in a room full of people; unaware of those around them, of Casper and the MF team hovering above them, and of Privates Peterson and Nelson three tables away.

They talked little, touched hands often, and gazed into each other's eyes. More than once, he told her how beautiful she looked as the candle light danced in her eyes. Their trance was broken occasionally as the waitress took their order and then delivered their dinners. They took the time to enjoy the food and agreed it was excellent. But when it came time for coffee and dessert they passed; anxious to leave this place for an even more enchanting one.

They left quickly passing through the large foyer barely noticing the piano player or the grand staircase. Earlier in the day, Nick had requested that no PIP's be located inside their room to give them a little personal privacy. A request Eric had no problem in granting. After all, he had one outside the door to the hall and one outside the balcony. No one was getting into the room without his knowledge.

The passion that had been building for months, rising to a fever pitch at dinner, exploded into a torrent of sensual kisses. They removed their clothing as if it were on fire and stood naked in each other's arms for a long moment before they went to one of the two queen sized beds. Then they made love as the skies cleared and the moon cast a soft light into the room.

Two hours later Kate was wide-awake as she lay next to Nick, who was fast asleep. And why not, he had been very passionate and yet gentle with her. Not once but twice. She wished the moment would never have to end. He looked so peaceful; this man she knew she could love deeply. She longed to be just Kate—a woman in love. But she couldn't be. There were others that she loved and owed a greater allegiance to.

Slowly she removed herself from his embrace, careful not to wake him. She slid out of bed, grabbed her clothes, and headed for the bathroom. She dressed quickly in the dark. She checked her Smith and Wesson 9mm pistol; grateful Eric had relented when Nick demanded they be allowed to have them for their own protection.

She waved in the air as she left the room knowing Eric, or one of his men, would be watching her through one of their little devices. She walked slowly, not wanting anyone to panic, as she made her way down the hall to the elevator. As she entered it so did Private Kincaid. At first she didn't recognize him dressed in civilian clothes and put her hand on the pistol in her pocket until he spoke.

"The Lieutenant would like to know where you are headed at midnight, Ms. Peters. And without Mr."

"I have a terrible headache and I am going to the front desk to see if they have any aspirin since the gift shop is closed. Nick is asleep and I didn't want to wake him."

"You shouldn't be out here alone."

"I'm not alone. Am I?" Kate said with a disarming smile.

"No, Ms. Peters, you're not," the Private said and then paused as he put his hand to his ear and received instructions from Lieutenant Johnson over their very private network. "Yes, sir," he said into the air and then addressed Kate again, "I've been instructed by the Lieutenant to allow you to proceed. I will be nearby."

"Someday you are going to have to show me how you do that," Kate said as the elevator doors opened to the lobby and she headed for the front desk and Private Kincaid melted into the background.

Along with Private Kincaid and whoever else was hidden in the lobby, she knew Eric Johnson was watching her up in his little ghost ship so she couldn't use one of the public phones. They would be certain to stop her. The night manager approached her and she hoped her plan would work. Giving him a big smile she said, "I'm sorry to bother you at this late hour, but I do hope you can help me?"

"I would certainly be happy to. If I can," said the young night manager. And he would if he could because it was the policy of the hotel to be as helpful to the guests as possible and because she was a beautiful woman. "What is it that you need?"

"First, I need some aspirin. I have a very bad headache."

"That's easy. I have some in the back office. I'll get them for you."

"Please wait. There's something else."

"Yes?"

"I need to make a personal call and don't want to use the telephones out in the lobby."

"Yes, I understand. They're not very private," the manager said with a slight hesitation in his voice.

Kate anticipated the question he didn't ask. "And I don't want to disturb my husband. Could I use that little office back there?" Kate gestured to an office with a computer, a printer, and a phone on a small desk.

The request was not unusual except it was usually the husband making a private call. "That will be no problem, either. Shall I charge it to the room." He anticipated the answer.

"No. I'd rather put it on a credit card. If you don't mind?"

"Certainly. Come right this way." The manager opened the half door and led Kate to the small office agreeing to let her close the door.

Kate quickly dialed the number afraid that Private Kincaid would be coming through the door at any moment; even though she had wedged the chair against the door. Seeing the door close, Private Kincaid headed for the office before Eric Johnson stopped him. The Lieutenant wanted Kate to make the telephone call, which is why she had gotten so far, so he instructed Private Kincaid to standby. Eric could monitor her activities and make sure she was safe from the transmissions of the PIP in the room with her. It also allowed him to hear what she was saying, although he could not hear the other side of the conversation. But that didn't matter. They had already tapped into the main telephone trunk line servicing the hotel. It was only a matter of a few seconds before they filtered out the relatively few other conversations and were able to hear and trace Kate's conversation.

"Yes." Yuri paused, as Malenkov held the phone to his ear, and then continued. "This is Yuri."

The breakdown in protocol and the strain in Yuri's voice distressed Kate. "Yuri, what's the matter? Are you all right? Where is Pasha?"

Ivan Malenkov took the telephone before Yuri could answer. "Hello, Ms. Petrov."

Kate took a deep breath trying to free the lump in her throat, "Who are you? What have you done to Yuri?"

"Be satisfied he is alive. And who I am is not important; except that I am the man who is going to kill him if you don't cooperate with us."

Kate's stomach turned from the thought of what these animals had done to poor Yuri. She had to help him somehow. "What do you want?"

"Please, Ms. Peters. Or should I call you Ms. Petrov. You see, Katya, we know everything. Everything but the code to launch the US missiles, which you will deliver to us in exchange for Yuri."

"You are Stepovich's men," the contempt for him was evident as Kate spoke. "How do I know you won't kill us both if I meet you.

"You will have to trust us or not only will your brother die, but so will your father."

Kate struggled hard to maintain control as her life unraveled. "My father would never allow himself to be taken by Boris Stepovich. He would die first."

"You are probably correct about that. And you are right we do not have him. But President Sokolov has him and it will only be a matter of time before he is turned over to Director Stepovich," Malenkov replied. "If you don't believe me, Yuri will confirm it. Listen." Ivan Malenkov then put the phone to Yuri's mouth, but he refused to speak. A nod from Malenkov and Skulsky gripped the fingers of Yuri's left hand and squeezed hard.

The pain in his scream cut deeply into Kate and almost made per sick, but he did not speak. Malenkov repeated his command, "Answer your sister or I will let Egor do whatever he likes."

"Please do as he says, Yuri," Kate pleaded. "Do they have father?"

There was a pause and then a painful voice that she barely recognized as her brother, "Yes."

"Now cooperate with us, Katya, or I will let Egor kill your brother and I promise you it will not be as quick and painless as when he killed your two friends."

Neither Kate nor Eric could see the smile on Egor Skulsky's face, or the gleam in his eyes, but they could hear the sadistic laugh of the hyena. It sent a cold chill through Kate and an intense hate engulfed Eric.

Kate's own anger now gave her the strength to continue. She was dealing with the worst of the old KGB and they would do whatever it took to get what they wanted—no matter how cruel. She knew they might only want to meet so they could kill her and let the code go to her grave with her, but normal procedure would say to capture her if possible and see whatever benefit could be derived by having her alive. The chance of either her or Yuri surviving was small, but there was a chance and she would take it. She could not leave her brother and father to die without trying everything she could. "I will meet you, but it must be in the daylight and in a semi-public place of my choosing." She had to insist on this to have any chance at all.

"That depends," Malenkov said. "What time and where is the place?"

"Ten in the morning at Perkins Cove in Ogunquit." Kate had read about Perkins Cove in one of the pamphlets the hotel had put in their room. It wasn't ideal since there was only one road in or out, but it was only two miles from the Cliff House, with a footpath connecting the two, so she could walk it.

Malenkov covered the phone and repeated the location to one of his men who knew the area. The man told him it was perfect since there was only one road in or out and it was accessible by boat. "All right, Katya," Malenkov agreed. "But be there or Yuri is a dead man." Then he hung up.

Eric Johnson stared at his console, reeling from what he just heard, as he hovered high above the hotel. His fury threatened to overwhelm him upon hearing that hideous laugh again. The animal that killed his younger brother was only minutes away and he couldn't let this opportunity slip by. It was risky and against standard operating procedures, but he was going to leave Nick and Kate with limited protection and go after his prey.

He turned to Private Brad Wilson, his navigator and in charge of tracing the call's location, and demanded, "Did you get it?"

"Yes, sir," Private Wilson responded. "I have the coordinates. It is in a town called Sanford, approximately fifteen miles from here."

"Good. Lock onto the location. We're going after them."

"Excuse me, sir," Corporal Semanski interrupted. "Do you think it is a good idea to leave our subjects without our protection?"

"It's a calculated risk that is worth taking," Eric Johnson answered. "We're only minutes away from them. We can make a pre-emptive strike that will secure our subjects. We will leave Private Kincaid in the hotel and Private Petersen watching the perimeter. We'll pick up Corporal Andersen and Private Nelson behind the farthest out building. We won't be gone for more than thirty to forty minutes. Now let's do it."

"Yes, sir," Corporal Semanski said and put Casper into motion. He agreed a pre-emptive strike, if successful, would go a long way to ensure the security of the subjects. He also knew Eric would not take the risk, under the circumstances, if it weren't for the chance to get his brother's killer. But he would have done the same thing.

Corporal Semanski maneuvered Casper to an open spot behind the most remote out-building and Lieutenant Johnson informed the team members on the ground what was taking place. Private Kincaid was to make sure Kate returned to the room safely and remained there. He was to keep watch on the hall outside. He and Private Petersen would be the only team members at the hotel so they would have to cover each other in the event anything happened.

They picked up Corporal Anderson and Private Nelson, rose to five thousand feet, and were on their way to the target. It was fifteen minutes since the call ended when they reached the coordinates designated by Private Wilson. As they descended to two hundred feet they scanned the entire area with infrared and heat seeking electronic equipment. There was heat in the main building and the cabin furthest in the woods. Because there was general heat in these buildings it was difficult to detect if there was life inside; especially if they remained still. The scan revealed there was no one on the grounds or in the woods for a radius of three hundred yards; there was a car at the main house and one at the cabin. The engines were cold and yet there was a trail of carbon monoxide leading from the road to the cabin; evidence a vehicle had recently passed that way.

On Lieutenant Johnson's orders, Corporal Semanski brought Casper to within twenty feet of the ground in the back of the main house and Corporal John Anderson and Private Brad Wilson leaped from the aircraft and landed safely with the help of their gyro-belts. They would slowly enter and secure the main house.

Then he turned Casper and was quickly at the back of the cabin. Eric Johnson and Private Martha Nelson leaped from the aircraft to enter and secure the cabin. The coordinates indicated the call came from the cabin and Eric hoped to find his killer there.

Corporal Semanski then positioned Casper between the two buildings and fifty feet off of the ground. From here he could monitor both buildings and warn the team members of any danger. He could also provide immediate fire power if necessary.

Both teams entered the buildings simultaneously as planned and were disappointed there was no one alive. In the main house they found the old couple lying beside one another. Their death had been quick and merciful with a single bullet to the back of the head. The cabin showed evidence of much more violence. First there was the body of a man with his face blown of who, from the trail of blood, had been killed in the center of the cabin and then dragged out of the way and left by the back door. A wooden chair in the center of the room with a rope still tied to it was evidence of further violence.

They had certainly been there and, just as certainly, were gone. Eric's disappointment quickly turned to panic as he realized they could be doing the same as he. They wouldn't have to be all that sophisticated to have Kate's call traced back to the Cliff House. It wasn't a secure line and would be easy to trace.

Lieutenant Johnson ordered Corporal Semanski to land and everyone to get on board immediately. As soon as he was on board he called Privates Kincaid and Petersen to see if there was anything unusual and to alert them to the possibility of visitors. It was too far for them to pick up any transmissions from the PIP's at the hotel, but Kincaid and Petersen could view the images and there was nothing to report. The only recent activity was two intoxicated men coming back from a night on the town by the looks of how they staggered into the hotel.

Then the call came from Private Petersen, "Lieutenant Johnson we have activity, sir."

A knot grew in Eric's stomach since they would not be on site for another seven minutes. "What type of activity?"

"I'm picking up four intruders; two each on the north and south perimeters. They are moving carefully, obviously trying not to be seen."

"Good, Petersen," Eric said. "Lock a PIP onto each group and then take the south perimeter. Do not engage unless absolutely necessary. But in no event allow them access to the hotel or the small ledge at the back of the hotel."

"Copy, sir," Private Petersen said.

"Private Kincaid did you copy that," Eric asked.

"Yes, sir."

"Then leave the corridor and defend the north perimeter with the same instructions."

"Yes, sir."

A worried Eric Johnson turned to his pilot, "Hurry, Dick. I'll alert Nick and Kate."

Having awoken to find Kate gone, Nick was in a panic, he dressed quickly, and was about to call Eric for a report when Kate returned. Like a parent he was at first angry, then relieved, and then demanding an explanation. He wanted to believe she just needed some aspirin so he did. He was still mildly reprimanding her when the call came over the cell phone from Eric. Nick took it and answered abruptly, "Yes?"

"Nick, this is Eric," the Lieutenant attempted to keep his voice from exposing his concern. "There is no reason to panic, but we have a small situation. Is Kate there with you?"

"Yes. What kind of a situation?" Nick knew an opening statement of not to panic usually meant there was reason to panic.

"We have some visitors on the outside of the hotel."

"Well, why don't we invite them in for a drink?"

"This is not the time for sarcasm, Nick."

"What's the problem, Eric? You have men covering the grounds, in the halls, and you are hovering above us in your super ship."

"Well, not quite."

"What the hell do you mean not quite? What part isn't quite right, Eric?"

"We have two men on the grounds, but no one in the hotel and we are on our way."

"On your way! What do you mean 'on your way'? Where the fuck are you?"

"We're only two minutes form you," Eric ignored Nick's justified outburst and spoke calmly. "Just in case an intruder does make it inside the hotel, I want you both to dress for going out in the weather and stay near the door to the balcony. And, for God's sake, make sure you both put on your gyro-belts. Don't worry about activating them, they will do that automatically if the need arises."

The two intoxicated men were in the elevator making their way to the third floor—Nick and Kate's floor. It had not been hard to get the young night manager to tell them the room number. The description fit the beautiful and mysterious woman who had just been in his office, and the six-inch blade at his throat was all the convincing he needed to provide the room number. Fortunately for him there was no need to kill him. A gag and rope were sufficient and less messy.

Exiting from the elevator they continued to act drunk until they were certain the corridor was empty, and then they quickly headed for the end of the hall and Nick and Kate's room. Making their way down the long corridor, they opened their coats and got their Glock pistols at the ready.

"Why do you want us to put on our gyro-belts? You don't expect us to jump from? It's three stories up and only a small ledge below before dropping over the cliff for Christ....."

Just then Casper had come into range and the hall PIP's indicated two men were rapidly approaching their room. "That's exactly what I expect and now. Do it now!"

"What the..."

"Damn it, Nick. Do it now!"

Fortunately Nick had already pushed Kate out the door and onto the balcony when he heard the key enter the lock. Knowing they were in trouble, he had no choice but to put his faith in Eric and his high-tech equipment. He grabbed Kate and they both leaped over the railing and off the balcony as the door swung open and the two intruders burst through with guns ready just in time to see their prey leap to their death or serious injury for certain.

Nick and Kate were petrified as they fell to earth feet first, but, to their amazement and relief, the gyro-belts fired a series of short bursts from the tiny rockets imbedded in the belts and one longer burst as they landed safely with only a small jolt. Unfortunately, they were not out of danger as the intruders fired their silenced pistols at the dark figures thirty feet below.

Nick felt the sting of the bullet in his back, thankful for the vest, just before he saw Kate stumble and fall towards the edge of the cliff. Ignoring his own pain, he leaped and grabbed for her. Casper appeared over the top of the hotel just in time for Eric to see Nick and Kate go head first over the cliff.

# CHAPTER 39

▼

# THE WHITE HOUSE WAR ROOM— WASHINGTON, D.C. EIGHT A.M., FRIDAY DECEMBER 31, 1999

## SIXTEEN HOURS TO <u>0</u> <u>0</u>

On the second sublevel beneath the White House, the President, his cabinet, the Joint Chiefs of Staff, and various military and other support personnel were all gathered in the War Room. They had started their meeting in the Situation Room located on the first sublevel but, after a preliminary review, they recessed for two hours and then reconvened in the War Room, which was better equipped and the Situation Room space was needed for others. During the recess, at the President's request, all of the individuals involved gathered their families and brought them to the situation room. It was unorthodox and crowded, but the President needed his key personnel to concentrate on the crisis on hand. If he had to keep them here so that they couldn't go to their families to protect them, then he would bring their families here and offer them the same protection as his own family, which was in the First Family Safe Room on the fourth sublevel. The remaining subbasement housed a medical room, a galley, and a fully equipped communications room.

Now that everyone was back, the President was anxious to continue. "I know it's a little early, but what's happening relative to Y2K?" He directed his question to Director Mathias and General Armstrong since the CIA and the military were simultaneously monitoring events as time advanced around the world bringing in the new millennium.

"The rollover to 2000 is just beginning so there isn't much to report yet," Donald Mathias responded. "New Zealand was the first major country to usher in 2000 and there have been some blackouts, but nothing serious. Eastern Australia was next and experienced much the same thing."

General Armstrong spoke by way of addition, not correction, "Of course New Zealand and Australia are expected to be two of the best prepared countries."

"That's true," Mathias agreed. "It really doesn't tell us much. There have been three provinces—Kamchatka, Magadan, and Vladivostok—in Russia's most eastern territories that have entered 2000."

"What happened?" President Stewart asked.

"Just as we expected," General Armstrong answered. "There appears to be a total power outage. Everything is shut down."

"In the next hour there will be two significant countries entering the new millennium—Korea and Japan," Mathias said. "What happens there will tell us a lot more."

"Speaking of Japan," interrupted Secretary of State Carlson, "They have information of the unusual activity at North Korea's missile sites and have made an informal inquiry about any information we have on it."

President Stewart had hoped the Japanese intelligence network had not pick up on the activity. "What was your response?"

"I told them I had no knowledge of any unusual activity, but I would make some inquiries and get back to them. They indicated they would be waiting for my call any time day or night."

"Good. That was the right answer. Now I want you to get back to them and tell them you've checked and there is no indication of anything unusual."

The Secretary of State was surprised. "But, sir. They could be sitting ducks. Shouldn't we at least warn them?"

"So they could do what, Judith? Evacuating Tokyo isn't possible and, even if they could, the North Koreans would just target another large city. If the Japanese attacked them the North Koreans would launch the missiles for sure."

"They could at least warn the North Koreans that any aggression would bring full retaliation." Secretary Carlson then added, "They would probably expect us to issue the same warning."

"You have already communicated with North Korea as I asked haven't you?" The President knew the answer, but it hadn't been shared with the others yet.

"Yes, sir, I have."

"And what was their response?"

"They denied any unusual activity. They said we have mistaken routine maintenance for something more."

"And you indicated our grave concern if it were not just routine maintenance?"

"Yes, I did."

"And that's all I want to do for now. Threats have little effect on them and I don't want the Japanese overreacting. The Pyongyang government has been using its missiles as bartering tools against the South Koreans, the Japanese, and us for some time now. Their people are starving and they are probably just trying to get some more humanitarian aid from us."

This was the opening Victor Noble had waited for and he quickly pounced on it. "That's just the problem. Their country is near starvation and their leaders will do anything to stay in power."

"Including risking annihilation?" asked Secretary of Defense Donovan.

"Yes, they would," Noble answered. "Especially if they expect that the Chinese would oppose any such retaliation. Remember the Chinese have been rattling their sabers about Taiwan for some time now, and we have sent very mixed signals on our commitment to Taiwan by granting China important trade concessions." Victor Noble let the statement sink in before adding, "And don't forget that the Chinese hatred of Japan runs very high. The atrocities of World War II are still very fresh in their minds."

"What are you suggesting?" asked General Armstrong.

"I'm suggesting what I would think you would agree with." Victor Noble was trying to put the General on the defensive. "Faced with the prospect of not having a nuclear missile capability at midnight tonight, I think we should launch a pre-emptive nuclear attack."

General Armstrong wasn't surprised by Victor Noble's attacking style, but he still didn't like it. "In the first place, a preemptive strike would most certainly cause North Korea to launch all of their missiles. We can annihilate them, but we can't prevent them from causing widespread damage to Japan and Taiwan. More importantly, the Russians and or the Chinese might interpret our launch of missiles as an attack against them and we would be initiating the destruction of the world."

The President had had enough and now wished he had eliminated Noble from the group. "That's enough talk of a preemptive strike. I can't believe that even North Korea is that crazy. They're just using their missiles as a trump card to get more aid. Besides, we have another sixteen hours before midnight. We have a lot more to worry about as the world deals with the Y2K problem.

# CHAPTER 40

▼

# MOSCOW—OFFICE OF THE PRESIDENT FOUR P.M., FRIDAY DECEMBER 31, 1999
## EIGHT HOURS TO <u>O</u> <u>O</u>

Entering the office of President Sokolov the Director of the FSS and his deputy were greeted cordially. Noticeably absent were Prime Minister Ivanov and his aid Stephan. When Boris Stepovich had provided the President with a copy of the tape of Stephan contacting Yuri it immediately got him a cell next to Dimitry. Because of this severe breach of security Prime Minister Ivanov was no longer a trusted member of the President's close circle and would be replaced shortly; he would be a good scapegoat for the problems in Dagestan.

The President thanked Stepovich again for catching the traitor within his office. When he had received the Director's request for a meeting he was only too glad to grant it. His interrogation of Dimitry had been physical and painful, but had not produced any results. The President had been preparing to contact Stepovich to hand over Dimitry when he had received the call from the Director indicating he had additional information that would be very useful in getting Dimitry to talk.

There was little time to waste so Boris Stepovich got right to the point. "I have information which will make Petrov give us the information. And give it to us right now. I guarantee it."

A cautious President Sokolov asked, "What do you have, Boris? Even your interrogation tactics do not work that quickly. And they are not guaranteed. Sometimes the subject dies without giving up the information, which is what I expect would happen with Dimitry Petrov."

The Director was not going to provide him with the information so quickly. He had Yuri Petrov and he was going to get more than a pat on the back for him. His plan to control the Russian nuclear missile system, while the US's system was crippled, had been sabotaged by Dimitry, but he would still gain power from what he now controlled. "I have his son Yuri, and I will soon have his daughter Katya."

"Where do you have them?" The President was excited.

"I have them in the United States. And I will have them killed if he does not cooperate; and he knows I will not hesitate to do it."

"Good. Let's bring him in then," President Sokolov said reaching for his intercom button. At the request of Boris Stepovich, Dimitry was being held in an adjoining room so he would be readily available.

"Not so quickly, Mr. President. If you please, I would like to discuss some other matters first."

While it was put as a request it was clear that the Director was not going to hand over his trump card without bartering for something for himself. The President expected as much and just hoped Stepovich would not ask for too much. His back was against the wall and he would have to grant him almost anything. If it were anyone else he would have had him arrested and gotten the information by other means. But this was not an option with Boris Stepovich; he was too powerful and had too many old school agents who were dedicated to him. "What is it, Boris."

Boris Stepovich leaned forward and spoke slowly and firmly, "You need a new Prime Minister. You can't trust a man who brings a spy into your office with such a powerful position. You will name me as your Prime Minister and will appoint Vladimir here as my replacement to be the Director of the FSS."

The President swallowed hard as he absorbed what Stepovich had just requested. His appointment to the post of Prime Minister would put him into the public arena and give him more power among the old hardliners and even the new moderates. Just as importantly, the appointment of Vladimir Kosloff as Director would mean that Boris Stepovich would still effectively control the FSS. And, unlike his four predecessors, he would not be able to be replaced at the will of the President. "But that would make you the fifth Prime Minister in the last seventeen months. I'm afraid of the reaction that it would cause. Especially with the appointment of a hard line communist." He knew it probably wouldn't work, but he had to try to persuade Boris Stepovich that this plan wouldn't work.

Boris Stepovich had expected this reaction, but would not be deterred. "Nonsense. Ivanov will make a great scapegoat for the problems in Dagestan. And I am a reformed communist who would make a good fit to help you bring stability and prosperity back to the country. Think about it. Would these terrorist bombings of apartment buildings have ever taken place under communism?"

"No. But....."

"Of course not. My appointment will show these terrorists and the Russian people you mean business and are in control. You must show them you are able and willing to control these hoodlums or you will have little chance of winning the July elections."

Sokolov knew there was some truth to what he said. He also knew there was little hope in talking him out of it. It was a good move for the Director to make if he could pull it off. The best he could do was to extract a commitment of support from him; for whatever that was worth. "So I can count on your support then?"

"Don't worry, Leonid, I know that I could never win a national election. But you have, and can again with my help. So do we have an agreement?"

Reluctantly, President Leonid Sokolov had to agree. "Yes, we have an agreement. But you should understand that I'm not going to launch a strike against the Americans. We could never be sure they didn't have enough capability left to cause significant damage to us. What I am going to do is use our temporary advantage to get concessions from them that will assure my win in July."

"I agree completely. Part of that should be to secretly encourage the North Koreans to launch their missiles by committing to them that we will strongly oppose any military retaliation by the United States and their allies. I know they already have the unofficial commitment of the Chinese."

"Are you sure of that?"

"Positive. The United States will be embarrassed they couldn't stop or retaliate against the Pyongyang government. The Chinese will never allow an armed invasion of North Korea. So the Americans will be between a rock and a hard place. They will lose the confidence and support of their allies. Eastern Europe will again be open for Russian influence, if not dominance."

"If that happens the election will be guaranteed. Yes, I'll unofficially give the North Koreans the assurance they need."

"Excellent. Let's bring in Petrov and get the code."

President Sokolov used the intercom to contact his chief of security who had Dimitry Petrov under heavy guard and ordered him brought in. His face was bruised and puffy and was unable to walk on his own and needed the assistance of two of the guards. He was escorted to a straight back wooden chair in the center of the room and put down hard by the guards. His eyes were half close and the pain was evident on his face.

Dimitry wasn't surprised to see Boris Stepovich; in fact, he had been expecting him. He wouldn't have given him this opportunity if they hadn't found his cyanide capsule. Now he would not only have to endure a terribly severe interrogation, but Boris Stepovich would have the pleasure of watching him suffer.

"Dimitry, my dear friend you don't look so good. What have you gotten yourself into?" Boris Stepovich took pleasure in his adversary's pain. "Of course you know it would be much worse if I had you."

Dimitry tried very hard not to let the pain come through his voice. "If that's why you're here now it's too late."

Boris Stepovich smiled, "Believe me, Dimitry, it's not too late. I will have the information we want within the next fifteen minutes."

Dimitry was afraid of what was coming next. Boris Stepovich did not make idle threats. He wished he could block out what he was about to hear.

"We have Yuri and we will soon have Katya as well."

"I don't believe it." Dimitry hoped he was bluffing, but he knew it was unlikely. "I must speak with him?"

"Of course you must. I wouldn't have expected anything different." Boris Stepovich then directed his attention to one of the guards, "Hold the phone to his ear. Remember, Dimitry, you will only have a moment."

As the phone was put to his ear he could hear his son on the other ended, "Father, I'm sorry."

The pain in his son's voice was unmistakable and sent shivers through him. Dimitry struggled through his own pain to try to reassure his son, "Do not be sorry, son. You have done everything I've asked. It will be all right now. Don't give up. Survive."

Boris Stepovich waived at the guard to take the phone away, "That's enough. Now you see we have your son. You should be proud, Dimitry, he is much like you. But it has cost him for not telling us the code."

"That's because he doesn't know it," Dimitry lied.

"Perhaps that is true, but it doesn't matter. You are going to tell us the code or we are going to kill both of your children and I promise you they will suffer."

"You have Katya? Let me speak to her."

"I will have her within a few hours because she cannot stand by and let her brother die. Can you?"

"If I tell you, you will kill them anyway."

"If you give us the code I give you my word they will not be harmed," Stepovich responded with as much sincerity as he could muster.

"That's not good enough," Dimitry said bluntly and then turned to face Sokolov. "I must have your word that my children will be safe and that they, and I, remain under your control as soon as possible." It was his only hope to save his children. He had reason to believe the President would keep his word, at least for now, he was not known as a man of unnecessary violence.

He wanted the code and he had no reason to want these people killed so President Sokolov didn't hesitate, "You have my word. And I will assure you that Director Stepovich will follow it."

It was the best he was going to get. He had put his children in this danger and he would have to do whatever he could to save them. "Then I will tell you the code.

Again at Boris Stepovich's request, they were standing by at the nuclear missile control headquarters and were prepared to do another test. Within an hour of receiving the code the test was successfully concluded and the results reported back to President Sokolov. Satisfied, he had Dimitry taken back to his cell, ordered Boris Stepovich to spare the lives of Yuri and Katya, and dismissed them so he could make his call to the Pyongyang government.

On their way back to the FSS headquarters Boris Stepovich instructed Vladimir Kosloff to contact Malenkov and have him capture Katya if at all possible. If he could get the code she had it would be useful in getting more concessions from Sokolov. But if they couldn't capture her then they must kill her. The Americans must not get the code to unlock their nuclear missiles.

# CHAPTER 41

▼

# ACADIA NATIONAL PARK, MAINE NINE A.M., FRIDAY DECEMBER 31, 1999

## FOURTEEN HOURS TO O O

The sight of Kate and Nick going head first off the cliff temporarily froze the Casper crew. They knew they had on gyro-belts, but could only hope they would not fight the automatic correction the belts would try to make. The gyro-belts were not intended for headfirst dives of a relatively short distance. And, if it did its job and corrected the fall, they could still land in the frigid water and be battered against the rocks.

Corporal Semanski gunned Casper and raced over the cliff and towards the water while Eric Johnson and Private Petersen got into their safety harnesses and prepared to go into the water to rescue them. As they cleared the side of the cliff, they were relieved to see Nick holding tightly onto Kate atop of a large rock. It was mid-tide and the rocks were surrounded by water, but they were not completely covered, as they would be at high tide. They were bruised, cold, and wet from the spray of the water crashing against the rocks, when Corporal Semanski maneuvered Casper close to them and Lieutenant Johnson and Private Petersen pulled them in.

Wet, cold, scared, and unable to return to the hotel, Eric Johnson had to find another place where they could get into dry clothes and get some rest so they headed north for Acadia National Park. The park was located a few miles off the Maine coast south of Portland and would be uninhabited at this time of year. There was a small Forest Ranger's lodge in the center of the island. It was accessible only by a dirt road, which would be impassable at this time of year.

At full throttle they were in the lodge in less than thirty minutes. The three-room lodge had a large room that served as a kitchen, dining room, and living area and two small bedrooms with a bathroom between them. They quickly set up portable electric heaters, which were powered by Casper, and changed into dry clothes. The near death experience of Kate and Nick had been emotionally exhausting for them and the MicroForce team: especially for Eric, who had almost blown it in his desire to get his brother's killer. Kate's answers to the barrage of questions asked on the flight to the island were vague and defensive and needed a great deal more explanation, but Eric knew the tensions were running high and they were exhausted so he ordered them all to get some badly needed rest.

Nick had protested that he was not tired and he needed to talk to Kate now and only relented when Eric had promised he would have time alone with Kate as soon as they all had some rest. He had agreed and, to his surprise, he slept as soundly as did the others and was startled when he was awoken at seven-thirty in the morning. True to his word, Eric ordered Nick and Kate to be woken so they could have a quick breakfast and have a little time to talk.

They were in one of the small bedrooms, Kate was sitting on the bed and Nick was sitting opposite her on a small wooden chair. Nick had a hundred questions that he wanted to ask all at once, but he fought against his natural tendency to do that. He also had a hundred different emotions running through his head: he was hurt, confused, angry, and sad. He had to control these emotions to get the answers he needed so he took a deep breath and began to talk to Kate, who was looking away from him. "What's going on Kate? When I agreed to come with you I knew there was something you weren't telling me, but what Eric said last night can't be true."

Kate still could not look at him as she uttered the words, "I'm afraid it is Nick.'

Nick felt like he had been kicked in the stomach by a mule. "A Russian spy? A God damned Russian spy?"

"Yes, Nick, a Russian spy. I told you not to come."

"You knew I had strong feelings for you, Kate. Or whatever your name is. And you used those feelings to get me to help you get this far, just like you used them last night." There was more pain than bitterness in Nick's voice.

She turned to face Nick, the trace of a tear in the corner of those beautiful dark eyes, and tried to assure him, "No, Nick, you have to believe me when I tell you it wasn't like that. Last night happened because I have those feelings too and gave in to them so we could share something beautiful before our world's came crashing down on us. You have to believe that, Nick. Please."

The anger in Nick took over, "I don't know what to believe. But I know your country is the enemy. It's as simple as that."

Kate continued to look directly at Nick and spoke softly as she gently shook her head, "No, it's not that simple. Nothing is that simple. I know you would like it to be, but everything is not black or white. Most things are different shades of gray. Long before I ever met you I had a family that I love and your country has been our enemy. I never meant to hurt you, but I had a commitment to my country and, more importantly, to my father."

"So your father is a spy, too." Nick couldn't control his anger. "So is he the one who planned the sabotage of our nuclear missile defenses."

Kate could understand his pain and anger, but he had to understand her side of it. "Yes, he did. But it was not to cause any harm to your country."

"No! What do you call leaving us vulnerable to attack by your country?"

"That's just it. He didn't leave your country vulnerable because he took it away from both countries. Remember, these aren't defensive they are offensive weapons."

"Do you expect me to believe your father had the Russian nuclear weapons system sabotaged as well?"

"Yes, that's exactly what he did."

"You expect me to believe that? Why would he do that?"

"He did it because the Y2K problem gave him the unique opportunity to have access to the ultimate security codes, of both countries, that were normally inaccessible. He knew that if he crippled the US system he would have to cripple Russia's too. Or else there would be those who would use the temporary imbalance in power to cause great destruction."

Confusion was now replacing Nick's anger, "But why bother at all? Why take the risk and put your life in jeopardy?"

"Because Russia is in serious trouble. Economically we are a disaster. In many ways we have gone from the status of a world power to a third world country.

And if we don't do something very quickly my father is afraid our democratic experience will be short lived and replaced by something worse than even the old hard line communists. I am afraid that has always been the history of my country."

Nick could sympathize with Kate, after all how would he feel if America was suddenly a third world power. "But surely you must see the danger of this plan. If one country gets the code, or fixes the system on its own, then the balance of nuclear power will be destroyed. There are men on both sides that would take advantage of such a situation. Maybe even annihilate the other."

"Yes, we see the danger. But you must remember that my country is in a desperate condition."

"And desperate men do desperate things?"

"That's right, Nick."

"So then give me the code," Nick pleaded. "I can use it to get you leniency."

She looked at him with a sadness in her dark eyes that made him want to grab her and hold her and make all the bad things go away. "I'm afraid it's not that simple."

"Yes, it is. Just give me the code and I can make it better."

"I can't.'

"Why not."

"Because the men who tried to kill us last night have my brother, and they will kill him if I don't meet with them. The code is all I have to bargain with to get the Lieutenant to allow me to go to the meeting."

"But a meeting with them would be committing suicide. Just look at what they tried to do last night. You can't trust them."

"I have no choice. I can't just let my brother die."

"There has to be another…….." Nick was interrupted as Eric Johnson knocked on the door and then opened it and entered with Corporal Semanski.

He looked at Nick, ignoring Kate, and said, "I'm sorry, but we are running out of time. We can't delay any longer." He then addressed Kate, his voice was cold, "I don't have much time so I am gong to be brief and I expect your answers to be the same. I believe your name is Katya. Is that correct?"

The coldness in his voice drove home the fact she was his enemy, but she had no resentment for what he was about to do. It was his job and she would do the same. "Yes. Katya Petrov."

"Cute. Kate Peters. Katya Petrov. Easier to remember that way, I suppose," Eric observed without amusement. "In short, you are a Russian spy who sabotaged our nuclear missile system and snuck away last night to arrange a meeting with your comrades. The same comrades that killed my brother."

Katya could see the fire in his eyes when he made this last statement. "Yes, I added a crucial security code to your missile system and, yes, I tried to make a call, but not a call to the men who came after me last night. The same men who have tried to kill or capture me four times now and, I believe, the men who are responsible for your brother's death. The call was to my brother who is in their hands, and will also die by their hands if I don't stop it somehow. My brother who disabled the Russian nuclear missile system just as I have yours."

"Whatever she has done, I don't believe she had anything to do with your brother's killing," Nick finally spoke. He then went on to quickly explain the ill-fated plan her father devised and was carried out by her and her brother.

"That's a good story. It may even be true, but the fact still remains that she is a spy and it is their plan that got my brother killed. She can never make that right, but she can try to make the sabotage right by giving us the code."

"I'm sorry, but I can't do that."

"Why not?" Eric demanded.

"Because then they will kill my brother for sure."

"I truly sympathize with you about that. But the fact is he wouldn't be in this danger if it weren't for you." Eric let that sink in for a moment before continuing, "Now you will give me the code voluntarily or I will take it from you."

Nick was shocked at what he just heard. "What do you mean take it from her? You're not going to torture her?"

"We are not going to torture her," Corporal Semanski responded. "Although, in the end, she may wish we had."

"What the hell are you talking about,' Nick demanded.

Eric would have preferred not discussing this with Nick, but now he had no choice. "All Corporal Semanski means is that we have a drug that will make her tell everything we want to know."

"Bull shit, Eric. He meant a lot more than that. What the hell is it?"

Eric realized he never should have let Nick stay this long and he ordered Corporal Semanski to remove him. But Nick pulled his gun and aimed at Eric's chest as Corporal Semanski quickly responded and had his gun inches form Nick's head. One wrong move by Nick or an order from Eric and he would be dead. Eric knew he could have Nick killed with little consequences. He was an amateur and would hesitate long enough to have his brains blown out before he could pull the trigger. And, even if he did pull the trigger, the worse that would happen is a broken rib. His special polymer enhanced Kevlar vest would ensure that. But Eric didn't want to have to kill a man like Nick. He understood the passion that drove a man to want to protect someone he loved.

"The drug is very effective, but it needs to be administered over a period of time to be safe. We started administering it a few days ago at the Quabbin Reservoir. That was the after taste you complained about, Kate. Unfortunately, you didn't eat enough and we didn't have a long enough time. To get the results we need now, we will have to administer a massive dose."

"And what will that do?" Nick asked.

"It will get her to tell us everything we need," Eric answered. "It may also leave her a vegetable. There' a fifty-fifty chance."

"Damn it, Eric. I won't let you do it. You'll have to kill me first."

"I don't want to have to do that. But, if I have to, I will."

"Wait, Eric," Katya pleaded. "Even if you get me to tell you the code, it won't do you any good. The system is very sophisticated. Besides the code it will need both my voice and iris recognition."

"Nice try, Katya. But how do I know you're not bluffing."

"You don't. And I'm not."

"Can you chance it?" Nick said. "Besides, there's another way."

"What?"

If it had to, Nick was prepared to have it end here. But he would try his best not to let that happen. "We can go forward with the meeting and try to rescue her brother. If we do that she will go with us to Washington to unlock the code."

"Is that true, Katya?" Eric asked.

"Yes. If you promise to try to save him like he was your own brother."

"It's a hell of a gamble, Lieutenant," Corporal Semanski said. "Our orders were to administer the drug by now."

"And what happens if she is telling the truth about the voice and iris identification?" Nick said. "Beside this will give you a chance to face your brother's killer." Nick was desperate and it wasn't hard to know what motivated Eric.

Corporal Semanski also knew what drove Eric so he appealed to his military reasoning, "Let's suppose she is telling the truth and this isn't just some scheme to try to escape. Why would they let her go? They aren't just going to believe she has told them the truth. And what if they know about, or suspect, this voice and iris identification?"

As much as he hated to admit it, Eric had to agree with Corporal Semanski. "He's right, Nick. They are either going to try to capture her or kill her. But they will never let her go. Isn't that right, Katya?"

Before Nick could speak, Katya answered, "Yes, that is probably right. But I've seen your team in action and you have unusual resources. I'm counting on that to save my brother and keep them from capturing me."

"I see," Eric said. "The problem, Katya, is that I can pretty much guarantee that we can keep them from capturing you. But I can't guarantee that they won't kill you. And I can't let that happen. Can I?"

"You can if I give you the code on a tape recording. Then if they kill me you can still bring my body back to Washington. Together with the tape you will be able to unlock the nuclear missiles. Technically all you need is one of my eyes, so all you have to do is keep them from completely blowing my head away."

"I still don't like it, Lieutenant," Corporal Semanski stated. "It's too risky."

Eric ignored him. "You'll give us the code on tape?"

"I'll give it to Nick, if you give me your word you will do everything in your power to save my brother."

"You have it. But there had better be no more lies, Katya," Eric said. "The problem is, after last night, we don't even know if there is a meeting, which was scheduled for less than an hour from now."

"Well, there is only one way to find out," Nick said. "Let's call."

Over Corporal Semanski's protest, Eric let Katya make the call. She was relieved when, on the third ring, it was answered by Ivan Malenkov. He would not let her talk to Yuri and they would not meet at ten as agreed. He would not discuss it. He wasn't going to give them time to trace the call. He agreed to a one o'clock meeting at the same place. If she were there fine, if not Yuri would be killed. If they saw the helicopter anywhere in the area Yuri would be killed. Then he hung up.

Malenkov had agreed to the meeting because they needed to either capture or kill Katya. He had hoped to accomplish this the night before and, because they failed, now he would need more time to arrange for their escape once they accomplished their task.

Corporal Semanski had protested more forcefully now that there was a further delay in time. Lieutenant Johnson overruled him and took full responsibility, and then he turned and looked straight into Katya's eyes.

"If this is a trap, or if you are lying to us in anyway, you and your brother will die instantly. I guarantee it."

# CHAPTER 42

▼

# THE WHITE HOUSE WAR ROOM— WASHINGTON, D.C. TEN A.M., FRIDAY DECEMBER 31, 1999

## FOURTEEN HOURS TO <u>0</u> <u>0</u>

President Stewart fidgeted in his chair, and continued to watch the large electronic map that occupied the entire opposite wall, as he waited for the report. The map plotted the advance of the new millennium as it progressed across the world. Japan and Korea had entered the Year 2000 some fifteen minutes earlier and the preliminary flash reports were being put together.

The satellite reports were the first to arrive and showed some power outages in both countries. The most significant was Tokyo; it was in total darkness. There were several other regional areas that appeared to have had power failures. The next report in was from the Ambassador to Japan who confirmed the power outage in Tokyo. He also indicated there were some reports of panic in the streets as a result. The government had feared this might happen because of the large crowds celebrating the New Year and had already declared a state of emergency.

"What about North Korea, Donald?" The President asked.

"Most of the country is in darkness," Director Mathias answered. "But that doesn't tell us much. They aren't in a position to be doing very much celebrating. Pyongyang is in total darkness. But, again, with them that could be intentional."

"What do you mean intentional? Why would they do that?" President Stewart asked.

"They may want us to think they have had a severe power outage."

"Why?"

"That's not clear, but it could be to use to their advantage somehow," General Armstrong offered. "We'll have to wait and see."

"What about their nuclear missiles?"

"They have their own generators, so if they really do have an outage, they will still be functional," Donald Mathias responded.

"The Japanese Ambassador has asked again if we know of any activity in North Korea," Secretary of State Carlson said. "I told them I have heard of nothing, but would check again."

"Good. I still don't want them told," the President responded. "There is nothing to be gained; especially now with Tokyo in darkness. We would just add to the chaos."

"Darren, how are we doing on the domestic front?"

The bags under his red eyes made the FBI Director look tired and drawn, "We've infiltrated and broken up at least a dozen planned terrorist attacks. But I have to tell you I'm very nervous about the celebrations going to take place tonight. There are huge outdoor celebrations planned across the country. They're expecting more than two million people in Times Square tonight and that's a terrorists' dream."

"I assume we have done everything we possibly can?" It was more of a statement than a question by the President.

"Yes we have, sir," Alexander responded. "We have every agent of the FBI, ATF, and DEA, every US Marshal and state and local police on full alert. In addition, we have coordinated with General Armstrong's staff and the state National Guards to have troops strategically located in all major cities."

"That's correct, sir," General Armstrong added. "All we will need is for you to declare marshal law and we will be there to take whatever action is needed."

"Thank you gentlemen," the President said. "But let's pray that that is not necessary."

Director Alexander added, "Let's pray that the lights don't go out in New York, or any other large city, or we will have chaos in the streets."

# CHAPTER 43

▼

# PERKINS COVE—OGUNQUIT, MAINE ONE P.M., FRIDAY DECEMBER 31, 1999

## ELEVEN HOURS TO 0 0

Nick drove the big Ford Explorer along the narrow road leading from the Shore Road to Perkins Cove. The vehicle had been left on a remote access road that serviced the back nine of the golf course and it had been easy for Casper to land undetected—engulfed in its own cloud. Nick and Katya quickly exited Casper and entered the vehicle; leaving behind Eric Johnson, Corporal Semanski and Private Petersen. The other four members of the MF team were already at Perkins Cove with the other SUV.

As they drove the distance on the short winding road, they searched for signs of the MF team as well as the enemy. Eric had refused to give them the locations of the other four members for fear they would give them away. All he would tell them is that they were there and would be dressed in the same camouflage outfit that he was wearing and would be carrying their distinctive rifles. He had provided both of them with bullet—proof vests and, at Nick's insistence, their pistols. Eric had warned Nick that giving Katya a weapon could be signing his own death warrant, but Nick insisted so Eric relented and warned her his team had orders to shoot her in the head if she made one wrong move.

He also gave them each a tiny microphone for their lapel and glued an ultra small receiver just inside their right ear. These extremely sensitive units were external versions of what each MicroForce member had surgically implanted. It took a little while for them to get used to the voice right in their ear, but with a little practice they were proficient enough to be able to listen to the voice in their ear and give no outward signs they were being communicated with.

As he drove onto the small peninsula that created Perkins Cove, Nick was struck by the how eerily quiet it was. In the summer, the picturesque little cove overflowed with tourists shopping in the quaint little gift shops and art galleries located at the far end of the peninsula or eating in one of its three restaurants located as you first entered the cove. But at this time of year it was deserted save for them, the four MF members, and God only knew how many Russian FSS agents. Even Casper was three thousand feet above them. Nick had questioned what good they would be able to do at that height and was told they would see everything and the computer controlled .50-caliber machine guns were deadly accurate at over two miles.

Nick pulled into the parking lot that occupied the center of the peninsula and pulled to the far end near the shops. He turned the vehicle around so that it faced the open lot and the only road out; its back was to the ocean. It wasn't a good position, but it was the best one they had. He kept the motor running for a quick get away, but he knew, in truth, their lives depended on MicroForce.

The MF unit was well positioned to defend them. Besides Casper hovering above, Private Nelson was in a small gift shop to their left, Private Wilson was in the other Explorer parked in a small wooden garage at the other end of the parking lot near the entrance to the cove, Private Kincaid was hidden in bushes on the cliff on the other side of the cove, and Corporal Anderson was located inside Barnacle Billy's restaurant, also at the entrance to the cove. Corporal Anderson had chosen the restaurant because it was the only building on the road and the water. Too bad he wouldn't get to taste the best clam chowder in Maine.

It was precisely five minutes after one o'clock when the dark van came down the winding road, drove passed Barnacle Billy's, and came to a halt at the far end of the parking lot about thirty yards from Nick and Katya. The side door on the passenger side of the vehicle slid open and two men got out. One man pulled the other from the van and then pushed him along in front of him until they were in front of the van and stopped. They man in front was obviously Yuri, his hands were heavily bandaged and he was unsteady, but they couldn't be sure because he had on a coat with the hood pulled up and the larger man held him by the back of his neck forcing his face to be tilted towards the ground. The larger man also held a gun to Yuri's head.

Nick and Katya got out of their vehicle; Nick on the driver's side and Katya on the passenger side. He quickly got by her side and held her by the arm to prevent her from racing to her brother.

"What have they done to my poor Yuri?" Katya whispered.

Nick could hear the despair in her voice and felt her pain. But he couldn't let himself be distracted. They had to be prepared to act quickly, and there was something wrong. "Didn't you tell me you thought they probably would have broken his fingers?"

"Yes. It is often used in the field. It is effective and also makes it difficult to escape. That is why Yuri's hands are bandaged."

With their microphones on Eric could hear everything they said, "What's the matter, Nick?"

"If his fingers were broken wouldn't they be bandaged too?" Nick questioned.

"Yes," Eric replied as he zoomed in on the man's hands.

"Well, they're not," Nick said jerking on Katya's arm; pulling her closer to him and stopping her forward progress. "It's not Yuri."

"You're right," Eric announced. Then commanded, "Abort! Abort!"

Before Nick and Katya could respond Egor Skulsky turned the gun on Katya and quickly fired a shot that struck her square in the chest. He fired only one shot because he knew the Teflon coated 356 magnum would pierce any vest she might be wearing. He also knew that was all the time he would have so he instinctively pulled his comrade in front of him just in time to have his chest smashed by the .50-caliber shell fired from Casper and meant for him.

Before the next shell could strike, Skulsky leaped into the open van as Ivan Malenkov floored it and turned sharply towards the water. Skulsky took aim at Nick, who was desperately trying to get Katya's limp body back into the SUV, and was ready to fire when Private Nelson emerged from her hiding spot in the little gift shop, located just behind and to the right of the SUV, exposing herself in order to get a clear shot at the van and direct fire away from Nick and Katya. Her efforts were successful as her bullets shattered the glass on the side of the van and kept Egor Skulsky from getting an accurate shot off. Unfortunately a sharpshooter, located on the small cliff across the cove, put a bullet in her right leg and immediately took her down. Private Kincaid eliminated the sharpshooter before he could fire a second shot.

As Lieutenant Johnson and Corporal Semanski had suspected, the helicopter that had been making a wide circle of the cove was now moving directly towards Nick and Katya, probably to make sure she was dead and then to assist their comrades on the ground. Eric ordered Corporal Semanski to intercept it at full throttle. As the enemy helicopter approached the SUV and prepared to fire, Eric used his computer guided laser to disable the craft and send it plummeting into the ocean.

One of the shots fired by Private Nelson pierced the drivers door and hit Malenkov in the leg causing him to crash into one of the small gift shops and leaving him unconscious and the vehicle disabled. Casper's pre-occupation with the other helicopter allowed Skulsky to escape and disappear among the maze of small buildings at the far end of the peninsula.

At the same time another black van came roaring down the narrow road stopping fifty yards short of Barnacle Billy's. It unloaded three of its occupants and then continued at high speed toward the parking lot with its remaining two occupants. This was the cue for Private Wilson to floor the Explorer and break through the flimsy wooden garage door and intercept the van. As he did so he came under heavy fire from the three men who were making their way towards the parking lot on foot. Corporal Anderson, from Barnacle Billy's, quickly returned the fire cutting one man down and forcing the others to cover.

Private Wilson had ignored the gunfire that had smashed into the side door and window of his vehicle, but had not penetrated. Concentrating on the van, he knew he couldn't let it get to Nick and Katya so he fired a small rocket concealed under the front bumper that exploded into the side of the van sending it off of the parking lot and down onto the small floating pier below. He then continued on to help Nick, Katya, and Private Nelson.

Corporal Anderson continued his firefight with the two men remaining from the van when he began to receive fire from a fishing boat on the water behind him. He radioed that he was in the middle of a crossfire and needed assistance. He received some help from Private Kincaid on the cliff, but he was under heavy fire from the boat himself.

Lieutenant Eric Johnson ordered Corporal Semanski to drop him by the van that crashed into the building and then to proceed to attack the boat. As Casper came to within thirty feet of the ground Eric leaped from its belly and landed behind the disabled van. He quickly determined that the driver was still alive, but unconscious, so he handcuffed him to the steering wheel. He then prepared to enter the maze and wished he had the use of Casper's heat seeking abilities. He would have to rely on his own judgment and the three PIP's he released into the air.

Nick was happy to see Private Wilson approaching and very pleased see the appearance of Casper. It had only been a few minutes since it all began, but it felt like an eternity. Kate was unconscious, but breathing. He didn't know how badly she was hurt; he couldn't find any blood. He had dragged her behind the SUV and had exposed himself again to drag Private Nelson behind the vehicle also.

Eric had no readings from any of his PIP's and knew operating procedure called for him to wait for assistance, preferably Casper, but he couldn't. He had to get this bastard so he slowly made his way around the first building. He saw nothing but fortunately heard the slight creak of a door two buildings away and immediately pulled back behind the building just in time to avoid the automatic weapons fire that tore away large chunks of wood from the corner of the building. From the sound and the power of the weapon he suspected his enemy was well armed with an AK47 assault rifle. Eric dropped low and returned the fire with a burst from his own weapon that jolted the door open allowing one of his PIP's to enter.

The video transmission showed the building was unoccupied and the back door was open. His opponent was smart; he moved as quickly as possible after firing. Rather than follow behind and go through the building into what might be a trap he circled to his right. It was a cat and mouse game, but it wasn't clear who was the cat and who was the mouse.

As he circled to the right, Eric caught a glimpse of his opponent and let loose with a burst of fire and then immediately took cover; barely managing to avoid the return fire. He quickly moved to his left in an attempt to circle his enemy from this direction. Unfortunately his opponent either anticipated this or just guessed right and was waiting for him. The two bullets that hit him in the chest didn't penetrate his vest but had enough power to knock him down and leave him out in the open temporarily dazed. His instincts made him fire his weapon in the direction of his enemy. But he didn't get lucky and emptied his clip without hitting him.

With his enemy lying on the ground in the open and out of ammunition, Egor Skulsky would take a moment to savor his kill. He stepped into the open with his gun aimed at Eric's head, "It was a mistake not to wait for assistance. You should never under estimate your enemy." Egor Skulsky then let out his hideous laugh as he prepared to fire.

The hyena's laugh made Eric furious and gave him the presence of mind to flip the switch. "No you shouldn't, asshole!" Pulling the trigger he sent a 20mm shell into Skulsky's chest blowing him to pieces.

With bullets bouncing off of Casper's skin, Corporal Semanski gave the occupants of the boat a chance to surrender—both in English and Russian. Refusing they tried to make a run for the open ocean and were easily blown out of the water. At the same time, Corporal Anderson had eliminated the remaining two men from the van.

Corporal Semanski landed Casper in the parking lot close to Nick, Katya, and Private Nelson. Private Wilson had already applied a pressure bandage to the leg of Private Marty Nelson, but she was still bleeding badly. Katya was now awake and breathing better, but she was in a lot of pain. The polymer strengthened Teflon vest had done its job not allowing the bullet to penetrate. However, the power of the high caliber bullet had bruised her sternum and knocked the wind out of her.

Eric Johnson went to the Russian van that had crashed into the small building and found Ivan Malenkov just beginning to regain consciousness. He was the last of the team of Russians left alive. Blood trickled from the welt on his head received when he hit the windshield. The bullet to his leg was only a flesh wound and the pressure bandage Eric applied easily controlled the bleeding. Eric then made him walk the short distance to join the others. His limp was pronounced, but Malenkov managed to cover the twenty yards with some prodding from Eric.

Eric Johnson then put his captive in the hands of Private Wilson and got a quick update from Corporal Semanski. "Her leg is broken and she is still bleeding in spite of the pressure bandages. We will have to get Marty to a hospital quickly or she could bleed to death."

Lieutenant Johnson put his hand on her shoulder to reassure her, "We can take her to the Naval base at Machiasport. It's the closest one we can go to and we can be there in less than thirty minutes. Get her on board." He then turned to Nick and Katya, "Hurry and get on board. We have to get Private Nelson medical treatment and then we have to head to Washington."

It was a bit of a struggle for Katya to talk, but she looked sternly at Eric and spoke as firmly as she could, "But what about my brother? You gave me your word."

"I told you we would try and we did. He obviously wasn't in the van, and if he was in the helicopter or the boat I'm afraid he is dead. If he wasn't here he may still be alive, but we don't have time to hunt for him. Not at least until after we go to Washington and take care of our business."

Katya's mind raced, as she looked for leverage to use against Eric, when she got a good look at the captured Russian. He looked familiar but she was having a hard time placing him and then she remembered. Her father had secretly sent her background and photographs of senior agents that she might need to know sometime. She was now thankful that her father was always thinking. "That man can tell us. He is senior agent Malenkov. Ivan Malenkov, I believe. My guess he is the senior agent in charge of this operation and the man who gave the direct order to have your brother killed."

The fire returned to Eric's eyes as he reached out and grabbed the man by the neck, "Is that right? Are you the bastard in charge of this?" Though he tried to deny it, it was too late. Eric had already seen the startled look on his face when Katya mentioned his name. "I'm going to kill you," Eric said through gritted teeth as he reached for his assault knife.

Nick grabbed his arm before he could draw his knife, "No, Eric, that's not the way; and he could still be useful."

"He knows where my brother is and you promised to do your best to help me free him," Katya pleaded. "You could use your drug on him."

At that point Corporal Semanski came back from helping secure Private Nelson in Casper, "I don't agree, but whatever we decide we should discuss it on our way to the naval base or Marty is going to bleed to death."

Lieutenant Johnson then order everyone into Casper except for Private's Wilson and Kincaid who would take the two Ford Explorers away from here and wait for his orders.

Nick helped Katya into Casper and she thanked him for intervening on her brother's behalf. He didn't respond, but held her closely and thought about the ache he felt when he thought she was dead.

# CHAPTER 44

▼

# THE WHITE HOUSE WAR ROOM— WASHINGTON, D.C. THREE P.M., FRIDAY DECEMBER 31, 1999

## NINE HOURS TO 0 0

Time continued its relentless march across the globe leaving varying degrees of problems in its wake. Evidence of this was displayed for President Stewart and his crisis team on the War Room's large electronic map and by the verbal communications being received from the field. The military's flying wings were doing their job effectively allowing the heads of the key governments, and the U.S. Ambassadors to those country's, to maintain communication with the White House in spite of the widespread power outages and communications disruptions they were experiencing.

In the past two hours China, Hong Kong and the Philippines had joined Japan, Korea and India as major countries who were experiencing power and communications problems, some of them significant. Beijing followed Tokyo,

Seoul, and New Deli as major cities that were in darkness except for the small amount provided by emergency generators. All flights had been cancelled to and from these cities and military now occupied the streets to prevent panic rioting.

Three quarters of Russia was now into the new millennium and with it came almost total darkness. Most of their generators had been sabotaged for parts or sale long ago. Soon Moscow would enter the new millennium and the President hoped he would still be able to communicate with his Russian counterpart. It wasn't possible to locate a flying wing over Moscow, but they had one hovering at the eastern end of the Balkan Sea if it was needed.

President Stewart had just finished another distressing conversation with President Sokolov. He took great offense at the suggestion that his country needed help from the United States to maintain its communication and emergency power systems; even though it was clear a number of Russia's nuclear reactors had lost the electric power that cooled their cores and the emergency back up generators were inoperable or non-existent. President Sokolov had ended the conversation with a statement that, before the new millennium was a day old, the United States would publicly commend him and his country for the vast progress they had made toward democracy and would lead the way in demanding the international loans, which had been cut off because of false accusations of theft and mismanagement, be restored. Not only would the U.S. lead the way in their restoration, but they would be greatly increased and would provide a great deal of the financing directly.

The President no sooner finished briefing the Security Council on the call from President Sokolov than Secretary of State Carlson received an urgent communication from North Korea.

"What is it, Judith?"

"I'm afraid it's from the North Koreans, sir. They demand to know why there is a nuclear submarine in the Sea of Japan infringing on their territorial waters."

"There is always a nuclear submarine in the Sea of Japan," General Armstrong responded. "It's standard operating procedure." He then nodded to one of his aides who pushed a button and eighteen orange lights lit up on the electronic map. These represented the United States' Trident class submarine fleet and were spread across the globe with one in the Sea of Japan off of the North Korean coast. As long as the Washington monument, the five hundred feet long and four story high submarine has twenty-four missiles that can carry as many as eight nuclear warheads, for a total of one hundred and ninety-two.

"But isn't the location of these submarines top secret?" the President asked.

"That's right, sir," General Armstrong replied.

"So how do they know it's there?"

"A good guess or a leak, sir."

"Or maybe the submarine was detected by the North Koreans," Victor Noble said.

The General was unperturbed by Noble's sarcasm, "That's possible, but highly unlikely."

"Whether they guessed or know doesn't matter at the moment, but this isn't the first time they have made this kind of complaint. Is it, Judith?"

"No it isn't, sir," Secretary of State Carlson said. "But this time is different. They are being much more vehement about it. They have even sent a special protest to the Secretary General of the UN."

"It sounds to me like they're laying the groundwork for a 'defensive' action," General Armstrong observed.

"Well, let's try not to give them any excuses, General," the President said. "Order the submarine out of the area as quickly as possible."

"Yes, sir."

"Excuse me, Mr. President, but shouldn't we be showing signs of strength rather than weakness," Victor Nobel said.

"Excuse me, Victor, but I don't want to give them any excuses or do anything to provoke them. Not at this critical time."

"I think we should be taking more aggressive action," Noble said.

"I know you do," the President responded firmly. "But that is all we are doing, for now."

"Time is running out," Noble said.

"But it hasn't,' a determined President Stewart responded. "Not yet."

# CHAPTER 45

▼

# NAVAL BASE— MACHIASPORT, MAINE
# SIX P.M., FRIDAY DECEMBER 31, 1999

## SIX HOURS TO 0 0

The young doctor at the Machiasport Naval Base infirmary successfully stopped the bleeding from Private Nelson's leg. While she was very weak from the loss of so much blood, Eric was relieved to hear she would make a full recovery, but she would have to remain here for now. He hurried back to Casper to tell the others and get out of there. He had been the only one to leave the aircraft when the ambulance came out to get her. He had been pleased when the base commander accepted his explanation that she had been injured in a freak training accident and they concentrated on her care. Now he wanted to get out of there before more questions were asked.

As he boarded Casper he wasted little time informing the others, "Private Nelson is going to be fine, but will have to remain here to recover. We'll make arrangements to get her moved as soon as she is able. Now let's get airborne Corporal before the base commander has a chance to ask questions."

"Yes, sir," Corporal Semanski replied as he prepared for lift off. They had not shut Casper down so they were in the air within two minutes of Lieutenant Johnson's order. "I assume the coordinates are to be set for Washington, D.C.? We're running out of time."

Eric Johnson's eyes revealed a trace of compassion as he looked at Katya, "Yes. It's time to complete our mission."

Katya was afraid of this and felt the desperation at the thought of what would happen to her brother. She couldn't give up yet, "But you promised to save my brother in return for the code."

"Yes. And that's why I let the meeting at Perkins Cove take place. I risked the safety of my team and it almost cost one of them her life. I can't ask them to do that again. Not for someone who is, or at least has been, our enemy."

Katya knew she had to plead to his sense of honor and his compassion. "But you said you would do everything you could. And you haven't done that. Would you quit if it were your brother?"

Reminding him of his brother made him both angry and sad. Fortunately for Katya the compassion won out, "What would you have me do, Katya? We don't know where he is, or if he is even alive, and we don't have time to find out."

Katya nodded toward Malenkov in the back of the cabin. "He knows. You could use the drug on him." She had no desire to hurt him for what he had done to her brother, but she would easily trade his life for Yuri's. "Remember, he may not have been the one to pull the trigger that killed your brother, but he was the one in charge of those who did."

The fire burned in his gut at the thought, and he wanted to kill him on the spot, so he decided he would keep his word and do all he could to save Katya's brother. "I'll give the drug one hour to work."

Corporal Semanski had to speak, "With all do respect, sir. We have already wasted a good part of the day and risked our lives. And you have avenged your brother's death. Now it's time to complete our mission."

"I'm afraid he is right, Katya. Even if we get the information in time, I can't ask these men to risk their lives again for something not critical to our mission."

"But if you don't, they'll kill him," Katya pleaded.

Nick saw the pain in Katya's eyes and heard the desperation in her voice and knew that, no matter what she had done, he loved her. "You're right, Eric. You can't ask your men to risk their lives to save him." He then looked into Katya's tear filled eyes and declared, "That's why I will do it."

She reached out and grabbed his hand, "No. I've done enough to you already. You're not trained for this. I can't let you."

He squeezed her hand, but looked at Eric as he spoke, "Now that you have Katya, I'm not critical to the mission and you are not responsible for me anymore. There were so many of them at Perkins Cove I can't believe there are more than one or two guarding him."

"Even so, Katya's right. You're not trained for this," Eric answered.

"I've managed to survive so far. Just give me one of those special rifles and the use of your fantastic technology. We can send a dozen PIP's in to get all the detail I will need and then you can back me up with Casper's firepower without putting any of your men at risk. That way you can keep your word and maybe save a life in the process."

"Or get you killed in the process."

"That risk is on me, not you."

"For such a smart guy I think you're making a stupid decision. You're thinking with your heart and not your head. But I'll give you this—you've got balls."

"Then you'll do it?"

"Yes, we'll do it," Eric answered. "Corporal head back to the southern part of the state. It's likely they're still somewhere in that area. I'll get started administering the drug."

"Can I have a moment to speak with him before you start?" Katya asked.

"Why?"

"Maybe I can reason with him."

"You can have a few minutes. But that's all."

Katya went to the back of the cabin and addressed him calmly, "Malenkov, they are going to use a drug on you that will guarantee that they get the information they want. The problem is that there is a good chance it will destroy your brain and leave you a vegetable. You should tell them and save yourself."

Ivan Malenkov listened to Katya and wanted to do it and end this whole thing. He never was fully behind this operation and he would be a dead man once Boris Stepovich found out he had failed, but he couldn't. "You may be right. But if I tell them I put my comrades who are guarding him at great risk."

On hearing this, Eric came closer to the two of them, "If you give us the location and details I can assure you we will use every effort to spare them. We have the technology and the equipment to do it."

"Believe him. I'm sure he is telling you the truth."

"I'd like to, but I can't take the risk. You'll have to do what you have to do."

Both Lieutenant Johnson and Corporal Semanski knew this was a good sign. The drug worked more quickly, and required less of a dose, when the subject's commitment to resist was weak to begin with. So Eric gave him half of the dose he was going to. As expected, it took only thirty minutes of questioning from the time of the initial injection until they had the information they needed. Yuri was being held at a safe house in a remote area in southern Maine and there were only two guards.

Eric Johnson gave Corporal Semanski the general area he had received from Malenkov and then contacted Privates Wilson and Kincaid and ordered them to drive to the area, but to stay back out of sight. Within an hour they had located the farmhouse described by Malenkov and were hovering five hundred above it. It was very dark as little of the moon's light penetrated the heavy cloud cover. They lowered to two hundred feet to get the best view through their night vision equipment and then made a series of slow, ever widening circles around the target.

This was a slow process that consumed more than thirty precious minutes before they were satisfied the farmhouse was in a remote location and there was no additional security in the immediate area. They then put Casper in a hovering position directly above the farmhouse and released a dozen PIP's to gather information on the security within the house. Directed by Corporal Anderson and Private Petersen, they surrounded the house but were having difficulty finding access. It was old but tight to the weather. Nothing could be seen inside the house through the heavy curtains drawn across the windows.

Corporal Anderson sent one PIP down the chimney but, as expected, it was consumed in the oil-fired furnace. They could smash through one of the cellar windows, but were afraid the noise might alert the occupants. Another fifteen minutes had been consumed before they saw it; the door to the cellar was old and warped and had a small space in the upper left-hand corner. They left four PIP's to cover the perimeter of the house and sent the remaining seven into the cellar. The cellar, with it's dirt floor, was used for little more than to house the furnace, oil tank, and some small garden tools. They were then directed up the stairs, through the space under the cellar door, and into the house. As programmed, they quickly dispersed to cover the entire house.

There was a guard in the front room armed with an AK47 to intercept anyone trying to come through the front door. In the back bedroom there was another heavily armed man sitting in a chair guarding the man in the bed. The man's legs were tied to the foot of the bed, but there was no need to bind his grotesquely distorted hands. They were useless and obviously causing the man great pain.

Katya gasped at the sight of her brother. "My poor Yuri. What have they done?"

Nick put his arm around her, "It's all right, Katya. He will be free soon."

With tears in her eyes she kissed him on the cheek, "I can't let you go. You'll be killed."

"There is no choice. And I won't be killed." His forced smile did nothing to comfort her.

"I must go with you."

"I'm afraid I can't allow that," interrupted Eric. "Nick may not be critical to the completion of the mission, but you are."

"But he can't go down there alone," Katya pleaded.

"No, he can't," agreed Eric. "That's why I'm going with him."

"I'll volunteer to go with you, sir," Corporal John Anderson immediately offered.

"Yes, I will too," added Private Petersen.

Eric saw the look of concern on Corporal Semanski's face. He appreciated his men's loyalty, but agreed with the Corporal that the mission was being put in enough jeopardy by just being here. "Thank you men, but I'm afraid I can't allow that. Even though it looks like he is only lightly guarded the place could be booby-trapped. And we don't have the time to properly investigate so we could be walking right into it."

"That's why you shouldn't go in either, sir," Corporal Semanski said.

"Perhaps. But Nick can't do it alone and I gave my word. If we do run into problems I don't want any involvement from Casper or any of the MF team. You're to pick up Privates Wilson and Kincaid and head straight for Washington. And that's an order, Corporal. Is that understood?"

"Yes, sir."

Then he turned to Katya, "If that happens you'll go with them and cooperate fully. Agreed?"

Katya hesitated, with fear in her eyes she looked at Nick, "Agreed."

"I have your word?"

"You have my word."

With that guarantee they quickly went to work. Eric put on his Kevlar vest and helmet with night vision goggles while Corporal Anderson helped Nick with his and checked his gyro-belt. While they were doing this, Private Petersen equipped the MF rifles with a special attachment that gave these weapons a third, less lethal, capability. They could now be used as stun guns by administering enough of an electric shock to temporarily incapacitate an enemy without causing serious injury, unless they had a bad heart. Also, the 20mm explosive shells were replaced with concussion shells. When exploded in a confined area these concussion shells would disorient anyone within twenty feet for five to ten minutes, depending on how close they were to the actual detonation point. Used together, the concussion shells and the stun guns could be quite effective. Eric had chosen to use these partly because he had promised Malenkov, but more importantly, because it would be a good live test in case they had to storm the White House.

Corporal Semanski then maneuvered Casper to the back of the house at an altitude of twenty feet. The PIP's had shown them that this was a blind spot from inside the house. This had obviously been an impromptu safe house as evidenced by the plywood nailed over the backdoor to eliminate that as an entrance to the house. On Corporal Anderson's signal, Eric and Nick leaped from the craft and landed softly on their feet and quickly moved to the back of the house. The plan called for Nick to position himself outside the window of the back bedroom and for Eric to take the front entrance.

Nick had insisted that he should take the front entrance in case it was booby-trapped since Eric was more critical to the mission. Eric thanked him but declined; he knew Nick would probably storm through the door once it was blown open and likely get himself killed. They found a small wooden box that Nick could use to give him a better angle to shoot through the window. When he asked Eric how he would know where to shoot with the curtain covering the window he was told to leave his goggles on and listen to instructions from Corporal Anderson. It would all soon become clear, but he was not to shoot or make any noise until he heard the explosion knocking in the front door.

Eric carefully placed the plastic explosive on the door handle and the three hinges to make sure the door would fall back into the room when he detonated the charges. All the while he was receiving reports of any activity inside, and there was none. He took a position ten feet in front of and to the left of the door and signaled Casper he was ready. Instantly Corporal Anderson sent a signal to each of them that turned their goggles into a small video screen. Nick was startled to see the inside of the bedroom showing the guard sitting in a straight backed wooden chair located in the corner of the room, with the wall to his back the guard could see the door, Yuri on the bed, and the window. His gun was beside him leaning against the wall; an important fact not lost on Nick. Eric could see that the guard in the front room was sitting in a large over stuffed chair located in the center of the room, facing the front door his gun was in his lap.

Nick was startled again when he heard Corporal Anderson's voice and almost fell off the wooden box. The corporal instructed Nick to aim his gun two feet above the guard's head and not to worry about the curtain. The 20mm shell would tear right through it at that distance. The corporal then instructed him to lower the rifle slightly until he told him to stop. He was instructed by the Corporal to hold it there until he heard the explosion and the order to fire from him. He was also warned to fight the natural tendency to look towards the direction of the explosion. Once he fired the concussion shell he was to fire the stun gun directly at the guard. There would be no time for the computer to assist his aim so he should keep firing until he hit him. There would be a light trail left by each electric charge fired to help him adjust his aim if necessary.

Corporal Anderson then instructed Eric that Nick was ready and he could proceed at his discretion. Eric hit the button that detonated the charges and blew the door inward. Simultaneously he fired a concussion shell, which was pre-set to explode two feet above the guard's head, and then rushed to the left of the open doorway. As he had expected, the guard was well trained and had instinctively pulled the trigger on his AK47 and held it so it would fire in the automatic mode directed at the door. Anyone coming through the door would have been cut to ribbons. But the concussion shell had done its job and, after the initial burst of fire, the guard was now staggering in circles firing aimlessly. Eric waited for the moment the reeling guard's back was to the doorway and dropped to one knee in the center of the doorway firing one electric charge that sent the guard convulsing to the floor, his weapon by his side—silent. Eric then removed his weapon and quickly shackled him head and foot and then headed for the bedroom.

As soon as he had heard the explosion and the order from Corporal Anderson, Nick fired his concussion shell that tore through the curtain and exploded just above the guard's head. Then, without hesitation, he fired three successive electric charges before hearing the order from Corporal Anderson to stop. The first two charges had hit the guard and the third only missed because the poor bastard was already on the floor writhing in pain.

Eric entered the bedroom only after he was certain Nick was under control and on his way in to help. By the time Nick entered the room the guard was shackled and Eric had the groaning Yuri over his shoulder and ready to leave. Within two minutes Casper was on the ground picking up the tree of them as well as Privates Wilson and Kincaid. The SUV's would be left behind their work was done.

There was a tearful reunion between Katya and Yuri and, while Corporal Anderson gave Yuri a shot of morphine, Katya also gave Nick a tearful hug.

Lieutenant Eric Johnson then gave the order to a pleased Corporal Semanski to head for Washington as quickly as possible. He would contact the Silver Fox and get clearance for them to make a straight run to the White House, at high speed and low altitude for maximum efficiency. It would be close, but they could be there before midnight.

▼

# CHAPTER 46

# THE WHITE HOUSE WAR ROOM— WASHINGTON, D.C. TEN P.M., FRIDAY DECEMBER 31, 1999

## TWO HOURS TO 0 0

President Stewart looked at the clock, it was ten p.m. and the entire world except for North and South American and the small Pacific Ocean Nations had entered the new millennium. All of Russia was in darkness except for the few emergency generators in Moscow that still worked. Like Russia, Eastern Europe had major power failures and only had emergency lights. Western Europe and the British Isles had widespread outages in the more rural areas and spotty outages in the major cities. Word was coming in from country after country that they were declaring a state of emergency and ordering all non-official citizens to return to their homes and remain there. Apparently there had been some small riots in at least Paris and London, and probably other cities, as the millennium celebrations were ended prematurely. FBI Director Alexander again expressed his concern about the celebrations taking place in the U.S. cities. He was particularly concerned about New York City. His reports indicated there were already two and a half million people in Times Square and the crowd was growing. His agents had already short-circuited one terrorist group and he was deathly afraid of what would happen if New York City lost power. The President told him he had been assured there would be no power problems and it was too late now anyway. If they tried to cancel the remainder of the millennium celebrations there would be panic and riots in the streets.

The worst news had come when General Armstrong took President Stewart to the President's small, private office and informed him of the discussion he had just had with the Silver Fox. There had been no word from the MicroForce unit led by Lieutenant Johnson all day and he could not be reached. They both agreed that either some catastrophe had befallen them or Lieutenant Johnson had let his personal vendetta take control of him and they were now truly a rogue element. In any event, they both concluded that the President needed to be told that it was very unlikely they would be able to produce the key to unlock the nuclear missile defense system by the midnight deadline. Unfortunately Colonel Clay's team was no closer to solving the problem than they were a week ago. The President's displeasure was obvious and for a few moments he vented his anger at the General. But he quickly composed himself and apologized to the General. He concluded that they would have to get by with the submarine based missiles, red sky, and a good poker face.

On the bright side, the grid of flying wings was working successfully in those countries that had lost their satellite feeds. In those areas where they were needed they replaced the existing communication system by relaying the signals to U.S. satellites and allowed Washington to remain in contact with all of the major governments across the globe. Indeed, at that moment a spokesman for the North Korean government was on the telephone with Secretary of State Judith Carlson.

After a short, tense discussion, Secretary Carlson put the call on hold and addressed the waiting President. "They are demanding that our submarine surface and allow one of its destroyers to approach and board it."

The President glanced at General Armstrong and then answered her, "They know we can't and won't do that."

"That's what I told him, but he demands that we do it." Judith Carlson hesitated and then continued, "If we don't, he says they will consider it an act of aggression and will respond accordingly. He didn't elaborate."

"Can't they see that the submarine is heading away from them?"

Judith Carlson pushed the button and spoke with her North Korean counterpart and then put the phone on hold again. "He says that their systems are telling them that the submarine is positioning itself to be in the best position to launch its missiles at his country."

"But that's impossible. We're moving away as fast as we can," the President responded. Then he turned to General Armstrong, "We are, aren't we, General?"

"Yes, sir, we are. Not only does the map show it, but I also have had it confirmed to me personally. I wanted to make sure there was no miscommunication on this. I'm afraid they are doing what I had feared earlier."

"They are going to claim a system failure related to Y2K?" the President asked. "Yes."

"But how can they do that?" Victor Noble demanded. "They entered the new millennium hours ago. How can they claim now to have a Y2K problem? And why wouldn't they have done it earlier, when they first entered the year 2000?"

It wasn't the questions the General resented, they were good questions, but it was the way he asked them. He could be sarcastic too. "Think for a moment, Victor. The answer to your first question is that they will say they got early warnings of a nuclear attack from our sub as they rolled over into the new millennium, but didn't react because they were afraid it was a Y2K problem. They will then contend they put themselves at great risk by taking the time to diagnose the problem and fix it. They'll claim they continued to get signals of an impending attack and did everything they could, including these telephone calls, to avoid a nuclear confrontation. But, unfortunately, they had to retaliate once they received the signal that nuclear missiles had been launched at them from our sub."

A smarting Victor Noble interrupted, "That's fine and makes some sense. But why would they wait in the first place."

"It makes a lot of sense. As I indicated, they waited to help build the case for how restrained they were, but more importantly they waited because they know our nuclear capability of land based missiles will cease to exist at midnight."

"Yes, that makes sense," the President said. "They and the Russians know. It's the only explanation for why they would act the way they have."

"But don't we have enough nuclear warheads on our sub to destroy North Korea?" Noble asked.

"Yes, we do," the General replied. "But that would give the Russian and the Chinese an excuse to retaliate against us and we don't have enough submarine based nuclear warheads to deter them. We could do significant damage but they would survive. We wouldn't"

"What should I tell him, Mr. President?" Judith Carlson interrupted.

"Tell him he has my word we are not attacking them, but we will not order our submarine to surface." Secretary Carlson immediately did as the President ordered.

"You have to use the sub's missiles to take North Korea out now," Victor Noble demanded.

The President looked angrily at Victor Noble, "And bring on our own destruction. Never."

Noble sat back in his chair as he responded, "You've just doomed Tokyo and Taiwan. And maybe the world."

# CHAPTER 47

▼

# CASPER—THE SKIES OVER NORTHERN MASSACHUSETTS TEN-THIRTY P.M., FRIDAY DECEMBER 31, 1999

## ONE HOUR AND THIRTY MINUTES TO 0̲ 0̲

Once airborne in southern Maine, they had spent some time gaining altitude until they were now at twenty thousand feet and holding off the coast of northern Massachusetts, and waiting for clearance to make a straight run to the White House. There was very light air traffic because of the time of night, it being a holiday, and the Y2K scare, so to go in at this height and full speed they risked being picked up by military as well as commercial radar, and also by military satellite.

They could go in at a much higher altitude and slower in order not to be detected, but might not make it in time.

Eric Johnson had finally managed to get through to the Silver Fox on his secure line to tell him their status and get the clearance they needed. He had expected him to be angry because he had shut off all communications for the past two days in order not to have to disobey a direct order. But he was not prepared for the level of the Silver Fox's anger.

The strain in his voice was evident as he tried not to yell, "Where the fuck have you been? And where the fuck are you now? And, if you lie to me, I'll have your balls on my trophy wall."

Somehow Eric knew this was more than an idle threat. He hoped the good news would appease him. "We are off the coast of Massachusetts. The good news is that we have the key to unlock the missile system."

That was good news and could save all of their asses as well as the country. "Tell me. And give me the short story."

"Kate Peters is really Katya Petrov. A Russian FSS agent.'

"And she sabotaged our missile system?"

"Yes."

"And she has given you the code?"

"I'm afraid it's not as simple as that."

"It never is. Is it?"

"No, sir. It isn't."

"Tell me. But be quick about it."

Eric then filled him in on Katya, Yuri, and their father's plan. Nick interjected that they had learned from Yuri that he was instructed to tell Katya to abort the mission and unlock the missiles, but the other FSS agents got to him first. And they were fully cooperating now.

After they finished, the Silver Fox thought for a moment before answering. "The plan is so bold it could have worked." They were all surprised when he asked if their father's name was Dimitry.

Apparently the Silver Fox new of Dimitry Petrov and there was a trace of a tone of respect in his voice so Nick decided to push his advantage. They still needed Katya's cooperation so now was the time to deal. "They deserve amnesty for agreeing to help us now."

"Are you trying to black mail us now, Mr. Logan?"

The stern voice told Nick not to make it an ultimatum, "No, sir, I'm not. They are going to help us no matter what. But they never meant to harm our country and I think they deserve it. Yuri was on his way to instruct Katya to abort the mission before we ever discovered their plan."

There was a hesitation then, "Lieutenant Johnson, do you believe that? Or could this be some kind of a trick?"

"I believe it. One look at Yuri and you know he has suffered painful torture. And the attempts on Katya's life have certainly been real."

"I see," said the Silver Fox. "Tell me, Eric. You lost a brother, as a result of this Russian plan, would you grant them amnesty?"

Eric looked at Katya, Yuri, and then Nick before he answered. He saw the look of hope in their eyes and had seen the love they had shown for one another and decided there had been enough death. Maybe some good could come of this and, besides, his brother had liked both Nick and Katya a lot. "Yes, sir. I would. They may have been part of this plan, but they weren't responsible for Jeremy's death."

"I see. Well it will be up to the President."

"But you'll support it?" Nick asked.

"Yes, I'll support it. But if you don't get here in time for us to have our missiles back it will be academic."

"We can be there in plenty of time if you can get us flight clearance straight through and we don't have to worry about being picked up on radar," Eric informed him.

"Well, you see, that's going to be a little problem," the Silver Fox responded. "I just got off the phone with General Armstrong and, because I hadn't heard from you and didn't know where you were, you and your team have been declared a rogue element to be shot on sight if you do not surrender."

"But can't you call him back and tell him the situation? That we have the key to unlock the missiles."

"I would if I could get through. I had been trying for two hours when the General called me. He wasn't happy that he had to place the call. I have the necessary clearances so I should have been able to get through even to the War Room, which is where they are now. I had a hard time convincing the General that I wasn't just stalling him. My fear is there is an enemy on the inside with the ability to control at least some, if not all, of the incoming calls. But hold on, I'll try again."

It wasn't more than five minutes before he came back on the line, but it seemed forever. "I still can't get through. I'm afraid you are on your own."

"If we have to take evasive action to avoid being detected it is going to be awfully close for us to make it by midnight," Eric informed him.

"I'm afraid you will have to take all necessary evasive action. Because of the heightened fear of terrorist activities, the military is on full alert. I'll head for the White House and see if I can gain entrance to the War Room or, at least, get a message through. In the meantime, we will keep our communication lines open and set at priority code zero. Only you and I will have access to that band. Is that clear?"

"Yes, sir. Priority code zero."

"I will also direct that Casper's computer be allowed access to the highest security level. That will allow you to have all of the information on the White House security and access codes. Including the War Room access codes and how to get there. And Eric?"

"Yes, sir."

"I know this will put you at additional risk, but you will have to use your stun guns and concussion shells unless it becomes absolutely necessary to use more lethal means. There are a lot of innocent people between you and the War Room. Besides, I don't want to have to explain why I authorized and assisted a full-scale military attack on the President and his Security Council. I'm sorry. I'll do my best to get there and get you clearance, but I will have to drive in as no flights are being authorized over Washington."

"We understand, sir. Good luck."

"Good luck to all of you. Remember we can't fail. It could mean the deaths of a lot of people."

It was very disappointing news to hear that they would not be able to get the clearance needed to insure they would get there before midnight and that they might have to actually storm the White House. But there was no use complaining about it, they would just have to make it work. The MicroForce team would do whatever it took. That's what they were trained for.

Eric Johnson took the co-pilot's seat next to Corporal Semanski and close to Private Wilson, the primary navigator. He also called over Corporal Anderson to join in the review of their options. The fastest route would be to hug the coastline and head straight south at five thousand feet to Washington. But that was out of the question, as it would take them over the air space of such major cities as Boston and New York. It was Corporal Semanski's suggestion that they all agreed was the best alternative.

For the first phase of the plan they headed out to sea in an easterly-southeasterly direction and on a path to climb to thirty thousand feet. This would mimic the flight path of a plane headed for Bermuda, seven hundred miles off of the North Carolina coast. Casper's footprint would resemble that of an Executive

Learjet and they would make no attempt to 'hide' from the military or civilian radar screens; although they had the ability to adjust the angles of the surface of the outer skin, made up of a series of flexible six-inch diamond shape panels, which could either diffuse or reflect the radar.

The urgent call from the air traffic control demanding they identify themselves had come only about a minute after they turned off the stealth protection and began their altitude climb. In somewhat slurred speech, Lieutenant Johnson gave them false call letters, indicated their destination was Bermuda to welcome in the new millennium, and confirmed they had indeed not filed a flight plan. An incredulous air controller gave them clearance to climb to thirty thousand feet, after a slight correction lowering their rate of ascent, and admonished them to save the rest of their celebration until they landed in Bermuda.

Forty-five minutes had elapsed from the time they first left southern Maine to now cruising towards Bermuda at thirty thousand feet and three hundred miles off the U.S. coast. There had been frequent transmissions from the air traffic controller giving course corrections to keep the crazy partygoers headed for Bermuda. It was now time to put phase two into action. Eric Johnson made a distress call to the now panicked air controller who, a second earlier, watched in horror as his screen showed the jet in a steep nosedive toward the Atlantic Ocean.

Nick and Katya had been warned of what was going to happen, but the speed and steep angle of the descent still came as a shock. The G force generated by the plummeting aircraft had them pinned back in their seats as Casper began to shutter and they thought she was going to come apart.

Kate held on to her unconscious brother and, in turn, was held by Nick. "I'm not sure we're going to make it."

Nick felt a chill run up his spine as the aircraft shook more violently and he tried to console her, "Don't worry. I'm sure these guys know what their doing. They won't let us crash."

"From what I've seen, I think these guys would gladly crash this aircraft into the sea if their mission required it."

"I agree, but that's just it. They will have failed in their mission if we crash. And that's why we won't."

"I hope you're right."

"Me, too."

"I'm sorry I got you into this. I wish I had kept you out of it. I would do anything if I could change it for you."

Nick held her tighter and kissed her on the forehead. "I wouldn't. You may have turned my life up side down and what is right and wrong are no longer as clear to me, but you have also shown me what it is like to truly love a woman. And that's worth everything."

They held on tight as Casper continued to dive towards the sea. The call from the troubled aircraft was a scream declaring they were going to crash and then went silent. The controller's desperate and repeated instructions for them to pull out went unanswered as he watched the plane plummet the thirty thousand feet and disappear from his screen as it crashed into the sea.

The steep dive had severely tested Casper's maneuverability and structural capabilities. It had also strained the nerves of all of Casper's occupants as the craft shuttered when Corporal Semanski attempted to take her out of the controlled dive. Fortunately Casper lived up to the expected performance and they were now streaking towards Washington at five hundred and seventy-five miles an hour at only fifty feet above the ocean's surface. At five thousand feet Corporal Semanski had started to pull out and at two hundred feet he adjusted the angles on the outside skin and 'turned on' Casper's stealth abilities. The affect was to convince the air traffic controller that the jet had crashed. Even though it looked like they were beginning to pull out, no business jet could survive such a steep dive and, when it disappeared off of the screen, he would have no way of knowing there was still two hundred feet of air left. A lot of effort would now be directed toward searching for any survivors, as unlikely as that was.

They could go much faster but they didn't want to create any sonic booms and, at fifty feet, they had to be careful not to run into any ships that might be in the area. Thirty minutes later they were approaching the mouth of the Potomac River and slowed to seventy-five miles an hour for their trip up the river highway. They were now running in full stealth mode to avoid being detected by not only the normal military and civilian radar, but by the additional radar that protected the capital in general and the White House in particular. They would soon be entering a no fly zone.

Even though it was an overcast night, they produced their own cloud that enveloped Casper. The engines were running at full baffle and one hundred percent after burn, which meant they were whisper quiet and left no vapor trail at all. The diamond shaped little polymer panels of outer skin were constantly moving to change their angle and to never provide a flat surface, making them virtually invisible to any radar. At just ten minutes until the new millennium there was very little traffic on the roads and time was running out for the MicroForce team so they decided to a abandon the Potomac, which curved to the west of the White House, in favor of a more direct route. They left the river at the East Potomac Golf Course, began gaining altitude as they flew directly over the course and then the George Washington Memorial Parkway. They were at three hundred feet as they went east of the Washington Monument, across Constitution Avenue, and followed 15th Street NW across Pennsylvania Avenue and past the White House on their left. They went past the target to see if there was any indication that they were detected. Through Casper's main computer, Privates Petersen and Kincaid were constantly scanning the communications of all of the agencies that were monitoring the area to see if they had detected any aircraft in the no fly zone. This included the Secret Service communications facility at the White House. There was no unusual activity reported by anyone.

Until just a few minutes earlier, no one on the MF team knew they had access to the Secret Service command center. And they didn't until ten minutes earlier when the Silver Fox gave Eric the access code. As he did so, he solemnly informed him that he probably just put the life of the President of the United States into the hands of him and his MF team. He also informed Eric that he was at the White House, but unable to gain access to the President or General Armstrong. He was convinced there was an enemy within and they were forced to take more drastic measures to gain entrance. The Silver Fox had a plan that he quickly outlined to Eric, who was relieved because his review of the computer schematics convinced him that penetration of the White House was possible, but of the War Room was highly improbable. When he was through, Eric was convinced the Silver Fox was someone who had spent many years in clandestine activities and he was very happy they were on the same side. He concluded by saying he was pleased that the entire crew were members of the Brethren of Dead Souls. They would need that kind of commitment because an assault on the White House using non-lethal weapons could prove suicidal. He wished them luck and promised he would be there with them

On the Lieutenant's orders, Corporal Semanski brought Casper to New York Avenue, banked left, and then hovered over Lafayette Park. They were at nine minutes and counting so they had to hurry. Locating the small brick pump house described by the Silver Fox, Casper was quickly lowered to within twenty-five feet of the ground, Corporal Anderson used the Secret Service computer to unlock the eight inch steel door, and then Lieutenant Eric Johnson, Private Kurt Kincaid, Katya Petrov, and Nick Logan leaped from the craft. As soon as he saw them disappear inside, Corporal Semanski raised the aircraft to two hundred feet and headed for the back of the White House.

The small group, led by Eric Johnson, made their way down the flight of stairs and quickly through another steel door leading to a long, dark corridor. This door had no outside handle and could only be opened manually from the inside or by remote control. Fortunately, Casper's main computer had gained access to the computer that controlled the Secret Service communications center and could now override that computer. Through a microphone in his helmet and a keypad on his wrist he could control everything in this secret escape tunnel. The MF computer had already copied the feedback from the tunnel's video monitors that showed a clear tunnel and was now continuously feeding this back to the Secret Service computer. The intruders would never be seen. The sensors in the floor and ceiling also would never detect them. More correctly, their detection would never be reported to the Secret Service because the MF computer would intercept them and forward a clear signal. That's why Eric was able to open the door.

Before they proceeded down the tunnel Eric released a half dozen PIP's to go ahead of them and make sure that they didn't run into some form of trap. This was a secret escape route in case the President had to abandon the White House, other than by helicopter or automobile, and one would expect to find some live guards at some point. The schematics showed that the tunnel led directly from the War Room to a small holding room and from there to the tunnel that went for one hundred and fifty yards before exiting in Lafayette Park. With Lieutenant Johnson in the lead and Private Kincaid guarding the rear, the four of them made their way just outside of the holding room to wait. There were just six minutes left.

After dropping off Lieutenant Johnson and the others, Corporal Semanski took Casper to a position two hundred feet directly above the White House and then slowly lowered her to within twenty feet of the roof. He had to lower the craft slowly to avoid detection from the guards on the roof. It was not that difficult since the spotlights were located at each of the four corners and directed outward and upward at an angle. The way they would expect a plane to come in. There was a cone of dead space directly in the center of the building because a helicopter could only access it and they would hear it in plenty of time to re-direct their lights.

Silently, Corporal Anderson and Privates Petersen and Wilson dropped behind the rooftop access door and waited for the signal. Corporal Semanski, with Yuri Petrov secured in the back, raced to a position fifty yards away on the White House south lawn and at a height of only ten feet he turned off all of the stealth technologies and immediately became visible to both the radar and the guards. Before they could react he opened fire with his .50-caliber machine guns and rockets. The firepower was considerable and the guards had no way of knowing it was being guided by Casper's computer to be non-lethal and minimally destructive. All they knew was the White House was under heavy attack.

This was the signal for Corporal Anderson and his men to enter the White House through the roof top access. Again the door was heavily steel plated but easily swung open since the Secret Service computer, as directed by Corporal Anderson, unlocked it. Descending the narrow stairs they knew exactly what to expect because they were also getting feedback from the security systems own monitors. The two Secret Service men stationed outside of the door to the roof staircase had gone to the nearest window to see what was happening. It was an easy thing to burst through the unlocked door and hit them with a burst from their stun guns, leaving them on the floor incapacitated. The MF team then made their way to the interior of the top floor and fired concussion and tear gas shells to cause as much noise and confusion as possible.

Outside, Corporal Semanski used Casper's agility and speed to dart around the White House and create the illusion there were multiple craft attacking them. He also used the internal computer to declare that both the east and west wings had been breached by many intruders.

Deep in the bowels of the White House the War Room became still as Secret Service Director Knight's emergency phone rang. Even Secretary Carlson, who was receiving additional demands and threats from the North Koreans, put her call on hold.

His face was ashen as James Knight stood and announced, "Mr. President, I'm afraid the White House is under siege. You must leave."

An incredulous President asked, "Under siege? By whom?"

"That's not clear at the moment. What is clear is that there are multiple aircraft involved and there are a number of intruders already inside the White House."

"But why leave? I thought the War Room was impenetrable. Even to nuclear attack."

The Director was already moving toward the President as he answered, "It is, sir. At least it is from an attack by air, but we're not so sure about a hand carried tactical nuclear device detonated directly outside the War Room."

"My God. Is that what we have here, Jim?"

"We're not sure, sir. I hope not, but we are getting some initial reports from our computer command center that the attack may be by terrorists with that capability."

FBI Director Alexander added, "I think we had better assume the worst. We have had reports of at least two terrorists groups with possible nuclear capabilities planning something as we enter the new millennium. Unfortunately we haven't been able to confirm or dispel the rumors."

As President Stewart was being ushered toward a large steel door, at the far end of the room, he continued to protest, "But what about the rest of you? And my family is down here."

James Knight still had his hand on the President's elbow and continued to direct him towards the door as he responded, "My family is here too, Mr. President. That's why I hope we're wrong. But we both have even bigger commitments. We have to do our jobs."

The President stopped and looked at his Secret Service Director. "Of course you're right, Jim." Then he turned to face the others and particularly Vice President Chandler. "Neil, if you have to take over listen to the General. He knows what to do. Good luck to all of you." He then turned and, with Director Knight at his side, followed the two Secret Service agents toward the door. Before entering the door he turned back and said, "General, it's time."

General Armstrong then went to a secure phone and gave the order that sent three unmanned aircraft into the air from a remote air force base in Alaska.

Waiting in the tunnel, Eric Johnson checked his watch and then the small video screen in his helmet. He could feel the perspiration begin to build on his brow, the PIP's left at the tunnel entrance showed the Special Forces squadron establishing a perimeter around the entrance while others descended the stairs, and the White House security camera showed no one had yet entered the holding room.

The appearance of the Special Forces team in the tunnel was not a surprise, but the quickness of their arrival was. The Silver Fox had revealed that this was the back up emergency plan to rescue the President if the security of the War Room was compromised. If that happened the President would be brought into the holding room to wait for the Special Forces to evacuate him to either Camp David or Air Force One, depending on the circumstances.

Unfortunately, they had to wait in the tunnel outside the holding room because the standard operating procedure called for a visual check of the holding room before allowing the President to enter. In order to accomplish this there was a double door with a small room in between, similar to an airlock on a space craft, that allowed an agent to enter the chamber and have the door locked behind him and then enter the holding room. If all were clear, then the President and the other Secret Service agents would do the same.

They didn't know if their plan to compromise the War Room had worked and, if it did, would it work in time. There were only five minutes left until the new millennium and even less before the Special Forces would arrive. The temptation was to unlock the door and enter the holding room to avoid them. But this would only leave them trapped. The door to the War Room from the chamber would be manually bolted form the inside and not even a command from the computer could open it.

They had to wait for the President to enter the room, but they were running out of time. Lieutenant Johnson and Private Kincaid looked at one another and both knew the advancing Special Forces team had to be slowed down to allow more time for the President to be ushered into the holding room.

It was Private Kincaid who spoke first, "I'll move up in the tunnel and try to hold them off until you can enter the holding room, sir."

"I can't order you to do that, Kurt. Nor can I order you not to use lethal force."

"I know, sir. But it has to be done and you have to stay here. And I won't use lethal force. These men are doing their jobs to save the President and won't die at my hands." Kurt Kincaid saw the sorrow in Eric's eyes and reminded him, "That's what BOD's is all about, Eric."

They shook hands and Private Kincaid silently started back through the tunnel. He would go about twenty-five yards and wait for the Special Forces to arrive and then use his stun gun and concussion grenades in an attempt to slow them down. There was no place to hide so he would lie flat on the floor as close to the wall as possible, but it would only be a matter of time before a bullet would find a vulnerable spot, most likely his head, or a grenade would do the job of silencing him.

Hearing their discussion Nick protested, "That's a suicide mission."

"We have no choice." Eric turned back to the door and focused his attention on the holding room.

"At least let me go with him to back him up."

"You've got guts, Nick. But that will only get you both killed. Besides, I need you here. And you'll get your chance to be a hero. When they do come into the holding room, there will be two agents in front of the President and one behind him. I'll be able to stun the two in front, but then the one behind will spin the President around and shield him. If I stun him the President will receive a significant jolt through contact with him."

"We can't do that to the President."

"No, we can't," Eric agreed. "That's why you are going to anticipate his spin and hit him hard enough to knock him against the far wall and then I will stun him. Try to avoid any contact with him after hitting him."

"Do you think this will work?" Nick questioned.

"Yes. But I won't guarantee you won't get stunned, too."

"Thanks."

"Just remember that I will shoot the agent on your side first so you can move as soon as I do. The other agent in front will shoot for me first, and that should give you an opportunity."

"Let's just hope he goes for a chest shot and not a head shot."

"Let's hope they come in the next thirty seconds. I might still be able to recall Private Kincaid," Eric responded.

Private Kincaid had taken his position on the floor about thirty yards away. He could hear them coming down the tunnel and it wouldn't be long now. He began to squeeze the trigger to send the first bolt of electricity bouncing off of the floor and walls when he heard the Lieutenant. "Abort. Abort. They're entering the room get back here on the double." The Private was immediately on his feet and rushing back to the holding room with the Special Forces team only thirty yards behind him.

Once the first Secret Service agent cleared the area, they wasted little time in getting the President into the holding room. As soon as the door to the chamber leading from the War Room was secured, Eric burst into the room and immobilized the first agent before he could react. As planned, Nick ignored the second agent, who put two bullets into the chest of Eric before he, too, was immobilized, and moved like a linebacker toward the third agent. He was able to hit the surprised agent hard enough to knock him against the far wall and clear from the President so that Eric could fire a jolt that sent him to the floor in a heap. Then Private Kincaid rushed into the room, pushing Katya in front of him, and closed the door behind him.

The President was surprised, but immediately recognized his attackers. "What the hell is this all about, Lieutenant?" He demanded. On seeing Kate and Nick, he didn't know if they were here to restore the nuclear missile system or if they had become terrorists themselves.

"Don't be alarmed Mr. President, we have not gone crazy and we are not here to harm you," Eric Johnson said.

The President looked down at the three men writhing in pain at his feet and then responded, "I don't think they would agree with you, Lieutenant."

"On the contrary, sir," Eric responded. "They are in pain but alive. We could have just as easily killed them. And you. If that were our desire, sir."

"How do I know you are not going to kill me or use me for a bargaining chip to get whatever you want?"

It was a frustrated Nick who responded, "If you only knew what hell we have been through to get here to finish the job we started you wouldn't ask that question. Sir."

"Easy, Nick," Eric said as he bent down and picked up one of the agent's handguns. "The President has a perfect right to question us. After all, we are late in providing him what he should have had a long time ago. And we are attacking the White House."

President Stewart swallowed hard and Nick prepared to step in front of him as Eric raised the gun toward the President. Then he turned the gun around and, holding it by the handle, handed it to him. "Here, Mr. President. Be careful the safety is off. Do you know how to shoot one of these?"

The President took the gun, "Yes, I do. The Secret Service strongly suggests training with these, and I took them up on it."

Eric knew that time was running out. The Special Forces outside the door would be working on blowing the door open and then all hell would break open, so he took the barrel of the gun and put it to his forehead. "If you believe we are the enemy then pull the trigger. Or you can take this phone and press nine."

"Who will I be talking to?"

He held out the phone, "A mutual friend. The Silver Fox."

President Stewart took the phone, pressed nine, and heard a familiar voice. But he was still cautious, "Who is this?'

Shielded by Corporal Anderson, he replied, "This is your humble servant, Mr. President. The Silver Fox."

The President was pleased and relieved to have his identity confirmed. "It's good to hear your voice. Where are you?"

"I'm at the first sub-level and making my way down with the MF team. I assume you're there with Lieutenant Johnson?"

The President still held the gun to Eric's head, "Yes, I am. And I'm not sure if he is friend or foe."

"Trust me, sir. He is a friend."

He knew time was running out and he had to make a decision. So he went with his gut and lowered the gun. "Okay. What do we do next?"

"We will patch you through to the War Room and you can order General Armstrong to let you back in. At the same time you can order the Secret Service to escort us to the War Room. You must use the General and his staff to take control. I am convinced there is one or more of our enemies within the War Room. I have been blocked from getting through to you. It could even be someone in the Secret Service."

"I don't believe that, but I trust the General with my life and I know he trusts you with his. So I will do what you ask." With that said, the President used the cell phone to contact the War Room on a line only known to him, the General, and the Vice President. A surprised General Armstrong answered the call, but he quickly grasped what was happening and did not hesitate to advise the President to do as the Silver Fox had instructed. The President agreed and ordered the chamber opened and the Silver Fox and his MF team to be escorted into the War Room.

The President, Eric, Nick, and Katya rushed inside the unlocked chamber door, leaving the three Secret Service agents lying unconscious on the floor, as the door to the holding room blew open and the Special Forces team stormed in. The chamber door to the War Room was then unlocked and they entered the War Room as the Silver Fox and his MF escort was being ushered in through the main door; Secret Service agents immediately surrounded both groups.

The General and Vice President Chandler were the first to greet him, and it was a concerned Neil Chandler who spoke first. "Are you all right, Mr. President?"

"Yes, Neil. I'm fine," the President said as he turned to General Armstrong. "General please contact your Special Forces commander and have them be prepared to take the Vice President out of here and to the safety of Camp David."

"But, Mr. President, you should be the one to get out of here," the Vice President protested.

An excited and angry Secret Service Director Knight agreed, "I agree, sir. And, forgive me for asking, what happened to the three agents with you and who are these armed men. I must demand that they turn over their weapons, sir."

"Easy, James. Your men are not seriously injured, and I believe if you check with your command post the mock attack is over." Indeed, Lieutenant Johnson had already ordered Corporal Semanski to break off the attack.

"Mock attack? Mr. President, I don't think this was any 'mock attack'." Director Knight did not want to face the embarrassment of ordering the President out of the War Room for a mock attack.

"If you check with your command center you'll find that none of your men were anymore seriously hurt than having been stunned by a non-lethal electric shock," Lieutenant Johnson added.

Director Knight was furious, "Who the hell are you? And turn over your weapons?"

The secret service agents around them moved to disarm them and Eric Johnson and Private Kincaid prepared to resist.

"That's enough! We don't have time for this. These men have had plenty of opportunity to kill me and haven't. And this woman is going to give us back our nuclear missiles. You can keep an agent with each of them, but remember they are not the enemy." The President then turned to his Vice President, "Neil, you have to go just in case we are not successful here and things go badly. I must stay to see this through."

"But, sir....."

"You must go now, Neil. I will have your family brought to you as soon as possible. Until then they will be as safe as my family. Now go." He was then escorted through the chamber by the Secret Service and joined the Special Forces team waiting in the holding room.

There were only two minutes left to 0 0 and they had to hurry. The President ordered Katya brought to the computer workstation that was tied into the nuclear missile command center and monitored by Colonel Clay and his staff.

Nick knew that there would be no better time to appeal to the President than now. "Excuse me, Mr. President. I know this is a difficult time, but I appeal to you to grant Katya and her brother Yuri amnesty and political asylum. I believe when you hear the story you will understand they never meant to endanger the United States."

"If they had anything to do with disabling our nuclear system they should be shot. Never mind granted asylum," Victor Noble said angrily. He was angry at the suggestion of forgiving them and because he hadn't found her first.

It was now time for the Silver Fox to come forward. As he did, CIA Director Donald Mathias and Assistant Director David Ford immediately recognized him. It was Zachary Andrews, the legendary CIA undercover agent who had dropped out of sight some five years earlier and was presumed dead. "Mr. President, if I may?"

"Certainly, Zachary," the President responded using his name for the first time; since he had shown himself there was no longer any need to use his code name.

"I believe that there is justification to consider amnesty and asylum for these two young people. I also think that there should be leniency for Nick Logan and Lieutenant Johnson. Release them into my custody with a commitment from them to serve the interests of the country until we are satisfied they have earned their unconditional release."

"Well, there is no way that either Lieutenant Johnson or Mr. Logan can ever work in an official government capacity again. If they, and Ms. Petrov and her brother, agree to serve you unconditionally then I will release them into your service."

With Katya committing her brother, they quickly agreed to the terms of their freedom. Katya could not have hoped for more for her and Yuri, Lieutenant Johnson was happy to be in the service of the Silver Fox and his BOD's organization, and Nick knew that, if he didn't agree, he would probably end up free but without the woman he loved.

Victor Noble protested, "You can't let the very person who sabotaged the system now have access to it to supposedly fix it. What if she totally destroys it?"

The President moved to stand beside Katya at the workstation and solemnly pronounced, "You destroy it—you die. You fix it—you walk." Katya nodded her head in understanding and she began to work as the President moved away to view the map and speak with the Secretary of State.

David Ford stood next to Victor Noble as President Stewart gave Katya the go ahead to proceed; seeing her start to fix the missile system he lost it and swore under his breath, "Traitor!" Then he reached for his gun as he moved toward her.

Victor Noble froze for a moment, not believing what he heard; then he realized the bitter truth of the man he had collaborated with and reacted. "Stop that man! He's the enemy. He's the mole."

David Ford quickly raised his gun, aimed at Katya's head, and pulled the trigger. She was a dead woman had Nick not already been moving to be beside her; the Secret Service agent's gun in his hand. He caught the bullet in the chest, but the Kevlar vest did its job once again. Staggering backward from the impact, Nick was able to get a shot off that caught Ford in the shoulder. The gun fell at the feet of Victor Noble, who quickly picked it up and shot Ford three times in the chest. One bullet pierced his heart and the traitor died instantly, and their relationship with him.

The Secret Service quickly took control of the situation and both of the guns. Eric Johnson and Privates Kincaid and Petersen surrounded Nick and Katya, forming a human shield, while Corporal Anderson and Private Wilson took positions at either end of the opposite wall so that everything was between the two groups. With only a minute to go, and Nick by her side, Katya immediately returned to her task.

The President turned to Secretary of State Carlson and ordered, "Judith get back on the line with the North Koreans and tell them that, no matter what they have heard, we are fully capable of blowing them off the face of the earth if they initiate a nuclear attack."

Secretary Carlson reached for the phone, "Yes, sir." Then she was startled as the map lit up over Southeast Asia and a warning signal sounded.

Then General Armstrong announced, "I'm afraid it's too late. The North Koreans have just launched their missiles."

There was a gasp from the group and Secretary of Defense Donovan said what everyone was thinking, "Those dumb bastards."

Judith Carlson's voice was barely audible as he spoke, "God help the people of Tokyo and Taiwan."

"God help us all," added the Vice President.

President Justin Stewart turned to General Armstrong, "It's all yours, General."

The General didn't hesitate as he took the secure phone from his aide and spoke to Colonel Clay at the Pentagon Command Center, "Colonel, operation Red Sky is a go. Release the hawks on the sparrows." Then he turned to the President, "It's done, sir."

Before the President could respond, the map lit up as the two missiles became intensely bright and then disappeared altogether. The unmanned drones had done their job to perfection. Hovering in the upper atmosphere above Southeast Asia, it took only five seconds, once the command was received, to lock onto the North Korean missiles. The sky turned red as each drone fired a laser beam and the missiles were instantly disintegrated.

"There is no further danger to Tokyo and Taiwan?" The President asked.

"No, sir. None," General Armstrong responded.

"What just happened here, sir?" Asked a surprised and confused Secretary Carlson.

"Did we just witness the destruction of those missiles?" Secretary of Defense Donovan asked.

"Yes," a relieved President answered. "You did."

A confused Secretary Carlson asked, "But how did we do that?"

"We did it with lasers, Judith."

"But President Bush pronounced Star Wars dead almost ten years ago," Secretary Carlson proclaimed. "Besides being opposed by most of the world's governments, including many of our allies, it was an extremely expensive plan and the technology turned out not to be feasible. I thought."

"The feasibility of the technology may or may not have been in question, but the rest was true," the President agreed. "But this isn't Star Wars. At least not the Star Wars you know." The President then turned to General Armstrong, "Perhaps you could give them the nickel tour, General?"

"Certainly, sir," the General responded. Then he addressed the others, "While we did destroy the North Korean missiles with laser beams fired from outer space, they weren't fired from satellites permanently stationed in outer space. They were fired from unmanned aircraft that are capable of taking off from any of our air force bases, reach the outer atmosphere, hit any target in space or on earth that we wish, and return to the air base all in less than forty-five minutes."

"I thought that they were still two years away from being operational?" Secretary Donovan asked.

"Well, sir, as far as being fully operational that's true. But the technology is perfected and we were able to get a limited number of aircraft operational on a crises basis. We didn't know if we would make it so we kept it as quiet as possible."

It was Secretary of State Carlson who spoke next, "Excuse me, but if we have this capability why are we so dependent on getting our nuclear missiles back on line?"

The President signaled to General Armstrong that he would answer this, "The problem is that we have only a few of these drones available for use. Not nearly enough to repel an all out Russian attack."

"I see, sir," said Judith Carlson.

Then the red phone sprang to life and began to ring, sending a chill through the occupants of the War Room. It was from the Russian President. President Stewart looked at the clock, he hadn't wasted much time, it was only three minutes past midnight. He looked over at Katya still working furiously at the computer terminal and then signaled his aid to have the Russian President put on the speakerphone. "Yes, President Sokolov."

"Mr. President, please explain what has just happened. Our intelligence tells us that your country has just detonated nuclear weapons over North Korea."

President Stewart smiled; he had to admire his counterpart's brass. "Mr. President, what we have just done is to save the world from a terrible tragedy. A tragedy of proportions that may well have plunged the world into total chaos."

The Russian President was adamant. "Our monitors have shown that you have engaged in an aggressive attack on our friends to the south. If you do not stand down our treaty with the North Koreans will require us to retaliate."

"President Sokolov, our satellite photos will clearly demonstrate that we have acted only in a defensive manner. The North Koreans were clearly launching an offensive attack on Tokyo and Taiwan," President Stewart said.

"They were only reacting to the signal that they were under attack from one of your nuclear submarines."

"Our satellite photos will confirm that there was no such attack and that we only acted in a defensive manner."

The Russian President was very agitated, "Well, our monitors show something very different and we are under extreme pressure to retaliate."

The strain in the Russian President's voice concerned President Stewart greatly. He sounded like a desperate man prepared to do a desperate thing. The President then moved until he was standing beside Katya and put the call on hold as he asked her, "Do we have control of our system yet, Ms. Petrov?'

"Yes, Mr. President, you do," she responded as she typed in the last instruction.

Then General Armstrong added, "Mr. President, Colonel Clay confirms that he has been able to get past the security alarms and arm the system."

President Stewart then turned to Nick and asked, "Well, Mr. Logan, I have the safety of the United States of America, and maybe the world, in my hands. Do you believe we have control of our nuclear missiles back?"

Nick Logan looked at the President and then at Katya, waited for a long moment, and then responded firmly, "Yes, sir. I do."

The President looked deeply into Nick Logan's eyes and then into Katya Petrov's before he opened the line to the Russian President, "Mr. President, I suggest that you stand down and listen to me."

"Why should I do that, Mr. President? You have clearly attacked our ally to the south, my monitors indicate that you are now attacking us, and my intelligence tells me you are not in a position to respond to our attack."

The President spoke calmly but firmly, "President Sokolov, listen to me carefully. First of all we did not attack North Korea without provocation. Our satellite photos will show that they had launched two missiles without provocation and our actions saved a terrible tragedy. Second, we are not attacking you and you have no evidence of that. And third, we have our full nuclear capability available to us and we will retaliate fully to any offensive gestures from your country."

"With all due respect, Mr. President, I don't believe you."

The President looked at General Armstrong, who was still on the line with Colonel Clay, and got the nod he was hoping for. "I didn't think you did. It is my understanding that your satellite is still operational and you can receive transmissions. Is that correct, sir?"

The Russian President was furious, "We are not a third world country. Of course we still have our satellite communications."

"Good. Please watch closely. We have launched a missile from its silo in Nebraska. It will reach the outer atmosphere in less than two minutes. You should be able to determine that it is targeted for the middle of the Pacific Ocean."

"We see it," President Sokolov answered, but he would not confirm that they did calculate the mid-Pacific as its target.

President Stewart knew that they would see it. The firing site and the trajectory were calculated to be clearly visible to the Russian satellite. "Watch closely, Mr. President. The missile will be breaking into the outer atmosphere any second now."

"Yes. We see it."

"Good. Now look up to the right."

"What the hell is that," demanded an excited President Sokolov.

"That's an unmanned plane capable of reaching outer space. Now watch closely."

In an instant the drone locked onto the missile, fired a bright red laser beam, and disintegrated the missile.

"Oh shit!"

"Yes, that's right, Mr. President. We are not only capable of launching our nuclear missiles, but we are also capable of destroying your missiles well before they can reach our shores. That's how we destroyed the North Korean missiles and those aircraft are now stationed in the outer atmosphere over your country. We are prepared to send up as many more as are needed."

It was a subdued President Sokolov that responded, "I see. What do you want?"

"I want you to stand down and disarm your nuclear weapons. I want you to condemn the North Koreans for their obvious aggression. And I want you to make a statement that the use of our advanced laser technology was not only appropriate but very fortunate in avoiding what could have been a major human tragedy."

"But the world will be on my side if I condemn the development and deployment of Star Wars. Even if it did avert a major tragedy, it will also put the world at great risk." The Russian President used the only bargaining chip he thought he had.

"That might be true if this were the old Star Wars technology, which had permanent satellites armed with lethal lasers hovering above the earth at all times. In such a case, a tragic accident or malfunction could have dire consequences. In sharp contrast, our 'Doves of Peace' are not constantly orbiting above us, but are kept safely on the ground. It is only with an imminent threat of attack are they launched, and then only in a defensive deployment."

"But there will be great political pressure if I do as you demand," the Russian President pleaded.

President Stewart understood his position and had no desire to force him out of office. "There will be even greater political pressure if you don't do as I ask. I doubt that even the Chinese will stand beside the North Koreans now. But, if they do, let them stand-alone. The rest of the world surely will denounce them. In return, I am prepared to have the United States initiate and support a major infusion of capital by the International Monetary Fund into your country. This should go a long way toward easing the pain and helping with your re-election." President Stewart then hesitated for a moment to let that sink in then continued. "Do we have a deal, Mr. President?"

His country was starved for capital and he could put a good spin on the terrible mistake that his friends, the North Koreans, had almost made. "Yes, Mr. President. You have a deal."

"Good." Before President Stewart could say anything else, he was approached by Zachary Andrews who whispered something in his ear. The President looked at General Armstrong who nodded his head and then continued, "There is one more thing, Mr. President."

"What else could you possibly want?"

"It is a small thing, and easily granted. I'm sure. You have a man by the name of Dimitry Petrov in your control and we want him."

"But why would you want him?"

"Just call it a favor to a friend. I can assure you that there will be no public mention of it. We will expect delivered to our embassy within the hour."

"Fine. You can have him. But I will expect you to get your people working on the IMF immediately. Good-bye, Mr. President."

"You have my word we will start right away. Good-bye." President Stewart then gave the signal to Zachary Andrews and turned to Nick, Katya and Eric, "In the end we have a great deal to thank you for. Together you have a unique combination of skills and I will expect you to further serve the country by following the directions of Zachary Andrews. Now go."

The Silver Fox led them and the rest of the MicroForce team to the holding room where they were met by the Special Forces team that would escort them to the end of the tunnel and the waiting Casper.

Lieutenant Eric Johnson felt some comfort on having avenged his brother's death and still be able to serve his country in whatever manner they chose for him. Katya Petrov was surprised and happy that, not only would she be re-united with her father and brother, she would be with the man she loved. Nick Logan's world was turned upside down and all the plans he had for his future were no longer relevant, and he didn't care. All that mattered now was that he would be with the woman he loved and would deal with the rest as it came.

0-595-30233-5